D0378912

Jul 2017

BOSSTOWN

BOSSTOWN

ADAM ABRAMOWITZ

THOMAS DUNNE BOOKS
ST. MARTIN'S PRESS
NEW YORK

THOMAS DUNNE BOOKS.
An imprint of St. Martin's Press.

BOSSTOWN. Copyright © 2017 by Adam Abramowitz. All rights reserved. Printed in the United States of America. For information, address St. Martin's Press, 175 Fifth Avenue, New York, N.Y. 10010.

Grateful acknowledgment is made for permission to
reprint lyrics from the following:

"Just What I Needed," words and music by Ric Ocasek. Copyright © 1978 by Lido Music, Inc. Published worldwide by Lido Music, Inc. All rights controlled and administered by Universal Music Corp. All rights reserved. Used by permission. Reprinted by permission of Hal Leonard LLC.

"On Dogz," words and music by Edo. G (Edward Anderson) from the album *The Truth Hurts*. Copyright © 2001. All rights controlled and administered by Edo. G. All rights reserved. Used by permission. Reprinted by permission of Ed O Music BMI.

www.thomasdunnebooks.com
www.stmartins.com

Designed by Omar Chapa

The Library of Congress Cataloging-in-Publication Data is
available upon request.

ISBN 978-1-250-07629-8 (hardcover)
ISBN 978-1-4668-8769-5 (e-book)

Our books may be purchased in bulk for promotional, educational, or business use. Please contact your local bookseller or the Macmillan Corporate and Premium Sales Department at 1-800-221-7945, extension 5442, or by e-mail at MacmillanSpecialMarkets@macmillan.com.

First Edition: August 2017

10 9 8 7 6 5 4 3 2 1

With love for Adrienne, Sam, and Antonia

AUTHOR'S NOTE

Boston as portrayed in this novel is pretty close to real, but I've taken liberties in my descriptions and the changes the city has undergone. The same goes for the events and characters presented in the story. I made all of this up.

BOSSTOWN

PROLOGUE

Everybody in the Game Thinks They're a Shark

This is how I see my father circa 1990: He sits in a high-backed chair, a deck of Bicycle playing cards nestled in the palm of his left hand, his right hand hovering over the deck like a magician summoning spirits. He is wearing a crisp white shirt unbuttoned at the collar, the sleeves folded into ruler-width rectangles that sit just above the elbows, framing his forearms and the coiled muscles that shift like snakes under his tanned brown skin. He is smiling, my father, exposing yin-yang upper teeth separated horizontally by a scraggly fault line where the bonding was attached but had yet to discolor to match the upper portion. His cheeks are #3 sandpaper, flecked with dull nickel silver only partially covering a lightning-bolt scar under his bottom lip. Smile lines run from the corners of his mouth into estuaries that reach the edges of his eyes, pools of battery acid lit with a galaxy of pinprick lights surrounding the pupils.

They are liar's eyes.

Most of my earliest memories are of poker games, my father caressing a deck of cards, the sound of chips hitting felt, darkened windows or drawn shades and rooms dense with smoke and men who, during breaks in the action, would practice staring into mirrors, trying to erase the light from their own eyes. On nights when my father couldn't find someone to sit with me and my brother, Zero, he would haul us to these games, where we would pass the time reading whatever books and papers were lying about, or if the game was somewhere with a kitchen or bar, Zero and I would fix the men sandwiches and drinks in exchange for tips. Most often though, we just sat behind—always behind—our father and watched the games unfold, luck give way to skill, friendly banter wind down into pressurized silence or muttered curses.

It wasn't unusual for Zero and me to appear in school directly from these marathon games, our pockets bulging with ones and fives, hair styled with palm sweat, clothes wrinkled and pungent with cigar and cigarette smoke. It was also not unusual for me to wake from a deep sleep in the nurse's office, Zero laid out beside me, his hands squeezing imaginary cards, dreams of royal flushes and quad aces dancing behind sealed lids. The Z Brothers they would call us. The Narcoleptic Twins (though Zero was nearly three years older).

Whether this midday catatonia brought my father grief from the school's administration is highly unlikely, since those he played with were often the school officials themselves or men otherwise hardwired to the city's machinery—politicians and their cronies, ward bosses and their street-corner protégés, cops and robbers, bag men, businessmen, and thieves—who could tell the difference? These were the men who made things happen and problems disappear. Dangerous men who brokered in favors and cautiously guarded secrets that secured their positions and livelihoods, a few of which, remarkably at odds with their public personas, weighed like liens on their conscience. Men who, I was to learn later, had sometimes found the weight of those secrets too great to keep and would look into my father's black eyes, those liar's eyes, and find whatever it was they sought. Forgiveness? Understanding?

In certain Central and South American countries—places where the governments rotate in and out of power seemingly through a revolving door directly connected to hell—there exists a cadre of men and women who hire themselves out as professional hostages, stand-ins for those taken from wealthy families and held for ransom. Though their loved ones have been removed from immediate danger, the families rarely fail to pay the ransom demands in order to preserve the honor of their word and their family's good name. Whether the hostages are mistreated or tortured, live or die, they could care less. In their world reputation is everything. My father operated under much the same principle, only minus the cold hard cash. His word was bond because, generally, it was all he had. My father was the place secrets went to die, never to see the light of day.

At least that's what everybody thought.

But then along came the Big Dig, Boston's $20-billion Central Artery Project slicing through the city's divided neighborhoods—Charlestown, South Boston, Chinatown and East Boston, the South End—tearing up the pavement and exposing the bodies everyone had figured were buried forever. What my father knew, or, rather, what he remembered as Alzheimer's crept in and rendered his past a grab bag of Etch A Sketch memories, seemed to shift as often as Boston's topography. The city and its history were turned inside out one heaping shovel load at a time; buildings that had stood mute witness to decades of fitful change were reduced to rubble overnight and carted off by convoys of trucks that shook the ground like mini earthquakes as they barreled toward the harbor docks. Two-way streets were choked into one-way passages, cement barriers eliminating turns. Exits and ramps were blocked or turned around and rerouted into makeshift outlets. Rotaries were halved, draining traffic back to the streets they had just escaped. Sidewalks vanished. Bridges led to nowhere. Streets disappeared completely. And as the earth rumbled, shifted, and coughed up its secrets, from every crack, hole, and crevice, the rats came out to play.

ONE

Boylston Street coming out of the Fenway runs for twelve blocks through Boston as straight as a sumo wrestler on the way to a buffet table before intersecting with Tremont, which in turn does a little improvisational dance into the rat maze that constitutes the Financial District—a place the sun never seems to shine below the twentieth floor.

There are eleven sets of traffic lights from one end of Boylston to where it hits Tremont, seven bus stops, forty-nine fire hydrants, and two mammoth potholes known to swallow small Hondas whole. There are no stop signs.

A leisurely drive down Boylston just taking in the sights—the granite mistake of the Prudential Center, Boston Public Library, Copley Square, Trinity Church and its Gothic reflection in the slate blue glass of the John Hancock Tower, a corner of the Public Garden blooming behind the cast-iron fence—would take about seven minutes, providing you didn't catch every red light along the way.

I know these and other meaningless facts about Boylston Street because it's a road I've traveled often, way more times than I care to remember, and in just about every condition imaginable, Boylston and just about every other strip of pavement masquerading as a street in this historic landfill. I get paid to travel them, you see. I deliver things. Pick things up. I'm a bicycle messenger. Hell on wheels. A pedestrian's worst nightmare.

On a social scale, that makes me right about even with the gum stuck to the bottom of your shoe. Maybe even the stuff stuck to the bottom of the gum. But I like it. There are even times I like it *because* of it. Sometimes I think it's a lot easier being the gum than the shoe. The life might be shorter, but it's full of flavor while it lasts.

To make up for my occasional bouts with a lack of professional self-esteem, I like to think of myself as Boston's lowest paid professional athlete. Though admittedly, I'd be hard-pressed to qualify, considering I've yet to submit to drug testing, be sued for paternity, or get stopped on the street for an autograph or handshake. And that's despite the fact my outfits are tighter than Tom Brady's game-day uniform and sometimes twice as flashy. I often contemplate hiring an agent. Just about every one of my ex-girlfriends—and there are plenty of those—thinks maybe I should get a real job.

But at this point such drastic measures are out of the question. I get enough of the ball-and-chain nine-to-five during my forays inside the endless cubicle cities and office cells. It's as close to real as I want to get. I decided a long time ago I needed a longer leash.

So I ride the streets. And the sidewalks. And the occasional lobby if it comes to that—caffeine fueled, adrenaline hyped, my stripped-down silver Fat Chance oiled and tuned to the bone. Almost out of habit it seems. No road too rough, no curb too high, no hangover too debilitating; on most days I never give much thought to what I'm doing or the streets flashing beneath my wheels.

Only this morning is different. This morning I have the time to think about where I am, which happens to be Boylston Street, long, wide, and one-way only. Because this morning in early June, sunny and bright, the birds singing like they've been paid in advance, Boylston Street is as backed up as John Goodman's arteries. Backed up solid. Plugged. Bumper to bumper and heading nowhere fast.

And I seem to be the cause of it. Because this morning I'm lying in the middle of Boylston at the intersection of Arlington, bleeding like I never knew I could. Like a river. Like a pro. Lots and lots of blood coming out from somewhere on my head, my face, my hip, and my leg, blood coming out red, warm, and sticky like someone turned on the faucet and left it running.

And all of a sudden, I'm not having such a swell day.

TWO

I blame it on the coffee. It was weak and old, the color of soaking rust, the filter a less than clean dish towel that had been lying around looking for a purposeful existence.

I gave it one.

I lined it inside my weary Melitta, poured in the suspect grounds, added water, and hoped for the best. I was the MacGyver of coffee. I searched the fridge for half-and-half but came up empty and emptier. A poke through cabinets and shelves turned up mass quantities of organic poverty: brown rice, tea bags, peanut butter, and ramen noodles, but no cream or anything remotely like it. This was real life. In real life there's no such thing as improvising cream.

So I drank it brown. It packed a wallop like Tinker Bell with twelve-ounce gloves and tasted just about how it looked, maybe a little too much like what the dish towel had wiped up a month earlier. I was halfway through a second cup when my Motorola started barking static on the strap of the bag hanging by the front door of the industrial South End loft I share with two roommates.

I ignored it and one-eyed the kitchen's apocalyptic mess: the sink piled high with plates and mismatched glasses, food and cigarette butts hardening onto their surfaces like glazed ceramic as the faucet *plip-plopp*ed cold water torture, drilling a hole through my pounding head. I knew better at that point than to try and fix it.

The faucet, I mean.

Our hot- and cold-water knobs are a distant memory, replaced by a pair of mismatched wrenches, which stick out at forty-five-degree angles and bleed toxic rust-orange streaks into the sink; to turn the water on, you have to tighten the grips on the wrenches and rotate them counterclockwise without skinning your knuckles on the wall. Hot water is hit or miss. The water heater, roughly three feet to the left of the sink and visible under the stairs, wears a sweater of pink insulation and an enormous black brassiere. We named her Joan. She's haughty and fickle and doles out hot water like UN rations, though a swift kick sometimes prods her into action. But for the most part, we wash in digit-numbing cold water, which might explain why our household tends to catch colds at the same time.

I cleared some room at the table, toppling empty Heineken bottles stripped naked, their labels having joined a hundred other brands in the alcoholic collage that wallpapers half the kitchen and speaks volumes about our overindulgences and lack of brand loyalty. *Beer is good,* our décor says. *You bring it, we'll drink it.*

That goes double for wine—preferably red—with each bottle

on the table bearing some mark of a pornographic alteration, crude figurines hand-carved into the amber glass with the sharp edge of a key.

My roommate Nicolette, a legit six feet, hard and lean from working as a welder and set designer, gets fairly creative when she drinks red wine, which is to say, often. When Nicolette isn't working steadily, she's prone to violent mood swings that come crashing through the loft in waves of activity masking despair.

Luckily, that activity often comes in the form of hastily thrown dinner parties, as was the case last night. Nicolette can be a handful, but the girl can *cook,* and on the cheap, too, which is no small thing in our little collective. Our other roommate, David, actually has something approaching a real job, in the sense that he gets up the same time most mornings, goes somewhere, and gets paid every two weeks (I've seen the checks). What exactly he does to earn those shekels is beyond me, except I know it's highly technical and based on the fact he's relentlessly cheerful, his life goal of achieving world domination through the production and dissemination of earsplitting techno beats must be progressing smoothly. David is short, hairy, and bespectacled; dresses like a ninja down to his polished eight-lace Doc Martens; and is one of the smartest, nicest, and funniest people I have ever known.

Last night, Nicolette threw together black beans with boiled dandelion greens she'd uprooted from the fenced-in alley that separates our block-long former factory building from the hardscrabble ball field behind us. The greens could be considered organic, I suppose, only the neighborhood drug addicts tend to urinate on them—the methadone clinic at Boston City is a zombie stroll away, and the Pine Street Inn, Boston's largest homeless shelter, is within sight of our front windows, our very own gloom with a view.

To the greens Nicolette added some unidentified spices,

chopped peppers, and tomatoes; wept bitter tears of an undetermined nature into a mountain of diced onions; and wrapped everything in pan-warmed tortillas sealed with a layer of burnt cheese.

The guests provided the booze, which in our household always amounts to fair trade. The playlist went a little something like this: Otis and Aretha, because we *always* start with some soul; Depeche Mode, Rage Against the Machine, Wu-Tang Clan, and Nirvana to take us through and home. At some point Nicolette dragged one of David's goth-leaning friends into her bedroom and forced him to do unspeakable things while the rest of us listened and played Guess the Position. His black leather Misfits jacket was still draped over one of the chairs, his pockets turned inside out and empty. I don't remember going to bed, but I know I went alone because that's how I woke up, nursing a ringing headache, the cat staring at me with scorn.

When my Motorola came to life again, my name surrounded by anatomic-themed curses, I unclipped it from my bag and pressed the side button.

"Argh," I said into it.

"Let me guess." It was Martha, my dispatcher, as always gnawing on something loudly. Martha's thin as a rail and has a mouth like the electrified third, and as far as I can tell, chewing is the only exercise she ever gets. "Red wine, rock and roll, and a whole lot of stick-it-to-the-man, fight-the-power bullshit."

"Argh," I said.

"I thought so." *Chew.* "You got a pickup at Black Hole Vinyl. ASAP."

"Martha." I rubbed my temples uselessly with one hand. "It's not even eight o'clock yet. Can you please not speak to me in acronyms?"

"Okey-dokey." *Chew.* "Black Hole Vinyl. Get your ass in gear. How's that?"

"Better. Isn't Black Hole Gus's account?"

"Your point?"

"You can't reach him?"

"Nope. Please tell me your slut of a roommate didn't snatch him up again."

"Snatch?" I said. "As in pussy?"

"Nooo." *Chew.* "Snatch, as in you're a pig. Is Gus there or not?"

"Not. Nicolette tapped someone else last night."

"Poor thing," Martha drawled, but I wasn't sure whether she meant Nicolette or Misfit. "You know where they're at?"

"Central Square, right?"

"Not anymore. Thirty-eight Newbury Street, sixth floor."

"Wow, movin' on up," I said, starting in on the theme song to *The Jeffersons*. "*To the apart-ment in the sky-I-I . . .*"

Martha chewed through my rendition, unimpressed. "You want it?" she said when I'd finished.

"I want it," I replied.

"You awake yet?"

"What's *that* got to do with anything?"

"Just checking," she said, swallowed, and faded to static.

I let the drain choke on what was left in my cup.

THREE

Thirty-eight Newbury Street is a seven-story red brick building that extends itself like a bookend to the corner of Berkeley Street. It's a high-rent building in a high-rent district, Brooks Brothers and Cartier providing a foundation of solid capital for the floors that rise above it.

One door over, in the darkened window of Alan Bilzerian, a pair of mannequins lurked in a thicket of bamboo poles, dressed in peasant straw hats and thousand-dollar silk Vietcong pajamas. I was admiring the antique Raleigh nestled between them when a man in a polyester tracksuit with five-pound weights strapped to his ankles stopped midstride and looked along with me.

"Look at this shit," he grunted, the "look" sounding like "Luke," a heavy Eastern European accent smudging the words. He had long sideburns and bristly black hair, a white towel wrapped around the back of his neck and stuffed into the front of his zipped-up jacket. "History is window dressing." He motioned to me with his chin. "You like?"

"Cool bike," I said.

"Yes. And look at the tits on that thing. Is like that on this street, eh? Everywhere I look is big tits and no heads."

"You're still talking about the mannequins, right?"

"That's a joke, eh? Very good. It makes for difficult run with three legs, no?"

I shook my head but saw his point. Sometimes the pageant that is Newbury Street makes wearing Lycra biking shorts a risky venture.

"Still, is good day to sweat, no?"

The man bounced lightly on his toes, worked a kink out of his neck. His eyes were bright, suffused with energy, the towel around his neck already damp with sweat. He shadow-boxed the air in front of him, cleared his throat, and spit through a gap in his front teeth to the base of the store window. "Fuck-*ing* Newbury Street."

I locked my bike to a parking meter, Boston's idea of a slot machine, and went in past a uniformed guard who tilted me a good morning nod but saved his smile for someone who could afford to tip him for his effort.

Black Hole Vinyl occupied half the sixth floor in front, three steps from the elevator, behind a glass door with brass handles that vibrated in my hands as I touched them. I'd heard the music coming up, but as I pulled the door open, sonic waves of Foo Fighters hammered the hallway.

The neighbors are going to love these guys.

The reception desk was vacant, the air thick with stale smoke, perfume, spilled beer, and some sort of cleaning detergent that had been employed to cloak the stench of vomit and failed miserably. Rugs that once prowled the Amazon sported fresh cigarette burns and crusty yellowish stains that didn't require CSI Boston to identify. Emptied boxes and moving supplies— blankets, straps, tumbleweed rolls of used tape—led to a closet-sized DJ booth, dual steel turntables flanked by muscular stacks of speakers. A pair of bright red headphones dangled from a hook on the front of the console, one ear marked with the letter "D," the other "J."

Taken in its entirety, the scene might have been lifted from some teenage wet dream: booze, a scent of babes, and just enough stereo to launch a nuclear missile out of the Back Bay; barely 8:00 A.M., the Foo Fighters giving way to the Beastie Boys blasting full throttle out of tiny Bose speakers hung inconspicuously from high corner moldings.

No! Sleep! Till Brook-lyn!

In the lone office with an open door, a vanilla vampire sat jabbing at the keys of an antiquated Underwood typewriter with long white fingernails sharp enough to be classified as weapons.

"Hello!" I yelled, but couldn't even hear my own voice.

The vampire had long slender arms a shade shy of Elmer's glue, a Medusa's head of dreadlocks twisted stiffly at the ends— blond, natural as NutraSweet. A single bone-white skull dangled off a silver chain just above where I always seem to get caught staring. On the windowsill behind her, a coffee machine pumped out steam, dripped something black and strong into a glass pot. It smelled nothing remotely like an old dish towel.

When Vanilla looked up suddenly and startled, it didn't take a lip reader to figure out what she'd said.

"Hey, I didn't mean to sneak up on you," I said too loudly, the music clicking off just as Adam Yauch was proclaiming his love for the outer boroughs and the joys of grabbing his ball-sac. "Nobody was at the desk." I threw a thumb behind me to clarify I hadn't scaled seven floors, scrambled in through a window.

"No worries." She smiled fangs, replaced a remote in the open drawer. "You need me to sign for something?"

"I got a call for a pickup," I said.

"From here? You sure?"

I wasn't sure of anything without a real cup of coffee behind me, but I didn't tell her that. "Black Hole Vinyl. Thirty-eight Newbury. That's you, right?"

"Straight outta Cambridge." Vanilla playfully flashed random gang signs that would get her shot in half a dozen Boston neighborhoods. "Only I didn't call you."

"Someone else maybe?" I pulled my aluminum case from my bag and scanned the paperwork I'd prepared.

"I doubt it. As if you couldn't tell, we had our little Welcome to the Neighborhood party last night. I don't expect anyone for a while." She stifled a yawn, wedged talons under a fist of keys stuck to the paper. "Sorry. I don't know what to tell you. . . ."

It's not so much my time is money per se—I get paid by the run, not by the hour—only with business tailing off and new clients harder to land than a Harvard scholarship, a blank start to my day was the last thing I needed.

"What about that note you're working on? That headed somewhere besides recycling?"

"No, I always screw these things up; it's part of the charm."

"And you don't believe in Wite-Out?"

"I think I found a better use for it." Vanilla smiled some of those high-wattage fangs, wiggled her fingers. "Anyhow, Ray Valentine has a thing for old-school, letters especially."

"Valentine your boss?"

"Lord and master of all you survey. Give or take a hungover blonde or two." Vanilla winked at me lewdly, and I had to move to keep the molecules in my Lycra shorts from activating in my crotch. "He figures people who're still into vinyl might appreciate a note that hasn't been edited with a fine-tooth electronic comb. It's, like, more, I dunno, personal?"

"No doubt, especially if you happen to misspell a few choice words." I pointed one out, followed by another, my eyes straying on their own again.

Bad eyes! *Bad!*

"Ooh, yeah, those I'll have to take care of. So what's the deal, Speed Racer? I mean, I *do* have something going out, but, like, I'm waiting on our regular courier."

"Which wouldn't happen to be Gus from Fleet, would it?"

"Yeah . . ." Suspicious. "How'd you know that?"

I explained that Gus and I share an office and dispatcher, not an unusual arrangement for the city's smaller, independent courier outfits. A couple years ago, we pooled with two other messengers and rented a basement in an alley off Berkeley Street. Martha operates as office manager so if someone gets swamped, needs a day off, or gets hurt, she farms the jobs out on a rotating basis and keeps track of the billing and paperwork.

"Listen, it's no big deal." I presented one of my business cards—Mercury trailing orange flames from the rear wheel of his bike. "Buzz if you want confirmation, only Martha was under the impression this job was chop-chop."

Vanilla bent me a wan smile, keeping the teeth in check this time, took my offered card, and tapped it with one of her talons. "So, Mercury Couriers? And you're—"

"Zesty Meyers," I said, saving her the trouble of reading the rest. "Fastest courier on the streets of Boston at your service."

"That a fact?" Vanilla made a show of reading the rest of the card. "It doesn't say anything about that here."

"The trophies are too big to put into print. Plus I didn't want to brag."

"You're not bragging now?"

"I'm just telling it like it is." I smiled, humility never one of my strongest suits and consecutive Messenger Alley Racing titles to rest my laurels on.

"O-kay then, Zesty, think you can cool your heels long enough for me to check on something?"

Vanilla tugged demurely at the low hem of her shrink-wrapped dress, came out from behind her desk, and sidled past me trailing vanilla vapors. I swear I tried not to stare at her as she ambled down the hall. Hell, I even counted to ten and inspected the ceiling. But it was a long hallway and a boring ceiling, and I guess it takes time to sashay ten yards on cork ramps hijacked from the Olympic ski-jump team.

"And help yourself to some coffee," she shouted, rounding a corner out of sight, but I was already in motion unscrewing the top from my thermos, planning ahead for once. Then, from a lineup of mismatched mugs beside the machine, I chose one with a thick red kiss smudged on the rim—what can I tell you, desperate times call for desperate measures—manned up, and drank the coffee black, the lipstick tasting like a morning smooch, something I'd been short of lately, morning, noon, and night. The cat doesn't count. His tongue's too rough.

Outside the windows, Newbury Street shrugged to life, clusters of well-dressed men and women sifting into nearby buildings to do whatever people in offices do all day when they're not updating Facebook. I had a view of my bike chained to the meter where I'd left it and watched as a trio of white poodles dragged one of the Taj bellhops out for a walk, stopping only long enough to sniff my toe clips and pee on my wheels.

Note to self: oil chain.

When a line on the phone console lit up, I walked my coffee into the lounge and killed some time leafing through the DJ's impressive collection of Boston vinyl, two full crates that included some pretty hard to find 45s, limited pressings, and rare independent releases from outfits and recording studios that no longer exist. The only person I know who owns a collection anywhere near this size is my brother, Zero, only he would never allow anyone this close to his prized discs, his diamond-encrusted stereophonic needle forever off-limits to my careless hands.

I let my fingers coast through alphabetized stacks—the Atlantics, Willie Alexander, fronting dozens of other local legends who'd rocked the city proud. A few even tasted a sliver of national fame or notoriety before flaming out or just fading meekly from the scene. I've been to hundreds of shows over the years, and I've seen a lot of these mostly obscure bands up close, even though arguably, by the time I was of legal drinking age, the Bosstown Sound was running on fumes, the city's heyday as a chart-busting rock-and-roll breeding ground fading into the rearview mirror.

My father, whose musical tastes straddled a generational and racial divide—he was a Chess Records and Motown devotee, a huge jazz and gospel fan—ran a speakeasy in the South End for a couple of years before moving on to manage a few rock bands in the early seventies.

The most successful of these groups was the band Mass, their claim to fame a muscular debut album that garnered the attention of Peter Grant, Led Zeppelin's manager, who'd slated Mass to open for Zeppelin in the winter of seventy-five as they toured in support of *Physical Graffiti,* released just weeks earlier and already topping the US charts.

It was the opportunity of a lifetime. But as it happened, fans allowed inside the old Boston Garden's normally restricted advance ticketing areas due to brutal February weather bum-rushed the turnstiles, trashed the Bruins rink ice, and grabbed every souvenir they could pry out of the old building. Zeppelin, not even on the East Coast at the time, was subsequently banned from playing any local venue for five years; not even my father's extensive contacts in the mayor's office were able to convince the city council that the combination of black light and velvet Zeppelin posters posed no long-term threat to the city and its inhabitants.

In a fit of pique, Grant cut Mass off the bill, and the band never realized their dream of sharing the stage with their heroes. And shortly after that debacle, with record sales fizzling in the wake of fan backlash over Zeppelin's Boston ban, Kirko "Kid" Klaussen, Mass's lead singer and songwriter, disappeared following a show at CBGB—stumbled out the back door of the famed New York club and has never been seen or heard from again.

I don't know if Klaussen's disappearance had anything to do with my father quitting the music business altogether, but shortly thereafter, he began parlaying his connections with local rock promoters and club owners, renting their spaces after hours for his Nathan Detroit–style poker games. Less a businessman than an opportunist, my father recognized a need and filled it, organizing and hosting cash-heavy games that brought together would-be or existing club owners with city hall operatives who could tug on the levers of local government and clear the way for any number of related transactions, from fire marshal approved capacity, to zoning regulations, to liquor licenses.

For the majority of these games, my father just dealt the cards, preferring to take his commission—usually 10 percent of the buy-in—up front and to save his considerable card skills for larger cash games where nothing more than money was at stake.

Take notice, Zesty, I can still hear my father saying to me, his yin yang grin firmly in place, *how smoothly things can run in this city after a night of winning poker by the right people.*

Whether this meant my father was manipulating the cards and therefore the outcomes of these games is unclear. Certainly nobody to my knowledge has ever accused my father of cheating, and I never witnessed any in-game sleight of hand—yet issues brought to his green felt docket were almost uniformly resolved, and the wheels of industry did in fact keep turning as they were meant to.

Of course, there was often a darker side to these games and backroom powwows when forces beyond city hall came calling for their cut of the pie, when men representing the interests of certain carting or construction companies with Irish or Italian surnames laid out the terms of tributes or protection fees with all the subtlety of a ball-peen hammer. These negotiations usually required a more nuanced approach by my father, who often assumed the role of mediator because the danger, everyone understood, far surpassed monetary ruin.

For the most part, as far as I could tell, things worked out with a minimum of bloodshed, though truthfully I wasn't paying much attention back then, distracted by the hi-fi buzz of a city that seemed wide open for the taking. After all, this was a period in our lives when Zero and I never had to pay a cover charge at any club, never had to produce any fake IDs and stand there sweating some bouncer's half-witted scrutiny (even though we were underage, and I definitely looked it). Clubs closed or burned seemingly every month, and just as quickly, new ones sprung from the ashes to take their places.

Boston rocked, and Zero and I drank and brawled our way through many a night, secure in the knowledge that if things ever truly got out of hand, we always had a rock-solid Get Out of Jail Free card—courtesy of our father—for just about anything that fell below a felony.

Of course, this was before the city began its conversion into a corporate and academic mega-mall. Gone is the black box of the Rathskeller in Kenmore Square, where bands like the Police and the Pretenders played their first Boston gigs to crowds in the dozens. Gone too is the Channel in Fort Point on the edge of South Boston, the club serving as a demilitarized buffer zone between one of the city's toughest neighborhoods (certainly one of the whitest) and the outskirts of the Financial District. The Channel could hold close to seventeen hundred people and often did as home-grown bands like Jon Butcher Axis, the Neighborhoods, and Mission of Burma played all-ages shows or opened for larger national acts. Same fate for Bunratty's in Allston, also known as Scumratty's for reasons that were, at the time, self-evident, where bands like the Lyres and the Real Kids gained their loyal followings.

There were too many to count really. The city is a haunted playground of clubs that went under as real estate skyrocketed and rents increased: Jumpin' Jack Flash in the Fens, the Penalty Box in the North End, Jack's on Mass Ave. Hardly a single bar Zero or I weren't justifiably kicked out of at some point, banned until new management took over or the bouncers forgot how hard Zero could hit.

Good crimes.

I was still waiting on the caffeine to kick in, lost in the liner notes of a Sex Execs single, when Vanilla returned clutching a heavily taped manila package between razor-tipped fingers. Maybe it was my imagination, but somehow her berry lips had lost their shine, as if the juice had been drained out of them.

"Sorry that took so long. How's that coffee?" she said.

"Awesome, thanks. There a problem?"

"Not if you like decaf there isn't."

Decaf!

"Easy now, Speed Racer." Vanilla shielded her grin with the envelope. "Contrary to the mess, we adhere to a strict no-spitting-in-the-office policy around here. Sorry." She winced. "I should have told you."

"Nah, it's no biggie," I lied, rallying past the urge to claw at my tongue. "Only I consider caffeine, like, one of my basic food groups, and today's just one of those days I need it bad."

"Which makes the two of us, then, only I've been on something of a quitting kick lately. Real coffee and cigarettes are down for the count, leaving only late-night junk food and trashy novels holding on for dear life."

"The last of the vices are last for a reason," I offered, sagely.

"Meaning . . ."

"Like maybe they're just not meant to be given up?"

Vanilla seemed to like that explanation. Not enough to unwrap herself from her dress maybe, but enough to recover her smile.

"Here, let me take that." She handed me the envelope and relieved me of my mug, where the smudged remnant of her kiss was still visible. "Dior Rouge, in case you were wondering."

"I knew that."

"I *bet* you did." She swiped her finger across the rim and dragged some color back to her puckered lips. I waited a couple of beats before following her into the office, holding the thick package down low in front.

"So, Mercury Couriers," she mouthed, cutting me a check. "That's a good name for a courier company. But refresh my Greek mythology for me. Mercury wasn't the one who flew too close to the sun, was he?"

"No. That was Icarus. Mercury's the god of commerce, dexterity, and eloquence. Not to mention speed, of course."

"I'm assuming you know where that is." She extended the check over the desk, pointing it toward an address scrawled across the front of the package in black marker. It was safe now to stow the envelope, slinging my bag to the small of my back.

"So, Zesty, was there some kind of course you had to take to get that name for yourself? You know, like some sort of dexterity and eloquence exam. Touch your toes, recite a poem? I mean, you claim to have the speed part of it down—"

"I thought this was a rush job," I said, eyeing the exit.

"You've got a few minutes."

"Will a limerick do? I've got some really dirty ones."

"I don't think so."

"How about some Charles Bukowski?" I offered. "He's always drunk and fun."

"After last night's Drinkapalooza? I think it's a little early." She tilted back in her chair, crossed her long legs. "Know any Octavio Paz?"

"Who?"

"Elizabeth Bishop? Mark Doty?"

"Can I interest you in some Lou Reed maybe?"

"I think I'd rather hear him do it."

"I don't blame you, I'm nine octaves high anyway. How about a deep knee bend followed by a crisp about-face. Would that suffice?"

"I think it'll have to." She frowned.

I went out past the same guard, freed my bike from the same meter, and poured the contents of my thermos over my wheels and chain, while the guard looked on stone-faced, like he saw this all the time. Foot traffic had picked up some, but it was still early. A handful of parking spaces were up for grabs; the Fashion Police had yet to make an appearance and issue citations. Give it an hour, the street would be mobbed, and you could make a nice living auctioning outdoor seats at Starbucks.

I draped the heavy link chain commando style off my shoulder and pedaled the wrong way up Newbury toward the Public Garden, blondes and coffee—preferably something high-octane—on my mind but not necessarily in that order.

Decaffeinated ghosts steamed off my wheels.

I hooked a right onto Arlington Street, cut through two lanes of traffic. With one hand, I plugged in my iPod, and Gang of Four kicked into a live recording of "I Found That Essence Rare," so I didn't so much hear as feel the loose-strut rattle of the battered Dodge van as it caromed out of a pothole behind me, careened past, and sideswiped the Subaru directly in front; two smoke-black fingers erupted from the pavement as the driver Flintstoned his brakes.

Fuck me.

I cut sharply across the skid, skimmed the Subaru's bumper with my front wheel, and flew blind into the next lane's angry traffic. When I gained the van's window, a pair of scarecrows in worn flannel were slam-dancing the windshield as Iron Maiden implored them to eat their young at twenty decibels.

"Hey, Numb Nuts!" I punched the door hard before spying the wake-and-bake joint burning steadily between the driver's lips, thick smoky pillows curling out the windows toward the street.

Breakfast of Champions.

"Wha?"

"Never mind." I pardoned the kids with a salute, inhaled a loose cloud, and rolled toward the intersection. When I spotted a break in the Boylston Street traffic, I ran the red light in front of us.

I don't know where the gold Buick came from.

Somewhere behind the stoners, I suppose. It gunned the red light like a heat-seeking missile with a bad case of the munchies, a blast furnace firing beneath the hood.

Accelerating!

I stood up on my pedals, leaned hard, and flew through the intersection at warp speed. The Buick's grill ate my back wheel like cotton candy, the crunch of metal reverberating like feedback, earsplitting, unforgiving. I thought I heard the lyric *run to the hills, run for your lives,* and then nothing at all as air thudded out of my lungs and something solid connected with my back, sending me hips over shoulders, still stuck in my toe clips. If my life flashed before my eyes, I either missed it or was so bored by the rerun I forgot it instantly, commercials and all.

The street flew by beneath me, black and calm, a darkened pitted sea. It was only after the acrid stench of hot asphalt and burning rubber filled my nostrils that I realized I'd already landed and might have sunk too deep.

And once the street has you, it never lets you go.

FOUR

Will Meyers is watching Harold and Maude *when the phone rings. There's something about* Harold and Maude *that speaks to him: young Harold, who has everything yet nothing, Maude, who's lost everything but manages to live with that, within that. Will's seen this movie a hundred times already, but the message still resonates. Once he was Harold; now he is Maude.*

The phone rings, and Will looks to Van Gogh Capizo, the cushions trench-sagging from a weight that doesn't just come from fat. Capizo is rounded but solid, a human stack of cannonballs topped by a gleaming bald dome reflecting the TV in surround-vision. Will could watch his head and not miss a thing if only he'd sit still.

Lot of water under the bridge between the two of them, not the least of which includes that AWOL ear. The details elude Will now—the random eraser of his Alzheimer's seeing to that—but still, he's got a notion if it hadn't been for something he'd done, intervened on Van Gogh's behalf, the rest of that giant melon would have gone along with it. That, at least, explains the man's vigilance, his drool-dog loyalty.

Van Gogh—it's a fuck-hard name to forget, and Will's thankful for that. Names are the low-hanging fruit on the memory tree, and once they're gone, they're gone for good.

"You gonna get that?"

"Get what?" Van Gogh shifts his double-barreled backside, the couch practically seesawing as the springs levitate in chain reaction.

"The phone. I can't hear the friggin' movie."

"The phone ain't ringing." Van Gogh frowns, looks to Will. "Anyhow, what's to hear? Just watch."

Will watches. The big man is agitated, but Will blocks out his waves of distraction. That's his gift—even now—to tune out the false signals, manufactured tics, even the unintended obfuscations, the natural signal jammers everybody throws off.

Focus: Harold. The noose. The crystal chandelier. Which is why, minutes later, it's Will who doesn't right off realize Van Gogh has vacated his cushioned hole, the house cell pressed tightly to his only ear.

Yes, now he remembers! Van Gogh doesn't listen, gambling debts, a runaway addiction to action—sports, not cards—bookies controlled by the DiMasis looking to set a meaningful example but settling for his ear, a symbolic message. Will doesn't wonder what Van Gogh's hearing now, what the man is saying on the other end. To him there's no mystery. The devil always calls collect.

Van Gogh hangs up, adjusts the gun in his belt, unable to get himself comfortable at the couch. So it's more for Van Gogh's sake than his own that Will asks, "Him again?"

"Him who?" Van Gogh pulls the gun from his waist, covers it

discreetly with a magazine. There's a strange look on his face, sweat dotting his brow. "It was a woman." Van Gogh shrugs, laces thick hands across his belly. A giant white pearl clamming up.

A woman?

"What did she say?"

"Nothing. She didn't make any sense," Van Gogh says. "Since when do they make any sense?"

"You hung up on her?"

Van Gogh reaches for the remote. "Are we watching the fuckin' movie or what?"

He restarts the film, Will watching the flickering images on Van Gogh's sweaty brow, Cat Stevens singing "Don't Be Shy," a song he wrote for the film, which went on to be a big hit for him. The phone rings, but this time it is Van Gogh who Zens it out. That myth about the other senses kicking into overdrive is a load of nonsense—Capizo reads with bifocals, has the taste buds of a teenager—but maybe Will's taught him something after all.

Will picks up the landline and listens. It's only when Will mutters a barely audible yes into the receiver that Van Gogh pays him any mind. "Yes." Will hangs up and sits back down; Van Gogh looks at him, a question in his eyes.

"It was my wife," Will says.

"Your wife." Van Gogh frowns deeply. "Diane?"

"Yes."

"I didn't hear the phone ring," Van Gogh says. "Are you sure it was ringing?"

"I just told you it was Diane." Will's voice is raised, angry. Since when does he get angry so quick, show everybody what he's thinking?

"Okay, take it easy. What'd she have to say?"

"That's none of your goddamn business, a private conversation between husband and wife."

"Okay." Van Gogh lets it go, turns back to the movie.

"She said she's dead."

Van Gogh sticks a finger into his one ear as if trying to remove an obstruction. "Dead?"

"That's what she said."

"Huh. Anything else? I mean anything that isn't, y'know, fuckin' privileged information?"

"Yes. She said that now that she's dead, I'll know what to do."

"That right? Do you?"

"Know what to do?"

"If that's what she said."

"Yes."

"Swell," *Van Gogh says.* "Now can we watch the movie?"

"Dead." *Will mouths the word, settling in, not so much saying it as trying to taste it, trying to get the feel of it inside him.*

Dead.

He looks to the television, Harold stepping into air, the noose snapping tight around his neck, Harold's mother entering to find him twisting from the chandelier, a look of severe disappointment crossing her face. She seats herself and dials a number from the same model rotary phone Will has just answered, the only difference being the inch of frayed wire jutting from Will's set, a ghost line plugged into nothing.

"I suppose you think that's very funny, Harold," *Harold's mother says in a clipped British accent, which causes Will to laugh aloud. Because for all her self-indulgence, her ignorance and vanity, for the first time Will recognizes that Harold's mother knows exactly what he knows: Nobody dies. He's come to understand that much, at least, as the plaque on his brain renders his memories a mosaic of sea glass, behind which everything goes mist.*

Nobody dies. Why is it Will's the only one around here who understands this? Nobody dies. They just disappear. Slowly at first. In pieces, a little at a time; then suddenly, completely.

And then they buy back in.

FIVE

Boston is a Celtics snow globe, a punch-drunk parade of green snow, blue sky, and pandemonium. I blink toward open blue, but what comes into focus is a short pink skirt over a pair of white lace panties high up on a set of strong legs. The legs seem highly tanned for early June, and they make the panties seem ridiculously white in contrast. Or maybe they are super white. It's hard to focus when little amoebas are doing the Slide and Hustle across my eyes.

Given a different set of circumstances, I'd say maybe this was my lucky day. Only Keith Moon's inside my head doing his best to dent his snare drum, the green snow morphing into a downpour of dead presidents all around me.

The woman with the panties is in excellent shape, knows how to use her elbows, and despite the frenzied competition, seems to be doing all right for herself. The intersection's a mosh pit, people skittering across the pavement chasing dollars and the dream, though it's Pink Skirt who worries me most, her high fuck-me pumps clicking inches from my face each time she lunges to snatch a bill from the air. Leave it to me to survive a collision with a Buick only to be shish-kebabbed by a pair of thousand-dollar Manolo Blahniks.

Something warm and wet rolls down my face as one bill, then another, swirls toward me and sticks to my forehead. Pinky glances at me, momentarily contemplating risk/reward before briskly stepping away. Money changes nothing; I have that effect on a lot of women.

I pull the paper off, blink at Ben Franklin and Andrew Jackson bleeding profusely from head wounds before stuffing them down my shorts. And as suddenly as the cash appeared, it's gone, the second wave of fortune hunters stumbling about as if they've collectively misplaced their wallets and car keys, the blood apparently not bothering them much. *My* blood. They plod around me as if I don't exist; it's a miracle nobody flips me over like a sofa cushion.

Fuck it.

I brace myself with my hands at my sides, tiny pebbles burning craters into my palms. Boylston Street, gridlocked for blocks, tilts sideways, and I have to admit it's a pleasing sight. Short of stump-jumping a Mercedes, it's every messenger's dream to control the flow of traffic for a change, instead of just reacting and avoiding it. Everything you've ever heard about Boston drivers is true: Signaling is for the weak. Side-view mirrors are purely decorative. Stop signs are optional.

Arlington and Boylston are parking lots, car doors flung open like pinball flippers, waves of heat—the staple of sitcom flashbacks—shimmering off blinding front hoods. It's enough to make me smile, only the ringing in my head is painful, a sharp, high-pitched static buzzing between my ears and driving me crazy.

My iPod.

I reach to yank the earbuds, but they're already gone, tossed with my bag, chain, and Motorola. Rotating my head to my shoulder brings the opening notes of a familiar song into proper frequency, but as I touch my chin to my chest, the tune fades into static, making it official: I've become a set of rabbit ears. Radio Shit Shack. A twisted coat hanger stuck at an odd angle to pick up an elusive signal.

I tilt into the opening beats of Stevie Wonder's "Living for the City," a lullaby my father would tuck Zero and me into bed with on the rare nights he was home. Only now it's accompanied by the reverb buzz of a hostile crowd realizing they've missed the windfall and are just late for work. But since there's nothing much I can do about it, I focus on my breathing instead, let my eyes drop closed, visualize the steady stream of ice-cold plasma and menu of prescription painkillers I'll soon call mine.

Stevie fades to static. I try opening my eyes, but they're glued shut. *Don't sweat it,* I tell myself, sinking into the pavement, into the deep black I just swam out of. The rush is over. The pain will pass; it's only a matter of acceptance now. The city and its mixed-up streets will have to wait on me for a change. They'll work themselves out. One way or another, they always do.

SIX

Will doesn't know the woman on his front porch, knows for sure he's never seen her before in his life. But there's a crackling buzz rising off her, which he recognizes as a frequency only people with dark secrets emit.

"Hello, William." The woman smiles through a drunken patchwork of crooked scars that make him think of zippers—what a face! And yet he doesn't avert his eyes as others must, doesn't look away or feign normalcy, and she seems to appreciate that. Although she doesn't say it, her coral gray eyes say it for her.

"It's been such a long time, William. You don't recognize me, do you?"

"No."

"I shouldn't be surprised. I don't look the same since, well . . ." She frames her face with her hands, flutters her arms as if to flap non-

existent wings before pirouetting quite nimbly for someone so large and soft. "Not a clue, huh?"

"No."

"That's all right. I figured as much. The years haven't been kind, which is why I brought pictures. Can I show you some pictures, William? Maybe that will help?" She reaches into her handbag and comes out with photographs and newspaper clippings. Will looks at the photographs; the clippings have black-and-white ones too at the bottom. Now, this woman, this woman he knows.

"Leila," he says with wonder, and looks harder at the pictures, almost like he's trying to see through them. "Leila Markovich."

How could this be? Leila Markovich is a beautiful young woman with dark skin and long straight auburn hair as in the pictures, not a face of zippers, a face of pink wormed scars and a thin-lipped mouth pasted into a pale strip. Yet Will looks into her eyes and knows this is exactly the same woman; there's not a doubt in his mind, and perhaps this is the one gift of his disease, not for Will necessarily, but certainly for the women he's known who have crossed into old age, into soft weight, wrinkles, and scars: He sees them only as they once were, forever young and beautiful.

"May I come in?" this new Leila Markovich asks. She is no longer smiling. Not the lips, not the eyes.

"You're going to stay?" That's the other thing the disease has given him: a directness that doesn't mince words, waste precious time. It's not quite a gift, but neither is it a curse.

"Just for a little while," Leila says. And as he opens the door wide, Will notices, for the first time, the black gun she holds in her hand.

SEVEN

Even through her rubber gloves, the EMT's hands are ice-cold, a minor fault I'm willing to overlook, considering the rest of her is straight-up Asian knockout: willowy, smooth skin, a geyser of oil-slick black hair sprouting high atop her head. She moves with urgency, those cold fingers riding the pulse in my neck before moving toward the throbbing pain above my right brow. Blood stains her gloves. Her eyes tell me she's been here before, seen worse. Unfortunately, the same can't be said for her partner, a steroid abuser with T. rex arms and a crew cut as flat as the bracing board he brought with him.

"Goddamn!" He whistles, catching sight of me before angling the board to shield his view. "Where do you want it?"

"On his other side," she directs him. "Where's the AED?"

"Oh, shit. We need it?"

"No." She glances down, beams me a well-trained smile. Rule Numero Uno they teach you at EMT school: Never let the patient know he's a goner. "But it should be here. And you left the van running. Hey, there, my name's Michaela, and I'll be your EMT today. Can you tell me your name, babe?"

"Zesty," I squeak. I'm back in middle school, and the prettiest girl just asked me to slow dance.

"Hi, Zesty. How're you feeling?"

"Nauseous," I tell her. "In love."

"That sounds about right. Can you feel where I'm touching you, Zesty?"

"Yes. Your hands are cold."

"They'll warm up." She winks, wraps a blood pressure cuff around my arm, ignoring the crowd circled in to share the reading. Finished, she shines a light in my eyes, has me wiggle fingers and toes. "Good. So, Zesty, aside from nauseous, how you doing?"

"How do I look?"

"Oh, I don't know. Sort of like an ATM that got run over. You know where you are, Zesty?"

I tell her.

"You know what day it is?"

"Feels like a Monday."

"That's cheating." Michaela fishes inside a red duffel, peels the cover off a gauze pad, and presses above my right eyebrow. "Can you tell me what happened?"

"I got run over by a gold Buick."

"Do you remember how you fell? What hit first?"

I close my eyes, the black street flying up to greet me again. "No."

"You remember losing consciousness?"

"No," I lie, knowing whatever hospital I'm destined for will insist on an overnight booking if I've been knocked out. I understand the precaution but prefer to recover in a nice quiet bar if I can manage it. Last I checked, a bottle of Jameson was still cheaper than an uninsured night in the hospital.

"Okay. Is there any place hurts really badly, more than another?"

"My head's pounding."

"No surprise. You've got a deep cut above your eye that's causing most of this blood. You'll need stitches, but it's not so bad, considering. Anything else?"

"I was hearing music," I say. "In my head."

Michaela raises her eyebrows to that.

"But mostly static. And this high-pitched noise like when you're spinning a dial, trying to hook a signal."

"And you're sure you didn't lose consciousness?"

"Positive." I flash my best poker face. "Maybe it was a car radio," I add belatedly, trying to throw her off the scent.

How can you tell a poker player is lying? Answer: *When his lips are moving.*

I don't say anything else as Popeye reappears with the AED and one of Boston's Finest in tow, a freckled redhead as tall as Popeye is thick. Red nods at me, almost as an afterthought, crouches opposite Michaela, and unleashes a big hound-toothy smile he probably reserves for sunny June mornings and exotic black-maned EMTs.

"So what are we looking at here?" From his shirt pocket he pulls out a notepad and lays it on my chest—Zesty the Human Coffee Table.

"A few superficial lacs, maybe a couple broken ribs. No loss of consciousness. Name's Zesty. Says he hears music."

"Every time I look at you," I croak.

They both ignore me.

"I just need your name, then we'll lead you out of here."

"She just gave it to you." I tap the notepad with a bloody finger. "You mind not writing on me? It hurts."

"I need your full name." He lifts the pad, flips to a clean page.

I tell him and watch the ill effects of a Boston Public School education rear its ugly head. Maybe the system's on an upswing these days, but his class must have gone from *Jack and Jill* to *Dick and Jane*; here's your diploma. Don't chew gum and operate heavy machinery at the same time. Join the police force. Steady bennies, tons of perks.

As I'm braced and boarded, I glimpse Popeye admiring his biceps, holding his end of my one-seventy with all the effort of a cat napping. Michaela, bent slightly with the strain, unwittingly gives Red an opportunity to steal a long look down her shirt.

Before the ambulance doors slam shut, I catch sight of what's left of my bike, the wheels twisted savagely, hanging spokes, the gear cables snapped, dangling like exposed nerves. The crank is shattered. The seat slumps like a limp dick.

My luck holds true to form as Michaela slips behind the wheel, leaving Popeye unsupervised to cut through my vintage Clash T-shirt, dreams of surgery dancing in his light blue eyes. The radio crackles. The bus lurches into gear. When my head static reasserts itself, it's reduced to background noise, no match for the siren broadcasting my pain to the rest of the town. It sounds different from inside, I realize as we pick up speed. But then again, what doesn't?

EIGHT

Beth Israel Deaconess Medical Center on Brookline Avenue is the place you hope they take you after getting hit by a gold Buick. It's clean, well lit, the halls lined with soothing prints of calm lakes and green forests, no doubt chosen by some interior designer who minored in psychology at school: Dull Your Patients to Health 101.

The emergency room is quiet as I'm wheeled in; people are either getting along or just aiming better. If you read the papers, you'd be inclined to believe the latter. Boston's inner-city neighborhoods, long balkanized primarily along color lines, are starting to drop bodies at a rate not seen since crack was king and Van Halen topped the charts with a song about wanting to bang your teacher.

Only here at Beth Israel, all is floral, the waiting room stocked with enough flowers to bury a war hero, a 1-800 number engraved on each vase in case you've only come calling with a lousy box of chocolates and some trashy magazines.

When Michaela finishes relaying my status to the intake nurse, an orderly with double-shift eyes bumps me through a set of swinging doors, and two hours, five X-rays, and one sleepwalking intern later, a supervising doctor is straight-up carving hieroglyphics on a prescription pad, his smile there but the rest of him already at the club preparing to tee the first hole. "Any questions, concerns?"

"I'm good." I don't tell him about the rough static I'm hearing, the high-pitched frequency floating another familiar song off the dial between my ears, "Where Is My Mind" by the Pixies.

The static is annoying, but my internal DJ rocks.

"The nurse will bring your initial dose. If you don't have a change of clothes, you're welcome to those scrubs on the bed."

It takes me five painful minutes to change into the surgical greens. It takes another three to pad barefoot to the nurse's station and beg the phone. Not surprisingly, nobody addresses me as doctor. Happily, nobody mistakes me for a pillar of salt.

Martha picks up on the fifth ring, still chewing with enthusiasm. "Mercury Couriers," she intones between bites.

"You forgot the jingle."

"You don't have a jingle. Where the hell are you?"

"Beth Israel," I tell her.

"Doing *what*?"

"Working my magic on Florence Nightingale." A nurse looks up from her paperwork, rolls her eyes toward her coworkers. I try winking at them, but the stitches are too painful.

"Yeah? Well, *I've* been busy farming your runs to Owen and Damien. We've been off the hook since an accident backed up Boylston. And why didn't you pick up at Black Hole?"

"What?" I say between static waves and a sharp pain that causes me to squint. "Say that again."

Martha obliges me between chews, and I counter with my own version of the morning, up until my head and the cash hit the street. I can tell she's riveted because the sound of chewing actually stops until I'm done. Or maybe she's just run out of food.

"Zesty, why would Black Hole claim you no-showed if you lost all that money?"

"I don't know. You ever get ahold of Gus?"

"No. Another reason we're swamped."

"Listen, if you get in touch, have him give me a call. No, scratch that," I say, realizing I no longer have a phone or the Motorola. "Just let him know I need to talk."

"You think Gus knows something about the money?" Martha hooks on to my line of thinking: Gus's client. Gus's run, only I got the call instead. I can almost hear the whirring of internal gears as Martha resumes chewing. "Zesty, what're you gonna do?"

"I don't know. Wait for the other shoe to drop. I've got insurance, right?"

Judging from the sound at the other end of the line, whatever Martha had been chewing might have just exited through her nose.

"I'll take that as a no," I say, glumly.

Martha recovers enough to explain that while I do carry insurance, the coverage maxes out somewhere in the neighborhood of two thousand dollars, a paltry sum in retrospect but more than enough to cover the daily slog of contracts, blueprints, and other paperwork that constitute the bread and butter of my assignments.

"I mean, how much money was there?"

I reach down the front of the surgical greens and lift the sticky bills from my cycling shorts. If the nurses weren't amused with me before, they're genuinely disgusted now. I look at the crumpled hundred and twenty in my hand. When I'd come around on Boylston, the sky was a downpour of bills just like them.

"Never mind, I'll dig up the paperwork. Only maybe you won't need it. . . ." Martha was uncharacteristically leaning bright-side: If the money stays unclaimed, I'll have nobody to repay.

"I guess we'll see. I'll get in touch as soon as I can." Figuring at the very least I have a built-in excuse to visit Vanilla Vampire again; give me time to rehearse my lines. *Sorry, the money's gone. What's with the bullshit? You busy Friday night?*

"Zesty . . ." Martha says something else, but heavy static clouds the connection.

"What? You're breaking up."

"I can . . . just fine."

I extend the receiver as far as the cord will stretch, but the static lingers. "I'll call you later," I shout at arm's length, as the nurses stare at me with defensive postures.

"Wrong number," I whisper, gently replacing the receiver.

I'm just starting to lace up my Adidas when my nurse arrives, Dixie-cup rattling my first dose of pain relief. "It says Tylenol and codeine." She barely glances at the prescription I try handing her. "You can start with these, gratis."

"You're joking, right?"

"Concerning what?"

"Check the chart. I got run over by a Buick! That's like an oversized ashtray with wheels. And," I add triumphantly, "I have an extra vertebra."

"Congratulations. You want those or not?"

I throw back the pills, choke them down dry while she delivers instructions in a monotone suggesting a dark knowledge that I won't be following them but here they are all the same.

"Any questions?"

"Yeah, what does someone have to do to get some Percocet around here?"

She concludes the question is rhetorical and exits between a pair of suits who come barging past her, the hot pursuit of their shadows apparently enough of a workout to leave the older of the two, heavyset and black, wheezing in the doorway, his rumpled blue wash-and-wear looking as if it's been getting more wear than wash as of late. The same could be said of his face, which is creased and stubbled, heavily stained under his eyes, giving him the sulking demeanor of a hungover bloodhound. His hair is cut close to his scalp, graying in patches. An unlit cigar protrudes from the corner of thick lips.

The younger man is another story altogether, wolf-lean and hard angled, his midnight suit assembled with Secret Service–like care. He has stubble on his face too, but it has clean-razored lines that come only with expensive manscaping. His hair is gelled, meticulously parted to one side by a team of Caltech engineers. There are no bags under his luminescent green eyes. His fingernails are buffed and polished. His tan is perfect. His shoes belong to Brad Pitt.

Gold Boston Detective shields hang from lanyards looped around their necks. They cross the threshold into the room, the older man kicking out the rubber doorstop behind him. I greet them with a frown. They pretend they're happy to see me.

NINE

They're lousy actors. Homicide detectives almost always are. By rule, it's the narcotics squad that gets all the theatrical types, the stand-up comedians. By comparison, the homicide dicks are the Ed McMahons of the police force—potted plants, spear holders, and cue card readers—players of two roles only and sometimes even those not so well.

The exception to that rule was poker.

In my father's illegal yet sanctioned poker games, the homicide detectives who played—always at the invitation of someone higher up the food chain, a department rabbi or someone dialed into the mayor's office—used their lack of range to their advantage, the gist being that it's awfully hard to read a potted plant. The homicides were also observant, quick to study other players' tendencies and body language, first to capitalize on tells while rooting out the false signals and manufactured tics sent up like smoke signals to obscure the strength or weakness of hands. Poker is a social game, and they were in the people business after all, both the living and the dead.

As a group, if there was one hole in their play, it lay in their dogged pursuit of a hand that needed to be released. The homicide players, almost to a man, were keen observers of others but could hardly recognize their own faults and weaknesses; they stuck around too long and often got burned.

I figure the young cop will lead, work the generational angle, the obvious shared love of fashion. I don't need anybody to tell me I look good in surgical greens.

"Zesty Meyers?" I'm wrong, the seasoned detective opens, leaving the younger detective to drift into the wings silently mouthing his lines. "I'm Detective Brill. Robbery homicide." He tilts his chin toward his gold shield. "My partner there, Detective Wells. How's the head feel?"

"Like it's been run over by a Buick," I tell him.

"So I hear. Doc was amazed it wasn't worse, considering."

"I guess I bounce well," I say, even though I don't really feel it.

"Or you got a hard head. How many stitches he sew into you?"

"About twenty."

"Mmm, not bad. Little war wound give you some character. Isn't that right, Detective Wells?" He addresses his partner's back, the detective busy clicking on the panel lights where my X-rays hang illuminated like haunted house decorations.

"What's that?" With a glowing finger, he traces the alignment of my spine into the area of the hip bones, places his palm flat against the bony stalactites of my fingers dripping off the larger bones of my arms.

"Character," Brill repeats, exasperated by his partner's lack of focus. "The stitches?"

"Yeah." Wells squints at the glowing film, tilts his head like the angle might help him see something he'd otherwise miss. "That's just what this guy needs, more character."

"Shoot. Don't mind Detective Wells, Zesty. He doesn't like hospitals is all. Makes him sort of—"

"Tense," Wells says, pivoting toward us, looking tense.

"Right." Brill rolls his shoulders. "Same with me too. And it's a funny thing, really. Like, I can walk into a morgue, smell of formaldehyde and all those chemicals they got in there, flip toe tags like I'm browsing a yard sale, feel just fine. *Relaxed* even. But here, even with all them pretty nurses, I get all—"

"Tense," I say, saving him the trouble.

"Squirmy," Brill continues as if I hadn't interrupted him. "Isn't that right, Detective?"

"Sure," Wells chimes in on cue. "In the morgue you can catch a nap."

Brill smiles benignly. "You know why I think that is, Zesty?"

"Because you're a homicide detective?"

"Because I'm a *robbery homicide* detective," Brill emphasizes. "But do you know *why,* Zesty?"

"Why don't you tell me, Detective."

"You interested?"

"Not particularly."

"Well, that's too bad. I like the morgue because it's quiet, Zesty."

"Dead quiet." Wells nails his beat, shrugging up his cuff to glance at his expensive watch.

"Peaceful. Nobody yelling 'Code Red,' 'Code Blue,' screaming and crying. The morgue . . ." Brill spreads his hands. "It's just me and the Popsicles, and the Popsicles don't tell no lies, Zesty, you feel me? They're like the last page of a book where everything's out in the open, everything's revealed."

"Depends on what you're reading," I say, just to say something.

"That's true." Brill concedes the point, taking the cigar out of his mouth for inspection. "Still, it's all there; might not know the whole story yet, but I sure as hell know the ending. And they're not going anywhere. . . ."

"Unlike the hospital?" I help him along, the Tylenol and codeine doing jack-shit for my pounding head.

"That's right. People in hospitals got their own agendas. Always in a hurry to get out, and I can't say I blame them. So they do anything, make up stories as they go along. I was here. I was there. I was giving my girl the high hard one, you ain't gonna tell my old lady, are ya?" Brill chuckles but narrows his eyes at me. "You following me here, Zesty?"

"I think so. You prefer the morgue over the hospital."

It's not the answer he's looking for, but it's a perfect segue for Wells to growl in my ear from behind. "Tell us about the accident." His hot breath smells childish. Bazooka bubble gum. "Whose money did you lose?"

I'd been expecting the question, but the length of the preamble and the fact that these are robbery homicide detectives doesn't add up. If Vanilla called Martha claiming I never picked up at Black Hole, I have to figure she didn't call the money in as a theft either. Which leaves what? The Buick killed somebody else after mowing me down?

"I was making a delivery," I say, deciding for now to wait on more cards to fall.

"From where?" Wells doing the talking now, Brill working a notepad he'd lifted from his jacket pocket.

"Black Hole Vinyl," I say, adding the address. "It's a local record company."

"*Record* meaning black vinyl discs, Detective," Brill says, without lifting his eyes off the notepad. "With grooves in them, which when played on a phonograph at a certain speed, the disc rotating under a fine needle produces the distinctive sounds of music. I can catch you up on this later if you're unclear on the concept."

Wells pretends not to hear his partner but slips a smile. "Who gave you the package?"

"Girl in the office, I didn't catch her name. It was a twelve-by-twenty-four manila envelope. Address on the front in black marker."

"Did I ask you that?"

"What?"

"Did I ask what the package was?" Wells stares at me.

What the fuck? I shrug, regretting the movement as pain shoots down my spine into my lower legs. I feel the static behind my eyes before I hear it. Black and white dots, needles, something sizzling in a cast-iron skillet.

"Can you describe the woman?" Brill gives me something else to focus on.

"Huh?"

"The one gave you the envelope?"

"Yeah, sure." I take my time doing it, working the details.

"I get the picture." Wells interrupts my poetic flow, turns to Brill. "You getting all this?"

"I underlined the word *hot*," Brill says. "Twice."

"She tell you what you were carrying?"

"No."

"You don't ask?"

"No."

"Don't care?"

"Long as it's not ticking," I say, which happens to be the truth. My job is simple. People call me to pick things up and deliver them. What I'm hauling across town is none of my business.

"Was there anyone else in the office when you got there?"

"No."

"See the whole thing?"

"Yes. No. Some doors were closed."

"So how do you know you were alone?"

"They had a party last night, and she said she was the first one in."

"Can anyone besides the girl confirm your being at the office?"

"There was a doorman. He saw me in and out." Did I sign a register at the front desk? I can't remember.

"But nobody *in* the office?"

"Not that I saw. There was some confusion on her part whether I was picking something up or dropping off."

"Yeah? Why's that?"

I explain to the detectives what I'd already explained once that morning: I'd been covering for Gus; our assignments are farmed out from our shared office off Berkeley.

"So it's not your regular run," Brill says.

"Exactly."

"Okay, you show up, the place is a mess, nobody knows if anything's coming or going. This sort of thing happen a lot?"

"More than I'd like." Especially in some of the larger firms where the chain of command isn't so clear and there are more rules than Parliament. Corporate confusion is not entirely without an upside, though: Reception lounge surfing is where I hone my chat-up skills.

"So what then?"

"She left for a few minutes, made a call to clear things up." Could she have given me the wrong package by mistake?

"She tell you that? That she was going to clear things up?"

"Something to that effect. One of you gonna tell me how any of this will help you find who ran me over?"

"We'll get to that in a minute. How do you know the girl dialed out? Maybe she was checking with someone in another part of the office."

"I saw a line on the phone light up."

"Maybe someone was calling the office."

"The phone didn't ring. Why's this so important?"

Wells ignores my question. "So what were you doing while she was on the phone?"

"Guzzling office coffee."

"Yeah?" Both detectives stir to attention.

"Decaf," I say.

"Jay-sus!"

"Tell me about it." I really do blame everything on the coffee. The day I can't outsprint a Buick across a busy intersection is the day I hang up my toe clips.

"And this was what time, did you say?"

"I didn't. I don't wear a watch."

"Sure. Who wants to be bothered with all that responsibility?"

Brill: "And where did you say the package was going?"

"I didn't say that either."

"So where was it going?"

I think about that for a longer moment, until it becomes a

string of moments and starts hurting my head. I can picture the envelope, but the address is a complete blank. "I don't know," I say, finally.

"You don't know?" Wells has to gather an errant bubble before he can continue. "You pick up a lot of packages and not know where the hell they're going? What, you just pick a spot, drop them off?"

I don't bother answering because there's nothing to say. I must've had a notion where I was headed when I tripped my way out of one Black Hole before falling into a deeper, darker one. Only now I can't remember a thing. Shades of things to come? Is this how my father felt when Alzheimer's crept inside his head, throwing a murky veil over the little things first? The car keys. The wallet. Whose deal is it? Setting the stage for the darker hours ahead. Did he lie in bed and wonder what was happening to him, chalk it up to stress, irregular hours, sketchy company? Doubtful. Far likelier, my dad's first response was to try and strike a bargain with the disease, broker a deal as he's always done.

Okay, here it is. You can have the car keys, the parking spot, and the wallet. I'll throw in all of Yastrzemski's at-bats, the comparison to Williams's statistics, the lyrics to "Sea of Love," and the time I played cards with Sinatra in Vegas.

Leave me my children's names.

Wells tires of waiting me out. "Besides the money, what else were you carrying when you got hit?"

I recite the short list, omitting the Altoids tin with a couple of loose joints I had knocking around.

"And you think, what, someone ripped off your pack when you went down?"

The pain from my last shrug reminds me to answer the question verbally, though I'm finding it hard to concentrate, another signal breaking through the static.

"Hey, Zesty, you all right?"

Sure, Detective. It's been twenty-four hours since I've had a real cup of coffee, and in that time, I've been run over, lost a wad of cash that doesn't belong to me, had my best bike twisted into a Dalí sculpture, and been given the equivalent of baby aspirin for my troubles. And oh yeah, I have no health insurance and a DJ's spinning records in my head. Things are great. Thanks for asking.

"What?"

"Was there anything in the package besides the money?"

"How should I know? Didn't we go over this already?"

"You ever deliver for Black Hole before?"

"No."

"Been to their offices before this morning?"

"No."

"Inside the building?"

"Maybe a few times. One of you gonna tell me what's going on here?"

"Just a couple more questions. So aside from the cash, there's no reason anyone would want to steal your bag, right?"

"Because it's there?"

"Or try to hit you?"

"Deliberately, no."

"Because you're there?" Brill says, without any mirth behind it.

"In this city?" I shake my head slowly, wince through a set of high-pitched frequency. The room starts to tilt.

"Ever been hit before?" Wells re-ups another brick of Bazooka, meticulously refolding the wrapper and placing it in his front pocket; likely a crime-scene habit—a place for everything and everything in its place. If I had to guess, his childhood home was an unholy mess, rusted cars littering the yard, rags for clothes, pale-skinned and anemic kids everywhere.

I lean forward, hooking the loose signal—bass and saxophone—a familiar tune filtering through. If the detectives think my movements are strange, they don't say so.

"Sure. Probably a half dozen times if you count getting doored. Boston drivers have a reputation to uphold, wouldn't want to disappoint anyone."

"Occupational hazard?" Brill says smiling.

Like bullets for you, I think but don't say. Only this is the first time my job included a grilling from a couple of homicides, and frankly, I've grown tired of it.

"Detectives, I don't mean to be rude, but let me point out *I'm* the fuckin' victim here. You want to write me a ticket for littering, jamming traffic, get on with it already and then go look for who ran me down."

Brill: "You trying to tell us how to do our jobs, Zesty?"

"I'm just figuring maybe you got better things to do with your time than add to my headache."

"Yeah? Like what?"

"I dunno, if BPD's got you double-timing robbery-homicide, you could always go to Roxbury, Mattapan, count real dead bodies or something."

"Bodies everywhere." Wells steps toward me into what my brother, Zero, would describe as my personal space. "Don't have to go to the Berry to find one."

Zero's always been big on personal space, and there're more than a handful of people walking Boston's streets with missing Chiclets who've had the misfortune of finding that out the hard way. Myself, I've always carried a more flexible bubble around my person. Spatial boundaries aren't nearly as sacrosanct to me, something the detective either seems to intuit or just doesn't give a flying fuck about.

I'm not claiming to be a Zen master, but patience I happen to have in spades, a trait my father always claimed was my strongest poker upside, this ability to ride the game's unpredictable rhythms, absorb the bad beats and amateur river pulls without going into full-tilt mode, to basically survive and wait for Lady Luck to rescind her temporary and fickle crush on somebody else.

So I'm hardly rattled with Wells's hot breath on my face, and anyhow, if it had a color it would be pink, and I happen to like pink (another reason Zero thinks I'm half gay). I don't back away. Partly because any movement is painful and partly because I'm getting clear reception for Morphine's Mark Sandman coming in over the top of a wounded saxophone on the opening notes of "Cure for Pain."

"Good for you, then," I tell Wells, my chin still pointing toward my chest. "Why don't you get out of my face and go play with one."

"Well, see, Zesty." Brill's cigar nearly takes out my eye as he steps between us. "That's the thing. We already got us a body. And a few of the bills you lost this morning too. Let me show you something." Brill produces two photographs and extends them to me. "You recognize this man?"

I look at the first picture, the type you might see on a license or company ID, cropped just to get the image from the chest up. The man in the photograph has close-shorn blond hair, thin bloodless lips, and weak eyes that seem to be avoiding the camera's direct stare. He's wearing a gray uniform with WELLS FARGO stitched above his right breast pocket. The second photograph is of the same man in the same uniform, except in this one he's slumped against the rear wheel of an armored truck, his head tilted at an odd angle toward his shoulder. One eye is open but vacant, and there's a bloody hole where his other eye should be. The front of his uniform is soaked in blood, a Rorschach splatter on the truck behind him, the picture taken while thick drops of gray matter still seemed to be sliding off the center splat.

I take a deep breath and give the detectives a long, hard look, vaguely aware that I've begun to rub the photos together like red-hot hole cards burning my fingertips. Though the detectives seem an odd pairing, what they share is the same implacable faces of overworked and underpaid cops everywhere, men and women sent out to do jobs nobody else really wanted or was capable of doing. I knew the look well enough—the cement-grinding jaws always chewing on a thought or angle, the cynical brows, doubting lips, and liar's eyes—I grew up around these types of faces. They are the faces of lowered expectations.

I squeeze the pictures one more time, Brill and Wells waiting patiently, their feet flat on the floor, eyes dull now with seeming disinterest. They are the city's dogs, and they don't expect a bone from anybody. And they certainly don't get one from me.

"No," I lie to them. "I don't know this guy."

TEN

Leila Markovich sits in the cratered cushions looking like she's fallen into a deep hole, the gun, a black .45 semiautomatic with a beavertail grip and carbon steel finish, on her lap now. Will knows how it feels to hold a gun like this in his hand. This knowledge is something he'd gladly trade in for something else, only his dementia isn't a menu of deletions and substitutions, allowing him to pick and choose what stays or goes.

"I spoke with Zero," Leila Markovich says. "He told me it wasn't the best time to see you. Only I couldn't wait, it's moving too fast."

"Zero," Will says.

"Your son."

"Yes. I have two sons. Zero and . . . and . . ."

"Zesty," Leila Markovich says.

"Yes. Zero and Zesty. They'll be home from school soon. Who did that to your face?"

"You don't remember?"

"No."

"It happened after I turned myself in. He still had influence then, people who feared him, even inside those walls. You know I've been in prison, don't you?"

"Yes. Somebody cut you with a razor?"

"There were two of them. These are only the scars you see. There are more of them on my body. I wasn't supposed to survive."

"But you did."

"I'm here, aren't I?"

Yes. But that doesn't mean as much as it once did. After all, everybody's here.

"And the people who did this to you?"

Leila Markovich conjures a thin smile, the only smile she can manage with what's left of her lips. A smile that sparks something else Will remembers about this woman, something that reveals her answer before she speaks it. Yes, Leila was always very dangerous. Beautiful and dangerous. And now her beauty is gone. So what does that leave?

"I killed them both," she says.

"In self-defense," Will says, and when Leila Markovich says nothing else, he adds, "To survive." Because Will knows a little something about dying to survive too.

"Perhaps," Leila says, looking through him to someplace far away, her fingers twitching on the gun. "You might say that."

ELEVEN

I catch a cab out in front of the hospital, the driver a gritty pug of a man, a city street version of Old Salty—seen it all, driven all over it. In fact, he could be one of Boston's last white cabbies, but it doesn't say that on the ID posted between the double-thick wall of cloudy Plexiglas that separates us.

"Charles Street," I tell him, easing back into spider-cracked leather.

"Which way?"

"Doesn't matter," I tell the cabbie. "I got money to burn."

We take Brookline Avenue past Simmons College, cross Park Drive, and roll into the Fenway, ramping Storrow Drive inbound, the sun-kissed Charles River sliding past my open window. There are a handful of joggers and rollerbladers circling the Charles, but they pass each other in opposite directions without incident. A man with two Labradors hurls a stick into the river, a flock of geese giving way as the dogs belly flop in hot pursuit. Traffic is light, the sky an endless expanse of open blue, and a Wells Fargo guard by the name of Collin Sullivan isn't enjoying any of it because five days ago, somebody put a bullet through his head.

The robbery had been the breathless lead-in on every local newscast—Boston loves itself a good armored car heist—and I'd read the *Globe* coverage in passing but don't recall whether the article named Sullivan as the guard who was killed. What I do remember is the truck was hit during its first drop of the day, the solitary shot that killed Sullivan coming only after his gun and the shotgun belonging to the guard riding the box had already been surrendered. The money was then loaded into a green Ford pickup that was found an hour later torched and empty down a steep embankment on the Jamaica Plain side of Franklin Park.

Beyond that, I know diddly, including why Wells and Brill would question me about Sullivan, whom I knew only in passing from working for Zero's Somerville-based moving company, a second job I sometimes take on when things are slow and I'm having a hard time making ends meet. Do the detectives know Sullivan moonlighted for my brother? I didn't get that vibe, since Zero's name didn't come up during questioning, but I'm not enjoying the six degrees of separation whittled to five, and if history's any guide, where there's money and trouble, odds are my brother's somewhere in the mix.

Salty curls off Storrow, a red light idling us around the bend from the Charles Street Jail. Of course, CSJ isn't a jail anymore—Boston taxpayers get awful ornery when inmates are afforded prime river views—it's been converted into a luxury hotel where rooms with steel bars cost extra, I shit you not. Slip the bellhop a fifty, he'll be happy to rake a billy club as you drift to sleep, give you that authentic jailhouse vibe.

As the cab cuts into the curb in front of the Sevens pub, I unfold Andrew Jackson and slip him into the cash slot, Salty glancing at the bloody bill before staring at me red-faced in the mirror.

"You didn't know Jackson was a hemophiliac? It's all I have. Keep the change."

Sam Budoff greets me swaying atop the landing of his four-story limp-up, an uneven skyline of black hair sprouting from his scalp at ridiculous angles, a paean to excessive Dippity-do and pillow-generated static electricity.

"I know you're confused," I tell him as he squints toward the skylight. "But what you're experiencing is called daylight. You work last night?" Which, in Budoff's case, means dragging his heels toward the longest-running doctoral thesis in MIT history. One day Sam will look back at grad school and think, *The finest ten years of my life.*

"Did some testing." Sam ushers me in with a quick glance down the stairwell, a symphony of locks clicking into place behind me.

One might assume Sam's work had taken place at the MIT labs, but I wouldn't wager money on it. The kitchen's open-ended dividing counter is littered with beakers and Bunsen burners, a long hose running from the sink into a small hole drilled into the center of the refrigerator door. In the middle of the studio, two ping-pong tables have been pulled together and are covered with an assortment of beakers, burners, microscopes, and a digital scale. In lieu of a living room, an undersize couch sits centered between two street-facing windows, stacks of newspapers propping a telescope that can spot naked women on Mars.

"You want coffee, I presume."

I do want coffee, and as I wait for it, I aim the telescope onto Charles Street, traffic bottlenecked to Charles Circle behind a black Pathfinder double-parked across the way. As I open the window for some air, someone across the street parts a set of curtains and does the same. I wave but don't get a response. I suppose it's because I'm not on a boat. People always wave to other people on boats. Except in Boston Harbor. In Boston Harbor they give you the finger.

"What are you looking at?" Sam sets a French press on the floor beside me, grounds floating to the top like grate-trapped sewer water.

"I think someone's scoping your apartment." I point out the windows.

"It's nothing to get excited about. Her name's Sheila; she bartends at the Pour House."

"I don't think it's a woman."

"Then it's her boyfriend. They like to fuck with the lights on and the shades up."

Which explains why the couch faces the window. *Ew!*

"You getting paranoid on me, Zesty?"

"Paranoid?" I pour the coffee and take a bite; it's not half bad. "You tell me."

I recount my day for Sam, squinting as a bolt of pain shoots over my right eye, making it feel like the stitches are about to pop free. Only as expected, Sam's interest centers mainly on the prescription I'd handed him, which he tears into tiny pieces and deposits over his shoulder.

"That's insane. I sprinkle Tylenol and codeine on my cornflakes, for fuck's sake."

"Which accounts for your always lucid demeanor," I say.

"Which accounts for your being here, dickweed."

"Good point," I concede. Because MIT has long held the reputation as Boston's premier Geek University, it might come as a surprise that on any given day, a sizeable portion of its student body can be found counting cards in illegal Chinatown casinos or figuring out unique ways to blow shit to smithereens. Sam's specialty happens to be boutique pharmacopeia, and therefore I tend to defer to his wisdom, his nondegree status notwithstanding.

"Your recommendation, Professor?"

"You could start by biking better. Other than that, I think I have something that'll do the trick. How's the noggin?"

"Hurts, but no more than anyplace else. I'm hearing music, though."

"Right now?" Sam concentrates in the direction of his Bose box, trying to pick up vibrations. If he were a pointer, his ears would be sticking straight up. As it is, it's just his hair.

"No. Now it's just static, like the HBO opening credit. It comes and goes."

"Like bad reception?"

"Exactly. And then music floats in behind it. Good tunes so far."

"Familiar?"

I run down the playlist.

"Maybe you're channeling Pandora. Anything else?"

"Body pain. Soreness. You have a theory on the music?"

"Just what I know from reading some Oliver Sacks. There's a condition that can take the form of musical hallucinations, which sounds like something you might be experiencing. Only it's rare and I don't remember anything suggesting it can be triggered by brain trauma. Stroke maybe. Seizures. Lightning. You black out?"

"Just for a few seconds. Twice I think."

"You tell them that at the ER?"

"Hell no."

"Because . . . ?"

"What're they gonna do, stick me in a hospital bed, wake me every couple hours to shine a light in my eyes, and then sic their bill collectors on me? I took a pass."

"Explain how you figured you were only out a couple seconds."

I have to concentrate for a moment to answer that question. "The money was still blowing when I came to the first time."

"And the second?"

"I'm not so sure, but I don't think it was long. You should've seen the responding EMT. She was capital H, *caliente*."

"You tell her that?"

"I tried."

"Big shocker. Score digits?"

"No."

"What, she wasn't into piñatas? Don't answer that. Let me hook you up with what you came for and then I'll run a search, call a neuro buddy of mine at Harvard, see what he says about the music. You have plans rest of the day?"

"I was thinking about checking into the office, see if maybe I can scare up some gear." There's always a mishmash of bike frames and parts lying around that I could piece together, augment my backup bike at home, maybe score another Motorola and a spare bag. And while I'm at it, I'll check in with Martha to see if she's heard anything from Gus, give Zero a heads-up he might be getting a visit from Boston's Finest, though something tells me he already knows.

"Eighty-six that. I've got your afternoon right here." Sam shakes a blue gel tablet from a plastic Advil bottle. "Don't be fooled by appearances."

I throw back the pill with the last of my coffee, my headache, I realize, already neutralized by the caffeine. How out of balance can a body get? Bulldozed by a two-ton gas-guzzler but suffering more from caffeine withdrawal.

"There's a good boy." Sam is only too happy to break down what I just ingested; the bogus gelcap contains a less than homeopathic blend of painkillers and muscle relaxants, certainly nothing I can't handle, considering my checkered resume.

"That's it?" It's not that I'm ungrateful, only Sam's grinning like an idiot.

"Well . . . maybe with a smidge of hallucinogen thrown in for fun." Sam is never as happy as when he gets to spread his chemical joy among friends. "Relax, Ace, it's nothing out of your league. As for your other problems, the one thing I *can* offer you is the spot where your girl from Black Hole crashes."

"You know her? Now, why doesn't that surprise me?"

"Because I'm popular?"

"That's only because you're a drug dealer."

"What'd I just say? Anyhow, I don't really know her per se,

but I've been to a couple after-hours at her place up around Mission Hill, right past the spot where that Stuart prick shot his wife? You can't miss it, seeing how the city planted some monster oak out front. All the bodies dropped in this town; one white lady gets killed in a black neighborhood, and they plant a tree in her memory? Fuck, Zesty, they do that for everyone, the damn city be Sherwood Forest by now. You could go camping in Mattapan, tap maple syrup in Roxbury. Be like Boy Scout heaven. Anyhow, her house is a two-family with double front porches out front, sagging like Dolly Parton's tits if she didn't get them lifted every year."

"Hey, I like Dolly Parton."

"What's not to like? I'm just saying."

"This girl got a name, Sam?"

"Britta . . . something. Gus would know. He was pretty sweet on her."

"They were an item?"

"What do I look like, the scorekeeper for eHarmony? Listen, Zesty, don't make me regret giving you the heads-up on this. My advice: Let this shit work itself out. Don't go *looking* for trouble."

"I'm not sure I can do that," I say.

"Why, because you think somehow your brother's got skin in this game?"

"What? What're you implying?"

"Come on, Zesty, wake the fuck up. You make it rain on Boylston, and next thing you know, a couple of homicide cops are flashing you pictures of this Wells Fargo guard? Do the math."

"Zero's not a killer," I say, with a little too much edge in my voice. Trying to convince Sam or myself?

"Nobody's saying he is. But you're not *listening,* Z. Britta laid it on Martha that you no-showed, she's either working her own thing or just following orders, right? Long as nobody's coming after *you* for the money, wherever it came from, I'd say you're in the clear. So stay that way. And as for Gus, I'm no hypocrite; we all have to make a little side-scratch to live in this town."

"What's *that* supposed to mean?"

"You're not hearing me, Zesty. Enough with the questions. All you have do right now is sit back and enjoy the ride. You think you can do that?"

I tell Sam I can do that, but while I still have my head about me, I start in with the telescope again. The shades are still drawn across the way, the Charles Street foot traffic thickening as the tourists and swells tumble down from the billion-dollar Beacon Hill town houses. The black Pathfinder pulls away before I can focus on the driver's-side window. A messenger I don't recognize weaves nimbly between cars, a silver canister wagging side to side as he navigates the stop-and-go flow; the tube probably holds blueprints or plans of some sort, and he's maybe heading down-town to a design studio or architecture firm. I doubt it's stuffed with hundred-dollar bills. Chances are he won't get run over by a gold Buick. Ten to one he won't be grilled by a couple of mur-der cops. Is that static on the horizon?

No. Sam's closed the bathroom door. It's the shower I'm hear-ing, only why so loud?

I start pulling out newspapers—the *Globe* put the Wells Fargo heist on Wednesday's front cover. I give the story a quick read, but it's getting hard to concentrate, the words falling off the page like they've been greased, Sam's magic pill starting to take effect. What am I looking for?

Sam has the papers stacked consecutively, and I run through them in order. The robbery got kicked to the Metro-Region section on Thursday, was buried deeper by Friday. But I'm not interested in any of it, not the robbery, not Collin Sullivan, who as far as I'm concerned is somebody else's headache. I'm just the messen-ger in the middle, and I didn't even deliver any of the bad news. Hell, I didn't deliver *anything*. What am I looking for?

I'm going the wrong way, that's the problem. I tip the pile, papers fanning out onto the floor, pull magic on my first try. I'd avoided reading the story as long as I could, only I knew I'd have to get to it sometime. As my father was fond of saying, *There are only so many loose threads you can ignore before you're standing naked in the wind*. I blink at the page and read:

FREEDOM FOR LEILA MARKOVICH:
MASSACHUSETTS PAROLE BOARD GRANTS RELEASE AFTER
TWENTY-ONE YEARS

Boston—Reopening a chapter in the history of Massachusetts and American radicalism, the Massachusetts Board of Parole yesterday voted to release Leila Markovich, 62, the 1980s radical and former cofounder of the Sparhawk Brigade. Ms. Markovich had been serving a sentence of twenty years to life after her conviction for her role in the 1986 robbery of the Allston branch of Bank of Boston and concurrent bombing of District 14 Headquarters that left a retired policeman and a bank manager dead and two officers severely wounded. Ms. Markovich is due to be released sometime this week, said Martin Flinck, a spokesman for the State Division of Parole.

The decision to grant Ms. Markovich parole came after two previous reviews by parole board commissioners, who had denied her parole request. It remains unclear what prompted the board's change of decision, but upon its announcement, Governor Gregory Hibert denounced the determination to free her. "This is a travesty of justice," Mr. Hibert said. "And certainly not a decision I would have made. The cold-blooded killings of Edward Kelleher and James Sheehan were horrific crimes and ones that should be punished to the fullest extent of the law." Aides to the governor, who had appointed both commissioners during his first term, vowed that he would actively explore ordering a recission hearing to appeal the decision.

Ms. Markovich's imminent release leaves only one surviving member of the Sparhawk Brigade yet to serve time behind bars, Diane Meyers, who remains underground and is still wanted on murder and armed robbery charges in connection with the same 1986 robbery. Ms. Meyers has been a fugitive from justice since March of 1981, when she was implicated in a bomb explosion on the campus of Harvard University that severely injured two administrators. Rachel Evans, the bank teller planted inside the Bank of Boston, had also eluded capture but died in a fall from a Delray Beach hotel balcony in 1988.

The FBI believes Ms. Meyers has used a variety of aliases during her time on the run, including the identity of one Jane Orr, who was murdered in Los Angeles in 2002, her body discovered beneath a highway overpass, her mouth crammed full of bills later traced to a 1979 Boston armored car robbery attributed to the Lockwood Brothers Gang that had operated out of South Boston. Johnny and Jimmy Lockwood were murdered in 1980, allegedly by Richard Ritter, Devlin McKenna's former triggerman, in a dispute over what is believed to be tribute payments related to that robbery.

There's more to the article, but I can't make out the words as they fall off the page, the paper dropping from my fingers. Collin Sullivan, Leila Markovich, my infamous mother, Jane Orr, Rachel Evans, Devlin McKenna and the Lockwood Brothers, banks and armored cars, blood, history, memory, a loose constellation falling from the sky.

I lie back on the couch, my legs dangling off the end. I wonder for a moment about who nabbed my gear and whether they're smoking my weed. I wonder if Britta has a steady boyfriend, and if she does, I wonder if he could kick my ass. Right now, I wonder who couldn't.

When the walls start breathing, I'm not alarmed. When a neon waterfall spills behind my eyelids, I go with the flow. When the neon splashes letters, the letters morphing into red hot words, the words forming an address, I know I should write them down, but my arms are on vacation and I can't feel my hands. I'll tell Sam the address when he's done with his static shower. He'll remember it or write it down for me. Sam's a good friend. I love Sam. I'll have to tell him that too. He can also write that down if he wants. It's good to keep a record of things.

A lot goes missing around here.

TWELVE

Will lets his mind drift because concentrating only draws the black tide faster. Leila Markovich is not the same person she once was. How old are his sons? What is his wife's name? Goddammit, where the hell is Van Gogh? Will's hands shake, but he manages to still them by visualizing a deck of cards, the feel of them on his fingertips, the way the pack fits snug in his palm. Silence doesn't bother him, nor does it seem to bother Leila Markovich. Silence is a commodity they recognize; they've both traded on it for a long time.

"Why are you here?" Will finally thinks to ask. And from the

grateful look on Leila's face, what's left of her face, he knows that it's the right question to break this silence, the only question.

"You don't know?" Leila studies him a moment before nodding, a different question left unasked, but answered nonetheless.

How could Will not know? He's been calling him, hasn't he, his voice like broken glass over the line. Yes, of course Will knows, it just takes him a moment. "Devlin McKenna," he says, the name acid on his tongue, bile in his throat.

"Yes."

"Devlin McKenna," he repeats, not because he likes the taste, but because it has *a taste. And taste for him is memory. "He calls me." Will points to the rotary phone; Leila registers the severed cord, the ghost line to nowhere.*

Nonetheless: "Do you talk to him?"

"No, I just listen. It feels like he's close."

"I think he is. What does he say?"

"He wants his money."

"Yes, the money," Leila Markovich says. "Do you have the money, William?"

"From the robbery?"

"Yes, from Bank of Boston. Do you still have it?"

"No," he says. "Yes," he says. No? Yes? What money? Which money? Whose money?

"I don't remember," he says.

"That's all right," Leila says, petting the gun in her lap. "Yes or no, it doesn't matter. He's back, but everything's changed, as he must realize. Still, money or no money, he will come for us. You understand that, don't you, William? He'll try to kill us like he killed Rachel, and Michael Drain, and Tara Agostini. He will try to finish my face, as it were."

Yes, Leila's face, what a poker face! To have a face nobody could bear to read. Only Will does; there's a lot of life left in that face, those eyes.

"Yes." Will understands McKenna will try to kill them both again. But what he is also thinking is that this time everything will be different. Because this time, Will has decided, he will kill McKenna first.

THIRTEEN

I wake up in my own bed. It's dark and the cat is curled beside me, asleep and snoring lightly. It looks like my cat. It has the same black body and white paws, the same easy and gentle snore that says, *I've never worked a day in my life and never will,* which is why I roll over him, my eyes adjusting to the darkness; everything in my room is as I left it or has been replaced by ingenious replicas, part of some diabolical plot meant to lull me into a false sense of security.

Just in case, I sit up vigilantly, try to piece together how I got home from Sam's Charles Street apartment. I remember swallowing what looked like Advil and then . . .

Never mind.

According to my wind-up Mickey, it's almost nine, making it roughly six hours since whatever I ingested put my nervous system on ice, which, even by my highly refined slacker standards, qualifies as a pretty long nap. My head feels spongy and the throbbing above my right eye is back, but the static between my ears is gone and I'm no longer picking up classic hits radio on my fillings.

As I snap, crackle, and pop my way to the bathroom, I pause long enough to pull the hall-light string but get nothing in return for my effort. I do the same in the bathroom, get the same nothing, strip, and shower in the dark, my cuts stinging like fresh knife wounds under lukewarm water. My mouth is sticky as a Roach Motel, so I brush twice for good measure and gargle with something I'm almost sure is mouthwash. My hair's a tangled, blood-clotted mess and there's no conditioner, so all I can do is run water through it before using a little leftover olive oil to help tie it back in a high samurai ponytail.

Banzai!

Back in my room I fumble through shelves, pull down boxer briefs, a pair of shorts and a T-shirt, grope the fuse box, and expend my sum knowledge of electricity flipping switches.

The loft stays dark.

I can only assume it has something to do with those bills stacked on my desk, specifically the envelopes marked TIME SENSITIVE in red ink. It's the red ones you have to look out for. The blue ones just mean they're on to you. The red ones mean the fix is in. All of which means I neglected to pay Boston Edison again, only life's too short to stress these sorts of things. Not the least because it's due to nothing beyond attrition and the vagabond nature of roommate situations that I've ended up responsible for most of the bills and anything related to the lease. Obviously, I use the word "responsible" loosely, but it's a more complicated matter than meets the eye because the loft is strictly commercially zoned and therefore unfit for residential occupation. Same goes for the bulk of properties on nearby Randolph and Albany Streets; ditto for parts of Bristol and Harrison Avenue, all of which exist in a no-man's-land of former manufacturing and industrial warehouses a stone's throw off the Central Expressway on the South End's outer border.

In the early 1990s these streets were Boston's skid row, the warehouses boarded up and vacant until artists and musicians began converting the giant factories into rehearsal spaces and studios, nailing up drywall, stripping bricks, and installing makeshift plumbing while Spagnola Realty Trust Co. turned a blind eye, ignoring that people were actually living in these spaces. The majority of rents were kept off the books, paid in cash, the trade-off an unspoken deal: *We pretend we don't live here, and you pretend not to notice we do.*

The few leases that actually exist are strictly commercial, and Mario Spagnola, playing the part of commercial landlord, cuts the heat promptly at six in the evenings and on Sundays doesn't turn it on at all. This past February was so cold I spent most of it sleeping in my winter coat, the cat's water bowl freezing nightly, and though it pained me deeply, I was forced to eliminate the line "your place or mine?" from my repertoire.

By the time I arrived on Thayer, there were few spaces that hadn't already been converted into some form of mixed-use loft; music from rehearsing bands or construction noises (sometimes it was hard to tell the difference) drifted into the street at all hours. Impromptu parties went deep into the night, nary a neighbor to be disturbed and call the cops. You could always find someone to lend you paint or brushes on Thayer Street, a darkroom in which to develop photos, and people to pose for them, or just stave off loneliness with a drink or a bong hit at the Rez, a dark and ratty basement speakeasy at the corner of Thayer and Albany, the site of massive after-hours parties and all-you-can-swill keggers headlined by acts like Bullet LaVolta, Malachite, and the Cavedogs.

Not everybody was an artist, of course, but the neighborhood had something for everyone: games of stickball and street hockey in the empty streets and parking lots, Sunday tag football games, atomic clouds of pot smoke emanating from prolonged huddles and mingling with the noxious exhaust from bumper-to-bumper traffic on the expressway. By all rights E-Z Wider should have paid us a sponsorship fee.

It was great while it lasted. But as the Big Dig ramped up and encroached on the neighborhood, construction equipment was routinely vandalized, leading to sporadic scuffles between construction workers and residents, drawing police attention and, finally, the city's all-in commitment.

What was the civics lesson learned? The most basic one of all: Not only can you not fight city hall, you can't even let them know you exist.

Evictions for fire code and safety violations were followed by rent increases, the real estate market heating up as gentrification, which had already swept through the South End proper, lapped steadily at our doors; pioneering merchants—a Chinese grocery, Korean nail salon, the requisite pawnshop—sticking their toes in the market on Albany, the high-end boutiques, coffee shops, and art galleries inevitably close behind.

For some people gentrification was as much an incentive as the construction to push them elsewhere—toward adulthood, real jobs, or wherever creative and dysfunctional people go when bills have to be paid. Like those scattered on my desk.

About that: Bills arrive with my name shining through the glassy envelope windows, and I tell my roomies what they owe toward their share. David is paycheck clockwork, but money from Nicolette trickles in sporadically, depending on whether she's landed work. My cash flow's steadier than Nicolette's, but it's often dependent on where my clients are in the billing cycle. Toward the end of a slow month, it's not unusual for me to pick up a few days' cash work with Zero.

But in the spirit of full disclosure, David's timely payments often get diverted to other necessities that, as de facto head of the collective, I've deemed more important than utilities or rent. Like food or marijuana. Personally, I don't have a problem with smoking in the dark.

I can't tell if anyone's home, but the kitchen's still a disaster, the sink-piled dishes taking on the permanence of sculpture. The cat usually comes running when he hears the pop of the can opener, but this time he waits until I have the door locked behind me lest he be forced to show gratitude for my effort; I hear the newly opened can skidding across the floor as I bounce my backup Yokota down the stairs.

In the loading dock beside the front stairs, a pile of blankets shifts, and even though I know it's Albert huddled under there in the pitch-dark, I twitch reflexively, a jolt of pain shooting down my back. Albert is homeless but a longstanding tenant of the loading dock at 42, sometimes even hanging a worn blanket across the front to mark his occupancy. By the time I arrived on Thayer Street, he was already a neighborhood fixture, ghost by day but arriving at some point each evening, a huddled sentry, a peekaboo gargoyle.

"You know, Albert"—I address the shifting mound—"one of these days you're gonna give me a heart attack and you'll feel real bad about it."

"That's what you always tell me, Zesty." Albert pops his head out of the blankets. His skin is the color of eggplant, mottled with dark moles, and covered by a thick beard littered with crumbs. "But you know I'm always here. Got a cigarette?"

"Have you ever seen me smoke a cigarette, Albert?"

"Weed?" he says hopefully.

"I wish." Albert, by his own admission, is a bit schizophrenic, his demons grown strong on years of drug and alcohol abuse. He's thin, but you wouldn't know it, multiple layers lending him a false thickness and outsize girth. I contemplate giving Albert one of Sam's blue pills, but it's probably not a good idea. At the moment he seems a little skittish; his head is jiggling like a hobo bobblehead. The smell coming from under the blankets is pretty funky too. His last shower must be at least a couple weeks behind him. Once in a while Nicolette or I will invite Albert to use the bathroom and clean up, maybe give him a bite to eat or a few dollars, but once he's inside, it's hard to get him out, and honestly, his stench lingers for days.

"How you been, Albert?"

"Good. Fine. Can't sleep, though." Albert blinks rapidly, narrows his eyes. "Damn, Zesty, what happened to you?"

"It's a long story."

"Mmm, I'm not much in the mood for long stories. Where you off to?"

"I got a few errands to run, then maybe over to Foley's. Quiet night?"

"Yeah, not like it used to be, right? I'd rather have it busy. Safer that way. Hey." Albert's voice turns conspiratorial, somewhere between a hiss and whisper. "Man come around couple hours ago looking for you. 'Spicious-looking. Why didn't you answer the door?"

"Part of the long story," I say. "He say anything to you?"

"Naw. He didn't see me. I can tell it's your bell he ringin', though. Got that annoying sound like when you answer wrong on a game show."

"You recognize him?"

"You got some weed, Zesty?"

"Like I said." I hold up empty hands.

"Oh yeah. Naw. I never seen him before. Black dude. Biiig. Like he made outta bricks."

"Okay."

"Big *black* bricks. Nigga bricks!"

"I get the picture, Albert." If Albert begins to stray in conversation, it usually turns weird.

"Nigga bricks." Albert mumbles to himself, his head shaking a little more, trying to jiggle a thought free. "Why's it we never see no black bricks nowhere? I seen white bricks. Yella bricks. Red—"

"I'll see you later, Albert."

"Pull up in a black Pathfinder. Not alone neither. Scoping your windows. I took one peep and turned myself into a pile of laundry, know'm saying?"

"They look like police?" Or is that a stupid question? For all I know, these are the cats the government sends to claw back their Pell Grants.

"I ain't seen them around before. Then again, ain't been straying too far and wide lately. Circling the shopping wagon, you might say." Albert smiles mismatched teeth at his pun. "Neighborhood's changing. Pretty soon you gonna have to win the lottery to stay 'round here."

"You play the lottery, Albert?"

"Fuck no! I'm homeless, Zesty, not stupid. Ain't got no money to piss away. You?"

I reach deep into my pocket, feel the crumpled hundred-dollar bill between my fingers. "Down to scratch myself," I tell him.

FOURTEEN

Mission Hill isn't considered a hot zone anymore, but like most Boston neighborhoods, it's cycled through its share of despair and renewal, the hillside overlooking Brigham and Women's faring better than the back end, which slopes dejectedly toward neglected Roxbury projects and run-down brick-fronted apartment buildings.

Britta's house is easy to spot, brown paint chipped and peeling, the intimation of a picket fence surrounding the property. A row of prickly thorn bushes lines the walk, but they seem to exist more as an afterthought, the stubborn perseverance of nature in the face of so-called civilization.

I lean my bike under an open window at the side of the house. The second-story room is dark, but Elvis Costello is drifting out, crooning about the dangers of the working week from *My Aim Is True*. The front door is a battered oak with a rectangle of wire mesh protecting stained glass at the top, a rusted mail slot sitting waist high blooming supermarket circulars. Buzzers to the right: A. Korvell on the bottom, B. Ingalls above. I pull one of the fliers.

Britta Ingalls.

Getting the swing of this detective work now, only a matter of time before I rent an office with frosted glass doors, a bottle of whiskey stashed in the top desk drawer, dames in furs waiting to throw themselves at me.

It's not late, but most of the houses on the opposite side of the street are also dark, people working overtime or maybe I'm not the only one with unpaid utility bills. Cars line the street, a few jammed in the narrow driveways between homes. I ring the top buzzer, hear it chime off-key somewhere upstairs. I ring the bottom buzzer, but nobody answers.

I've already leaned twice on the buzzer next door, getting set to leave when a woman's raspy voice exclaims, "Hold on. You young people don't give an old lady a chance to do anything."

The door opens the width of a chain, one rheumy eye peering below it, a slice of stringy gray hair held back by a bright yellow barrette.

"I'm sorry to bother you, ma'am, but I'm looking for Britta next door. Do you know your neighbors?" I point to Britta's house.

"What?"

"Britta," I repeat. "Ingalls. She lives next door."

"She lives next door." The woman throws caution to the

wind, slips the chain off the lock. An oversized men's dress shirt reaches below her knees. "Is that what you just said? Well, that's what happens when you have the same set of ears for eighty-four years; I'm not going to apologize for them. You'll just have to speak louder. And straighten up, young man, or you'll look like me before it's your time."

I do as I'm told, pulling my shoulders back. "Have you seen her today?"

"No. Once a week she stops by with the girl downstairs, helps me water my plants. Those I can't reach." She opens the door wider to show me overflowing planters hanging off hooks drilled into the ceiling. "I broke my hip trying to water those spiders. Now I don't move so well. I tell all my friends I broke it ice-skating. I used to skate the most lovely figure eights. Who did you say you were?"

"A friend of Britta's." The lie slides easily across my lips. Murder police, little old ladies, makes no difference.

"Then how come I've never seen you before?" She narrows her eyes to bring me into better focus.

"You know, I was just thinking the same about you."

"Hmm." She allows herself a small chuckle at that notion. "Don't go thinking I'm some fuddy-duddy, young man. It's just an old lady in this neighborhood has to watch out for her comely young neighbors. My ears might be going, but my memory is just fine. And don't think you're the first to come knocking for Britta either. If I'd any sense, I'd pin a note on my door 'if you're looking for Britta, I don't know where she is.' Save me the trouble of seeing all your disappointed faces. Which, if you don't mind my asking, what happened to yours?"

"I fell off my bicycle," I say.

"Oh dear. But got right back on I see."

"You say someone came looking for Britta before me?" I try steering the woman back on course.

"Why yes, dear. As a matter of fact, he looked a good deal like you." A thought occurs to the woman, and she flaps a playful elbow my way. "Trying to get an inside track on your competition, eh?" She winks knowingly at me.

"Something like that," I admit, reasonably sure she might be talking about Gus or roughly half the messengers in town.

"Well, I can see she likes the long hair on a man. She told me so herself. What's your name again?"

"Zesty," I say to her for the first time—this old lady is working me like a two-way street. I fish a card out of my bag and hand it to her.

"Anyhow, like I told the other fella, I haven't seen Britta today. Peculiar."

"What is?"

"He'd driven up in her car and then parked along the side of the house but didn't know where she was. You're not worried, are you?"

"No, ma'am. But would you do me a great big favor? If you see Britta, would you give her this card and tell her to call the number on it right away? It's kind of important."

"I'm sure it is." The old woman throws me Groucho Marx eyebrows.

"No, really."

"Keep your tight britches on, young man. If I see her I'll tell her. Only don't you think it might be wise to give your face a chance to heal? Women like pretty faces too, and you have wonderful bone structure, even though you slouch. You know, it's not all buns and muscles, washbasin stomachs and all that."

In lieu of a washboard stomach and probably a few inches short of "all that," I give her a big smile and walk to the opposite side of Britta's house, where I'd missed seeing a car covered by a heavy tarp parked as far back from the street as possible. A light mounted to the side of the house flicks on as I step into the gravel driveway, and a wave of nausea passes through me as I lift the front corner to look at a scratched chrome fender, a long metallic scrape the color of my mangled Fat Chance running toward the center. I fold the entire corner back and the tarp snaps off like an ill-fitting sheet, revealing the gold Buick shining in the spotlight.

I leave the sheet where it fell, try the car doors and the trunk, barely suppressing the urge to kick in the window, the sound of breaking glass sure to attract unwanted attention.

When the light clicks off, I circle around to the back door, but it's locked. I find my bike where I left it and step from the frame to the seat and boost myself to standing. I gain a toehold where a shingle's missing, reach a grip on Britta's window ledge, and chin myself up, my legs speed-cycling over the outer wall as I get my elbows and forearms over the sill.

The stench hits me before I tumble onto what's left of a futon, the stuffing everywhere except where I needed it to cushion my fall. "Britta?" I have to retrieve my tongue before it can flush itself down my throat. Flies strafe the air, kamikaze window glass.

This would seem an opportune time to panic. But I've been dragged to a Phish concert before, so it's not the first time I've smelled this much patchouli, only never in such high concentration; the futon is soaked with the oil. I rush to strip off my shirt, my eyes stinging wet, my cuts and scrapes burning like they're on fire. Waves of hippie waft off my skin. I hear nothing. Not even Elvis, whom I must have unplugged midlyric, the cord hot to the touch; no telling how long he's been playing.

Sift uninvited through the belongings of someone you don't know, you're a private eye. Grunt, lift, and charge by the hour, you're a mover. And if nothing else, working for Zero has given me the ability to gauge a person simply by strolling through their home, giving their belongings a quick once-over. Britta Ingalls is no exception. Except her things have been largely destroyed, making them just a little harder to read.

So what does Britta's shabby chic with a dose of kitsch tell me? What do I learn from her gutted futon, shattered mosaic coffee table, colorful Bakelite ashtrays, a scattering of batik-dyed throw pillows, threadbare kilim rugs, just about everything destined to decorate the curb come trash day?

Nothing helpful, except that whoever tossed the place has done a thorough job of it, debris in the hallway leading to destruction in the living room. Even the fridge is cleared out, except for a bottle of Amstel, which I pop open to swig the taste of patchouli out of my mouth before pouring some over my head and neck. Now I just smell like Harvard Square on a Saturday night.

From under the living room shades, there's just enough light to admire Britta's collection of vintage rock posters, an obvious perk of her job at Black Hole and worth a small eBay fortune: The Modern Lovers. The Zulus. Robin Lane and the Chartbusters. The Neighborhoods. The Mighty Mighty Bosstones. There's a scattering of work papers and old-style Polaroids strewn about the floor, receipts, pay stubs, apartment lease, credit card bills. Big credit card bills.

There's more than one picture of Britta and Gus together, which doesn't surprise me, Gus being the lead singer of the unfortunately named but not altogether terrible Gizzard Blizzard, last year's second-place finishers in the long-running WBCN-sponsored Boston Rock & Roll Rumble and signed to a record deal at Black Hole, which is how he landed the messenger account in the first place.

I stick a couple of pictures into my bag and sit in the center of the room, where the destruction is minimal, to think this mess through. Somebody was looking for something, and judging by the noise they must have made tearing the place apart, knew nobody was coming home anytime soon. But how did they get in? Definitely not the way I did. And how is it both the front and back doors are locked solid, showing no signs of being broken or picked?

A key would do the trick, I suppose. There aren't any outward signs of a struggle, by which I mean no blood or holes punched in the walls, not that there would be necessarily. Which leaves what? An opportunity to drink beer. Boredom. The realization that just because I sit posed like Rodin's *Thinker* doesn't mean that anything brilliant will materialize between my ears. Not a damn thing. Except for the squawk of shoulder-mounted walkie-talkies.

Shit.

I wedge my chair under the knob of the front door, peep out the window to see the old woman standing on her porch, pointing toward the side of the house. From Britta's room, I hear gravel crunch, one of the cops passing under the open window where I left my bike.

The cruiser came with lights flashing but the siren off. There are two to a squad car, meaning they've split up, one in back and one in front to squeeze me out. Chances are they already have their service revolvers drawn, and I'm not digging the bad karma circle, the Carol DiMaiti memorial tree out front in early bloom giving me the heeby-jeebies.

Aside from the possibility of getting shot, this is not a situation I want to be caught up in, my father's influence too long gone, and detectives Brill and Wells probably only too happy to have me tied tighter to whatever mess I've been yanked into. They'll think I tore the place apart, and they'll hold me at least until Britta turns up.

I hear glass break in the back stairwell, shards tinkling as I lose the beer and throw on a shirt that was lying on the floor. It fits just fine. It's black and on the front in bold red letters says PARADOX IS THE THRESHOLD OF TRUTH. I have no idea what that means, but this is no time to be choosy.

I'm hanging from my fingertips, halfway out the window, when the old woman lets loose a high warbling scream. I push off with my feet to clear my bike and land awkwardly, my ankle on fire, but instead of flying the short route out front, I run-hop the bike around back, hoping the second officer is still navigating the darkness after smashing the glass to get in.

No such luck. "Stop!" He's on the porch, gun and flashlight out. "Police!"

"I know!" I break the light beam, mounting on the run as I turn the corner alongside the gold Buick. "Don't shoot! White guy!" I yell, aware it's a shitty thing to say but preferring a karmic rebuke to a bullet in the back.

"He's out!" The cop tears after me but manages to hold his fire. "Stop!"

"Okay!" I yell, one foot in the clip as Cop Two comes crashing off the front porch, my wheels skidding a cutback toward the broken section of the bush-propped fence. The cop's knees buckle as I cut behind him, kicking the flashlight out of his hand as he tries to shove it between my spokes.

I make the street as the cop from the rear hurdles his fallen partner but can't land the quick-shuffle footwork to do the same over the fence: His back foot catches the top of a post, and his gun skitters toward my front wheel as he tastes tar for his efforts. I scoop the gun on the go and shove it down the front of my shorts, dipping into the descent of Calumet Street, turning once to see the fence-hurdling cop on his knees, a rivulet of blood gushing from his mouth, his partner barking into his shoulder walkie as the old woman comes off the sidewalk waving in my direction, my Mercury Couriers business card flapping between her fingers.

Brilliant.

FIFTEEN

I'm a bullet off Mission Hill. One bad pothole and I'm toast, the only upside being that if I crash and manage not to shoot my privates off, I can always euthanize myself, save the police the trouble.

I burn brake pads toward the bottom, a genie puff of smoke lifting off the wheel as I scrape the corner onto Huntington, destination downtown, the cover of evening crowds and one-way streets. On Huntington I hit a minor downhill grade, my chain red hot as I crank it through the derailleur, my ankle on fire begging for mercy, the world liquid in my periphery.

There's a break in the tracks if I cut hard onto Louis Street, but that road's a straight shot into the Fens, risky if more cars join the hunt from other directions. My only choice then would be limited to jumping the grass into the Fenway's tall blow-job weeds, a notorious gay cruising ground within walking distance of the Ramrod, Boston's toughest gay bar. How do I know these things? Open mind. Got to keep an open mind. Banking right's not an option either; I could try ditching the cruisers on the Northeastern campus, but the university's stocked with retired police who'd be only too thrilled to join the chase, break up the monotony of disbanding keg parties and confiscating bongs.

Squad cars race toward me, but they're stuck on the outbound side of the MBTA tracks until they hit Museum, and I'm almost where I need to be, the Christian Science pool and Prudential Center within sight, packs of Northeastern students crossing carelessly, the glow of phones—ghost faces, radioactive hands—

more visible than their bodies. I stay locked on Huntington, sometimes no choice being the best choice of all.

Pedestrians pose a daily threat to my safety, but momentum has its distinct advantages. You just have to accept up front that Boston biking is less a matter of *whether* than *when*. A car door is out there waiting for everyone, and if the flippers don't get you, the swerve into traffic will. Downtown especially, there's a flow to the hustle, a metronome rhythm that can be tapped into with experience even as the untrained eye sees nothing but all hell breaking loose. Reacting is never enough, though; you have to be a visionary, see the future before it strolls into the crosswalk with its head up its ass.

You gotta *feel* it.

They come in all forms: The Crosswalk Wanderer. The Car Sobber. Or worst of all, the Squirrel Crosser, who starts to dance, one step forward, one step back. Clowns to the left of me, jokers to the right, you know the rest.

Anticipate.

Blue disco lights arc across my bike, glint off my wheels. A Huntington train, students stacked at the rear and middle doors, stops in front of the Y where I play my hardcore pickup basketball games.

See the future.

The accordion doors wing open. I squeeze my brakes, but they're useless, melted to slag on the Mission Hill plunge. The cars in front of me tap brake-light Morse code, unsure of what to do with the sirens bearing down behind them. One car veers to the right, burns rubber in the crosswalk; the other guns through, the YMCA pack crossing in its wake.

Speed kills, but indecision maims.

"Pull over!"

I flip the squad car the finger behind my back, lock onto a solitary redhead jabbering into her phone.

Timing. Front? Back? Front! My right hand out and open, I clip the phone so fast, her last words are delivered into thin air.

I kamikaze through the horns and curses of Mass Ave., cut upstream toward the South End, counting on the cruisers that had been stuck on the Museum side to hit the underpass hoping to head me off before I make Copley Square. I jump the sidewalk and roll across Columbus, dropping the phone into my bag, blending into the South End flow, outdoor cafés and young professionals pushing five-hundred-dollar baby strollers past gay couples and packs of mixed-race teenagers, the old and new co-existing like a city planner's dream.

I cruise onto Tremont, the sirens moving off in the distance, my adrenaline sweat drying in the warm breeze, plenty of other bikes to attract the eye, a spoke in a haystack, far too many to start pulling people over.

The door to the black Pathfinder comes almost as a relief. There's no way to avoid it, no point in even trying, and lord knows I can use the rest. Black leather interior, tinted windows rolled most of the way down; at least glass won't be an issue.

Anticipate, I remind myself as I fold into the impact. *See the future.*

Only problem is, the future's black.

SIXTEEN

"Do you remember Rachel Evans?"
"No."
"No? You saved her life once."
"Okay."

"And then McKenna found her. I don't know how, but he has his ways; otherwise, he wouldn't have been able to evade capture for so long. And poor Rachel was never really cut out for the life, was she?"

"No," Will says, and leaves it at that, though Leila's words grate on him like a bounced check. Life as he's always seen it boils down to a test of wills, how many times you're willing to get up after being driven to ground. He doesn't wish to be cruel, but sizing people up was his gift, and Rachel Evans, Will knew from the moment he laid eyes on her, was a puppet waiting for someone to come along and cut the strings.

"I know I'm not being fair to you, William. Perhaps forgetting is a gift sometimes and all I'm doing is dredging up things you'd rather forget."

Fair? What's fair? The phone rang and he answered it. Devlin McKenna was calling. Somebody else called too, who was it?

"When he found Rachel, I knew he'd find me next. We'd been in contact, prearranged times and locations, new places, new identities, but the same life. Life on the run is a prison of its own kind, and once McKenna had Rachel, I realized the only safe place for me anymore was inside those prison walls. The irony wasn't lost on me. And as it turns out, I was wrong anyway."

Relax. Let it come, Will thinks. He's already checked his hole cards, no need to peek at them again; they haven't changed.

"Diane," he says aloud, his wife's name spinning to him like the odds-defying river card filling his full house, his inside straight.

Leila looks up at him, confused.

"Diane," he says again, delighting in the sound off his lips, the happy tell sparking his eyes. When you're holding the nuts, who gives a fuck what people think?

Leila is expectant, waiting for more, but doesn't speak.

"My wife, Diane," Will explains. "She called."

But in his pot-raking contentment, Will's mistaken the look on

Leila Markovich's face, and suddenly it's come apart at the seams, tears leaking from her eyes, reminding him of a high-stakes game he used to run out of Narcissus, where one of the players had kept a worn picture wedged under his chips that he would gaze at, his eyes perpetually wet and unreadable. The man played winning poker, but Will remembers thinking, at what cost?

Yes, Diane called. Why did Will think Leila would be happy to hear this news?

"Don't cry, Leila," he says, noting an iridescent sheen sliding down Leila's gun barrel. "Why are you crying?"

"Because Diane is dead, William." *Leila has turned to sobbing, and really, Will can't understand why. Diane disappeared, and now she's dead. It all makes perfect sense to him.*

"Yes," he says. "Diane's dead. I know that."

"You know? How is that possible that you know?"

Actually, Will thinks, the better question is: How could it be possible he wouldn't know? But that's not what he says. What he says, in a whisper as if to a child that needs to hear hard things softly, is "I told you, Leila. She called. She told me so herself."

SEVENTEEN

"*Got-damn muthafucka!*" A voice echoes off the walls of a blacked-out tunnel.

"Shit." A different voice responds minus the reverb. "That ain't nuthin'."

A triangle of iridescent light consolidates into a shapeless smudge somewhere in front of my face.

"Nuthin'? Nigga, you call *that* nuthin'?"

"I'm okay," I mumble, looking vertically at a soggy street-lamp above me. "I'm all right."

"Just use some of that, whatchamacallit, Armor All spray, wipe it down. Be good as new."

"No spray," I say. "No new."

"Didn't you say you was about to trade it in anyhow?"

"Resale value, son. This shit's gotta shine."

"So get Loppy to detail it for you."

"No detail too small," I say still looking at black, only this time in the form of Brick standing over me, his enormous frame shielding me from street view, the car double-parked, taking care of the sidewalk. "Just a scratch," I say to him. "I'll be all right."

Brick spits into his hand and wipes a spot on the interior door leather.

"See?" I say, sitting up. "Good as new."

"See?" Brick's partner is switchblade thin, shiny dark. Shaka Zulu in Adidas sweats and black flat-billed Red Sox "B" cap. He leans across the front seat from the passenger side. "Good as new."

"New, huh?" Brick turns and kicks me hard in the chest, knocking me back to the street.

"Totally unnecessary," I wheeze, curling up in a ball, the police-issued Glock dropping deeper down my shorts, threatening radical vasectomy. From this angle I can see my Yokota stuck halfway under the Pathfinder, the front wheel warped beyond repair, an industrial flower blooming spokes off the center.

"Nigga, get up and get the fuck in." Brick yanks me off the asphalt as Switchblade, taller than me by a good three inches, pulls the bike free and tosses it to the curb. It's like *Groundhog Day* around here, only with new actors and less money. One endless day, two bikes, misdemeanors and felonies stacking up like firewood.

Switchblade latches a vise-like grip on my elbow, places me in front.

"Take your bag off." He folds himself into the rear seat behind me, sticks the muzzle of a gun into the corner of my eye. "Slowly. Then pass it back."

Brick gets in and pulls away from the curb, adjusting the rearview mirror. Switchblade takes my pack and gently taps the side of my head.

"Turn around and put your seat belt on."

"Where we going?"

"And shut the fuck up."

Brick tunes the radio to 88.9 WERS Emerson College Radio, the low volume an insult to his custom Boston speakers stacked in the rear.

I reach to the dial and turn it up, Brick scrunching his face in disbelief. "It's Edo. G," I say by way of explanation.

If I'm a ride
I'm a ride by high
Fuck the rules ain't shit we abide by
We live and die by
The same thing that you do
Edo. G rock the B hat and FUBU
Somethin' to move to
Boston's finest, skills remain timeless
Bullshit behind us
Runnin' through your crib like interior designers

Brick clicks it off.

"Runnin' through your crib like interior designers. I love that line. Speaking of cribs, where we going? One-oh-four Cabot, right?" The lost delivery address for the Black Hole package drops into place, a manila envelope scrawled with black Sharpie flashing in my mind's eye. "Cabot . . . That'd be off Dudley Square?"

Brick slides his eyes to the rearview mirror, Switchblade shaking his head, his gun out of sight. I keep my hands away from my shorts, not even contemplating trying to shoot my way out.

At a red light Brick sniffs the air, powers down a window.

"Didn't I tell you?" Switchblade volunteers from behind. "White people smell like dog when they wet."

"Yeah, well, this dog smells like he peed hisself."

"It's patchouli," I say.

"It's bitch pussy what it is. Now, roll down your window and shut the fuck up."

One-oh-four Cabot is a refurbished brownstone off Dudley Square, the longtime heart of Boston's black community and a stone's throw from Junior White's, Boston's funkiest record store and one of my original accounts. My father hooked me up with that connect, having never made the switch off vinyl.

We park out front, Brick mugging full-faced to the security camera mounted inside a clear Plexiglas box before using his own set of keys to unlock the double front doors. They sandwich me up two flights of stairs and through another locked door into a bright loft-style apartment with wide plank wood floors and three windows offering views of the square. There's a large oak desk in the far corner, centered on a bright Persian carpet. Crates of albums line the brick walls, a familiar-looking DJ's turntable, red headphones, and stacks of speakers massed on the opposite side. The muscular black man behind the desk looks familiar too, but it takes me a second to place him this far out of context.

"Darryl?" I say. Brick and Switchblade look at each other quickly. "Man, I can't tell you how happy I am to see you. Nice place. Yours?"

"Zesty." Darryl runs his hands over his face. He shakes his head but not as an answer to my question. "Really, C?"

"You told us scoop the nigga that lost the money. What we do? Here's the nigga."

"O?"

"Like he said."

Darryl says, "This ain't him. He looks like him, I'll grant you that, but this ain't him. You don't recognize this white boy? For real, C? From the courts at the Y . . . ? *All* white muthafuckas look alike to you?"

"Gunner?" Brick says tentatively, shooting Switchblade a crushing *what'd I tell you?* look.

"There you go," Darryl says expansively. "Gunner. Nigga never saw an outside shot he didn't like."

"What can I say, I'm always open."

"Right! You a beneficiary of the black man's conundrum. Cover you tight and you drill from twenty feet; make your man look foolish and he's gonna hear it from his teammates. Leave you wide open and you drill from twenty; black man just lazy but we all lazy from time to time. Mind you, I ain't talkin' about myself," Darryl says with a smile.

"He got handle?" Switchblade shows some renewed interest now, maybe trying to picture me with a basketball in my hands.

"You mean's he the next coming of Manu Ginóbili? Hell no. But he got just enough to squeeze his shot off. Ain't that right, Z?"

"I'm not one to boast," I say.

"Shit, what's to boast about? I just called you a one-dimensional baller."

"I've been called worse. You want to tell me what's going on, D?"

"I don't think so. What's he holding there?"

Switchblade makes a show of finger walking through my belongings, pulling things up for Darryl's inspection, holding up one of several pictures of Britta Ingalls I'd lifted off her wall. "We seen him at her crib tonight?" Switchblade pops the picture with his index finger. "Rolled out when po-po showed, figured they done got his ass. But then here comes Slick, rolling Tremont like he ain't got a care in the world."

"Climbed in through her window like a damn monkey," Brick puts in. "I'm telling you, D, this the nigger lost your money, right here."

"*Your* money?" I say, the picture getting a little clearer but no less dangerous. "By the way, nice collection you got there. You always DJ the Black Hole parties? I gotta admit I didn't peg you for a rock-and-roll guy."

"Black people can't like rock?" Darryl talks toward the window but meets my eyes in the reflection.

"Puts you in the minority. And not a whole lot of black rock bands to follow either."

"No? Maybe you just don't know your music." Darryl turns, counting off fingers. "TV on the Radio, Bad Brains, Living Colour—"

"Okay, I get the point. It's just the racist white boy in me. Once in a while I let him out to play. And speaking of white, you ever shop Junior White's off the Square?" Darryl slides his eyes toward his men, getting almost imperceptible negative head shakes in response. "No? The place is awesome, but their organization's for shit. You gotta have beaucoup time on your hands to find what you're looking for, but there's gold in them thar records."

"What do you want, Zesty?"

"What do *I* want? That's a funny question, considering. But since you asked, D, why am I here?"

"Simple case of mistaken identity. You want to leave, be my guest."

"Just like that? This is Gus's regular run, right?"

"What's it to you?"

"I want to know who ran me down," I say. Though at this

point all signs point to Gus driving Britta's Buick. But does Darryl know this?

"Then we both after the same thing. How'd you end up with that package this morning?"

"Luck of the draw." I explain to Darryl what I explained earlier to the detectives. "Shit happens, right? What can you do?"

"Bike better." Darryl joins the chorus of my critics.

"Easy to say, D, only getting run down on Boylston wasn't an accident. But you already know this."

"How you figure?"

"Because your boys have been on my tail since I got out of the hospital. And Gus is missing. You responsible for that, too?"

Darryl ignores my question, but I already have the answer. They wanted Gus, got me instead.

"So why were you at Britta's place?" Darryl asks. "What'd you expect to find?"

"Honestly, I don't know, D. I'm just groping around at this point, but Britta flat-out lied telling my dispatch I never showed to pick anything up. Those your orders she's following? Britta just doing what you expect of her, that being your money." Darryl turns slowly and glares at Brick. "That's a lot of cash to be moving around, D. You got an aversion to online banking?"

"What do you want, Zesty?"

"I was thinking maybe we could work out some type of re-payment plan."

"You can't fuckin' be serious. You just told me you don't know shit, got set up, and now you want to pay back the money you lost?"

"My package, my bad. I got professional pride, D."

"You also got fifty large lying around, Z?"

"That what it was? You must be one hell of a DJ if that's your going rate."

"Right." Darryl lifts his chin toward the door, giving Brick and Switchblade the signal to leave. "Hold up. O, give the man his bag."

Switchblade pivots in the doorway and pump-fakes once before shoving the bag hard into my chest.

"Notice I didn't flinch for his fake," I say to Darryl after the door clicks shut.

"He's too fast is why, like I always tell him. You got to sell it slow to muthafuckas don't have them fast-twitch muscles working. Play with their heads. Young guns don't never listen." Darryl paces the floor, stops and looks contemplatively out the window toward Dudley Square.

"Okay. So what now?"

"That's what I'm trying to figure. But I gotta be honest with you, Zesty, the businessman in me just says shoot you and that's the ball game right there. . . ."

"But . . . ," I say, hoping there's a "but" coming.

"You come with too many strings attached, right?"

"Sounds good to me," I say, though I don't really know what he's talking about until I do. "Yeah, Zero can be a handful." I find Darryl's eyes in the darkened window, disappointed but not entirely surprised to have my brother surfacing in this mess.

"And I'm assuming five-oh sweat you after the money shower?"

"Detectives," I say, before adding, "Robbery homicide," giving Darryl something else to consider, but holding tight to their line of questioning that led to the Wells Fargo heist and my Collin Sullivan connection.

"So there's two reasons," Darryl says glumly.

"And we've been playing ball a couple of years makes three." I figure the more reasons I can give Darryl *not* to shoot me, the better.

"You a hacker," Darryl says. "Let's just leave it at two."

"Whatever does the trick." Which still begs the question: "So what's next?"

"Next we get you another shirt because you smell like ass. Then we take a ride." Darryl whistles loudly, drawing Brick and Switchblade back into the room.

"Whassup, D? I get to shoot this nigga now?"

"Not today." Darryl stands up, scratches his beard absently, and throws me a T-shirt from one of his crates. "You search him before you brought him to me, C?"

"Huh?"

"What, you harda hearin' all of a sudden?" Darryl is almost a foot shorter than Brick but nearly as thick, a narrow waist exploding up into a bulky chest, muscled arms, and shoulders with shoulders on them. I might be a pain to guard on the basketball court because I don't mind running around to find my shot, but when I end up covering Darryl, there's little I can do to keep his rear out of the paint, his combination of ballhandling and brawn usually leaving me sore, my ribs a pounded slab of beef. Darryl's right, I am a hacker. Only on the court it's called survival.

"We took his bag," Brick says defensively, his body retreating without actually taking a step back.

"But no pat down, right? No dickie check." Looking hard at Brick.

"No."

"Yeah, well the muthafucka's packing a cannon down the front of his damn shorts, and I'd like to know how the fuck y'all missed that?" Darryl points emphatically at my crotch, where the gun is wedged awkwardly and outlined in the Lycra like the cucumber in *This Is Spinal Tap.*

"I mean, *got-damn,* Cedrick. You *ever* known a white guy hung like fucking Godzilla over here? *Ever?*"

"Hey." I adjust the Glock from outside my shorts, letting them see my hands as I move. "Least I can jump."

EIGHTEEN

We pile into Cedrick's Pathfinder, Switchblade glancing rear-view, his eyes registering my hand resting on the waffled butt of the 9mm inside my bag.

"Music?" Cedrick asks.

"Just drive." Darryl stares out the tinted window.

"Corners?"

"Nigga, what I say?"

We drive deep into the heart of Roxbury, Dudley to Zeigler to I don't know where, the streets dark and mostly empty, a couple of hoodies marching briskly, hands deep in kangaroo front pockets, empty lots, boarded-up houses, steel-awning bodegas and metal-ribbed liquor stores, check-cashing joints and store-front ministries. Pizza shop, Chinese, barbecue, liquor store. Dollar store, Nation of Islam, check-cashing joint, liquor store, Baptist church. Left, right, left, the open-air nightlife of the revitalized South End only a mile or so away, but it might as well be a thousand, the renovation bomb having missed this section of the Berry completely. We glide by gang-tagged walls, urban slices of crumbling and neglected asphalt pie spoken for with bullets, RIP murals—blood and roses, crucifixes, basketballs, pit bulls, and hand cannons—layered six coats deep, hard and glossy in the theatrical vapor glow of streetlamps.

We hit corners, activity amidst desolation. Teenagers in white tees sewn for giants, worn by scarecrows, Celtics jerseys, black "B" baseball caps, shorts hanging down to the tongue tops of Air Jordans, slack-eyed crews snapping to life as the Pathfinder rolls past, elaborate birdcalls, hand signals, shadows darting into alleys. Brick powers down his window to give them all a long cold stare, his hand dangling idly, middle, index, and thumb in the form of a gun, message received loud and clear: Hold down the corner.

Darryl rests his forehead on the blackened glass. I don't figure we're visible from the outside; Brick's presence is enough to jump-start the crews to action.

"Yours?" I say to Darryl as he turns to me, distracted, like he's completely forgotten I was there.

"The crews, they're mine. The corners?" He shrugs. "It's like real estate everywhere else, changing hands for whoever can hold it down."

"For sure we holding them down now," Cedrick says. "And tomorrow and the next day. For real."

"For real for now." Darryl sucks his teeth, slumping back to the glass, the weight of the world. "But a month from now? A year? We still gonna be humping these corners change of season come?"

"We do what we gotta do, D. If we want 'em."

"See, there's the magic words." Darryl comes off the window, finds Brick's eyes in the rearview. "*If* we want 'em."

"You don't want 'em, D? We spreadin' out, ain't we, from Humboldt to Seaver, nigga get your Glocks out!"

"Damn, C, I told you, this push ain't nuthin' but a one-off." Darryl is almost hissing now, the buzz of his voice even causing O to flinch out of his low-lid coma. "Have we been strategizing corners?"

"Corners the mainstay," O murmurs from under his "B" hat bill. "Bread 'n' butter."

"Okay, corners the starter kit, no doubt. But we've been expanding our horizons, ain't we? Wonder Bread square, but the world's round, right? Get that through your damn thick heads already. Round like a basketball. Find me a corner on a basketball, C. Hold me down a corner you're so fond of, the corner be all yours."

"Ain't no corners *to* hold down, D. I get what you're saying, only like . . . like . . . Yo, O!" Brick punches O hard in the shoulder, though it doesn't seem to hurt him, more steel inside that tracksuit than one would suspect. "You gon' help a nigga out or what?"

"Change be hard," O says from beneath his cap. Ghetto sage.

"There you go!" Cedrick, expansive. "Fish outta water. Nigga out the hood. This is what we *do,* D. I hear you 'bout spreading our wings and shit, but look how *that's* shaping up." Brick tosses his eyes in my direction. "I still don't get why you won't let me just cap his ass and be done with it. This dude's a loose cannon, D, you know that, right? He's all up in our business from Black Hole to the white bitch, our money on the street. All due respect to y'all playing hoops together, but there's gotta be another white boy out there you can school."

"Word." From O.

"Word. And you know that Glock he holding be a mutha-fuckin' *cop* gun, and here we are driving his ass around. We get pulled over, you *know* how that shit's gonna go down. I ain't questioning you, D, I'm just saying—"

"What, one and done?"

"Exactly!" Brick is fully animated now, a fine mist of spittle flying toward the windshield. "One and done. Hell, use the damn cop gun. You know they be happy to get it back."

"And what do we do about his brother?" Darryl says, O back to slouch-napping in the front seat, his inactivity about as comforting as a viper lying in wait.

"I cap him too if I have to. Who's his brother?"

"Go ahead, tell him, Zesty. But first, do me a favor and take your hand out of your bag. If I thought having you dead was a good idea, believe me, it'd be done already."

"His name's Zero Meyers," I say, my hand coming out slow and empty.

"Oh dag! For real?" Brick checks me in the mirror again as if he expects to see a different person. "Zero Meyers, huh? I din't know he had a faggot ass brother. *Goddamn,* D, they don't look nothing alike at all." Cedrick shakes his head in disbelief. "So *now* what?"

"South End," Darryl says, turning to me. "Cathedral. What's wrong with you?"

"Headache." I stick my thumb into the soft spot above my good eyebrow, not bothering to explain the static building up again, the presong pain worsening as a familiar guitar riff wedges a foothold between my ears.

"Yo, me too," Cedric declares from the front. "This shit's gotten mad complicated. Zero muthafuckin' Meyers!"

"So take something and quit whining, both y'all. Didn't I see a bottle of Advil in your bag, Z?"

"I'm trying to lay off. It messes with my stomach. You want one, C? No hard feelings, cap my ass and whatnot."

"Be much obliged." Brick extends his hand palm up behind him, and I shake one of Sam's magic blue capsules into his mitt. He glances at it, pops it into his mouth, and puts his hand back again. "I usually take two."

"If you insist."

Darryl motions for me to get out at the corner of Washington and Monsignor, the Gothic Cathedral of the Holy Cross dwarfing the low-rise orange bricks of the Cathedral housing projects and Cathedral High. To my surprise, Darryl slides out behind me and taps the Pathfinder, sending it on its way.

I start walking a bit just to get loose, the opening guitar strut of the Del Fuegos' "Don't Run Wild" providing me a little gimp rhythm, staying close to the buildings, wary of police cruisers probably out there looking to pick me up on my bike. All-points bulletin: Zesty Meyers, armed and stupid fucking dangerous.

"How you going to get home, D?" The Pathfinder's brake lights flash once, disappear around a corner.

"Which home?" Darryl keeps my snail's pace, holding the outside position on the sidewalk. "I don't mean to sound boastful, but I got a few spots I can lay my head."

"One of them Britta Ingalls's place?"

Darryl stops in his tracks, leaving me exposed until I step back to retrieve his muscled cover. "Nah, it's nothing like that, just business."

"So you're like what, the Company Store? She works for you, rents one of your places."

"What?"

"Please. I saw her lease. It had your Cabot address on it, and anyway it's the only thing that makes any sense. Like Cedrick said, I had to climb through a window to get in. Cops had to break the glass to come up the rear. No busted locks means your boys must have had a key, walked right in, torn the place apart, and locked up behind themselves."

"Maybe Britta just a slob."

"I don't think so." We keep walking Washington, the skeleton frames of half-built buildings rising out of precast concrete, soaking up the moonlight. "I suppose they could've just been watching the house waiting on Britta, but they don't exactly strike me as sit-around type of guys."

"No, I'll give them that, all right," Darryl says. "They're *doers* in every sense of the word."

"They find what they were looking for?"

"You think they'd stick around if they did?"

"I guess not. You got a lot on your plate, D."

"A brotha got to be diversified in these uncertain times, Zesty. Lot of changes going on around here."

"No doubt. Only I still don't get it. If that money I lost is yours, D, why have a messenger run it across town for you? Why don't you or your boys just pick it up at Black Hole?"

"C'mon, Zesty. *Think,* now."

I do the thinking out loud, the required concentration pushing back the static that was hurting my head, the guitar riff still there but comforting, everything clicking now. "Distance," I practically sing. "There were pictures in Britta's place, looked like parties, promotional events; you were in the background in a lot of them, doing your thing. I didn't recognize you outright because I wasn't really looking at you. As far as anybody knows, you're just the handpicked DJ for parties and events. That's how you keep face time to a minimum, come and go without attracting too much attention. Which probably means you've got some sort of stake in the business. Pretty smart."

"What is?"

"Figuring that if you're tied into a rap label you're going to get looked at tighter? IRS. Feds. But straight-up rock and roll? A black guy in Boston? No way. That's why Britta lied about the package. So the money isn't tied back to Black Hole. Tied back to you." And that's what I have to assume she's also told Brill and Wells, their only lead at that point circling back to me and, inevitably, Zero. So why's Britta ducking Darryl and his men? What are they looking for? Is there more of Darryl's money unaccounted for?

"Britta works for you," I say, trying to talk my way into clarity. "Gus has the Black Hole courier account. Maybe after a while Gus figures out what he's delivering and tries to take some of it off you. Him and Britta. They set me up. Together."

"And you know that because?"

"The car that hit me, Britta's car, is sitting in your driveway. And I know Cedrick and O have been tailing me since I left the hospital, already trashed Britta's apartment, and were sitting on it waiting for her to show when I got there." I leave out Albert's sighting on Thayer Street; a well-concealed set of eyes is always a good thing to have on a darkened Thayer Street.

"Okay," Darryl says. "Go on."

"Only whatever plan Gus and Britta had went south when the money hit the street. Maybe they just wanted me down so they could lift the cash, come back to you, and say, 'Shitty break, Boston drivers.' How'm I doing?"

"Fucked if I know." Darryl shrugs. "There's more?"

I step into a doorway as a cruiser passes, leaving Darryl to absorb their drive-by eye-fuck on his own, a world away from the pickup games we play three times a week with as diverse a group of guys gathered in a city known as much for its racial and ethnic divisions as it is for its historic and crooked streets.

That Darryl's turned out to be a corner kingpin neither disturbs nor surprises me. The scourge of hard drugs on inner city neighborhoods is an ethical weight Darryl has to deal with on his own, and I'm pretty sure that he tells himself if it wasn't him running corners, it'd be someone else, the game unstoppable, no matter who's calling the shots. In the time I've known him, I figure he's smart enough to realize his shelf life is limited, prison or an early grave waiting for him somewhere down the line, which might account for the business sermon handed down to his lieutenants, diversification and expansion obviously carrying its own growing pains.

"You can come out now." Darryl thumb texts briefly on his cell.

"So." I get back to it, trying to keep the story straight. "The money's everything, right? You're running blow through Black Hole."

"Like hell I am. I told you I was diversified, Z. Why would I mix my corners with Black Hole and draw that kind of heat? Two different worlds, kid."

Well, not entirely, considering the money I lost pulled in a couple of robbery homicide detectives working the Wells Fargo job. Only I have a hard time picturing Darryl and his crew going from corner-slinging on their home turf to taking down an armored car in broad daylight. So what's the connection?

"There any real money in the record business, Darryl?"

"Might be with the right band. I thought maybe Gus was that golden goose, but it looks like he done fucked that up. Anyhow, *this* is where the real money's at, Zesty." Darryl spreads his arms above him. "You just got to open your eyes to the possibilities."

"Real estate?" I say, incredulous.

"*Real* estate." Darryl relishes the word. "Brick and mortar, baby. I mean, look around. The Cathedral Projects are right *there*. Villa Victoria just down the block a ways, projects left and right, but the Big Dig's changed everything. Soon there won't be an empty lot or broke-down building for a mile. My corner boys are steel, but they've got fear in their hearts because the big boys are coming and they know there's no stopping them. Forget rock, forget heroin and meth and all that other shit. Soon niggas gonna be speaking Starbucks *I*-talian, grande this and venti that, hooked on lattes and raspberry scones, and, Zesty, you know how many calories in one of them fucking scones? It's going from coca to coffee beans around here, and this is one nigger who is not gonna be left behind. Are you, Zesty?"

"Am I *what*?"

"Are you in or out?"

"You offering me Gus's account, D? I'm gonna be your messenger boy now?"

"Why not? I can use a set of eyes and ears I can trust. Why you laughing?"

"You might want to check my references first."

"So that's a no?"

"It's more like I prefer being my own boss, D. I think you can understand that."

"And what, you expect me to just let you walk away, knowing what you know? 'Thanks for the offer, D, but I gotta decline'? We *still* in the street, Zesty. I mean, I know I got to deal with Zero if I feel like I gotta take you out of the equation, and that's a whole 'nother set of complications right there, frankly, I ain't too keen to take on right now. The operative words being *right now*. Like Cedrick said, and I'm gonna paraphrase a little here, I gotta do what I gotta do."

"Like you did Collin Sullivan, D?"

"Say that again." Darryl's nostrils flare.

"The money," I say, instead.

"Aw shit." Darryl darkens. "See, there you go, Zesty. Stepping over lines that should not be crossed. You don't know shit about Collin Sullivan, Zesty. Not a damn thing."

"I know the money I got hit with—according to you, *your* money—bought me a visit from a couple of homicide cops working the Wells Fargo heist. You telling me that's a coincidence? Black Hole's books in good enough shape for a police audit?"

"Don't make a difference." Darryl shrugs. "Ain't nothing with my name on it up there. Any heat gonna come down on Ray Valentine, not me."

"And you don't think Valentine'll flip if he's staring down time?"

"For what?"

"Oh, I don't know, money laundering?"

"Not if he enjoys breathing. And anyhow, Valentine doesn't know shit. Far's he's concerned, he living out his rock-and-roll fantasy, bankrolled by some cagey nigger who doesn't know the music biz from his A-hole."

"It's that simple, huh?"

"It ain't simple, Z. It's just business."

"Not if it includes the Wells Fargo job, it isn't. That's murder, D."

"Yeah, well, I ain't got nothing to do with it. I hold down corners, and I deal in money, Zesty, like a regular businessman. I don't ask where the money comes from, just like J. Crew doesn't grill their customers where they got five hundred dollars for a pair of shiny-ass shoes. Sale's a sale."

"And all sales are final?" I say, thinking of Sullivan lying stone cold in the morgue, a marked-down tag dangling off his blue toe. "You know, D, you think you're a player now? You'd be ten times more dangerous armed with an MBA."

"Shit, Zesty, I already got *that*. It's called a Masters of Bitch Ass."

"Right, from the University of the Berry. And you majored in streets. I get it. I just don't get why you're washing someone else's money, then."

"Come again?"

"You just told me corners and cash, but that money I got hit with, at least some of it, must have come from the Wells Fargo job, or why else would the police come see me? You say you got nothing to do with it, you're just plowing money into Black Hole. That's good enough for me, but I gotta wonder how you got hold of it and why you're not asking the question you really need answered."

"Which is what?"

"How come the money I got hit with pulled the cops in so fast? Somebody not doing their job, D? Good help that hard to find?"

Darryl chews the inside of his lower lip, giving that some thought.

"And I only got hit with, what, fifty Gs? That's a lot of coin left over from that haul, but you don't have it. That's what Cedrick and O are looking for, right?"

Darryl ponders my question, looking over my shoulder.

"You think Britta and Gus stole it? Is that it?" But then why is Gus looking for Britta too? Is there nobody in this fucking city who isn't trying to screw somebody over?

"This conversation's over, Zesty." Darryl steps to my inside as the Pathfinder glides to the curb.

"I thought you were staying in town," I say, swinging my bag over my shoulder, but not quick enough. Darryl hits me with a forearm clothesline, knocking me toward the car, where Cedrick reaches out the window, wrapping his thick arm around my neck as O comes loping around the fender holding a bright-yellow-handled lock cutter, its metal pincers wide open and hungry.

"Change in plans," Darryl says.

NINETEEN

Will and Diane have just returned from the banks of the Charles River, leaving behind the nearly half million revelers who'd gathered along its shores anticipating the moment when the Boston Symphony Orchestra would launch into Weber's Jubilee Overture, followed by Tchaikovsky's Concerto No. 1 in B-flat minor. It's a special Boston night, but they've seen the show before; they'll catch the fireworks from the roof.

That had been the plan—at least before Will recognized the specter of Richie Ritter loitering like a bad infection on the front stairs and walked in to find Devlin McKenna sitting at his kitchen table, the obvious bulge of a holstered gun under his shamrock Members Only jacket.

Will is there again now, back in the game.

"I hear congratulations are in order, William. Would this be the new missus now? So, is it Mrs. Meyers now, Diane? Or in the privacy of your own home do you prefer to be addressed by your maiden name, the one the boys at the Federal Bureau of Investigations use for you in your file?"

TWENTY

Darryl punches me in the stomach, my knees coming up too late to protect my midsection. I'd double over to puke, but Cedrick starts choking me, and whatever came up from my stomach is forced back down as I try to dig my chin under his grip, my bag pinned awkwardly at my side, my vision swimming.

O tosses Darryl the lock cutter. I claw at Cedrick's leather jacket, but it's no use. His other arm comes across and traps my wrists at my neck, from a distance probably looking like I'm choking myself with my own two hands.

"This might hurt a little, Zesty, but you'll thank me for it later. Pin the muthafucka's legs, O, he's spazzing out. And don't choke him to death, he's turning colors!"

Cedrick loosens his grip and twists me sideways, while Darryl comes at my skull with a sweeping arc, raking the lock cutter across my scalp. My hair is pulled as much as cut off my head.

"No!" I gurgle.

"Got-damn, Zesty, hold still already. I gotta get the other side. Let'm breathe, C."

I gag as Cedrick loosens his grip and O steps away, either afraid of getting thrown up on or realizing I'm not going to kick Darryl off. Half a haircut is not a look I'm likely to rock.

"Wait." I hold out the hair for him. "At least try and make it straight."

Darryl switches sides and cuts across the length, leaving me holding a clotted mess of long brown strands two feet long.

"There. Feel better now?"

"Fuck you. That took me three years to grow." I'm not so much angry as relieved to still have both my ears attached to my head, only I'm not about to thank him for it. "What the fuck, D?"

"Change is good, Zesty." Darryl steps back to admire his handiwork. I tuck what's left behind my ears. "Look like a man now at least. And there goes the match the police are looking for, right?"

He has a point there. No bike, short hair, just another citizen blending into the brickwork. Except I need wheels like a baby needs his pacifier. I take a look around the empty street. "Let me borrow that a minute?"

"Yo, D!" Cedrick, on high alert, jumps out of the truck as Darryl hands me the lock cutter.

"What, you forgot about that Glock in his pack? He ain't up to nothing."

Well, not exactly nothing. There's a gleaming silver Trek hooked to a no parking sign in front of a new luxury condo, the lock a rubber-coated Kryptonite that, purchased new, comes with more paperwork than a Russian adoptee. I fit the pincers where it meets the top corner and snap down hard; the cutter jumps out of my hands, only the rubber cut through.

"Gimme that." Cedrick boxes me off the sidewalk and chomps down at the same spot, a vein bulging at his neck as he leverages his weight until the lock snaps and falls to the sidewalk. Cedrick spits on the ground, looks at me, and winks, his pupils suddenly coming up slot-machine question marks, the initial effects of Sam's magic capsules hitting him. A bubble of spittle forms on his lower lip. His knees go wobbly as he stumbles back to the car, tosses O the keys, and throws up over the rear tire.

Darryl makes the universal *if he keeps throwing up I'm going to throw up too* face and says, "There, now we even for the bike we messed up."

"Leaving only the fifty grand I owe you."

"Zesty, haven't you been listening? You're off the books for the fifty."

"What about Gus and Britta?"

"You ain't responsible for them either. Never were."

"I am for Gus." I know it sounds corny before it leaves my lips, but I say it anyway: "He's my friend."

"Your friend!" Darryl's eyes nearly pop out of his face. "Your friend set you up and ran over your ass!"

"Maybe."

"No maybe about it. You explained it pretty clear."

Darryl glances at the Pathfinder, where Cedrick is alternately laughing and crying, kissing the polished surfaces of the car and trying to wrap the vehicle in a hug. *What the fuck!* he mouths to O, who shrugs clueless somewhere deep in his sweats.

"We ate Thai tonight?" O says.

"How can I make things right?" I draw Darryl back to me.

"Make things *right*? Zesty, that greedy muthafucka maybe fucked up everything I worked my black ass off for. Him disappearing would make things right, but I'll take care of that myself."

"What if I could make that happen for you?"

"You shitting me? I just offered you a *J-O-B,* and you said, 'I'm sorry, I'm going to have to decline.'" Darryl switches to his imitation white voice for that line. "And you gonna what, whack somebody for me now?"

"I didn't say that. But what if I could make him go away? Britta too."

"Now you dreaming. But hell, you want to be the Disappearing Man, be my guest, only it still doesn't account for my money. I want my money, Z."

"Whose money?"

"Fuck you."

"Okay, fuck me. But if you get it back, you don't need Gus and Britta, right? Everything washes out."

"Naw, I see what you're thinking, but it doesn't work like that. That money, even if you end up getting it back, there are too many loose ends. I do something, put my mind to it, I like to lock it up tight. And hell, Zesty, what's *wrong* with you? Gus and that bitch ran you down for a lousy fifty Gs, and you're trying to *negotiate* some peace-loving exchange? They tried to kill you, boy! Ain't you got some pride in you? Hell, if you anything at all like Zero, you'd have flames coming out your eyeballs right now."

"The money for Gus and Britta," I say, my hand slipping inside my pack, finding the waffled butt of the Glock, the curve of the trigger guard.

"Oh shit." Darryl rears back. "You are out of your damn mind." Our eyes lock for what feels like a long time before Darryl drifts his gaze toward O, who without my noticing, has edged to within three feet of me, his pistol aimed squarely at my head.

"We got ourselves a deal, Darryl?"

"Hell no, we ain't got no deal! Now, take your hand out the fuckin' bag before O shoots you for practice."

I slip the safety off the Glock, Darryl hearing the click, a single line of sweat dropping down the side of his temple.

"Tell O to put down his gun," a voice I don't recognize says.

"Fuck you, Zesty." Another line of sweat forms on Darryl's other temple and runs its way past his ear. It's a muggy evening, but I don't think that's what's causing Darryl to sweat. "You ain't gonna shoot me."

"That a fact, D? Maybe I've got more of my brother in me than you give me credit for." I let my index finger slide gently along the trigger, the curved metal warm to the touch, the gun having its own needs.

Shoot him! it screams.

I glance at O, who yawns and smiles without showing his teeth. If he shoots me in the head, he'll be watching Netflix an hour from now, munching on Fritos. But as my father was fond of saying, you play the cards you're dealt, or you fold and get out of the game. Only who listens to their parents?

"You talk about pride, D, righteous anger?" I say, manufacturing some on my own. "Let's talk about nothing to lose instead. I got cops on my ass tied to this Wells Fargo thing, cops probably waiting for me at my place, covering my office, so I'm pretty much fucked already. I shoot you, at least one of my problems goes away. You feeling *me,* Darryl? You seeing things the way I'm seeing them? White-on-black crime, all things being equal now in the new South End."

"Fuck you, Zesty," Darryl says but he's smiling now. O disappears his gun as quickly as he produced it—now you see it, now you don't, those long fingers trouble in a card game.

"Fuck me indeed." I let my finger slide from the trigger, as relieved as any finger's ever been. "But we have ourselves a deal, right? The money for Gus and the girl?"

"Naw. No deal. More like an arrangement subject to change. And here's the fine print for you. The money *clean* for Gus and the girl within twenty-four hours, or I do things my way. Washed, dried, and folded, because I'm not taking dirty money into my retirement years, no way, no fucking how. I want my million, and I want it untraceable."

"Whose money?"

"Nah, I'm not going there. You want to play Monty Hall, be my guest, but we do it on my terms, you got that?"

"Sure. Why not?" I pull my empty hand out of my bag and extend it toward Darryl like I've done at the Y a hundred times before, win or lose; on the same team or as foes; blood, sweat, and fouls. Promise the stars, promise the moon, might as well throw in the sun as well.

Darryl takes my hand and pulls me off balance into a man hug, his other hand grabbing hard at the back of my neck but not meant to hurt.

"Gunner," he whispers in my ear, his breath as clean as a summer's breeze. "I always knew you had it in you."

TWENTY-ONE

McKenna was not yet the reigning crime boss he would become, but he'd begun to branch out on his own, carve his slice of the growing city pie. Will learned this firsthand when McKenna tried to extort protection money from his nascent poker game, a nearly fatal miscalculation because Will was already paying tribute to the DiMasis to operate within their broad jurisdiction, already piecing off the action.

Will had compounded McKenna's error with one of his own by complaining about the protection touch, prompting a Prince Street sit-down with McKenna's principal employers. And though matters were squared, Will might as well have drawn a bull's-eye on his forehead, judging by the way McKenna's dead eyes bored into his.

So this is on him now, McKenna sitting in Will's kitchen. Will didn't think things through, didn't practice the long game he always preached when the cards began to sour. If McKenna knows Diane's true identity, then it goes without saying he knows far more, her TNT talents, her radical past. The Polaroids he produces of Leila Markovich, also still underground and unrepentant after the Harvard bombing, are just so much showing off, an unnecessary flourish that Will files away for future use.

How McKenna knows these things is not important, Will tells himself. How is misspent energy, distraction. These are his cards. How will he play them?

And to his credit as a reader of faces, as a manipulator of his own features, those dark lying eyes of his, he chooses to play the rube. That is, a feigned tic of his lids, a stiffness of body to mimic that genetically ingrained moment between flight or fight—not directed at McKenna, of course, that would amount to suicide, but toward the flowered Medusa who cuckolded him with a manufactured alias, grown thorns as sharp as razor wire. This, Will decides, is the only play he has, the ultimate bluff for their very lives.

"You didn't know, William?" Devlin McKenna laughs because this, it turns out, is far richer than what he had hoped to gain from this moment. Laughs because he has bought at least this part of his bluff and in doing so will extend the play. Because when you win, when the cards fall just right, you never want to stop playing the game.

"Oh, this is rich!" McKenna is delighted, but playing it for mock regret. "The FBI, no less, would be quite happy to know where your young bride is hiding out. And here I am telling you what I assumed she'd told you herself? Maybe she doesn't trust you, William? Not quite the ideal way to start a marriage. Now, is that a wee bump you're showing, Diane, or have you just gained a little weight lately?"

TWENTY-TWO

I cruise up Harrison, crossing into Chinatown to the corner of Washington and LaGrange, where Gus has a loft a few doors past the Glass Slipper, one of the last strip joints operating within Boston city limits, the street dealers slouching out of the brickwork, warming to their hustle as I approach. I don't figure Gus to be home, but I'd be remiss not to try, and anyhow the street is pleasant, lined with relics of the Combat Zone—faded nudie posters, aging glossies—posted on lamp poles, brick walls, construction plywood.

I ring once, twice, three times a lady. No answer.

I cut down Beach Street, order a bowl of tofu and ginger noodles from Xinh Xinh Vietnamese, and eat it sitting on the curb, Chinese pop music filtering down from the hanging black garden of fire escape balconies, the tune just lousy enough to make me appreciate the artistry of Britney Spears.

A tangle of white lanterns is strung along the fire escapes on the corner of Beach and Knapp, giving Knapp—more cut-through alley than street—a serene glow, offsetting the dark and heavy permanence of sentinel Dumpsters lining the curb, and beside them, the up-down firefly glow of cigarettes, restaurant workers alternately standing and squatting, catching a smoke between shifts, between dishes, just between.

What have I gotten myself into? It's hard to tell, but it has a familiar feel to it: the first few times my father allowed me to risk my own money at the poker table when he was short a player in one of his games—a minnow at the table with sharks. What did

I learn from those nights aside from my penchant for punishment? That sometimes it's more important to catch the rhythm of the game than to catch cards, essentially to quit fighting the current and find a way to cut into the flow. In other words, follow the money.

I lose fifty grand that I pick up from Black Hole Vinyl and instantly draw a couple of robbery homicide detectives working the Wells Fargo armored car robbery. How did Brill and Wells know to come see me at Beth Israel? Were they just stumbling around blind, hoping to get lucky, or were they playing me, already aware of the link between Sullivan and Zero? Or was it more about Black Hole, Darryl already on the police radar, which is the feeling I'm starting to get, the cash taking center stage, as always.

But if Darryl's to be believed, that he's got nothing to do with the Wells Fargo robbery, how did that tainted money get into the coffers of Black Hole Vinyl? And did the few bills the detectives claimed to have recovered mean the whole stack was tainted? One more step back: I worked with Collin Sullivan, both of us moonlighting for Zero. Zen Movers is stocked with enough ex-cons to field a rugby team. Do the detectives already know this? Do they believe in coincidences? One shake of my illustrious family tree, there's no telling what will fall out—my brother, mother, and father all dangling from the branches like overripe fruit, a worm in every bite.

My mother: a Bosstown legend, who, prior to the Harvard bombing and Bank of Boston, was known for little more than her steady presence protesting US Central American policy and co-founding Boston's first food co-op. How long has my mother been gone? Long enough that I rely on photographs to know her face. So what am I missing, too close to see the money for the trees?

Zero is sketchy, there's no denying it. His pirate band of movers covers just about every form of felonious misconduct on the books. Only I have a hard time picturing him orchestrating this mess, even as the detectives inevitably follow that line; aside from me and the money, it's the only solid reel they've got to tug on.

So tally time: I've got half the Boston force looking for me, a gun I need to ditch, a promise made that I have no idea how to deliver on, and Zero, to whom I neglected to give a heads-up as the day picked up speed. Leaving me where?

Craving weed. Marijuana's not addictive—it's the Doritos that steer you to rehab—but the introspection I get from smoking might be. I like being a messenger just fine, but there's nothing quite like being a stoned messenger. And I've noticed nobody runs over the stoned messenger. He's like the court jester on loan—two-minute bits and out the door before the crowd sours.

Barring that, a drink will have to do. So after I deposit the gun in a mailbox at the corner of Tremont and Harrison, I'm leaning my new bike in the alley behind J. J. Foley's, the neighborhood's last standing bucket of blood and a longtime cop bar and filling station for the *Herald* staff who toil a block up Harrison. There's a second Foley's on Stanhope Street downtown, but that watering hole caters to an entirely different clientele, suit and tie during daylight hours before shifting to the tattooed and pierced crowd as the evening drops in. It also happens to be Messenger Central; on busy nights there's not a free signpost or parking meter on which to lock a bike for blocks.

Not the case here. And depending on how you feel about the combination of cops, guns, and alcohol, it is, at any given time, either the safest or most dangerous place in the city and quite possibly, I figure, the last place they'll be looking for me once they connect the Britta Ingalls break-in to Black Hole Vinyl and then to the money I papered Boylston with.

I take my chances at the long L-shaped cigarette-scarred bar. There's fresh sawdust on the green and white checkerboard floor, plenty of open tables and chairs, but they're too close to five burly men in blue jeans and loosely zipped BPD Windbreakers whose conversation stalls briefly as I enter, resuming to full volume only as I slide into an empty seat. Shot glasses and beer bottles cover the two tables they've pulled together; except for a couple of hard hats probably off from working the Big Dig, I have the bar and bartender to myself.

"Be right there," Jerry the barkeep and owner says, separating bills in the register, his back to me. Jerry works mostly nights, usually with one of his three sons, but he looks to be winging it solo for the time being.

"Jameson and a Guinness when you get the chance," I tell him.

"Feelin' Irish tonight are ye, pal?" Jerry says in his soft Irish lilt, glancing at me in the bar mirror, noting my new lock-cutter haircut before resuming his counting.

Pal. Nothing beats that. I've been in here two hundred times, been served by Jerry a hundred times before. Welcome to Foley's. Cheers is for losers.

"Just trying to fit in, Jerry."

"Yeah? How's that working out for you, Zesty?"

I make a show of looking around the bar: street signs nailed above the front door pointing toward Dublin and other Irish towns I can't pronounce unless properly drunk. On the walls, a photo gallery of Boston politicos, ballplayers, and cops through the ages. Cops and servicemen. Cops and celebrities. Cops and Ireland. You get the picture.

"I think I'm in the wrong Foley's," I say.

"Ah, well, long as your money's green." Jerry, master of subliminal advertising, sets the drinks before me on a pair of Guinness coasters.

"Would you settle for greenish?" I plunk down the blood-stained hundred, make a show of smoothing it out. Jerry blinks at the bill and takes a long look at my face. If it's my stitches he's counting, he'll need a third hand for the job. But to Jerry's credit, he doesn't say anything and doesn't ask any questions—it's the new millennium, *pal,* and the bartenders don't want to hear any of your troubles; they've got enough of their own. My father always claimed Jerry would make one heck of a poker player.

I take a long pull from the beer and throw down the shot behind it, studying my new reflection in the shadowy bar mirror. The T-shirt Darryl gave me is light red, bordering on pink that matches the color of the swelling above my right eye. It's a fine outfit for the South End proper, but a little out of place here, and if Jerry didn't know me, I wouldn't hold it against him if he made me for an unhappy victim of a recent gay bashing. Too much of that going around lately, tempers flaring as new money rubs up against empty pockets.

I salute my gay reflection with a raised pinkie toast and settle in to watch the corner TV tuned to a West Coast ball game, my beloved Red Sox battling the Seattle Mariners, Ichiro gliding around the bases after slapping the ball into the corner.

"Now, there's a fucking ballplayer!" one of the Crown Vic cops exclaims. "Feetfirst like you're supposed to."

"Pete Rose used to slide headfirst," one of his drinking partners imparts.

"It's wrong."

"Charlie Hustle's *wrong*?"

I watch Ichiro get stranded at third and hardly think about Black Hole Vinyl and all the money I lost. Ortiz leads off the Sox half with a homer to left, and I give nary a thought to Collin Sullivan, the murdered Wells Fargo guard I only knew from working for Zero's moving company. Sullivan was likely moonlighting for some extra cash, like I often do.

Varitek drills a double to left-center, and I practically forget the mismatched detectives, Brill and Wells, to whom I lied due to my inherent mistrust of institutional authority and to cover for Zero until I knew how thick he was with Sullivan, the booze blending nicely now with the residual knockout punch of whatever Sam had concocted in his home lab.

During a commercial break, my crash-triggered antennae pick up static again, the frequency making me wince. Only this time the noise fades before delivering a song; maybe my gift is losing wattage as I recover.

We are experiencing technical difficulties.

I watch another inning of listless baseball and notice the hands on the Miller Beer clock above the rear doorway sitting squarely on midnight.

"Is that right?" I wake Jerry from his standing nap.

"On the money," Jerry assures me.

I order another Guinness, and before I know it, Ichiro is up again, apparently taking on the Sox single-handedly. The bar fills up as shifts change on the Big Dig and nearby Shawmut Avenue police station. Men in loose construction clothing, jeans and sweatshirts or cheap suits with noticeable bulges under their left arms; a few women peppered in among them, pistol- and mace-loaded handbags slung over shoulders within easy reach. Two ladies take their seats near me, and we all watch as Ichiro bloops a double just over Youkilis's reach at first.

"Halfway to the cycle!" shouts the same cop who admired Ichiro's slide a couple innings before.

"Remember Pearl Harbor," grumbles the man sitting across from him.

"What the fuck's that supposed to mean?"

"I'm just sayin'."

"This is just like being at Fenway." The woman beside me blatantly looks me up and down before swiveling to her friend. "The seats are lousy, the beer guy's never around when you want him, everybody's soused off their ass or on their way, and every other word you hear's either 'fuck' or 'shit.'"

"No fucking shit," her friend responds, without a hint of sarcasm. "If I ever tell you I'm getting hitched to anyone in this room, shoot me before the rock gets on my finger."

I get up after Ichiro's stranded again and head for the bathroom in back. When I return, I point toward the clock, which hasn't moved at all. "Fuckin' A, Jerry."

"Hey, you just asked me if it's right. Not if it's working." Jerry folds his arms, the bar rag draped over his shoulder. "What's that they say about a broken clock, Detective?" He grins sideways at Wells who, with a Rolling Rock in hand, sits in the seat I'd vacated.

"If you can't take the heat, get out of the kitchen?" Wells says. "That's the one."

I'm definitely in the wrong Foley's, I think to myself.

TWENTY-THREE

Boston's a small city, but not so small I'd just run into Wells out of the blue, notwithstanding Foley's status as a longtime cop bar and Wells being a homicide detective. That he's got my purple and black messenger bag on the bar in front of him only confirms it, which in turn means he's been following me. But for how long and from where?

"Your friend Albert told me you might be here." Wells clarifies that mystery, sliding the bag toward me. The plastic snaps at the front have been scraped into jagged prongs dangling uselessly from nylon straps. I peel back the flap and find my metal clipboard sporting the mother of all dents on the front cover, my tin of weed, and one of Zero's Zen Moving Company T-shirts I don't remember being there this morning. With my hands inside the pack, I flip open the tin and peek at the joints still inside.

"Brother"—Wells peers at me over his bottle—"if you've got the brain cells to spare, all the power to you."

Wells's enlightened view prompts me to look at him with new eyes, and what I notice first off is the detective's still wearing the same suit from this morning, only now, on closer inspection, I see his sculpted beard beginning to creep like weeds escaping their cultivated lines, a slight gap at the neck where his tie's knotted, missing too many meals as he chases down leads. He's still tan, but his skin is dry, matching bags forming under increasingly puffy eyes.

"You know how much room we'd have in prisons for people who belong there if we legalized that shit?" The detective tilts his chin toward my bag as Jerry brings him a vodka with ice and limes, sets it down in front of him.

"You're preaching to the choir," I tell him.

"No kidding, except the choir conveniently forgot to sing about that stash when we asked what went missing this morning."

"I plead short-term memory loss."

"From the smoke or the Buick?"

"Now I plead the Fifth."

"I bet. Everything else is gone, though, right?"

I pry open the clipboard. "Including the paperwork and the check they cut me at Black Hole. Where'd the bag turn up?"

"Under a car towed off Commonwealth, which qualifies as a small miracle in my book." Wells drinks off half the vodka, mashes ice in his back teeth.

"What do you want, Detective?"

"Collin Sullivan." Fatigue settles into Wells's voice for the first time. Or maybe it was there from the start and I'm just noticing it now.

"What makes you think I know anything about him?"

"The badge reads *detective*. You need me to show you again?"

"No." I finish my Guinness, decide against another; I'll be sore enough in the morning without adding a hangover. His drink also finished, Wells just sits and glowers at me.

"You know Charlestown, Zesty?"

"What about it?"

"Population Irish? Least before all the yuppies who look like me moved in."

"So?" I ghost sip my empty drink. When did I finish it?

"Not even a couple square miles, the place produces more bank robbers, armored car hitters than anywhere else in the world."

"Fascinating," I say.

"You'd figure somebody in this town would've banged out a dissertation on it by now, right? Tight community. Nobody talks to cops, even though everybody's related to one. Like it's the first thing they learn growing up. We root for the B's, the C's, depending on how many coons they got on the team, the BoSox. Here's the Code: Don't talk to cops. Or else."

"You?" I say.

"Me what?"

"You didn't grow up around here?"

"Do I *sound* like I grew up around here? I actually like the letter *r*. It's worth pronouncing once in a while. Why do you ask?"

"Because you make it sound like Charlestown's so different from every other place, but it's just like any neighborhood in any city big or small. As for the Irish and banks? They're a smart people, and that's where the money is. There's no mystery to it."

"Short thesis." Wells points at my empty glass.

I shake my head.

"Anyhow, like I was saying . . . Jesus, what was I saying? I need a nap."

"I'm assuming you were talking about Sullivan," I say.

"Right. Our man Sully. Grows up in the bank robbery capital of the world and lands a job working for Wells Fargo. It doesn't add up."

"A job's a job," I say, without really meaning it. I do what I do because it's what I'm cut out for. I'm built for speed the same way Wells is uniquely suited to his job; not everyone can speak for the dead. "What's your point, Detective?"

"Temptation, Zesty." Wells taps the bar for emphasis. "All that money talking to him every day and the neighborhood whispering in his ear. Sullivan was dirty. It just didn't work out the way he planned."

"So what? I still don't get why you're telling *me* this."

"Ah, there we go. *That's* where I was. So me and Brill, we've been to Sullivan's place before, and by *we,* I mean the lab guys, forensics, FBI. Been over every inch of that apartment, and there's nothing there you wouldn't expect from a guy bringing home a little over twelve hundred every couple weeks. No fancy flat screen, no keys to a spanking Mustang, just Working Man shit, family pictures, porn, Xbox. We learn nothing. And then lo and behold, you come around and there's cash flying through the air. That money you were hit with? We know at least some of it came from the Wells Fargo job. Except it pretty much dead-ends with you, so back we go to Sullivan's place."

"Before talking to anyone at Black Hole?"

"I'll get to that in a minute. How much you figure you were carrying—twenty, thirty grand?"

"I told you at the hospital, I wouldn't know," I half lie, knowing now it was fifty thousand.

"Right, anyhow, to Sully's depressing one-bedroom manhole we go. And guess what we missed the first time around?"

"I don't have a clue." My brain tells my mouth to say that, but

I see where he's going, my stomach sending me a totally different message.

Zero's Zen Moving T-shirt.

Wells reaches into my bag and lays the dead man's shirt out on the bar, thick cotton, black as a starless night, spun heavy and stitched tight to absorb the sweat and hard labor of moving furniture. I have the same shirt, except mine's paper thin, soft and worn from hundreds of moves, the black dye bleached into an uneven charcoal gray by my sweat.

"I recognize Sullivan, but I didn't *know* him," I say. "He worked for my brother, moonlighting I guess, like me when he needs the help or I need some quick cash." I slide the shirt closer to Wells, but he doesn't move to take it back, too busy rubbing his hands with nervous energy, sparks practically flying from his fingers. Maybe later he'll take out that DETECTIVES tin and shine it up, blind himself in one eye.

"At Zero's place, you work off the books?"

"You homicide or IRS?" I say with enough of an edge to let the detective know how far I'm willing to go in this conversation. If Wells's late-night talk is going to veer deep into my family, then the discussion, for me, is through.

"Why'd you lie about Sullivan this morning?"

"Because I don't like getting stuck in the middle of something I have nothing to do with."

"Bullshit."

"Yeah, okay. Maybe I just didn't like the way you were asking. You like that answer any better?"

"No. But you know what, Zesty? You need to toughen the fuck up, because as far as I'm concerned, we came at you easy this morning. I don't know what kind of pull your father has in the department or with Brill, for that matter, but it was way before my time, and I don't owe anybody shit, you hear me? BPD signs my checks, but I work for Collin Sullivan, the dirty cocksucker, and the way I see it—no, the way *we* see it—is you owe us one."

"Is that right?" I say. "You don't know who my father is? He's right there." I pivot in my seat, pointing to a photograph on the wall: my father with Jerry's dad, a trim, snow-capped Irishman, posed alongside then Boston mayor Kevin White and Barney Frank, who at the time was an aide to White and would become a senior-ranking Massachusetts congressman. The picture was probably taken in the early seventies, and it was beginning to show its age, yellowing at the borders, the corners curling toward the glass frame. My father looks happy, or at least in his element, those liquid black eyes of his shining.

"Your father was a fixer. I figured that out. He knew people, got things taken care of. Beyond that . . . ?" Wells shrugs, the heat draining from him as swiftly as it had arrived. "He still alive?"

"He's got Alzheimer's. Just like the mayor there, coincidentally. Maybe it's this city, it makes you want to forget shit."

"Ah, don't be like that, Zesty," Jerry says, hearing the edge in my voice. He leans both elbows on the bar, pointedly ignoring two slumming stockbrokers waving fistfuls of money down the other end. "They just didn't drink enough, what it was. Listen, my pa, God rest his soul, used to tell this story—after Mr. White was out of office, of course—how the honorable mayor would grace this establishment ostensibly to drink and negotiate with the powers that be. Stop me if you've heard this one, Zesty."

"Go on," I say, smiling.

"Well, White, he'd always be the first to arrive, and when he'd come in, he'd request a dishrag from my da, a dry one, and he'd wipe down the bar in front of him like he was waxing his car in the driveway. 'Jaysus!' my father would say, his face like a pomegranate, least the first few times this happened. 'Mr. Mayor, the stick's clean as a whistle! You could eat a steak off it. Whattaya have to go wiping it down for?' The mayor would just regale him with some nonsense, shoulder the rag like he's keepin' it in case of spills, like he worked here. And my da would stalk away, have my uncle James or Joe Marshall serve him. He was so angry he couldn't even look at him. You probably don't remember Joe Marshall, Zesty, but he worked the stick here fifty years for my father. Fifty years! Anyhow, the mayor would keep the rag, but at some point in all the drinking, it would disappear from his shoulder like magic. What nobody noticed is that the mayor dropped the rag to the rail under the bar and all through the night, as everybody got good and hammered, the mayor would be tipping his drinks toward the floor. Shot after shot, to the rail, to the rag, everybody getting plastered, and the mayor straight as a razor and twice as sharp. Hizzoner cut many a deal in his favor right here, with your father in attendance quite often, I might add, Zesty, for your da was never far from the action, was he?"

"No, sir."

"I doubt the mayor's sleight of hand escaped your pa's notice, being the cardsharp he was himself, all due respect. Anyhow, at the end of the night as everybody stumbled home, their heads ringing into the wee morning, there was the dishrag, the mayor's unholy cloth we called it, soaked with whiskey, which my father refused to touch. . . ."

"And?" Wells prods, tries his best to look uninterested.

"Well, Joe would squeeze it out, of course." Jerry corkscrews the rag that had lain over his shoulder. "Where do you think well drinks come from?" He winks at me, feigns surprise to see the stockbrokers still waving their bailout money. "Gentlemen! What'll it be?"

The detective picks up his empty drink, sniffs the glass.

"You were saying?"

Wells looks at me hard but doesn't find any resistance to feed off of. Maybe Jerry's story gave him a little historical perspective to mull things over.

"How many times you work with Sullivan?"

"Maybe twice, three times? Guys come and go at Zero's. It's a tough job, harder than it looks. If he worked any more than that, my brother would have a record of it." Or not. Cash moves are encouraged by Zero's crews, and those jobs tend to disappear from the books. The moving business in Boston is no joke; you find whatever edge you can to turn a profit. Probably only Zero's main rival, Gentle Giant, keeps accurate records.

"Sullivan never mentioned working for Wells Fargo?"

"Not that I remember."

"Short-term memory loss again?"

"More like there was nothing to it. We worked, shot the shit, and that was that. Seemed like an okay guy. Worked hard. Next thing I know, you're showing me pictures and his brains are all over the side of his van."

Wells maintains focus on me for what I guess passes for long and hard, his Truth-O-Meter clocking overtime, trying to decide whether I'm holding out on him.

"You come from a pretty interesting family, Zesty."

"What's that supposed to mean?" He has my full attention now.

"We run a check on *you* after the hospital visit, and we get nothing, not even a parking ticket, probably on account you don't even have a driver's license. And there's your father's influence to consider, but like I said, that's before my time. You have your courier's license—expired, by the way—so there's something I can hang on you. But aside from that, you're either a model citizen or just real lucky. Zero, on the other hand, pops up all over the fucking map, though granted, always in a tertiary manner."

"Tertiary," I say. "Nice."

"Yeah. I'm a cunning linguist," Wells says.

"Did someone say cunnilingus?" One of the two lady cops who'd parked themselves next to us slides off her seat.

"Not exactly." Wells rubs his temples with both hands.

"That's a shame," the lady officer coos, running her finger down the length of Wells's expensive tie.

"I once flew Air Cunnilingus," the other lady officer says, a catlike smile on her face. "All the way to Ireland."

"Nonstop?" I say.

"Of course, darlin'. Except back then it was called Don't Ever Stop." She reaches out and strokes my thigh. "Come see me when you're healed, baby."

"One day I'll make a TV show about you," I say, catching her as she tips toward the bar, unsteady on her heels. "It'll be called *Lady Cop,* and it's gonna go something like this: *Lady Cop*! She was a lady first. But *first* she was a cop."

"I like it," Lady Cop purrs, tossing her long curls.

"Friday nights," I tell her. "After a very special episode of *Bones.*"

"Ohh, I love that show."

"Remind me to drag you downtown next time," Wells says. "This place is like storytime for drunks. So Zero. As in zero arrests, like you. And yet his name keeps popping up in everything from the Gardner Museum extortion thing to the BU payroll job. Called in for questioning a handful of times, but nothing sticks."

"My brother owns a moving company," I say, and leave it at that.

"Zero's Zen Moving? Are you kidding me? Practically everybody working there's an ex-con or some local hard case with a sheet so long you could use it for packing paper. He should call it Recidivist Moving, see what that does for business."

"Ex-cons shouldn't work? He gives guys second chances."

"Oh, that's what he does. He doesn't, like, say, hire somebody good at safes, case out a house on a job, then come back to finish things off?"

"You've got a hell of an imagination. You want to go partners on that *Lady Cop* thing, pitch it somewhere?"

"No."

"Me neither. My brother's a mover and a businessman, and I own my own courier company." What's left of it. "What are you getting at?"

"Your father—"

"Like I said, my father has Alzheimer's. So you can leave my father the fuck out of this discussion. My mother too, as far as that's concerned, because that's where you're headed next, right? I don't *know* my mother, don't know where the hell she is or even if she's alive, so you can keep her the fuck out of it too."

I don't know when during my soliloquy I got up out of my seat, but I'm standing now. The lady cops and Crown Vic guys aren't watching the game anymore, their antennae twitching to a possibility of action. In fact, the whole bar's a little hushed, and I can hear the baseball announcer working himself into his own frenzy, Ichiro striding to the plate from the on-deck circle just a homer shy of hitting for the cycle.

"Sit down," Wells says evenly.

"I don't think so." I lower my voice but keep my eyes on the TV. "I told you what I know about Sullivan. My family's my family; it's the only one I got. Now go chase your tail." Ichiro steps into the batter's box, points his bat, tugs on his sleeve, and fouls the first pitch back to the screen.

"Best ballplayer in America," Ichiro's biggest fan says loudly, setting the bar back into motion. "Selfless. Down by two, needs to park one for the cycle, and he's slappin' at the ball, just tryin' get on base."

"That's how he swings at everything," says his partner.

"You, my friend, are a moron. Mo-ron!"

"It's time you wake up to what's going on around you, Zesty. What happened to you this morning wasn't an accident."

"You figure that out all by yourself?"

"Hell no. That's why I work with a partner. If you haven't noticed, I'm the good-looking one. But here's the thing. The money you got hit with, whether it came from Black Hole or not, hardly makes a difference. You hearing me, Zesty?"

"I'm listening," I say, though what I'm really hearing is the static filtering its way back into my head, the Cars dropping in stereo between my ears.

I don't mind you comin' here
And wastin' all my time
'Cause when you're standin' oh so near
I kinda lose my mind.

Ichiro fouls another ball near his feet, this time barely making contact. The phone behind the bar starts ringing. Jerry answers it, glances our way.

"You've managed to step neck deep into a pile of shit here, Zesty, so you'd better be telling me the truth about Sullivan. We having an understanding on this?"

"Get to it," I say, probably too loudly, the song at full volume between my ears now.

"We went over to Black Hole to corroborate your story, and there's no record of any pickup for a delivery, nothing signed, a check missing but the copy blank. You following the bouncing ball, Zesty?"

"Yes, he's here." Jerry winces into the receiver. "Now how am I to know why he doesn't answer his damn cell, Detective?"

"So maybe you're just a liar or maybe you got set up this morning, only either way, I don't need to be a fortune-teller to see where this shit's heading. I'd watch my back if I were you, Zesty, because your life just got a whole lot more complicated."

I don't mind you hangin' out
And talkin' in your sleep
It doesn't matter where you've been
As long as it was deep, yeah.

"Detective." Jerry extends the phone to Wells.

"Hold on a sec. What?" Wells grunts into the receiver. "Really? No, you heard right. I got him right here. Tell me again. Okay. Got it." Wells hands the phone back to Jerry as Ichiro knifes away from a ball inside. "Where were we?"

"My complicated life."

"Right. Forget that part about not having to be a fortune-teller. Turn around and put your hands on the bar, Zesty."

"What?"

"You're under arrest."

"For what?"

"I don't know. Breaking and entering on Mission Hill ringing any bells? Possession of marijuana? Assaulting a police officer?"

"Heavens to Betsy!" Jerry clutches his chest, staggers backward.

Ichiro takes a ball down low. I turn around, place my hands flat on the bar. "I changed my mind, Jerry. I'll have another Jameson."

Wells guides my arms behind me, cuffs me at the wrists.

"Ohh, kinky." The curly-headed policewoman nudges her drinking partner. "Need assistance patting him down, Ociffer?"

"Make that two Jamesons," Wells says. "And two for the ladies."

Jerry lines up five shot glasses from under the bar and fills them. "What are we toasting to?"

"Anyone ever been arrested inside your fine establishment, Jerry?"

"*Inside?* Why, I don't believe so." Jerry picks up two shots, hands them to the women, and slides one along the bar to Wells.

"Then to firsts," Wells says.

"To firsts." They all clink glasses, Jerry doing the honors for me as the bar erupts to the crack of a bat. *There it goes! Way back . . . !*

I tilt my chin to the ceiling. Jerry pours the shot down my throat. Lady Cop with the long curls presses against me and, with a hand at the back of my neck, pulls my head down to kiss me hard on the mouth, her tongue sliding long and hot across my teeth.

I guess you're just what I needed
(just what I needed)
I needed someone to bleed.

"Oh baby!" She looks up into my eyes. "You know, I'm not that drunk." She winks, dabs the corner of her glistening lips with the tip of her finger.

Just my fucking luck, I think as Wells pushes me out the door.

TWENTY-FOUR

Wells's car is a black Audi sedan with tinted windows, walnut trim, and enough dashboard gadgets to order a set of Ginsu knives off Amazon. We head out of the South End crossing into Roxbury, bowfront brick turning to public housing as we cut Mass Ave.

"You forgot to read me my rights," I say from the front seat beside him. The cuffs are loose, but my shoulders are cramping. Sam's magic pill evidently maxes out at nine hours. At the corner of Ruggles and Tremont, we glide past the glass cubes of the new Boston Police Headquarters. There's nothing else here, but maybe that's by design. Isolationville.

"So I'm not really under arrest?"

Wells blinks at me, runs a red light. "Keep those cuffs off my leather, or I'll beat you with a rubber hose."

"I have a client in Bay Village who makes good money saying shit like that to people."

"So?" Wells shrugs, unimpressed. "I'm on the clock."

"Yeah, but you're not wearing stilettos and a studded dog collar. No siren?"

Wells slides his window down, twirls his finger in the air. "Woo woo," he says. "Music."

The radio comes to life with a Coldplay song. Wells seems to like it, picks up speed on the guitar solo. If I had a choice, I'd take the beating with the rubber hose.

"What were you doing at Britta Ingalls's house?"

"I don't know what you're talking about."

"Don't be an idiot. We have your description, your business card. Soon we'll have your prints in the house. Where's the gun?"

"I still don't know what you're talking about, but check the mailbox on the corner of Tremont and Harrison, maybe you'll get lucky."

"You want to talk lucky?" Wells looks at me for too long, the Audi drifting over the yellow dividing line. Wells might be a transplanted Bostonian, but he's got the driving habits down. Next thing you know, he'll be skinny-dipping in Walden Pond, smoking clove cigarettes in Harvard Yard, and complaining about Cape traffic. "That gun you clipped came off the commissioner's nephew. If it happens to turn up unfired, you slip out of that noose, because there's no missing-gun report yet. No missing gun, no felony assault. You following me here, Zesty?"

"Yeah," I say. "Nepotism rules. You see the gold Buick in Britta's driveway?"

"Duly noted. And the lab will match paint chips from the front fender to your bike. We get that. The girl, Britta, and maybe your buddy Gus Molten set you up. That why you were at her place, looking for payback?"

"I don't plan that far in advance."

"What were you looking for?"

"Her."

"Bullshit. Why'd you wreck the place if you weren't looking for something?"

"That wasn't me. It was like that when I got there."

"So who did?"

"You're turning me into a broken record," I say. "You're the detective, live up to the billing already. Find Britta or find Gus, and maybe you'll find the rest of the money and a lead to Sullivan." *And do it before Darryl gets to them,* I think, for the time being keeping Darryl's name out of it, not wanting to give Wells another lane toward Zero. The two of them obviously cross-pollinated at some point, and God only knows how deep my brother might actually be in this fucking mess.

"How much was the score from the truck?" it finally occurs to me to ask.

"Shade over two million," Wells says after a slight pause.

"Is that how much those trucks regularly carry?" That's double the figure Darryl said he was trying to recoup.

"No. Matter of fact, it's about twice the usual for that partic- ular run, and most of it was destined for automated cash ma- chines, which is why you were able to carry so much in such a relatively small package and why we were able to trace it so fast. The money's serialized and compressed so the machines can spit it out. When you got hit, the bills pretty much exploded. What aren't you telling me?"

"I'm a Pisces? Where're we going?"

"Right here." Wells turns the corner and slides nose first between two cruisers parked half up the curb in a V formation, his car forming the shaft of an arrow pointing toward a dark basketball court. His headlights flash on a crowd of mostly black and brown faces, a hundred disembodied fingers laced through chainlink fence, a lineup of noses poking through trying to get a better view of what's inside. The small park is nestled into a corner lot at the tail end of a decrepit apartment building, electric and telephone lines running overhead, a dozen sneakers twisting in the soft breeze. There's a fast-food restaurant called Fritters across the street in what looks like a failed Burger King; some of the old franchise signage is still up, crowns and kings, the promise of having things your way. On the roof a ten-foot carnival bucket glows red and white, a pile of neon drumsticks poking over the rim, casting a greasy light that smudges the court.

"Nothing like a midnight block party." Wells leans me forward, unlocks the cuffs, and replaces them around his belt. He unbuttons his suit jacket, cranes his neck to look up at the neon chicken bucket. "What the hell is Fritters?"

"It's what you're doing with my time. Why am I here?"

"You'll see. Stay close enough so I can see you. Don't talk. You ever see a dead body before?"

Crime scene tape is going up around the chain-link, a couple uniforms elbowing the crowd off the wire, gift wrapping an unwanted municipal present. I think about what Sam said about a tree planted for every murder victim, that image holding more permanence than the dozens of bright RIP murals that color-dot the city and fade over time; when the roots eventually pushed themselves up through the court, they would simultaneously serve as a civic punishment and reminder, the ghost of victims forever whistling through branches, blocking all jumpers, everybody forced to take it hard to the hole.

There's another officer walking along the street, pausing at parked cars, jotting down plate numbers. Despite the late hour, the crowd's three deep, mostly young men and teenagers, a handful of baby mamas pushing strollers, a couple of men towing shopping carts loaded with bottles.

"This way." We have a direct line to the court entrance, where Brill is speaking into a cell phone, only Wells has me follow him to the opposite side where he penetrates the last row of gawkers. "Who got it?" he drawls to no one in particular.

"One minute he takin' it to the hole," a shirtless teenager responds out the side of his mouth. "Next, he be leakin' from 'em."

"He a player?"

The teenager turns around, sucks his teeth as he catches sight of Wells. "I dunno. He din't have no jump shot if that's what you mean, *De*-tective."

"He was a good guy, though, right? Who'd want to cap him?" Wells knows he's pushing it, throws up half a smile with the question.

"Nah. I dunno." The kid starts to look uncomfortable, people edging their eyes at him. "I just got here. . . . Who got shot up?"

"Who's on first," Wells says.

"Wha?"

"Wha's on second." Brushing past, Wells slides his card into the kid's back pocket, a skilled sleight of hand that must have taken some practice. I let him work his way through the crowd alone—"'Scuse me, 'scuse me, who got shot up?"—fishing his play on the long side of the cage, drawing only stares and vaguely hostile mumbles. I break off to join Brill, who is huddling now with a tall black uniformed officer and a slim teenager slouching in a ribbed wifebeater, basketball shorts down to his ankles, a flat-rimmed Cincinnati Reds baseball cap tilted over long cornrows.

"Zesty. Nice haircut." Brill pockets his phone, turns to the kid. "What's happening, Q?"

"Same old. Who the chalk?" The kid chin-points toward the court, where a sheet covers a body sprawled across the foul lane. Retro Air Jordans stick out one end, crossed at the ankles, heels up like somebody put a move on him from which he couldn't untangle himself.

"You tell me."

"Naw. I ain't never seen him before." The kid pauses to scratch an itch between his rows, adjust his cap. "Least before this week."

"New to the hood?"

The kid shrugs. "New to me."

"I thought you knew everybody, Q."

"Yeah, well, on the block maybe."

"Block by block?" Brill says.

"You know how it is. Who dat?" The kid angles his baseball cap my way.

"Undercover," Brill says, straight-faced.

"You shittin' me?"

"Deep."

"Don't touch anything." Wells joins us, limboing under the strung tape. "Walk in my footsteps. What'd you have for supper tonight?"

"Supper?" I have to think about it for a second. "Jameson, Guinness, and noodles."

"Swell. If you're gonna puke, do it away from the body."

Brill ducks between the tape, turns back to the uniformed officer. "Listen, Rasheed, nice call on the hammer. Let it be known your contribution doesn't go unnoticed."

"You'll tell the loot?"

"I'll make sure a birdie whispers in his ear." He winks poorly. Rasheed looks disappointed.

"What?"

"He's not gonna show?"

"For this? Rasheed, c'mon, now. Who runs this street?"

"Ray Ray's crew, far's I know."

"They in the middle of something?"

"Fireworks near every night. It's hot out here, but you know I'm wearing my Kevlar."

"Colors?"

Officer Rasheed makes a face, turns to Q.

"Purple?" Q says, which dials up a smile to Brill's face.

"What, all the tough-guy colors were taken?"

"They like the Colorado Rockies."

"So do I. For hiking."

Q indicates his cap.

"Yeah, I got it. Purple, huh? Who's got pink?"

"Ax your undercover," Q says, smirking gold fronts. "He the one wearing lipstick."

"Who, him?" Brill squints at me, gulps back a smile. "Don't be casting aspersions, Q. He's tougher than he looks. Legend has it, this morning he ate a Buick for breakfast."

"What, and it was wearing lipstick?"

"Tell him, Zesty," Brill says as I wipe my mouth.

"*Zesty?*" The kid with gold fronts rolls his eyes. "Now I *know* you playin' me."

"What time the lights go out here?" Brill points to one of two rusted light stanchions positioned at each end of the court.

"Midnight most nights. Same time Fritters closes."

"Fritters, huh? It looks like a Burger King someone topped with a bucket of chicken."

"See, that's why you a detective," Q says.

"You telling me a Burger King failed in *this* neighborhood?"

"I know! Everything going *up*scale."

Wells and Brill share a look, somehow managing to keep the amusement in their eyes off their mouths. "You eat there?"

"Hells no. Chicken costs *cheddar*. Anyhow, I'm a vegetarian."

"No shit? So how you know they close midnight?"

Q huffs audibly through his nose, points toward the restaurant, a sign on the window reading: OPEN TILL 12 AM.

"Gotcha. Court lights on during the shooting?"

"You think they running full in the dark?" Q takes a deep breath. "Why's I gotta do all the work for you?"

"'Cause I'm getting old. Hey, Rasheed. You want to see if you can get somebody turn these things back on?"

"Like who?"

"I dunno. Ask Q, he's got all the answers."

There's a half dozen plainclothes around the body, four barroom bouncers I recognize as members of the antigang crime unit, J. J. Foley's regulars, hard drinkers, brawlers, street cleaners. The other two men, round, bald, and glum, are in sports jackets that look all the worse in comparison to Wells's natty suit and polished shoes. I assume they're homicide, though I don't garner an introduction. Neither Brill nor Wells makes a move toward the body, maybe adhering to some sort of etiquette.

"Let's make this quick," one of the bald guys says, yawning. "You really think you got something here?"

"All guns, Matty." Wells shrugs. "What do we know?"

"What I got . . ." The bald detective flips open his pad. "Is shirts and skins running full court, couple guys warming the benches. Kid strolls . . ." The detective squints at his handwriting, brings the pad closer to his face. "Excuse me, *rolls* by north/south on one of those small circus bikes, whaddaya call them . . . ?"

"BMX," I say.

"Who's he?"

"Resident bike expert," Wells says.

"All-access pass, huh? Enjoy the show. BMX." The bald detective jots in his pad. "Anyhoo, black tee like with a tattoo design on the shoulders? Jean shorts, black White Sox cap over black do-rag, empties a clip, rides off hi-ho, Silver. We got shell casings outside the court, but soon as our shooter's off, it's a game of kick the can, casings everywhere they shouldn't be."

"Who wears White Sox?" Brill directs his question to one of the gang unit cops juggling a cell phone and cigarette.

"Humboldt," he says through smoke.

"They at war with the Rockies?"

"Interleague play?" He closes his phone. "I fucking hate interleague play. No, not as far as I know. This is too far from their turf. Maybe some little banger trying to make bones, didn't want to shit too close to home?"

"You don't recognize the vic?" Wells says.

"Nah. Neither one."

"*Neither one?* There's another?"

"Yeah." The cop points to three orange cones triangulating a dark smear near the top of the three-point line. "You just missed the bus to City. He ain't making it though. . . ."

"Was *he* wearing colors?"

"BoSox. Black. Not to be confused with BoSox red."

"Now this is getting confusing. Who wears BoSox black?"

"Darryl Jenkins's crew. This isn't exactly their turf either, per se, but they got a long reach and they're ambitious, more so lately. Jenkins runs his crews twenty-four-seven *and* he's hiring."

"You on top of them?"

"On *top*? Shit, we're just rolling with the tide, waiting to see who gets beached. Lot of product on the street, though, I'll tell you that. Every snitch I got says all of a sudden it's like junkie Dow Jones, prices falling through the floor and everyone's buying."

"So who here's the intended, you think?"

"Hard to tell. Matty there's the man with the pad."

"And the pad says who the fuck knows. Rasheed was the responding; second vic was talking, but couldn't tell him shit beyond what I just gave you. All he got was boom boom on a bicycle roll-by."

"Better for the environment," Brill says. "Smaller carbon footprint."

"I don't know how you work with him."

"Finely honed selective hearing. Shells?"

"Nine mill. We picked six, but there's probably more. You want to take a look already?"

"Yeah. Hey, Zesty, snap out of it." Wells dons a pair of latex gloves, and as if on cue, the court is flooded with light, Q hooking up Officer Rasheed with his neighborhood connects. The crowd that had been undeterred by the yellow crime scene tape comes off the chain-link as if it was electrified. The light has something of the same effect on the gathered police, though to their credit, they stand their ground even as they obviously feel exposed. The gang crime unit perp-walk themselves toward the perimeter of the court; the uniforms go all OCD, touch-tapping the Glocks secured at their hips. Only the homicide guys are unfazed by the mortuary brightness, though the light does them no favors exposing their wax-figured fatigue.

Wells flips his tie over his shoulder, squats beside the body. He lifts the corner of the sheet, and Brill comes up behind him to take a look before curling his index finger at me. The victim is light-skinned, lying stomach down, one arm awkwardly jammed beneath him, his cheek tucked into the crook of the other arm. Except for the blood pooled around him, he looks like he's just been hacked going to the hoop and decided not to get up. A small diamond dots the one ear I can see.

"Yes or no?" Wells looks at me over his shoulder, his eyes in electric polygraph mode again.

"No," I say. "Why would I?"

"History." Wells turns toward the bald homicide. "I can dance with him?"

"Sooner the better. The crowd don't like the lights with all the unis hovering, but they'll get over it. We know what we got here, gang crime already took their snaps, they don't know him, but he's got jailhouse tats on his left wrist, so he's on the books somewhere. Also, there's a wad of cash, and that arm there—looks like he's grabbing his balls on his way to the afterlife? There's your hammer. Pull it if you want. What is it you're looking for again?"

"Python." Wells squats on his toes now, getting leverage, and rolls the body over before ducking down even farther to see what's under.

"*Python?* Shit, I haven't seen one of those cannons in ages."

"Count your blessings," Brill says. "Whatta we got, pod-nah?"

"What we got is . . ." Wells reaches under the man's torso, tosses a tight band of bloodied bills, which lands at my feet with a wet slap. He reaches again, this time lifting out a large handgun by the trigger-guard, holding it up for inspection as the body rolls loosely back into napping position. "Bingo, we're in business. Let's bag this shit and get a move on."

"Mazel tov." Baldy closes his pad with finality. "And not a moment too soon." He raises his eyebrows, indicating a battalion of reporters rolling out of news vans, adjusting ties and hemlines, smoothing down hair you could take a chisel to. "Remember to smile for the cameras."

"Fuck that noise. Your catch," Brill says, not looking too upset about it. "Let's go, Zesty. I'll drive you home. Anybody tell you, you look like you got run over by a Zamboni?"

TWENTY-FIVE

Like his suit, Brill's car isn't as fancy as his partner's, but his taste in music more than makes up for it. Plus, he splurged for killer speakers. Etta James sings "I'd Rather Go Blind" and means it as we cross back into the South End, Brill steering with the heel of his hand, choosing to drift neighborhood streets, well-maintained stoops, block after block of handsome repointed brick buildings with flowering window boxes tucked in for the night.

You can't do much better than Etta James, but she sounds all the sweeter not coming from inside my own head, my postcrash internal ear not as finely tuned as Brill's stereo. Brill keeps glancing at me—I can see his dark reflection in my window—whatever thoughts creasing his brow not quite making it to his lips. We pull to a stop in front of a granite stoop, dark purple bougainvillea curling over the railing. Brill shifts the car into park, leaves the engine running. Etta starts singing "Tell Mama," offering herself up again to someone who doesn't deserve her.

"I don't live here," I say.

Brill nods like he's reached some sort of conclusion, turns the music down just a touch. "You know, Etta put together 'I'd Rather Go Blind' visiting Ellington Jordan doing a bid in San Quentin for armed robbery? Talk about your diverse talents. He'd already written the lyrics but titled it 'I'd Rather Be A Blind Man.' Now, of course that didn't fit Etta so much, so she reworked the song from his outline, put the finishing touches on it herself."

"Great story." I look out onto the stoop, familiar to me for some reason.

"I'm not done yet. See, now Etta, at that time, mid to late sixties, had a nasty heroin addiction *and* tax problems on top of that. So for accounting purposes, she signs songwriting credit to her boyfriend, Billy Foster, over at Chess Records. Can you imagine, having a hand in writing a song like that and not being able to take any credit for it, never mind the royalties. . . ." Brill lets out a low whistle and shakes his head, but I jump in before he can resume his narrative.

"Chess Records releases *Tell Mama* as an album and the title song, same name, as a forty-five with 'I'd Rather Go Blind' on the B-side, and it sells like crazy. Big whoop."

"That's right." Brill gives no indication he's impressed with my soul music knowledge, another line of wisdom my father had imparted to Zero and me to accompany our poker educations.

I recognize the stairs. There are two pictures sharing a single frame in my father's house: my father sitting with a trio of tuxedo-clad, long-haired, wild-eyed white guys mixed in with a dozen or so black men in suits and fedoras, a group of neighborhood children squatting at the bottom of the stairs. The other photograph is the same group, but everyone stripped down to his undershirt, the street urchins out of the frame, abandoning their poses for some other neighborhood distraction.

"You knew my father," I say.

"Knew?" Brill screws the cigar out of downturned lips. "He passed?"

"Not exactly. More like lately he's *all* past."

"What's that supposed to mean?"

"He's got Alzheimer's. All his yesterdays are today. Shit, Detective, if you knew my father back in the day, then you *are* old."

Brill barks a laugh. "Tell me something I don't know." He reaches over and clicks off the stereo. "Except I'm not *that* old. I knew your father from the block when I was a kid." Brill points to the stoop directly across the street. "Lived right there with my uncle and his kids. But it wasn't until my late teens I got to know the man for real. See, my uncle had this little blues joint near the corner of Columbus and Mass Ave. Just this one long room, street level, but the acoustics were phenomenal, even better in the bathroom in back—so much so that some guys actually played from the toilet with the door open. Your dad used to come in fairly often, alone mostly, but sometimes with other people, rock-and-roll types, giving them a little blues education, a taste of the street. Brought your mom in too." Brill lifts his eyebrows, anticipating some kind of reaction, but getting none, he lets them fall back into place.

"Pretty lady. Lot younger than your dad. Course I didn't know who she was at the time, but talking to my uncle years later, I got the distinct impression a lot of people did. You get what I'm telling you, Zesty?"

"She was protected?"

"Don't make it sound like a dirty word, son. She was *community.*" Brill puts emphasis on the word, explaining something without having to explain it. "And because she was with your father and your father been around these parts a long time. Did a lot of favors for people."

"My father play poker in your uncle's place?"

"Nope. And I'm glad you asked that question. Now, I don't have to tell you my uncle's place was a nee-gro place, do I? We're talking early eighties here, which makes it—"

"After the Harvard bombing but before my mother robbed Bank of Boston. I get your point."

"I have a point?"

"My father didn't mix business and pleasure." I try to move the detective along, my eyes getting heavy, the ratty butt-indented seat suddenly way too comfortable, molding to my weight.

"To a degree, maybe. Except back then, the South End was

something of a free-for-all, rubbing up against Roxbury, which
Jerry Dapolito controlled; Southie, which was soon to be all Devlin McKenna's; and Boston proper, which the DiMasis ran all the
way from the North End through to the Back Bay. The South
End was a problem, see, because it was a stew to begin with and
getting more mixed by the day. Jerry ran the gays when they
started coming in, remodeling. Bathhouses, dance clubs, and the
like. McKenna started making inroads on the numbers, coke and
heroin, and the DiMasis wanted a piece of everything because
they were the DiMasis and it was so close to home."

"My dad mediated for your uncle."

"You got it. City hall for the license and everybody else for
everything else, garbage collection, liquor wholesale—"

"Protection, drugs—"

"Nuh-uh." Brill had begun shaking his head even before the
words were out of my mouth. "My uncle was a *church*goin' man,
you understand? And he wasn't a hypocrite, either. But all the
same, he was a businessman, which means he was a realist. He
couldn't control everything. I mean, you have to put it in context.
We just flipped the seventies; every day it was something else. I'm
not saying people didn't run their games, smoke their reefer; after
all, it was a music bar. And, man, we had us some names come
through there: Pinetop Perkins, Bettye LaVette, even, singing
'Let Me Down Easy.' Still brings tears to my eyes. . . ." Brill takes
a moment to compose himself, lights up his cigar, maybe to hide
behind blue smoke.

"But rules were rules. Working girls understood they were
welcome to come in, soak up the vibe, but they couldn't run their
johns out of the bar. Heavy hitters had to check hardware with
my uncle or leave it home. The bathrooms were off-limits for
junkies, and anyhow, like I said, someone was usually blowing a
horn out of it. I'll tell you, that was the cleanest bathroom in the

city." Brill allows himself a smile at the memory. "My uncle paid what he had to, but it was more like pay *not* to play, and your daddy was the only one who could make that happen. So when he came in, there was always a table or a spot at the bar and a drink at the ready, though he wasn't much of a drinker either. I guess you can even say he and my uncle were friends."

"Which makes us, what, friends-in-law? What's the lesson, Detective? It's way past my bedtime."

"The lesson is don't be a middleman, Mis-tah Meyers. There's no percentage in it, and it doesn't suit you. That clear enough for you?"

"Clear as day. Now can you take me home?"

Brill looks at me for a hard moment. He reaches to shift the car into gear but instead cuts the ignition and screws his cigar back into his mouth, looking out his window away from me.

"Naw, you know what? I think I'm gonna stay here awhile, reminisce on my own. Oh, and my *original* point concerning Ms. Etta James before I was so rudely interrupted is this: Take credit where credit's due, understand? Take responsibility. Don't let someone write your script for you and hope to get yourself flipped to hit it on the B-side. Now go fuck yourself, Zesty. You can walk from here."

TWENTY-SIX

Some days are better than others. Days when Will feels the years that have slipped by, haven't just left him inhabiting a shell of what he'd once been, robbed him of his ability to manage the entanglements his life has accrued. As his well empties, having a voice in his final days is what matters to him, even if that voice has now been choked to a whisper.

The irony of his predicament isn't lost on him—he built his life on a foundation of silence, survived by holding his tongue, sealing those lips. Now he wants to speak? It's almost laughable.

Some days are better than others.

Only this is one of those days when the shadows edge closer than ever, when a stranger, his body smelling of damp earth and ozone, pulls up a seat and starts stacking chips as the deck that was so famil- iar to Will morphs into fifty-two double-edged razor blades, a cut in every shuffle, blood from every turn.

This is the day Devlin McKenna lets Will know who runs this city and takes from him the only thing a player can ever truly control—that decision to fold, to lay down the cards and get out of harm's way. Will can couch it any way he pleases, but the cold, hard truth of the matter is Will has a boss now and the only card that really counts is the card he punches clocking hours under his permanent midnight shift.

Welcome to the new Bosstown, motherfucker. It's no wonder he's in a hurry to forget.

TWENTY-SEVEN

Tuesday's optimistic sunshine forces its way through my eyelids like a crowbar on a rusted lock, the open sky a blank canvas for some early-morning skywriter taking advantage of a captive rush- hour audience. The pilot isn't very good, though, or maybe it's just windy, the bloated marshmallow script unreadable. If it was a heaven-sent message destined for my eyes, I imagine it would have said something along the lines of *sorry about yesterday. Care to try again?*

My answer to that would be *not particularly.* But there remains the matter of those bills on my desk, the shut-off electric, and the question of what to do about the Black Hole money I papered Boylston with. As for Gus and Britta, I don't know where to go next. I just have to hope Brill and Wells find them or they've realized the enormity of their fuckup and have put some serious distance between here and Darryl.

On top of that, it's Tuesday, a day I reserve for visiting my father at his rented home in Brookline, where he gets round-the-clock care from arguably the most unusual assortment of caregivers ever assembled, a hodgepodge of former "colleagues" from my father's poker games and a few longtime trusted employees of Zero's. Needless to say, I don't make much of a financial contribution to my father's care—Zero handles his bills and rent—but I do what I can, and Tuesday is generally my day to give everyone a break.

So I will myself out of bed, change my bandages, and pick a standard working outfit: black cycling shorts, black Dogmatics T-shirt, Adidas high-tops. I open my reclaimed bag, rake the cascade of bills into the main hold, and pop another can for the cat before making the mistake of opening the refrigerator for a habitual peek inside. I'm not sure what I expected to find—groceries have never magically appeared before—but what I get would make a coroner gag. Not that it hampers the cat's appetite. He keeps himself busy face-walking the can across the floor.

Today's a new day, I tell myself. *Every day is a new start. Onward and upward. Carpe diem.* Here's the plan: I'll drink enough coffee to float a battleship, call Martha to reroute work for the day, and find out what my insurance situation is. I'll go see my father, give Zero a heads-up about Brill and Wells coming around to chase the Collin Sullivan connection if they haven't done so already, and finally, drop by Black Hole to get a handle on their story and maybe a lead to Britta.

But first things first.

I get my coffee at the bakery on the corner of Shawmut Avenue and Union Park, served by a girl with a pink Mohawk and diamond-studded nose ring, who swears it isn't decaf and won't taste anything like an old dish towel.

I take it outside under the bakery's roll-top awning, where an abandoned copy of the *Globe* already blankets the dime-sized table, saving me a dollar and a walk around the corner to the 7-Eleven discreetly tucked in among the high-end shops that have sprung like wild mushrooms up and down Washington Street.

The smells of baking bread and freshly ground coffee hang pleasantly in the air, every once in a while pushed along by a light breeze that adds the scent of the grass being mowed by a thick man with a gleaming bald head inside Union Park. It's not really hot yet, but you wouldn't know it watching Kojak sweat. Cherry blossoms curl and fall into the street.

I drink my coffee, trying to ignore the stiffness rooting in my spine, the chair from the Marquis de Sade Collection not helping matters as it was clearly designed to stimulate table turnover. *Meditate on the positive,* I tell myself, flipping the newspaper open. *Ignorance is bliss. Yesterday never happened.* In fact, I'm not in Boston anymore. I'm sitting at an outdoor café in Paris, waiting to deliver the next batch of baguettes somewhere. To another café with even stronger coffee and softer chairs. Somewhere Buicks don't eat bicycles for breakfast.

What's eating me? Is it the fact that I don't have a clue what to do next or that yesterday's delivery was the first I'd ever failed to make? Through heat waves and hangovers, busted tires and blizzards, if there's one thing I could be counted on for, it was that I always made the pickup when called, always went all out to get where I needed to go—God help the pedestrian who didn't look both ways. Why do I feel like the guy who couldn't get it up when the hottest girl in town finally gives him a chance? Could it be that somewhere along the line I developed a work ethic? A sense of professional pride? Do I actually have a *job* now?

Screw that noise.

Drink more coffee. What's the problem? Is it the bills I can't pay? Or that until I fell on my head again, I couldn't recall yesterday's delivery address, much the same way my father can't remember how old he is or where he lives or how to drive a car? Could a couple of concussions cause the early onset of Alzheimer's like it's triggered my internal radio?

It's a self-indulgent question, really, and one that serves no purpose other than to remind me that somewhere in my DNA the same fate as my father's might be waiting for me, my memories destined to swirl that same dark drain, only to spit up chunks in no discernible order, the ghosts of my past released to walk the earth as if they'd never left.

Drink more coffee. Think positive. I dump the bills and deal them out into three piles. The phone company wants 142 dollars. The electric company has me down for three hundred and change, and UMass Boston's registrar's office, an equal-opportunity harasser, is demanding five figures while withholding credits.

I slip the electric and phone bills under my coffee cup, create a new pile for the rest, and wade in again until I come across a series of envelopes with only my name and loft number handwritten on the front. The first letter's backdated to last month, essentially the warning shot across the bow. The second and third notes are a series of code violations brought to light by city inspections. The fourth is a signed and notarized eviction notice.

I dump everything back in my bag and give the *Globe* a couple of minutes, but the headlines alone are misery. Suicide bombers in Pakistan, death squads made up of moonlighting police officers in Brazil, the Midwest underwater, large swaths of

California and Arizona in flames. Lacking any natural disaster, Massachusetts manufactures its own brand of calamity: a state lottery official indicted on charges of fixing winning scratch tickets, a director of public works arrested for selling road salt reserves, which led to deaths on icy roads.

Thankfully, last night's Red Sox debacle had ended too late for the paper to record. Habit would have demanded I try to glean some insight from the loss, which, according to my father, is what we're supposed to do with life's bad beats—the sports pages are an ongoing lesson, much like listening to Etta or Ella or Billie singing the blues, something to be learned from, through tears if necessary, blood if it comes to that.

A steady parade of fit, well-dressed men come and go from the bakery, cruising each other shamelessly. Nobody lisps. Nobody calls anybody Mary or Miss Thang. I find my name in two column inches buried inside the Metro-Region section. Mercury Couriers gets a plug I don't figure on adding to my business cards anytime soon. I flip pages, but there's no follow-up to the Wells Fargo heist, no connections made to the money on the street or the Roxbury shooting, the paper empty as Mother Teresa's rap sheet.

Darryl said I was off the hook for the fifty grand. So why am I having trouble letting it go? Because I'm a professional is why. And in my business, that means you pay and I deliver. So for starters, I cross the street to the doorway of the Union Park Laundry under a busted sign that once said WASH AND FOLD and now just says FOLD. Good advice in a poker game when the cards aren't falling your way. Not particularly helpful as a life philosophy.

TWENTY-EIGHT

"Zesty, Zesty, please molest me." Martha masticates loudly into the receiver. "Where the hell are you now?"

"Gee, I'm fine, Martha. And how are you?"

"Swamped. Gus is still a no-show, Owen's hung over, and Damien *said* he got a flat and now he's ignoring his phone. Is anybody interested in working around here anymore?"

"Not me," I say. "It's Tuesday."

"Oh yeah, sorry. Give your dad a kiss for me."

"I will, but later. Zero's got people who can hold the fort till then."

"So you'll make some runs?" Martha's so hopeful she even stops chewing a second.

"I didn't say that."

"Great. So *where* are you?"

"Union Park Laundry, watching clothes go round and round."

"Sounds thrilling."

"You should see some of this underwear. I think they're running some kind of stripper special." I stick another quarter in the pay phone while Martha's chewing is replaced by the hiss and pop of a bubble. Gum has long been a staple of Martha's diet, but lately she's taken to Swedish fish, which tend to leave little pieces of red jelly between her teeth, giving her rare smile a carnivorous look.

"Oh hey, before I forget, a couple of detectives were here yesterday asking all kinds of questions about you."

"Black and white guys?"

"Like an interracial Mutt and Jeff. How'd you know that?"

"Been here, done me," I say. "In a manner of speaking. What'd they want to know?"

"Like who handled the Black Hole account? What your schedule was, as if you had one, a complete list of your accounts."

"They say why?"

"I didn't ask, just assumed it had something to do with yesterday. By the way, you see the *Herald* this morning? You're Boston's most famous bike messenger. There's a picture and everything."

"That'll be swell for business. Anything else?"

"I don't know. They came at a bad time; the phones were jamming. Really I just wanted to get rid of them. They also asked where you hung out and who with."

"And you told them?"

"What's to tell? You're a long-haired freak who likes to ride, smoke pot, and chill with other people who do the same."

"Great job of reducing me to a stereotype, Martha."

"Spare me. People put more revealing crap on their Myspace page. I tell it like it is."

"Which is why I love you."

"By the way, nice work leaving the bong out in plain sight."

"Martha, how many times do I have to tell you that's a water sculpture?"

"Right. That younger cop was super cute. I mean, for a cop. I wish he'd sniffed a little closer in my direction."

"Why, so you could eat him?"

"Mmm, I would at that."

"Anything else?"

"They seemed pretty curious about how much money you pulled in and how you got by on so few jobs."

"Did you tell them by the skin of my teeth?"

"Something along those lines."

"You gave up my accounts?"

"Roger that. What've you got to hide, right? I mean besides the Cullen account."

The Cullen account is a buddy of mine who runs pot out of a loft in Jamaica Plain above the warehouse of Food Not Bombs, an organization that distributes food to the Boston area homeless. I don't deliver large amounts for Dani, who's by far my steadiest client, and I never see the goods because they're already packaged when I pick them up, but I'm well aware of what I'm delivering, and, boy, are people happy to see me come walking through that door.

"Anyhow," Martha says, "I left Dani off what I gave the detectives, so you can relax."

"Good girl." I mentally cross Dani's name from the list of heads-up calls I have to make today. "Hey, just wondering, but the cops didn't flash a warrant, did they?"

"They showed me their badges?" Martha says apologetically. "I guess I got kind of flustered, figured I had to give them something."

Which is what they'd intended, though there wasn't much Brill and Wells could have done to compel Martha to volunteer any information if she'd decided to clam up. Persuasion, my father preached to Zero and me from early on, has little to do with carrying any official emblem of authority. The badge is even a hindrance, he'd argue, because it is a symbol with too many negative associations for some people. My father espoused the need to read people individually, in and out of context and situation, not just listen to their words, because the words are often nothing more than distraction.

Focus. Eyes. Hands. How are they sitting or standing? It's not so much the pitch that counts, it's the delivery.

Other kids get the birds and the bees. Zero and I got winning poker. Except I realize now he wasn't just talking cards.

"It's no big deal, Martha. Anything else?"

"They asked a lot of questions about Gus too. And took his client list, which is *way* longer than yours, by the way."

"But everyone knows my dick's bigger." Black Hole being Gus's account, it makes sense they're chasing down his angle. So why do I feel my pulse quickening, a fibrillating buzz through my veins?

"What's going on, Zesty? Are you and Gus in some kind of trouble?"

"I can't speak for Gus. Hold on." I stick another quarter into the pay phone, spy a police cruiser idling at the curb. Keeping an eye on me? "So what kind of questions, specifically, about me and Gus?"

"I dunno, it seemed pretty vague—like, how would I characterize your relationship? I told them you weren't his type."

"What do you mean, type?"

"You know, like what type he'd be interested in if you swung both ways."

"Hold up a second, Martha. You're telling me Gus is bi?"

"It's not like it's some kind of secret."

"It's news to me."

"Puh-lease. Tell me you've never heard 'Do Me Two Ways'?" Martha, a huge Gizzard fan, starts singing into the receiver, the word "hole" featuring prominently in the vocals, though it wouldn't surprise me if she was just spicing it up for my benefit. Somewhere out there fiber-optic cables are curling.

"And all this time I've been dialing one nine hundred for a cheap thrill," I interrupt her. "But it's just a song, Martha. You know for a fact Gus is bi? Like, all the power to him, it's just he's never really struck me as the type to—"

"What, suck dick? Or take it in the butt?"

"Well, both, actually. If you want to put it that way."

"Well . . ." Martha's mocking me, her voice dropping from hoarse to seductive. "How would you like me to put it, Zesty?"

"I think you put it fine, Martha." What the hell?

"Mmm-hmm."

Mmm-hmm? "Mmm-hmm *what,* Martha?"

"Mmm-hmm I'm getting wet, Zesty." Martha's breathing rises to prank call heavy, a cacophony of phones ringing unanswered in the background, the sound of jobs slipping through cracks.

"Oh, Christ, Martha!"

"Say something dirty, Zesty!"

"Martha, I'm in a fucking Laundromat! This is where people come to clean things!"

"Louder, baby, I'm touching myself. Tell me about the fucking Laundromat, Zesty! Tell me!"

Unbelievable.

The police cruiser lets out a whoop and peels out from the curb. I drop another quarter and dial Zero's cell, but he doesn't pick up. I recover a *Herald* from the trash outside and bring it back to the leopard-spotted bras, crotchless lace panties, and Day-Glo thongs tumbling through my reflection in the dryer's porthole window. The *Herald* has me on page three, a headline writer's dream:

SPECIAL DELIVERY: MESSENGER LOSES 20G AS GRIDLOCK

BREAKS OUT ON BOYLSTON ST.

How the paper came up with that cash tally is beyond me. Maybe they talked to one of the looters and multiplied the take by the cars backed up to Copley Square. There's not much more to the article other than what the *Globe* had reported, except for a picture of me being loaded into the ambulance.

"Do me a favor," I say when Martha, exuding relaxation, picks up the line again.

"Anything, Zesty."

"You have copies of those client lists you gave the detectives?"

"I can print them out for you."

"I just need Gus's."

"Why?"

"Will you just do that for me, please?"

I have to wait on something crunchy before I get my answer, most likely chocolate-covered espresso beans—Martha prefers her caffeine in crunchable form. "Okay. Wait a sec, duty calls."

I listen to Martha answer ringing phones, marking addresses and handing out wildly optimistic delivery-time estimates.

"Zesty? I just put some girl looking for Gus on hold."

"So?"

"Do you want to work?"

"Not really," I say, but then a thought occurs to me, as they sometimes do. "You recognize the number?"

"Not offhand." Martha punches keys on her computer. "Okay. I've got Gus's file up. No, the number's not here."

"She ask for Gus specifically?"

"Yep."

"I'll take it," I say. "You think she's seen Gus before?"

"How would I know?"

If the number was on file, it would qualify her as a regular account. And if the caller knows Gus outside of work, then she could have called him directly at his place on LaGrange or his cell. Maybe she already dialed those numbers and, getting no response, decided to try him at work.

"Is this Gus's first call since yesterday morning?"

"Are you kidding? It's been off the hook for him since yesterday when I sent you out. I even called Flash looking to get a bead on him, but they haven't seen him either. I figured maybe he just turned his cell off for a bit." Martha pauses to think things over. "It's not like him to be gone so long."

"Listen, Martha. Print up that list, and I'll make the run, okay? If the girl's upset it's not him, I'll tell her he's out sick, and that'll be the end of it."

"I don't know, Zesty. What are you up to?"

"What am I up to? I'm up to my fucking ears in bills and staring down an eviction notice. Cut me some slack here. I make this run, get paid, then I check in with you. Tell you what, I'll even sweeten the deal, throw something your way when I come in."

"Yeah?" Martha's receptive but a stickler for details. "Like what?"

Like what? Good question. "Like . . ." I hold the receiver at arm's length, look around the deserted Laundromat. The dryer buzzes and takes a final spin, erotic feathers floating to the bottom of the cylinder. "Like panty heaven, baby," I purr into the receiver. "Like panty fucking heaven."

"Oh boy."

TWENTY-NINE

That McKenna is not a card player, his black talents of a more forceful nature, is of small solace because what he possesses is the patience of a grinder, and the grinders are always dangerous because they believe with near-religious fervor that today's the day they catch lightning in a bottle. McKenna having unearthed Diane's identity shouldn't come as such a shock, considering the sad fact that Diane's former comrades had at times relied on criminal elements to arm themselves or purchase drugs, the undercurrency of every protest movement. The federales must have loved that catbird seat: Watch the crooks who sold to the kids, who bombed the buildings. Everybody in one big net.

So Will was in the game now.

And two months later, sitting in a high leather booth at Hunan Garden, overlooking the spill of neon over Central Square, McKenna deals out another hand; every card has something to say if he'll just open up and listen.

"Now that you have your house in order, we can finally get down to business. Marriage does that for some men."

"Does what?" Will says.

"Makes them more manageable, agreeable? Maybe it's because now they realize they have somebody else they're responsible for. Am I making myself clear?"

Will doesn't answer, as women, their hair pinned with a spike of dark wood through the bun, bring steaming plates of food, which they set at the table's center. Tea is poured into small cups with no handles, hot to the touch.

"Do you enjoy travel, Will?" McKenna works the chopsticks with surprisingly nimble fingers. There are deep red scrapes on his knuckles.

"Sure. Where're we going?"

"Not we, boyo, only you."

"Where am I going, then?"

"All over. It's a big country; you'll be seeing a lot of it."

"Okay." Will sips the scalding tea.

"That's it?" McKenna peers over his chopsticks. "Just okay? No questions?"

"Doing what?" Will says, only because McKenna's inviting the query.

"Investing in the future."

"I don't understand."

"I don't expect you to." McKenna talks with his mouth full. "And anyhow, that's not your job. You're going to be putting my money away for me, William. Someplace safe."

"Why?" Will puzzles aloud, groping to find an angle. "I mean, why me? Why don't you do it yourself?"

"If only I could. But there are too many prying eyes on me, both the jackal and the hyena, you might say. Neither of whom I trust. It's hard for me to get out of town unnoticed, much less to a restaurant for a civilized meal. As for you, William, you know everybody, but you also know—now—to keep your mouth shut. That lone mistake with the DiMasis is unlikely to happen again. Am I right, William?"

"Yes."

"Am I a good judge of character? Do I have the right man for the job?"

"Yes," Will says, like a man without traction, like a man falling backward. "You have the right man for the job."

"Yes." McKenna peers into Will's black eyes. "I believe I do. Because what we have, what we've created, is a perfect symmetry of confidences, you might say. Your lovely Diane on one end, my interests on the other. As long as one is safe . . . ? And just to be perfectly clear, William, the fact your wife isn't rotting behind bars while she's got a bun in the oven, isn't getting gang-raped by a pack of up-county bull dykes, is my doing alone. Understand that, boyo. It's not a matter of my friends knowing; it's a matter of them choosing not to act on what they know."

"The FBI," Will says.

"Balance is everything." McKenna holds a clump of white rice at the end of his chopsticks to illustrate his point. "Without balance, nobody eats."

"I get it," Will says.

"Do you?"

"Yes." He understands McKenna perfectly. When you live in a

house of cards, balance is everything. But also Will understands this: When you're all in, when you've pushed every chip you have into the center of the table, there's no turning back. And when you're at your weakest, when you've lost the feel for the game, sometimes all in is the only play that's left.

Will drinks the tea, even though it blisters his throat. It's better that way. Something tells him he'll need to build up a tolerance for pain, for scars.

"When do I start?"

THIRTY

Marlborough Street in the Back Bay is tree lined, and dominated by turn-of-the-century red brick town houses, which stand in relative architectural harmony with one another like soldiers at inspection. Two-thirty-one Marlborough is near the corner of Exeter Street, four stories high, with bowfront windows and arched doorways identical to its neighbor. A blue jay is standing guard on the rim of a scrolled iron birdbath, shaking down membership fees from the other neighborhood chirpies.

I flick water at him as I pass, get clicked into a tight marble lobby with a large chandelier dripping crystals from the ceiling, distracting the eye from the surveillance camera tucked in neatly above the doorway.

There's no elevator. Boston's older buildings rarely have them. Before the town house was chopped into condos, the butler climbed more steps than a Sherpa. I follow in his worn footsteps. The first-floor landing is dominated by a painting of a foxhunt spread across a green expanse of British countryside; on the second floor, a hunter takes aim at a flock of geese flying in formation overhead.

On the third floor, the girl who opens the door is very tall and ultra thin, dragging hard on a cigarette between lips as full as collagen implants will make them.

"You're missing a painting." I motion toward the blank square of off-colored wallpaper beside me. It had probably been something quaint, like a nice oil of the Boston Massacre.

"Yeah. It fell. I guess it's in the frame shop." The end-glow of her cigarette ignites green-tinted cat-eye contacts. She blows casual smoke past my shoulder, tucks stringy blond hair behind tiny ears. Her look is dirty and oily, but I'm pretty sure it's just a look and probably an expensive one at that. "You're Gus?"

I don't contradict her, following as she leads me down a narrow hall into a bright living room that, despite the gleaming parquet floor, conveys all the comfort of a physics lab. There's furniture to sit on, only it's all hard angles and symmetry, glass, chrome, and plastics salvaged from a Superfund site. The television's a razor blade mounted above a fireplace painted glossy white; the only decoration is a series of framed magazine covers featuring my host wearing even less than the slip she has on now, her large eyes making love to the camera. Evidently, she's a master pouter, only the pictures are either airbrushed or old because her nose looks perfect, doesn't have the same red raw puffiness her nostrils sport now.

"You want a glass of water or something?"

"No thanks. What's so funny?"

The girl stifles a giggle, glancing toward the opposite end of the apartment, where I hear the muffled strains of tacky music that usually accompanies porn flick sex scenes. Don't ask me how I know these things, I just do.

"Roommate?"

"Friends." What sounds like live grunting starts backing up

the waka-waka score. The girl takes another massive drag on her cigarette, holds up an index finger, turns, and scampers down the hall. "He can hear you!" she shrieks into the room.

"So?" a man's voice says. "Fuck him. Give him the goddamn money, and let's *par-tay*!"

"Oh, ick!" The girl returns with a handful of cash. "Don't look at those pictures! I look terrible."

"You look fine," I assure her. "Why does this one look familiar?"

"It was on a billboard in Kenmore Square. This month I'm in something for *GQ*. You read *GQ*?"

"Once in a while," I lie, the truth being I get my magazines from a neighbor's recycling bin and use them to line the litter box. I don't know what it is, but I swear the cat shits better on pictures of Nicole Kidman and Tom Cruise.

"So, I don't really know how this works. . . ." The girl touches the back of her hand to her red nose, the distraction of her cigarette gone. Or maybe it's just dawned on her she's practically naked in front of a man who looks like he's been through a meat grinder. "I mean, like, Ray gave me your numbers?"

"Ray," I say, alarm bells going off in my head, yesterday's radio static igniting a signal in the distance, the room starting to blur.

"He said it was cool." The girl starts chewing a fingernail.

"Ray?" I say again, but already have a good idea who she's talking about. "From . . . ?"

"Black Hole Vinyl? Omigod, I mean, he said it was cool! Fuck, I'm so sorry—"

"No, no worries. If it's cool with Ray, right? You were at the party the other night?"

"On Newbury! Yes! You were there?"

"Just for a bit. You probably didn't see me."

She's about to say something else when the sound of giggling picks up, followed by more of the tacky porn soundtrack. She lifts the back of her hand to her nose again, comes away with a small red dot, which she rubs onto the edge of her slip.

"So what do you need?" I say. "I don't mean to be rude, but I'm kind of in a hurry."

"Two eight balls. Is it any good?"

"I'm not in the advertising business, honey, the shit sells itself. It's good enough for Ray." I shrug, but the line doesn't seem to inspire much confidence. Maybe Ray's not such the connoisseur of blow I imagine him to be. I gauge what's in her hand and shoot for the moon. "That'll run you eight hundred."

"Can I see it? I mean, I'm sure it's, like, good but—"

"Ray didn't tell you?"

"Tell me what?" The girl's grip on the money is tight, her knuckles white except where the blood's streaked across her fingers.

"I don't carry the shit. It's money first and then I come back with it. Fucking Ray. He didn't tell you that? I'm outta here."

"You don't have it on you?" She grabs at my sleeve.

"It's too risky. You want it or not?"

"Is it close?"

I give her a reassuring smile that tugs my stitches and brings a cloudy tear to my eye. My father always claimed I was a lousy liar—which is to say, unlike him—that I possessed an assortment of tells he could easily decipher. Just what those particular tells were, he never said, preferring to let me puzzle it out on my own, as he did most things. But I imagine it has something to do with the eyes, those windows to a cliché, and right now mine are swimming and, if not unreadable, at the very least smudged.

The girl peels off sixteen fifty-dollar bills, and I fold the money and stick it in my bag as she leads me back down the hall. The man in the bedroom curses loudly as something shatters on the floor, a woman yelps theatrically as her Hollywood dream slips away, while another failed thespian at least gets her line right and says, "On my face, baby, on my face," followed by more of the music reaching a crescendo. I look at the girl in the slip. Blood stains the edge of the fabric. The only thing blushing is her nose.

"Fifteen minutes," I tell her, and slip out past the carnage.

THIRTY-ONE

"Those," I say, tapping the glass case, directing the salesman's attention toward a pair of silver-framed orange-tinted Oakley Iridium sunglasses. I know I don't look like money, but the salesman turns a key and slides the glass door on his side. Before I can ask how much they cost, I'm serenaded on the joys associated with owning a pair of Oakley sunglasses. I slip them on and look in the mirror.

"State-of-the-art styling, urbanized materials redefining eyewear today as we know it," the salesman says.

The world is one big tangerine. The glasses fit just fine and cover most of the stitches and bruising around my eye. They also, I have to admit, considerably up my cool quotient. "I'll take them."

They're damned expensive. I pay with six crisp fifty-dollar bills; to hell with Boston Edison and my student loans.

"You did *what*?" Martha's mouth hangs slack, a phone cradled between shoulder and ear, a bag of Cracker Jack open on her lap.

"Chew and swallow," I tell her.

"Dude, I love it when they chew and swallow," Damien croaks from the couch, his bag propped behind his head. "Well, less chew and more swallow." He looks hungover but peaceful, not exactly a poster boy of industry.

"Go back to sleep," I tell him.

"I can't. The phones keep waking me up."

"You wouldn't hear them if you were out there working, douchebag. No, not you," Martha says into the receiver. "I'm soo sorry!" Martha shoots Damien the finger, but he's too busy curling into a ball to notice.

Our cozy bomb shelter of an office comprises two rooms, which you have to duck into after descending three stairs from the alleyway and dodging the severed pipes, potentially lethal to vital bodily organs, sticking out from various points in the walls and low ceiling. As a safety precaution, we covered the ends with foam rubber and spray painted them in Day-Glo colors, but every now and then, especially when we're tired or stoned, we still manage to impale ourselves.

There's a set of battered gym lockers beside the stairs, a bike stand attached to a cement block with a red Fuji frame awaiting repairs, built-in shelves covered with cannibalized bike parts. The walls are plastered with overlapping stickers and posters of naked women and other things that go fast.

The sunken second room is largely Martha's domain, a large desk running the width of the far wall, covered with paperwork in an order known only to Martha—touch at your own risk—and the couch where Damien now resides, reeking of alcohol. Strings of multicolored Christmas lights hang from the ceiling. There aren't any windows, so we usually keep the door open for air and whatever natural light we can squeeze from the shadow-draped alley. Martha doesn't mind the dearth of vitamin D. She works on her pale the way other people work on their tans.

I settle in and help answer phones until the rush passes. With Damien out of commission and Gus AWOL, only Owen is working, forcing Martha to siphon the bulk of our runs to Flash

Couriers, our main competitor. Even though Martha gets a commission for every job, regardless of whom it goes to, she's not happy about it. The risk Martha, and by extension, all of us run is that if a client develops a relationship with one of the Flash messengers, they're likely to change services altogether. Once you lose an account, it's practically impossible to get it back, and it's no secret the Flash messengers project a more corporate-minded image and actively recruit our customers, so none of our clan can really afford to lose any business. Only you wouldn't know it looking at us.

In between calls, I crush scrap paper and pepper Damien snoring into the folds of his bag, a sloppy crown beginning to form around his head. Martha hangs up the final call and glares at me. I hadn't noticed before, but she's been holding the same card Detective Wells gave me, angrily flicking it between her fingers.

"Hey, you never said you liked my shades." I opt for diversionary tactics.

"They're fantastic." Martha reaches into the bag of Cracker Jack she'd set aside during the rush. "Absolutely gorgeous."

"You don't like them," I say.

"You really don't care, do you?" A wet sheen slides over Martha's eyes. The Oakleys definitely not at issue anymore.

"About *what*?" I say.

"That Gus is dealing coke and God only knows what else through this office. Through *me*."

"Oh, that."

"Yeah, *that*," Martha apes, bitterly. "And you lost a delivery yesterday, which might end up costing you your business. That the police have come around asking questions, and you just don't seem to give a damn. What the hell is wrong with you, Zesty?"

"I never said I don't give a damn." I slip the sunglasses back on, mindful of my father's poker-face rebuke, my telltale eyes.

"You don't have to. You stole, what, like a thousand dollars from some ninny and then just shrug it off like it's no big thing. Hey, I'll pretend I'm Gus and take this girl's money while her nose runs on the carpet. I mean, why not, right? What's to lose? Isn't *that* what you said?"

I don't really have an answer, so I don't say anything for a change.

"And if that shit list isn't bad enough, I just farmed out half the jobs to Flash while you're sitting around answering phones, which is *my* job, not yours, and Damien here sleeps another one off, and nobody knows where Gus is." Martha takes a deep breath, two solitary drops racing down her cheek.

"Don't touch me!" She swats my hand as I reach for her cheek, her eyes bright with anger, her index finger leveled toward my face. "And you . . . you almost died yesterday, and you act like it never happened. Like you're indestructible, and here you are, still no helmet, back in the saddle and not even to goddamn work, but to fuck around in Gus's place."

"What do you want me to do, Martha?"

"I don't know! I want you to care."

"About what?"

"About yourself. About the shit you do so cavalierly, the choices you make. All this." Martha sweeps her arm around the room. "Your business and friends. Doesn't it bother you, even a little bit, that Gus is dealing blow, putting everyone here at risk? Did you think of that, Zesty?"

"No," I admit. "I didn't. Because don't you think it'd be just a little hypocritical for me to come down on Gus when I'm running weed all over town? You ever consider that?"

"As a matter of fact I have, and they're entirely separate issues."

"How's that?" I ask, not in the least enjoying playing devil's advocate against what I consider my most gentle of vices.

"Because it's Dani, and we know where her stuff comes from and how they live up there in organic Hippyville. And don't even get me started on the politics of it."

"Wow," I say. "When did you join NORML?" But in fact, I've never even seen Martha smoke a joint, and I thank God for that. I'd hate to see the damage she'd do with a bad case of the munchies.

"Is Gus your friend?"

"Sure." I hesitate, Martha's sudden switch in gears throwing me, which I guess says it all. "I don't know, Martha. According to you, I'm the only fool in town who didn't know Gus was bi, so what does that tell you? And you know what? If this is confession time, truth is maybe I'm a little jealous of Gus and his band and all that gets you in this town. I'm tired of this fucking place. It's starting to grind on me."

"*You're* jealous of Gus?" For some reason, Martha finds this hard to believe.

"Martha, look at me. I'm practically homeless, broke, morally ambivalent, and a borderline pothead. What's not to love?"

"Zesty—"

"Martha, you're asking me to think through something I just don't generally put a frame around." I throw up my hands. "Gus is a musician and a good one. He gets a lot out of that, and if he's lucky, he'll go someplace with it. I don't begrudge him for it, but yeah, I guess I'm a little envious. Shit, I'm even envious of Damien, and look at him—he's a fucking mess. But we both know he can fix a bike like there's no tomorrow. He can *lean* on that. What am I good at?"

"You know how to talk to women." Martha comes out of her seat to kiss me on the forehead.

"Sweet. Like that never gets me into any trouble."

"And let's not forget you're Boston's fastest messenger, with the hardware to prove it." She points to my trophies gathering dust amidst cannibalized bike parts.

"There's that," I concede. "But I'm not feeling so speedy at the moment."

"No? Feel like working anyway?"

"Do I really have a choice?" I frown at the sight of Damien curled on the couch.

"Not if you want to stay in business. But first go see your dad. We'll manage a few more hours without you. And before I forget, call Sam. He's been trying to reach you. Something about music in your head. Care to explain?"

"I'll take care of it."

"He said it was important."

"I got it."

"Yeah, well, then one more thing. Grab Damien's Motorola and a helmet on the way out. Your glasses *are* sweet, but your new hair's a hot fucking mess. Honestly, I can't look at it anymore. And when you get back out there, Zesty, find Gus before the police do. You hear me? I don't have a good feeling about this."

THIRTY-TWO

Beacon Street into Kenmore Square is flat and wide, and I burst into sunshine zipping past the behemoth BU Bookstore, working up an easy sweat, the pain draining from my pores as I click into lower gears, the amalgam buzz of the city distilled to the steady rhythm of my breath and the hiss of my tires on hot asphalt. The stolen Trek's starting to grow on me too. It's not as sleek or light as my Fat Chance, but the frame is rock-steady and easy to handle as I let my legs do their work, hopping a few curbs here and there to get back into sync, building momentum as I cross into Brookline, my postcrash static dialing in again, the search-and-destroy frequency driving a nail behind my eyes, filling my ears with hornets. I try outracing the signal until I recognize the thunder roll of Public Enemy dropping in off the dial, making it work for me now.

Bring da noise! Bring da pain!

White dashes blur beneath my wheels. Milky red roses bloom through gauze bandages.

Sid, a long-standing crew chief in Zero's moving company, crushes me in a hug before I take two steps through the back door into my father's home. In his early fifties, Sid is generally considered old for a mover but runs at a higher RPM than guys half his age and, despite his towering build, has a nimble grace that serves him well on the winding staircases and narrow doorways of many a Boston residence.

Sid is patient with my father, gentle even, probably because of his experience dealing with his own father, whom he suspects died of Alzheimer's or Parkinson's-related dementia, though it hadn't been diagnosed as such back then. "He was off his nut" is how Sid once explained his father to me. "But it's hard to say when it really started 'cause my old man was always a little off his nut, the crazy bastard. The fruit don't fall far from the tree, right?"

"Least you have a built-in excuse," I told him.

"You should talk."

In what must seem like another lifetime, Sid drove a bus for the MBTA, but came undone after a case of commuter suicide on an early morning route. When the mandatory postcrash test turned up traces of cocaine, Sid was convicted of manslaughter and served a two-year bid in MCI–Cedar Junction at Walpole, where his oldest son, Pete, now resides. Therefore, Sid generally prefers to talk about women, which is what he launches into as soon as he releases me from his grip.

"Zesty! How's it hangin'?"

"I'm good, Sid."

"Not as good as me, brotha!" Sid ignores my cuts and stitches; he's heard enough crash-test-dummy stories to last a lifetime. "You shoulda seen this broad I was with the other night. I'm tellin' you, I would have made love to this woman if she was stone dead she was so beautiful." Sid pauses to contemplate what he just uttered. "Actually, if that there was allowed. . . . Whattayacallit?"

"Necrophilia?" I say.

"Ya. There'd be a lot of dead women out there in the bushes calling my name!"

"Sid, that's fucked up."

"Ya, well don't tell Petey I said that. What's up? You're early."

"I don't think I can stay today, but I wanted to look in on him. How's he doing?"

"He's all right, but it ain't one of his best days. I mean he had breakfast this morning with *his* father, your grandfather, that would be. You ever meet your grandfather, Z?"

"No, he died before I was born. Good conversation?"

"One-sided to my ears, but your dad had a lot to say to him."

"He eat anything? I mean my dad."

"What, because I'd fuck dead women in the bushes, I'm crazy? I know who you mean, Z. Yeah, he ate a little. Toast. An egg. He's okay, except . . ."

"What is it, Sid?"

"I dunno. Zero's been acting all cagey lately, got us on high alert on account of these crank calls we been getting? And then this lady visited, and your dad's been all agitated ever since."

"Lady from the nursing service?"

"Nah. Van Gogh said she had a face looked like it was melted wax and stitched with barbed wire. Nice, right? Anybody you know?"

"Not offhand. My dad see her?"

"Ya. Let her in and told Capizo to make himself scarce. Only he's been talkin' wackadoodle since then."

"My dad answer any of these calls, Sid?"

"Nah. You know the house phone's off-limits to him." A precaution we took to protect him from bottom-feeding scammers who target the elderly, fishing for personal and financial information. "Your pop's just doing his thing, watching one of his movies."

"*Rounders* again?" I can hear the TV playing in the living room, Matt Damon saying, *Listen, here's the thing. If you can't spot the sucker in the first half hour at the table, then you are the sucker.* There are no reruns in the Alzheimer's mind—the film's poker scenes probably ignite a neural party somewhere deep in his brain, his gambler's instinct still alive in there.

"Snatcherally. You know how your dad fuckin' loves Matt Damon."

"The poker son he never had."

"You can't always come up aces, right? Listen, Z, I was thinking, I know a guy patched into Damon, like, his agent's agent? Maybe we can get him up here, play a few hands with the old man, splash a little blood in the water. Whattaya say?"

"It's a nice thought, Sid."

"Take some of that Hollywood money, right?"

"You know it." If he still recognizes the cards.

"Ya, well, listen, after one of those calls I back-dialed the number? Only whoever answered wasn't saying nothin'. I called a couple times, and there was always different sounds in the background, so like, I'm assuming it's a cell phone, the prick on the move?"

"You say anything to him?"

"Ya. I told him if he keeps calling, I'll rip his fuckin' head off and piss down his neck."

"What if you don't have to go?" I say.

"Shit, Zesty, at my age I always gotta go."

I follow Sid into the living room, where the shades are drawn. My father's reliance on daylight has been eclipsed by a permanent fog that's rendered his circadian rhythms obsolete. Scattered on the table next to him are a few of the many framed photos spread throughout the house, each one affixed with a piece of tape on which Zero and I have painstakingly written small reminders: *This is you and Mom getting married on the lush outfield grass at Fenway Park. This is you as a child. These are your two sons, Zero and Zesty. These are your parents. This is you as a young man.*

I'm not sure the tape makes a difference anymore. His Alzheimer's at this point produces a daily theater of the absurd, my father conjuring up children he never had, historical and minor characters appearing for walk-on roles and one-liners, ghostly extras whom he directs and addresses and never mentions again.

"Hey, Mr. Meyers, look who's here to see you—your boy, Zesty."

My father doesn't respond, and I sit beside him on the couch, listen to his labored breathing, hard and raspy as if he's just climbed a flight of stairs. He lets me take his hands and hold them, his palms cornstarch smooth, his nails longer than they should be.

"It's time," my father says, turning to look at me for the first time. On the TV, Matt Damon pulls wads of cash from hiding places around his apartment.

"Time for what, Pops?"

"I can hear it in his voice. That's all there is, the voice."

I look to Sid, who points to the TV and shrugs.

"He calls me," my father says.

"Who?"

"Whattaya mean who?" My father works his tongue against his bottom gums, his lightning-bolt scar flashing as he presses his lip forward. His eyes are reflective lenses, his face without nuance, the rough edges in his voice worn smooth, even his Boston accent polished of any personality; not my father at all, and I'm not ready, don't know if I'll ever be ready for this. How do you talk to a man who wakes each morning in the portal of a time machine, who communes with ghosts? How do you help a man who doesn't realize he's fallen get up off the ground?

"He wants his money," my dad says, turning back to the screen.

"See?" Sid says.

"Diane took the rest."

"Diane," I say. "That's great, Pops. You've been talking to Mom?"

"What?" My father begins to rock himself, gently at first and then harder, as if trying to gain momentum to rise from the couch. "He wants to meet. But not tonight. Tonight's not good. Tomorrow."

"Meet you where?"

"I told him I buried it. . . ."

His rocking subsides as on the TV, cards are dealt around a poker table. His eyes darken, something akin to recognition, a return to self, flashing momentarily. It's a lot to ask for, too much, as my dad continues, "He said he'd bring a shovel. He's had practice over the years. It's true. Lots of practice. . . ."

"And so it goes. Listen, I'll call Zero, get somebody down here to relieve me, or I'll just stick around, I ain't got nothing going on. Go do what you gotta do, Z. Everything okay?"

"Fine, Sid. Thanks, you're the best." I kiss my father's cheek, but his eyes stay glued to the television.

"Yeah? Tell that to Petey when he gets out. You'll get an earful."

"Don't be so hard on yourself, Sid. Just keep in mind necrophilia's considered a crime against humanity."

"Yeah? So what? I'll just add it to my list, then."

THIRTY-THREE

My first run sends me downtown into the shaded canyon of the Financial District, the city's well-dressed foot soldiers providing me with plenty of cover as I make a concerted effort to avoid any roving bike police patrolling for jaywalkers and expired courier tags. For logistical purposes, Martha keeps me downtown, cleaning up the backlog of steady and long-term clients that accumulated while Damien slept off his hangover and I scammed eight hundred dollars from some girl whose next plastic surgery would be to repair blown-out sinus cavities.

Gus's clients are peppered into the mix, but they're all scrubbed and corporate—legal writs, notarized forms, ball game tickets—nobody I encounter is cold sweating or sniffling blood into a tissue. If the receptionists and lobby bouncers even realize Gus is missing, they don't show it, and I'm reminded that in the everyday scheme of things, we're pretty much interchangeable parts. The delivery's the thing, and if it's eye candy they're looking for, they'll have to wait until I'm healed. I keep the sunglasses on, make it a point not to sweat on the suits.

Since the first Big Dig shovels hit the streets, downtown traffic's been an ever-changing mess, construction diverting cars and pedestrians to wayward destinations. A walk around the block can turn into a Himalayan trek through restricted hard-hat zones; nobody gets a direct route to where they want to go. Even a pedestrian change of direction is difficult, bordering on dangerous, as crowds are aggressively herded through orange bucket embankments by uniformed traffic division crossing guards, the more loose-limbed members of their hostile fraternity practically break-dancing in the streets.

I leave them all behind, cutting diagonally across the Boston Commons, the Statehouse dome blinging like a Brahmin rapper's solid gold tooth. I catch a wave of optimism as I approach a DPW crew patching up a pothole, but on closer inspection, it's business as usual: five guys in orange vests, two doing all the work, the other three supervising to make sure it's done poorly so they'll have to come back tomorrow and do it all over again. White dashes fly beneath my wheels like a string of undotted *i*'s.

Ah, Beantown.

The same guard is manning the door at 38 Newbury, except today he's jazzed up the uniform, added a dark blue commando sweater to go with his single-striped navy pants. Something in his demeanor suggests a heightened sense of awareness or anticipation. Then again, maybe he's just got gas.

"So I happened to be reading the papers this morning . . . ," he says as I reach for the door.

"Okay," I say, backtracking.

"That you got hit yesterday?"

I take off my sunglasses, figuring an eyeful of stitches is worth at least a thousand words.

"You weren't wearing a helmet yesterday," he observes.

"Nope."

"And now you are. Isn't that a little like locking the barn doors after the horses are loose already?"

"Stable," I say. "Horses are kept in stables."

"All right, cowboy."

I take a deep breath, look up to the sky. "Actually, I'm just covering up a bad hair day."

"You too?" He lifts his blue cap, revealing a shock of corkscrew curls. "Why back so soon?"

I point toward the Black Hole windows.

"Was it really that much green you lost yesterday?" He twists the cap back on, wrestling his hair into submission.

"I couldn't tell you. I just pick shit up and deliver it." My tone comes out sharper than I meant it.

"Hey, don't shoot the messenger, right?"

"Exactly." Why waste bullets when you can run him down with a gold Buick? "Here's a question for you. You notice any police around here yesterday? Maybe a couple of guys visiting the sixth floor?"

"Black and white guys, not more than a few hours after you left," he says. "Detectives."

"They badge you?"

"Didn't have to. They all carry themselves like they got something shoved up their ass. Ah, fuck, I shouldn't have said that. I got family on the force in Medford, and my brother-in-law's a stand-up guy. I'm just a little sore today—ignore me, everybody else on this street does. All this standing around, my leg's killing me."

"Me too," I say. "We could start a club."

"Trust me, brother, you don't want to be in my club." He pulls up his right pant leg, revealing a flesh-colored metal and plastic prosthesis that runs from somewhere above his knee all the way into his custom-made black shoe.

I nod like an idiot. "Where?"

"Iraq." He shrugs, looking off into space, avoiding my eyes. "Place called Hamdiyah, some little shithole you probably never heard of. I shouldn't be complaining. I was one of the lucky ones."

"Zesty Meyers," I say, holding out my hand.

"Charles Valdes. But my friends call me Charlie." He takes my hand, thoughtful enough not to crush it; bright red pebble-sized indentations still dot my palms.

"Good to meet you, Charlie."

"I said my *friends*." Charlie carves himself a stone-face, but his ears have risen a millimeter, tilting his cap to shade smiling eyes.

"Man, I hope you don't play poker," I warn him.

"Hells no. I only spend my money on the necessities: wine, women, and song. The rest—"

"I blow on useless shit."

"Oh, you heard that one already?"

"Really, you're gonna make me say it . . . ?"

"Don't quit my day job?" Charlie winces into the line, turns himself in a tight little circle on his one good leg. "Shit, what's to quit? Listen, Zesty, go on up, do what you gotta do and don't worry about your bike over there. I guarantee no dogs'll be pissing on your wheels today. And those detectives? I told them you were here but I couldn't tell them what office you visited on account of you never signed the register."

"It's no problem," I say, chewing on a thought before figuring, what the hell. "You able to ride with that leg of yours, Charlie?"

"You mean like a bike? Shit, I did some stationary rehabbing at Walter Reed, only I didn't have to balance."

I dangle a set of phantom keys from my hand.

"Maan . . ." Charlie bends a look up and down Newbury, contemplating the repercussions of skipping out on his post. "What the hell. I get canned, they'll be doing me a favor. I'm freakin' bored out of my skull."

"You could always be a messenger," I say cheerfully. "The hours are long, the work's dangerous, but the pay sucks."

"Sounds about right." Charlie mounts the seat and pushes off the curb with his good leg. "You better hope I come back," he wolfs, a cab swerving violently to avoid his swaying takeoff. "I ain't joking neither. I think I got this!"

They've made significant progress at Black Hole, the whiff of beers and babes overwhelmed by the cleaning crew and some antiseptic spray; Joey Ramone is rocking out a cover of Louis Armstrong's "What a Wonderful World," only the volume isn't enough to burst an eardrum. The downstairs neighbors must be relieved as hell.

They've also finished unpacking, and the front desk is manned by the yin to Britta's yang, a short, not unattractive girl with black bangs cut straight across her forehead, black fingernail polish, eyeliner, and purple lipstick highlighting a messenger-devouring smile. She's a goth Betty Boop, and she looks vaguely familiar. I've seen her out before, the Middle East on Mass Ave. or Bill's Bar on Lansdowne—Darcy, Daley, something like that, vaguely slutty, risky, high-maintenance, kinky rewards. Bad timing with all my cuts and bruises; she shows me only business interest.

"Dropping off?" she says.

"Dropping by. Is Britta here?" Not that Darcy/Daley's lacking curves herself. Like I said, she's short, so I have the angle on her, only half guilty for looking because she hasn't put a lot of effort into hiding anything. The difference is I don't get caught this time, my eyes steady masked by the orange-tinted Oakleys.

"She's not in today," she says, frowning.

"How about Gus?"

"No. Do you—"

"What about Ray?"

"Is he expecting you?"

"Nope."

"He's in a meeting right now."

"With who?"

"I don't think that's any of your business."

"Yeah? You'd be amazed."

"I doubt it. Anyway, I can't interrupt him."

"Trust me, he wants to see me."

The girl twists up her face, the punctuation marks of her features skewing at odd angles. "Hey, you can't go back there! He's in a meeting!"

The unpacking extends to the rest of the office. The moving supplies and blankets are gone; a magnet board is already tacked three deep with laser-printed photographs from the party. I grab two shots and slide them into my pack, passing toward Ray Valentine's frosted-glass corner office.

"Give those back!" Darcy/Daley uses her outside voice; she's hot on my tail as Whac-A-Mole heads pop out the tops and sides of cubicles. "He just stole pictures from the party! Somebody call security!"

"We have security?" A telemarketing headset cuts across a Flock of Seagulls revival haircut.

"What number do we call?" says another through a yawn.

"A picture?" says a third. "God, I hope it's not of me. I was plastered!"

I don't bother knocking, and I'm surprised the door's unlocked, considering Ray Valentine's hunched over his desk snorting a massive line of cocaine off a black vinyl disc, a white mound piled precipitously close to the center hole.

"What the fuck!" Valentine rears up from huffing. His eyes, as much as I can see of them, lit, his optic stalks fried to their roots, his right eye dimming fast as it swells shut under fresh bruises.

Valentine's also sporting a large bump on the left side of his temple, an almost comical swelling like a thought balloon fighting to escape his head and float free above him. His bottom lip is split down the middle, a single dollop of blood dropping onto his half-snorted line; the powdered worm sizzles as it mixes with whatever the coke was cut with.

"Who the fuck are *you*?"

"He's asking for Britta and Gus," Darcy/Daley says, a crowd gathering behind her.

"Close the door!" he roars.

"I'll get security."

"What? No! Close the door! He can stay."

Darcy/Daley is a portrait of confused but does as she's told, her coworkers reduced to milling shadows before dispersing to light up the rumor hotline. It wouldn't surprise me if someone had snapped a picture in the ten seconds the door was open; there's nothing like a shot of your boss snorting Mount Everest to help you negotiate your next pay raise.

Valentine looks me over, comes to some sort of conclusion, and lowers himself to vacuum the rest of the line, holding his longish brown hair off his forehead with one hand, plugging his unoccupied nostril with the other—a talent to behold. And not an ungracious one either. Finished, he cuts another line and extends the bill toward me.

"Wow. Yesterday I can't even get a cup of real coffee in this joint, and today I get rocket fuel. No thanks." I wave him off. If I wanted to grind my teeth all day, I'd get myself a real job.

My refusal gives Valentine pause. "Straightedge?"

"Hardly," I disappoint him. "You know who I am?"

"Hey, that's *my* line." Valentine laughs, the movement producing an avalanche of powder onto the front of his shirt. If the blow wasn't sitting right there in front of him, I'd think he'd just been careless with a powdered donut.

"You're certainly not Gus," he says, tap-touching his shirt with his index finger before wiping the residue over the swelling surrounding his eye. It doesn't strike me as such a smart move, but maybe he's got the same medical coverage I do. "Gus would have his shnozola a foot deep in this pile if I offered it to him."

"Wouldn't that cut into his profits, since he's the one selling it?"

"Well, you might have a point there." Valentine smiles numbly, showing me horse's teeth. "So what do you want? No, let me guess. You're in a band, right? Guitarist? Nah, not guitar, you got the arms of a drummer but the attitude to just crash in here, upset poor Darcy just trying to do her job. That right there says to me front and center, lead singer, spotlight, where's the fucking spotlight!" Valentine springs from his seat. "Am I right? Tell me I'm not right. You looking for a record deal . . . ?"

"Zesty," I say.

"Zesty! Oh, that's perfect right there. Wouldn't have to change a thing. You looking for a record deal, Zesty?"

"No."

"Really? That's a first. Aren't all you messengers something else besides twelve-speed wheel jockeys?"

"You tell me."

"Yeah, man, I'm just doing this till I hit it big-time, right? Oops, I hit a nerve? Shit, I could make a million dollars with you, Zesty. Would you like a million dollars?"

"It would solve a few problems," I admit.

"Yes it would! Only there's one hitch, Zesty, one major fucking obstacle. Know what that is?"

"Enlighten me."

"There's a thousand clowns out there who look just like you, and they all want the same thing, Zesty. Ten thousand clowns. Bring in the clowns!"

"Like Gus?" I say.

"Well, see, now I gotta tell you, Gus might be the exception.

Gus actually has some bona-fide talent, but at heart he's a fuckup, plain and simple. Are you a fuckup, Zesty?"

"It's too early to tell. I'll have to get back to you on that one."

"Yeah, well, Gus is a fuckup. Aside from the fact that band name sucks and he's too loyal to the retards he plays with, Gus doesn't listen. Do you listen, Zesty?"

"I'm sorry, you were saying something?"

"See, that's what I'm talking about. Sarcasm is a cancer. It'll eat you alive."

Then I'm a walking dead man. "What happened to your face?" I leave the sarcasm out of my voice just in case.

"What happened to yours?"

"I'll get to that in a minute. Gus is signed to your label, right?"

"To my everlasting regret."

"Why? Didn't you just tell me he has talent?"

"See, you weren't listening! I just told you he was a fuckup. Capital *F,* capital *U.*"

"Is dealing blow one of his fuckups, or is that on you?"

"You mean do *I* deal blow? Hell no. I'm in the record business, Zesty. Look around you. I got an office on Newbury Street with all the trimmings. Secretaries, talent scouts, a warehouse full of merchandise. Want a T-shirt? The blow's just a fringe benefit; you should know that." Valentine again extends the bill, but I shake my head. "You mind?" He gestures to the mound.

"Knock yourself out," I tell him.

Valentine throws himself back into his seat and busies himself separating a line from the pile with a platinum Amex card, scratching the vinyl apparently not a concern.

"So what's the problem with Gus, then? You signed his band, and I know you're steering business his way, so the two of you should be getting along just great."

"Says who?" Valentine sits up, shivering as the drug ignites something in his bloodstream.

I reach into my pack and flip the picture of my Marlborough Street model onto his desk.

"Oh her. You know, for someone who makes a living getting her picture taken, that bitch talks too much."

"Actually, she snorts too much. Do you know where Gus is right now?"

"No. Why would I?"

"Did Darryl beat you up?"

"*What?* Who? No. Nobody beat me up. I was in a fender bender."

"Was your face *on* the fender?"

"Was yours?"

"Actually, yeah. That's why I'm here."

Valentine closes the one eye he has control of, managing somehow to sit still, which must take a great deal of concentration, considering the amount of cocaine coursing through his system. It's hard to get an accurate read of his face beneath the cuts and swelling, but my guess is he's pretty much what you'd expect a young rock-and-roll impresario to look like: four days' worth of just-so stubble, hair cut long and jagged, tan and healthy skin, at least where he hasn't been pounded, suggesting a jaunt to the Caribbean or a long Vineyard weekend. He's lean but not scrawny, which I attribute to practice on the yoga mat leaning in the corner, handsome in the way that confidence carries the day: Levi's, dark gray Converse T-shirt under a thin and supple midnight leather jacket.

Valentine sinks into his Buddha act, hands resting palms down on his desk, his shoulders losing their high-clavicle tension. I'm not sure if he's meditating, but whatever state he's managed to adopt seems to do him good.

"What can I do for you, Zesty?" His one good eye clicks open, his brown pupil focusing on me.

"Where's Britta?"

Even Valentine's ballooning lip doesn't prevent a smile from lifting the corners of his mouth. "Zesty, you're a piece of work. Anybody ever tell you that?"

"Sure, only not so nicely."

"A piece of fucking work. I don't know what you *think* is going on, but let me give you some advice: Stay away from it. You don't know the people you're dealing with here. You seem like a smart guy, I shouldn't have to tell you that."

"Do you know where Gus is?"

"I'm not a babysitter. How the fuck should I know?"

"You're invested in him, aren't you?"

"Now you're pissing me off, Zesty."

"What about Britta?"

Valentine starts to look queasy, his one good eye swimming. "What about her?"

"She's the one who forked over the money yesterday, and today she's gone."

"What money?" Valentine looks at me hard a moment, the light in his good eye flickering before extinguishing altogether. "You were never here yesterday. Deal with it."

"Fuck you. I already know where the money was heading and who it was going to."

"So why're you here, then?"

"I want the rest of it."

"You're out of your fucking mind."

Maybe, but I press on anyway. "Whose money did I lose?"

Valentine just sits there, an almost imperceptible movement of his head starting up. He hunches forward, his hands moving automatically toward the cocaine, his platinum Amex scraping the vinyl, electrifying the hairs at the back of my neck.

Slowly, Valentine lowers himself, mumbling something I can't make out, another thick white worm disappearing up the conical bill.

"Say that again." I take a step toward him.

"You're a dead man." Valentine obliges me, his neck stretched out on the back of the chair like an offering for the chopping block, the postnasal drip from the cocaine thickening his voice, his tongue flicking over front teeth that probably feel like they're no longer there.

"Yeah? Fuck you, *Ray*. You're a day late and a Buick short. Dead man cycling was yesterday, and I'm still here. And today I *had* my coffee before coming to this joke palace. So fuck you and your bullshit record company. Shove it up your ass."

But my anger's wasted on him. He's not listening, his one good eye dialed back to black, as devoid of emotion as the perforated ceiling panel above him.

"I guess this isn't a good time to ask for free tickets," I say to Darcy, who is stewing at the reception desk, her angry eyes checking the points of the black knives attached to the tips of her fingers. Between Darcy, Britta, and a coked-up Valentine, this place is turning out to be downright dangerous.

"Go fuck yourself," she says flatly.

"That's funny. Yesterday a doctor told me basically I should be able to do just that. Something about an extra vertebra. Darcy," I say, "think of the possibilities."

"Good for you, Zesty. Why are you wasting your time here, then?"

Zesty. By name. "You know me, Darcy?"

Darcy loses interest in her nails. "I've seen you around."

"Hear anything good?"

"Wasn't asking."

"When does Blizzard's album come out?"

Darcy's thrown off by the question, takes a moment to recover her attitude. "It's been delayed. What's it to you?"

"Delayed why?" I know enough about the music business to

know that you strike while the iron's hot, Gus's second-place Rumble finish and accompanying step-up in airplay qualifying on a local level.

"It's not a decision I get to make," she says, literally tongue in cheek.

"But the album's finished?"

"And mixed. They even brought in Nichols as a producer. You know who that is?"

"No, I'm not that cool."

"Way to state the obvious." Darcy makes a face to screw home the point. "He's worked with Dropkick Murphys and a bunch of other bands. I know he didn't come cheap."

"Whose end did that come out of?"

"You mean who paid for him? Gizzard split the fee with Ray."

"That how it usually works?"

"There is no *usually*. You cut the best deal you can or take your chances somewhere else."

But the sharks are everywhere in show business. At the poker table, at least they're sitting in front of you where you can keep an eye on them. The more time I spend around the music business, the more it resembles a bloody chum bucket. It's no wonder my father got out.

"So half the producer's fee came from Gizzard's advance. How much was that?"

"Low six figures. It sounds like a lot, but after the producer, studio time, equipment, and then split it four ways with the band, it's not that much."

Not enough for Gus to quit biking or trying to pick up extra drug money on top of that. But why sit on the record if it's already cut and the money already spent? And more important, Darcy's right: What's it to me?

Random thought: "Who has access to the safe in Valentine's office?"

Darcy looks at me quizzically, like she's about to tell me to go fuck myself again, but instead says, "Far as I know, it's just me, Britta, and Ray. Hey, Zesty, you okay? You don't look so good all of a sudden."

THIRTY-FOUR

By the time I'm downstairs, Charlie's resumed his post with vigor, his left pant leg cuffed to just below his knee, revealing a shock-white calf zippered with at least a dozen heavy pink scars running horizontally across the skin, likely a residual gift of the shrapnel that had taken his right leg off at the thigh. There's a light sheen of sweat on Charlie's upper lip, a lit cigarette dangling from his mouth, and his popcorn curls are glistening like they've been buttered.

"That's a new look."

"This close, Zesty. I was this close to not coming back."

"And yet here you are."

"Only 'cause I told you I'd watch your bike. Man, people around here drive like shit. I almost got doored coming around Berkeley, which would've been a laugh. Live through Iraq, die under the wheel of a VW."

"Semper fi," I say. "Welcome to my world."

Charlie takes a last hit off his cigarette, flicks it to the curb. "So how'd it go up there?"

"It's complicated. Hey, at the risk of sounding racist, you

happen to notice a couple cagey-looking black guys come in today, go up to Black Hole?"

"Define cagey." Charlie requires more than skin color, which tells me something about him.

"They would've been driving a black Pathfinder. One guy really big . . ." I think back to Albert's description of Cedrick. "Bear with me here: made of big black bricks? Can I sound any more like a peckerwood?"

"Not really. But I know who you're talking about. I probably wouldn't have noticed except they got a parking space right out front, which is like winning the lottery around here. Pathfinder. Two guys. You described one of them pretty accurate."

"What about the other?"

"Taller. Thin. Definitely a baller."

"Now who's a racist?" I say, grinning.

"Fuck you. He was athletic, what I'm saying. Had that walk. They were here about an hour ago."

Which explains the fresh beating on Valentine's face. How long does it take to beat up a guy? Depends on the guy, I suppose, and whether there's any snappy dialogue before the smackdown. Either way, I'm a step slow on everybody, in to the river on every pot, drawing toward inside straights and slim-odds flushes. In other words, nowhere. And now my aches and pains returning, too long off my bike, the bandwidth of my skull hooking yet another single from out there on the airwaves.

The band is Madness. The song: "Our House." Which reminds me, I'm about to get evicted.

Sing along, everybody.

THIRTY-FIVE

Mario Spagnola's Harrison Avenue outer office is all exposed brick, iron beams, and oiled cherry Mission furniture. Sepia-toned photographs and linear architectural drawings hang on the walls, my address among them—Thayer Street, Albany, Harrison Avenue. I've been in Spagnola's office before, making a general nuisance of myself when things in the loft need attention, ruining the retro-industrial vibe for the assorted bankers, architects, and lawyers waiting patiently for an audience with Spagnola in the flesh.

"Karla." I greet the dragon at the gate, a well-maintained brunette with an air of easy confidence and consistent disdain for my now-and-again presence for no reason that comes to mind other than it might be an integral part of her job description. "Working late, I see. You look awesome. You color your hair? It's shining."

"Zesty." Karla sizes me up, doesn't find any upgrades worth noting. "What took you so long?"

"I'm expected?"

"You received your eviction notice?"

"I did."

"Well, there you have it." She tosses me a razor smile.

"He in?"

"He is." We exchange gunslinger stares.

"Aren't you supposed to offer me coffee or something while I wait?"

"There's a coffee shop downstairs. They're about to close, but

I'm sure they'll sell you the dregs. You're probably used to them by now."

"Hey, that's not what you say to everybody else."

Just as I'm settled into one of the club chairs, Karla announces, "You can go in now."

"So soon? Aren't you supposed to keep me waiting awhile?"

"Actually, I am. Only I don't think I can stomach the sight of you anymore. Have you checked a mirror lately? You look like somebody chewed you up and spit you out."

"Wow, Karla, you've got it bad for me."

"Sure, that's what it is."

"Don't worry. I'll let him know how rude you were to me."

"You do that, Zesty. I'm due for a raise."

Spagnola's probably somewhere in his early fifties but works hard to keep the years from piling up. He's tan, bulky through the chest, his hair peppered with silver, cut short and close-cropped around the ears. Two months ago, he attended a tenants meeting in running shorts and sweat-drenched T-shirt and spent the entire time contorting himself in a variety of stretches, the show a wordless put-down of the tenants assembled, a clear message that their concerns and grievances weren't even worthy of a feigned formality.

Spagnola's dressed pretty much the same today, tank top, shorts, probably just come up from the Gold's Gym in the basement.

"Been lifting?" I start friendly, tapping my biceps.

"Ten thousand," Spagnola says.

"That sounds like a bit of an exaggeration. I bench about one-forty, but I tell everyone one-sixty because it sounds believable, right?"

"Dollars." Spagnola's eyes register an idiot in his presence. "Ten thousand dollars."

"Wow, you're that rich you lift money? How many reps you do with it?"

My landlord rubs his face hard with his hands, and we're just getting started.

"To leave, Zesty. Ten thousand dollars to vacate your little rat's nest."

"Really? How soon can you get the money?"

"I'll cut you a check right now. We have a deal?"

"That's ten thousand each?" I say.

"Each what?"

"I've got two roommates."

"Oh, right. The drunk and the zombie. No, I don't think so. You're the only name on the lease. Going once—"

"Ten grand? You know what Starbucks charges for a pound of coffee? I'll be destitute in a month."

"Then make it twenty. Split it any way you want or keep it all for yourself, I don't care." Spagnola opens a desk drawer, tosses a checkbook onto the blotter. "You telling me you can't use twenty thousand dollars?"

"You don't know the half of it."

"And to show you no hard feelings, I'll forgive the two months' back rent you owe. We have a deal?"

Twenty thousand dollars. I chew on that number for a moment. Twenty large gets me a new place to live, pays my overdue bills, puts a dent in what I owe Darryl. *You've got yourself a deal,* my brain says.

"No." My mouth decides to speak on its own. *No?* What just happened?

"Then I withdraw my offer," Spagnola says sharply. "You *are* going to move, Zesty. I'm not making this offer again. You're practically the last ones left, and that eviction notice is going to stick, I guarantee it. Your days are numbered. You hear me?" Heated now. "Numbered!"

"You know, you're not the first person to tell me that today."

Spagnola's not interested. "Have you looked around this neighborhood lately, Zesty? The construction? You see anyone who looks like you, has a job like yours? Bike messenger. How long you think that's going to last? Either your body's going to go"—he taps above his own eye, signifying my stitches—"or technology's going to beat the street to it. How much money do you have in the bank, Zesty?"

"What's a bank?" I say.

"Joke all you want, you're moving out. Even if I have to have the building condemned around you, you're gone. People like you are meant to be pushed around."

Oh boy.

"People like me?"

"You a reader, Zesty?"

"I like the comics in *The New Yorker*," I say. "Sometimes I even understand them."

"How about de Tocqueville? No, I don't suppose you have. But that's okay. I'll give you a little synopsis. See, de Tocqueville wrote a lot about the nature of democracy and ownership, but he also had this premise that people choose their livelihoods based *not* on what their interests are but what they internally, maybe even subconsciously, think their standing in life is—basically, where they fall on the food chain. You following me here?"

"There going to be a quiz on this later?"

Spagnola nods, but it's more of a response to an internal question of his own than to mine.

"It's why you see so many people follow in their parents' footsteps: second- and third-generation cops, schoolteachers, athletes. It's not all genetics; more like an instinct, an internal measure of status. So really, if you take a good look at it, it makes perfect sense you make a living on a bicycle—mobile, transient, easily displaced."

"And all this time I thought it was 'you are what you eat.'"

"No disrespect, Zesty, and I apologize in advance if I'm wrong, but back in the day, didn't your father run card games all over the city?"

"What about it?"

"You don't see the connection? From one place to another? From bar to club, empty theaters? You, from office to office, here to there. No? That too much of a stretch for you? How about this? My father used to play in some of those card games. How's that for a connection?"

"Solid," I say. "He win or lose?"

"My father was a degenerate. Ponies, sports, you name it, he bet it. You couldn't depend on him for shit. My father was a loser."

"And look at you," I say, not enjoying the way this conversation's veered personal and into the past, feeling like forward movement is all I can afford right now. "Doesn't quite fall in line with your de Tocqueville theory, does it?"

Spagnola, like every proselytizer I've ever encountered, shakes off the point.

"I know what *you people* say about me, Zesty. All you tragic hipsters and that maniac fucking neighbor of yours, John Whatsis, with the three kids and the wife pregnant again, living in an industrial loft cranking out religious icons. He . . ." Spagnola loses his words, color rising through his neck. "Outside my church. You know what I'm talking about?"

"Maybe."

"Waiting for me, in front of the priest and everybody, slandering me, shouting how I'm a slumlord, claiming I'm all mobbed up, the fucking religious fanatic, because I'm Italian, I'm a patsy for the Mob. You think I'm in the Mob, Zesty?" Spagnola sticks out his chin, waiting for it. White dots of spittle have formed at the corners of his mouth.

"Honestly? I think you're a one-man Mob all by yourself," I say.

"You're damn fucking right I am. I'm a goddamn wrecking ball! But if you want to see the real Mob in action, go to city hall. You want graft and protection, licenses, permits, zoning changes? See how far you get with that bunch empty-handed. I'll show you the fucking Mob. You can't stand in the way of progress, Zesty."

"Progress? You call this progress? Luxury lofts and three-hundred-dollar-a-pop hair salons? You think pushing aside any-body that doesn't have a million dollars to spend on a roof over their heads is progress?"

"I made this neighborhood safer—"

"No, see, that's where you're wrong," I say, the timbre of my voice surprising me as it echoes off the vaulted beam ceilings and gloss bricked walls. "I did that. Me and the drunk and the zom-bie and everybody who moved here and built up this forgotten shithole when nobody wanted it. When you neglected it. With-out us, you don't have your condos, your restaurants. You don't have shit."

Spagnola sticks to his talking points. "I make this place cleaner, safer, a better place to live."

"For people who can afford it."

"For people who've *earned* it."

"That's utter fucking nonsense," I say, but I'm out of gas, the futility of arguing housing and community with the man hitting me like a spike between my eyes.

"You have till the end of the month. Or I guarantee all your shit will be on the curb, and there's nothing your cheap-suit pro bono can do for you except recommend a moving company." Sp-agnola throws the checkbook into a drawer and slams it shut. "Oh, and another thing? Go look in the dictionary at the definition of 'progress.' No. Better yet, I'll tell you. Webster's defines 'progress' as *moving* forward, to *proceed* and *develop* to a higher stage. Emphasis added, duly noted, but when you leave here, open your eyes and take a good look around and tell me I'm not progress, Zesty. I should be the picture next to progress. And hey, like I said before, no hard feelings. You've kept the neighborhood warm long enough. Nobody owes you anything. Now it's just time for you to go."

THIRTY-SIX

The garage that houses Zero's moving company could pass as a theatrical set for a moving company, the proscenium edge of the stage staring into the open black boxes of the Zen-logoed trucks. The ceilings are twenty feet high, the walls lined with Erector Set shelves stocked with pallets of flattened boxes and giant bins filled with moving straps, bands, and blankets. There's a weight bench in the center of the floor—I mean, who *wouldn't* want to pump iron after moving heavy shit all day?—surrounded by assorted dumbbells on jigsaw floor padding.

I'm not surprised to find the garage door lifted after dark (Zero's crews often work late), but the sight of two elaborately inked ex-cons alternating sledgehammer blows on an ATM is something new.

"Yo, Zesty Meyers in da house!" Jeremy sticks fingers in his mouth, lets out a shrill whistle that snaps his partner's head in my direction. The floor is littered with plastic fragments and bits of metal as if a bomb had detonated at their feet.

"Really, Jeremy? Are you fucking serious?"

"Nah, it ain't what it looks like, Z." Jeremy is a former stickup artist who's perpetually slouched, as if he's been poured into bodily form and has yet to solidify. Think Gumby with tattoos—hellfire, demons—that sort of thing. "Well, I mean, it *is,* but it ain't what it seems. Tell him, Smitty."

Smitty grins bashfully, wipes his brow with a colorful sleeve of Satan's itinerary and the same black ink spot that's stamped on the underside of Jeremy's wrist, the infamous Southie dot, considered by many a Boston hood as an open invitation to rumble. "We just trying to get paid, Z."

"I can see that. You do know that thing's got a GPS on it?"

"Really?" Smitty shoulders his hammer. "Where you think it's at?"

"My guess, inside the box. How long you been at this?"

"About an hour. We're almost there, though." He points to a large dent in the side. "Every safe's got a weak spot, right, Jeremy?"

"You know it." Jeremy smiles through hockey enforcer's teeth. "Zesty, you remember Davey Coley from Old Colony?"

"No," I say. "Not my neighborhood."

"Cross the bridge from the South End's, like, a million miles, right? Anyhow, one time Coley and this other chucklehead Jimmy Rolle get wind there's this guy been selling fireworks by the gross out the trunk of his car, got a pipeline, like, outta New Hampshire? Cherry bombs, M80s, Roman—"

"I get the picture, Jeremy."

"Ya, so they, like, follow the guy, case his house in Everett? Sure enough, they find a safe in his closet bolted to the floor. Now, neither one of these jamooks knows how to pop a safe, right? They rob houses, ain't got torch skills. So what do they do? They pry up the floorboards, the wood still attached to the bottom of the box—like, they're hauling around half the Garden floor, but still no way to open it. The safe's gotta weigh in the neighborhood of, like, three hundred pounds, and they get it in the trunk of this old Tercel Rolle used to have, and the thing's practically doing a wheely going over the Tobin, the tailpipe scrapin' the road, sparks flyin' everywhere.

"They get back to Southie, but they don't wanna attract too much attention, so Rolle, he sees Fat Joey on the corner by Triple O's, and he says, 'Joey, get in, I'll buy you a case a Twinkies—no, not the back, get in front.' So now there's the three of them mashed up front, Coley on Fat Joey's lap, his head stickin' out the window, no more sparks, but it's like Clown Car Hour except the back-seat's empty.

"So Rolle, he goes up and down Broadway looking for a torch, but you know how it is, everybody wants a piece of the action, and Jimmy, he's only offering, like, a small percentage because they don't even know what's inside the box and he doesn't wanna risk getting in and end up *owing* money. And you know they gotta piece off some already to McKenna 'cause he always gets his cut."

"Makes sense." I smile, enjoying the story.

"I suppose. But what does he do? Him and Davey hump that mother up six flights in the building Davey's mom lives at. Only by then, word's spread Davey and Jimmy are gonna drop a safe off the roof, and a crowd's gathered below, kids running wild, the old hags got their beach chairs out, Stevie the Greek with his Good Humor truck parked on the corner—it's a fuckin' carnival. So of course the cops show, squad cars everywhere, Davey and Jimmy are fucked, right? Except the cops want to see the safe fly too, because you know how it is, sometimes the heavy shit coming down's harder than going up and the cops don't want any part of it, throw out their backs before the Fourth and fireworks, all that easy OT coming their way. So they move the crowd back, and Davey and Jimmy figure 'What the fuck, we're fucked anyway. . . .'"

"And . . . ?" I say because that's my line.

"The thing cracks open like an egg, cash and coin everywhere, and the crowd goes wild. Last I saw, there's still that same, like, crater in the sidewalk where the safe hit. It's practically a neighborhood shrine with flowers and shit growing out of it."

"Coley and Rolle got arrested?"

"Whattaya, kiddin' me, Z? The crowd woulda ripped the cops apart. They pinched them later getting hammered at the Cornerstone; not a fuckin' dollar between them, but it didn't matter, their money was no good that night. Fuckin' legends."

I find Zero at his desk, absently riffing a deck of Bicycles, to the untrained eye a straight-up shuffle, only the odds rearranging themselves as his long fingers manipulate the placement of cards. I'd closed the door behind me, but I can feel the heavy banging below, the floor shaking through the bottom of my Adidas.

"Take a seat." Zero deals out three hands of Texas Hold'em, two cards apiece. "Pick a hand."

"I'll take yours," I say.

"No you won't." Zero smiles like a big cat showing his teeth before he eats you, as much a preview of things to come as a greeting.

I slide the cards off the desk, peek pocket kings, a monster starting hand in any game, especially Hold'em. Zero appears tanned and healthy, the tattoos on his arms out of sight under a powder blue dress shirt. His head is shaved and gleaming, the shallow pools of his granite eyes beaming neutrality, revealing nothing.

"You know they're never gonna get that thing open." Zero burns three cards, sets them aside.

"What's the tallest building around here?"

"What?"

I shake my head. "So why do you keep letting them pound it?"

"What's the harm? Let them work off some steam. They'll sleep like babies. You?"

"Me what?"

"You getting any rest?" Zero flops three cards, a king and a pair of eights. "What with all your cuts and bruises." Zero points to the ghost hand, and I flip over the two cards to reveal a queen and an eight.

"You gonna ask me how I got them?"

"Don't have to." Zero burns another card, turns over an ace. "You in some deep shit?"

"I'm on top of it," I say.

"Yeah? You don't need some backup, help you straighten things out?"

"I'm all right," I say.

"Like you're all right not giving me a heads-up a couple of homicides might be showing up trying to pull my records, rattle my guys?"

Fuck.

"Like you got things figured out, like you're holding the winning hand there?"

"I'm sorry," I say. "I meant to call you earlier but—"

"You pulled a Zesty on me. Whatever. What are you holding?" Zero raises his chin toward my cards, and I turn them over. "Lookit that. You flopped a kings boat full of eights, the world's your oyster; all you're thinking is how'm I gonna eat it, fast or slow until the ace comes up to give you indigestion. This guy next to you flopped a set of eights, thinks he's sitting catbird, but who's kidding who—nobody likes to see an ace if they're not holding one. To the river we go. I didn't give the cunts shit."

"Because there's nothing to give?" I make sure not to let an accusatory tone enter my voice.

"This Sullivan kid?" he says sharply, his eyes fixed on mine. "I didn't know him for shit. Crazy Eddie brings him in one day, says he wants to work, and I needed some bodies on account of Johnny Thunder and Dumberto got into a tussle at the Tap with some of the Giant guys and were cooling out in county for the weekend."

"What about the Giant guys?"

"Get real, Zesty, we're talking JT and Dumberto. The purple people were guests of Mount Auburn ER, all five of them." Zero shrugs dismissively.

"Who started it?"

Zero's eyes go wide. "What difference does it make? The question's always who *finished* it."

Except I already know that answer. "Eddie vouched for Sullivan?"

"There an echo in here?"

"What'd Eddie have to say?"

Zero smiles bitterly, flops a deuce of clubs—no help, but no harm to me or the ghost player with a set of eights.

"He swore Sullivan was a citizen with legit bills to pay. Homicide thinks this kid was dirty?"

"Why do you say that?"

"Sorry, bro, for a minute there I forgot who I was talking to. Welcome to the ballpark. By the way, it's like the eighth inning already." Zero flips his hole cards to reveal pocket aces and the predictable pot-busting aces full of eights. "I don't like getting used." He points at me in warning.

"By who?"

"Who do you think? This Sullivan fuck."

"I'm not following you. Last I saw, Sullivan had one eye and his brains were dripping down the back of a truck."

"Wrap your head around it, Z. If this kid's about to pull in, what, like half a million as the inside man on this armored car thing, what's he need a few extra hundred dollars off the books for?"

"Maybe he's not dirty." I go for logical but come off naive, even to my ears.

"Don't be an idiot." Zero takes a deep breath, his patience with me waning. "Sullivan knew he was going under the microscope after he got hit. They all know that's where the investigation starts. So what better way to shade things in his favor than picking up some side work to say, 'Hey, I'm just trying to pay my bills here. Why else would I be moonlighting *extra* if I'm in on this thing?' It's subtle, but it's smart, I'll give him that."

"How well did Eddie know him?"

"Neighborhood. Said he used to fuck his cousin."

"Terrific. How well did Sullivan know Crazy Eddie?"

Zero mulls over my question. "You mean like what if Sullivan didn't know what a bunch of angels we got working here? Picked the wrong place to OT?"

That's what I mean. Crazy Eddie is a recovering addict who steals to pay for his addictions, but he's a far cry from a hardened criminal like some of the other guys on Zero's payroll. Maybe Eddie just told Sullivan it was honest cash labor and nothing else. But at the same time, I also have to acknowledge Zero could be right, the extra work not only a curve to throw the investigators Sullivan knew would be nosing around after the robbery but also plenty of the usual suspects on Zero's payroll to throw them off the scent.

"Detective Wells," I say. "The younger homicide? He told me you should rename yourself Recidivist Movers, see what it does for business."

"Yeah? He didn't tell me that to my face, but it's pretty funny." Zero sticks his pinky into his mouth and starts working a nail, something I've never seen him do before. "You know, I recognized the other guy. He got old fast, but I think Dad knows—sorry, *knew*—him from the old neighborhood."

"I heard about it last night. His uncle used to own a blues joint on Mass Ave. I guess Dad used to hang there some, maybe smoothed a few things over."

"Yeah, well, small world. Speaking of Dad, all this nonsense why you're not covering home tonight?"

"I stopped by to let Sid know," I say defensively.

"And Sid called me. It's too much for you?" Zero says.

"What's too much?"

"One overnight a week and you gotta get Sid to cover for you? It's not like this is the first time."

I look at Zero, trying to pick up his vibrations, but the less time we spend together, the harder he becomes to read, the connective tissue of our misspent youth frayed by the demands of trying to keep our heads above water and our necks off the chopping block.

I've come to accept that I'm pretty much an open book, and the easy read sometimes costs me, but Zero's a tougher nut to crack on all fronts. Only it's not Zero's words I'm focused on; it's his body, the tilt of his head, the tell coming from the cartilage in his jaw just below his ears.

"It's getting harder." I decide it's safe enough to broach the topic. "I'm not sure we're doing what's best for Pops anymore. Half the time, he doesn't even know who I am, and the shit he says. . . . Today he thinks he's talked to his dad and to Mom. And there's physical issues now too, bathroom stuff, the front stairs—"

"And what, you want to warehouse him?" Zero's face reddens, but I look past it, focus on the jaw.

"There are places," I say, unable to drum up as much conviction as I'd hoped to hear, trying to convince myself as I convince Zero. "People trained to deal with this disease, give him what he needs around the clock. I've looked into it some—"

"What the fuck's wrong with you, Zesty? Looked into it? Pop's all we got, and we take care of him on our own until there's nothing left to be taken care of. To the end. I gotta explain this to you? We deal with shit ourselves; all *you* got to do is get your fucking priorities straight." Zero's eyes cloud over, signaling the point of diminishing returns.

"And on that note, get the wax outta your ears, because I'm only gonna tell you this one time. I got nothing to do with this armored car thing and this Sullivan kid beyond what I told you. You got that? Nada. BPD wants to see my files, they'll have to get a warrant on *principle,* because I can't afford to have it look like I just roll over and beg for a biscuit every time Big Blue wants something outta me. As of right now, I don't have this Sullivan kid on paper. If your pot-soaked brain can remember, you were the one worked with him, and they were all cash jobs. So as far as I'm concerned, they never happened until they have to happen on the books."

"So you have it down somewhere," I say.

"Of course. I keep records. Hell, sometimes I even pay taxes. And another thing, in the spirit of full disclosure here, I hooked Sullivan up with whatever crew you happened to be working because I know sometimes you don't like humping with some of these knuckleheads, maybe you don't have much in common? I figured Sullivan for the same on account of what Eddie told me, didn't want to throw him to the wolves off the bat, let him get a feel for the place first, the work. Fuckin' love the way that worked out. Next rookie up I'll stick him with a crew of Vic the Quick and Tommy Bones, and he can listen to them dissertate why getting hummers in the joint don't make them gay. As far's Dad's concerned? I'm not blind, okay? Maybe we need some outside help on this, get a trained nurse for some shifts, look into some of the newer medications. But we gotta ante up too, right? Isn't that what he taught us, the long run?"

"Among other things."

"Among other things." Zero nods acceptance. "We square on this, Dad and all this other shit?"

"We're square," I say.

"Okay, then." Zero drums his hands on the edge of his desk. "Now you wanna explain why I got a visit from the FBI this morning and all *they* wanna talk about is Devlin fuckin' McKenna?"

THIRTY-SEVEN

This is what Will sees when he opens his eyes: heavy blinds drawn across the windows, a fissure of light splitting a seam that slices the bed in two. What's that movie? If It's Tuesday, This Must Be Belgium *starring a young Suzanne Pleshette, before most Americans got to know her as Bob Newhart's wife. Who else? Ian McShane. Ben Gazzara. Donovan sang "Lord of the Reedy River."*

Why is it Will remembers this brain-cluttering nonsense, these trivial bits like metal shavings stuck to a magnet, insignificant, adding up to shit? He sits up in bed, feels for the gun under the pillow. Lately he can't shake the feeling he's being tailed, but it's just nerves; Diane's taught him how to cover his tracks, ditch surveillance if someone's picked him up.

The chain is across the door. The briefcase is beside the bed. He's alone. And yes, it might be Tuesday, but St. Louis is more likely than Belgium. Florida. Wisconsin. He's become accustomed to the travel but not the places; they lack the sharp edges of Boston, sprawl in place of density, not quite suburbs, certainly not cities.

It's harder for Will to acclimate himself when McKenna does the choosing, which he does at first, before he trusts him fully, trusts his trap. He started closer to home as would be expected—Nashua, Stowe, Poughkeepsie—and then fanned out in a wider arc, the guns and money where Will said he'd deposited them, either McKenna

*himself darting out under cover of darkness to verify or maybe send-
ing Ritter, who sizes Will up like a tailor eyeballing a suit for a corpse
as he delivers McKenna's parcels.*

*Storage lockers in Topeka, Raleigh, Flint, one year paid in ad-
vance and after that, the money wired through Western Union, filtered through out-of-town PO boxes. Guns in Sacramento. Cash in
Taos. Treasure maps marked with skulls and X's. The rule is keep to
small cities, avoid the glare of large metropolises—Chicago, Miami,
New York—too many players, knowing eyes, crime buffs; same
goes for small towns where a new face brings scrutiny, lazy porch
banter, hayseed theorizing. Will has become a traveling salesman
with nothing to sell, the Fuller Brush Man with a negative quota: Lose
everything. Or else.*

*The gun is under his pillow. The gun is in his hand. For the life
of him, he can't remember where he is.*

THIRTY-EIGHT

It's early, but my body tells me it's late, half past rigor mortis, any
energy I had draining from me as the static returns full blast. My
cuts and bruises reassert themselves, the primacy of pain top dog
again.

I ride Harrison Avenue toward Thayer, cutting down Randolph to approach via Albany Street, the Expressway at my back
so I don't worry about getting spotted from behind, no telling if
Darryl's changed his tune and wants another pound of flesh for
his troubles. There's a squad car parked at the stairs of my loft,
the cab glowing with the electric blue of a computer, a single sil-
houette visible on the driver's side. Albert's nowhere to be seen.

At the corner of Thayer and Albany, I step into a dark doorway and use the card Detective Wells gave me to dial his number.

"Wells." He answers on the first ring.

"You find Britta Ingalls, Detective?" Wells doesn't respond, but I hear movement over the line, other voices.

"Zesty," he says wearily. "When I said you were up to your neck in shit, it wasn't meant as an invitation to dive off into the deep end."

"I don't know what you're talking about, but you want to tell me why there's a cruiser sitting in front of my loft?"

"You're in a world of trouble, Zesty." He repeats my name louder than the rest of the conversation, probably alerting Brill or others to the call. In the background a car door slams.

"You're not at headquarters?"

"No."

"Your partner with you?"

"He's about to be."

"I have something for you."

"Hold on a second." I listen to movement and another car door shutting, Wells settling into his seat and then the same sounds again, probably Brill sliding in beside him. "Now, you listen good, Zesty," Wells's voice comes fast and angry. "I don't know what the hell you think you're doing, but shit is piling up so fast around you, you're liable to drown in it."

"Make it quick," I say. "Your metaphors suck, and I'm about to hang up."

"Wait! Where are you? I'll pick you up."

"No thanks. I didn't like the feel of your cuffs the first time."

"Then fuckit," Brill shouts into Wells's phone, somebody besides me sounding like they need a nap. "Tell us something we need to know like—"

I shut the phone off, edge around the corner to look over an empty street, the cruiser gone. I turn the phone back on, and when Wells answers, I say, "Black Hole Vinyl. They run dirty money through the record business."

"'They' being . . . ?"

"I don't know." I still keep Darryl's name out of it, nothing to gain yet by pointing in his direction. "That's for you to figure out. Gus was dealing cocaine, but I think it was his own thing and doesn't have anything to do with Wells Fargo. If you find Britta, I'm betting you'll find the bulk of the Fargo money." I give up Gus and Britta, figuring that with the pair of them in custody, they'll be out of harm's way from Darryl, or if by some minor miracle I find the money—I can exchange it for the promise of their safety. If Darryl's a man of his word. Too many ifs.

"Well, if you're right about any of that," Wells says evenly, passing over my put-down, "you're only half right, then."

"How's that?"

"We have your buddy Molten already. He doesn't have the money, isn't carrying any blow, and he's not talking. Got any other suggestions?"

"You have him there right now?"

"As a matter of fact, I do."

"Let me talk to him."

"You going to come meet us, or are we still playing Where's Waldo?"

"I'll come to you," I say. "Where are you?"

"LaGrange Street," Wells says. "This is Molten's place, right?"

"Yeah. I'm actually pretty close. Can I talk to Gus a minute before I get going?"

"No you cannot," Brill barks over the line. "'Less you can float a fucking séance to reach him. Your boy Gus is dead. Now, you gonna come see him off or not?"

THIRTY-NINE

If nothing else, Will admires McKenna's long game. It reflects a realistic view; he knows the day will come when he'll be forced to abdicate his crown of thorns. He doesn't come right out and say it, but Will knows he likens himself to a general at war, and why not? There're enough bodies to back that up, unmarked graves, blood on the beaches. Will knows of two: Wollaston. Tenean.

Only McKenna is not planning to win any war, just the skirmishes, as he plans exit strategies, quotes passages from Sun Tzu, from Demosthenes. "He who fights and runs away, lives to fight another day." Will prefers the Bob Marley version. Or better still, Rolling Stones: Exile on Main Street.

Will assembles a marked deck only he and McKenna can read, though he has trouble picturing McKenna winding his way through these Middle American waiting rooms, collecting his blood money, flattening his heavy Boston accent to fade into retirement and anonymity.

It doesn't seem likely to happen anytime soon. One by one, McKenna's adversaries fold. The DiMasis are defanged by the FBI riding their wiretaps; Ritter is set loose to do what he does best: Jerry Dapolito bound in the trunk of a Pontiac, a bullet through his brain. Johnny Lockwood in the bed of a tanning salon of all places, his Irish blood bubbling on the hot glass; his brother practically decapitated in a Lowell barber shop, a little too much off the top. McKenna consolidates power as the rest of the city bleeds.

McKenna must be a target of law enforcement, the state if not

*the feds, but it's Keystone Kops every time, Inspector Clouseau meets
DA Magoo. McKenna's name tumbles off every indictment, wriggles
out of every legal noose, witnesses recanting, decomposing, every at-
tempt on his life a bungled card trick by double amputees.*

*That Will is bound to McKenna seems inconceivable. His lips
are sealed. He runs his table. Omaha Hi-Lo. Seven Stud. Texas
Hold'em. If nothing else, McKenna has focused him, put everything
in perspective. He knows his role, keeps dealing from the top of the
deck. He has a family to provide for. Now is not the time to shave
odds. Not yet. Rake the chips, wash the cards, and deal.*

Like it or not, McKenna's the only game in town.

FORTY

The crime scene is lit like a movie scene, like a bad dream—
police cruisers and unmarked cars, yellow tape, crime scene ana-
lysts, a crowd of extras, a silver roach-coach parked as close as the
blues will allow, opportunities everywhere, you just have to find
your niche. I half expect Mark Wahlberg or one of the Affleck
brothers to show up on set, start yammering in an exaggerated
Boston accent: *Whatta we got he-yah?* Or *Someone pahked a couple
a monstah slugs in our vic and we-yah workin' on an ID. Pretty
fuckin' wom out he-yah.*

Instead I get Wells and Brill stripping disposable gloves, huddling with a slick Asian suit. Not as slick as Wells's fitted Armani,
or whatever it is he's changed into since last night, but nice enough.
The uniforms are working the crowd, notepads out like waiters
listing daily specials. Brill makes a circular motion with his hand

as I roll up and one of the unis lets me glide under the tape, setting off a rumbling from the onlookers angling for a better view.

"Why's he so fuckin' special?" one guy snapping pictures yells out, framing me in his lens.

Before I can answer, Brill grabs me by the shoulders, spins me around, and cuffs my wrists behind my back, the bike rattling to the curb. His pat-down has a personal feel to it, rougher than it has to be. Wells retrieves the Trek and rolls it to a tech wearing white paper booties and matching gloves working out of the back of a mobile crime scene truck. He motions with his chin to a strip of taped-off pavement pointing up Tremont.

The Weegee of phone photography clicks away, yells, "Hey, what's your e-mail? I'll send you pictures."

Brill leans me face forward against the unmarked Crown Vic, lifts my pack over my head, and rummages through it.

"You ever afraid of being typecast, Zesty?" Brill finds my eyes. "You know, like forever one of those goofy characters they march out on sitcoms for a cheap laugh." He pulls out the leopard-spotted underwear I've forgotten to give Martha, lets it dangle off his finger. "Question withdrawn."

By all rights I should be wired, but stress makes me want to curl up and go to sleep, the metal hood of the Crown Vic as inviting as a pillow. The buzzers for Gus's building are protected by an outdoor cell of paint-glopped iron bars, a door cut seamlessly into the frame. I close my eyes to avoid looking at Gus, but I've already seen him laid out inside the gated foyer, the sole of one Converse All Star pointing straight up at the end of his extended leg, his other sneaker twisted up behind him as if death had come just as he was busting some hellacious dance move.

"Am I boring you, Zesty?" Brill's voice snaps me back to the artificial light.

"Am I under arrest?"

"Shit. What do you think?"

"I haven't been Mirandized yet, and I watch *Law & Order,* so I'd have to say no."

"Then Mirandize your own goddamn self, if you know the script."

Wells returns from the van and turns me around. "You have the right to remain stupid. . . ." He opens the front door, guides me in with his hand on top of my head.

The Asian suit is in the backseat already; I hadn't noticed where he'd disappeared to or felt any of the doors open or close as I was leaning on the car. I look at him in the rearview mirror instead of twisting around, the cuffs at my wrists too tight, digging into flesh.

I hate to say it, but the Asian guy looks, well, inscrutable. Maybe it's because he's sitting as if a board's been jammed down the back of his suit jacket, his mirror image flat as the jack on a playing card, his lips no more than a line drawn across his face, dark hair shaved close to the skull, his nose a visual sleight of hand to suggest a depth that isn't there. In fact, if he weren't wearing that expensive suit, he'd be as animated as a cardboard cutout.

"Zesty Meyers," he says in a similarly flat voice, betraying no regional or ethnic accent whatsoever. "My name is Wellington Lee. It's been quite a while since someone from the bureau's spoken to you, hasn't it?"

"You're FBI?"

"What has it been, a little over two years now?"

"I don't count the days. Anyhow, if you're with the bureau, I figure that D. B. Cooper thing's still keeping you busy."

"Detective Wells informed me that you fancy yourself quite the comedian." Lee's frown drags his caterpillar eyebrows down for a triplicate image of disapproval.

"Really? I'd say I'm more pithy than funny, but funny gets the girls, so okay."

"The agent whom you spoke to last, Grossman, do you remember him?"

"Sure."

"Said the same thing. He even thought it worth mentioning in your file."

"Sweet. So two out of three law enforcement officials agree I'm funny. What are you selling, Agent Lee? Am I in your custody now?"

"We'll get to that in a moment. But first, it has come to my attention that you are peripherally involved in a matter involving the robbery of that Wells Fargo truck a week ago, at least a portion of the money you were delivering from an outfit by the name of Black Hole Vinyl originating from said robbery."

"Whoopee."

"I'm told that you knew Collin Sullivan, the guard who was killed, in a corollary manner, which is to say, in passing. You worked with him at your brother's place of employ, twice, which your brother's statement confirms, though he declined to turn over any written record. Do I have your full attention now? Why are you smiling?"

"You're the one talked to Zero?" When we spoke, Zero didn't tell me anything about the agent himself; I just assumed it was the regular patrician suit with the bad comb-over.

"Yes, of course."

"So you get around."

"Yes. You sound surprised."

"I'm just taking mental notes. The timing doesn't surprise me," I say.

"No? How so?"

"Leila Markovich's parole."

"Ah, very astute. What about it?"

"Whenever anyone who so much as claims to have smoked a

joint with my mother pops up, I get a visit from you guys. Least I used to."

"Leila Markovich did much more than smoke a joint with your mother. They were the founding members of Sparhawk, were responsible for the Harvard bombing—"

"And they both robbed banks. I get it. What do you want, Agent Lee?"

"You don't know?"

"I could guess, but jumping into the FBI's fantasy isn't such a turn-on for me. Hey, Lee, do I smell like a Grateful Dead concert to you? You know who they are, right? Because Zero's got this collection of old albums used to belong to my dad, and every time he plays 'Box of Rain,' I can't help but picture my mom planting that bomb in Harvard Yard."

"Your point being?"

"That you'd catch a better lead from a pint of Cherry Garcia than wasting your time with me. Now are we done here? Because I'd like to get on with this arrest already. The cuffs are killing me, and I don't like wearing bracelets, I think they look a little feminine on me. Or maybe it's just the color?"

Lee takes a deep breath, presses on. "I noticed your brother's not quite as committed to humor as you are. Or do you think it was just me?"

"That's just Zero being Zero."

"Brothers are often different." Agent Lee nods in understanding. "My older brother is a very successful gynecologist in Philadelphia."

"Good for him."

"Not according to my brother. I believe his profession severely limits his dinner conversations. Anyhow, at this point it's the bureau's determination that you've been led into your current predicament through no fault of your own, although your continued meddling has perhaps . . . I want to get the right word here . . . accelerated events. And I'm sorry to say, for your friend Gus Molten, it has accelerated consequences."

"Gus getting killed is *my* fault now?"

"I didn't say that." Lee taps his ear to keep me on point. "But things are certainly moving quickly, are they not? And in that you are perhaps culpable. Would Mr. Molten have met the same fate without your involvement? In my opinion, it is probable. The people that he, and by proxy, you are dealing with are dangerous and violent criminals. This is how things often end if you are not adept or equipped to handle them."

Way to state the obvious, I think, but keep to myself, seeing as it's neither funny nor pithy, and I'd hate to ruin such a cultivated image with one sarcastic remark. Probably not a lot of FBI files list "funny" in the personal description column.

"Do you know a man by the name of Darryl Jenkins?" Lee finds my eyes in the mirror.

I look away too quickly, kicking myself for being caught off-guard.

Growing up, whenever Zero and I would sit down to play cards, the deal rotating among us, our father would admonish us, *Control yourselves. You think your eyes are just there to look at pretty girls? Your eyes have muscles. Work them. Fill them with smoke, polish them to mirrors.*

Zero proved to be a better student of the game, only behind his smoke and mirrors was a flame that tended to get the better of him in the long run. I had the gift of patience but enjoyed the sound of my own voice too much, meaning I tend to lie with my lips moving. "I know Darryl," I say. "Assuming we're talking about the same guy."

"It is the same," Lee assures me. "He utilizes a number of vehicles but is primarily driven in a black Pathfinder by his lieutenants Cedrick Overstreet and Otis Byrd. Together they run a narcotics distribution enterprise in Roxbury and parts of the South End. Darryl Jenkins also owns a number of legitimate businesses and residences, a dry cleaners in Mattapan, a two-family rental unit in Mission Hill, and most pertinent to your predicament, a recording company on Newbury Street, through which he launders his corner drug money. Quite successfully, I might add, until recently, when he made one enormous miscalculation."

"And what would that be?" I'm fully alert now, my head spinning with what Lee's telling me: Darryl's empire built on a foundation of quicksand, our little arrangement already voided with Gus dead, the city's federal and blue tide rolling in on him fast. Has Valentine flipped already, or is there something I'm missing entirely?

"Why, the money from the Wells Fargo robbery," Lee says. "Isn't it obvious?"

At one of the police vans, Wells is talking to the paper-booted tech he'd handed my bike to, the tech handing it back, shrugging. Brill has wandered off, working the crowd's periphery as Wells had done in Roxbury, arms spread like an open invitation for random hugs, a lit cigar dangling from the corner of his mouth, homicide's very own game show host: Step right up and win the dead guy.

"You're telling me Darryl and his crew robbed the Fargo truck? That's a hell of a step up from running corners."

"Darryl Jenkins has proven himself to be quite the entrepreneur, but no, he wasn't involved in the robbery of the armored vehicle. Just the attempted laundering of the money."

Two million dollars. Darryl's missing stake only a million, meaning he *is* cleaning the cash for someone else, fifty cents on the dollar to have it come out pressed and dry. So who's the partner? And where's the other million if Gus or Britta are only responsible for one in Darryl's eyes? Still on the street, as of yet unconverted from dope to cash?

"So what you're telling me," I say after thinking it through a moment, "is whoever hit the truck was smart enough to know the money was too hot to spend and brought it to Darryl to clean?"

"Yes." Lee actually smiles. "The problem is not unique among bank thieves who manage such a large score, which might contain serialized bills, nor is it insurmountable. They pay their street debts with it, take road trips to Atlantic City or Foxwoods, gambling junkets to Vegas, purchase drugs or sex or throw it into local high-stakes poker games—I imagine you know quite a bit regarding that sort of endeavor. That is, assuming they're patient and have time to piece it off a little at a time, avoid the big-ticket items that would catch the attention of law enforcement. What is highly unusual is for a group to bundle the stolen money and entrust it to another individual to launder it for them. They are, after all, every one of them, thieves. And who can trust a thief? Which leads me to conclude that whoever was behind the robbery was also in a hurry to have clean money to spend without attracting undue attention."

"But you don't know who robbed the armored truck and brought Darryl the money."

"No." Lee shakes his head. "I know that too."

"Then why're you wasting your time talking to me?"

"Because I am unable to talk to them." Lee shrugs up his suit cuffs, reaches into his jacket, and produces three photographs, which he spreads onto the seat beside me. "Seeing how they are all thoroughly dead."

FORTY-ONE

Will knows something's wrong as soon as the spectral form of Richie Ritter slips empty-handed through the covered side entrance at Man-Ray to occupy the only vacant seat as he deals to a collection of out-of-town convention rubes whose Rotary Club hosts had fronted their initial buy-in action and who have since dipped, more than once, into their pockets again.

Will stacks a thousand dollars in chips, the burnt filaments of Ritter's eyes flaring as he lights a warped cigarette smelling faintly of opiates and something that makes Will think of ground bones, the noxious smoke swirling around him as he drags the chips into his well without comment or counting.

The men don't know Ritter—why would they?—but they're attuned enough to feel a shift of ions in the room, something akin to a precipitous loss of oxygen. The man to Ritter's left starts squeezing the cards so hard, his hands begin to shake. The man to his right accidentally turns over his down cards for all to see. After several more hands, none of which Ritter plays, Will is forced to prompt the action with words sharper than he'd intended, a prairie dog nipping at the heels of wayward steer, and thirty minutes later, the men have all gone, leaving Ritter tapping ashes into his well, ignoring the copper trays built into the table. Will's never been comfortable with Ritter's presence—in the physical sense, Ritter feels like a stain Will can't rub off his skin—but he's grown accustomed to his unannounced appearances, luggage in tow, the wordless exchange. Only he's already noted Ritter is empty-handed.

Will deals a hand of Texas Hold'em, two down cards for each of them, three burn cards on the worn green felt. What is it Will wants from this game? Time, he tells himself. For the smoke around Ritter to dissipate. To read those dead eyes of his.

"He wants to see you." Ritter leaves his hand untouched. "And if you didn't fuckin' notice already, I don't play cards."

"It's the same game I was dealing before. Were you paying attention?"

"I didn't say I didn't know how to play." Ritter parts his curtain of smoke.

"So one hand, then. What've you got to lose?"

"Nothing." Ritter mucks his cards, a pair of jacks flipping up over the burn cards.

"That's fitting," Will says and waits, looking straight into the depth of Ritter's vacancy, into eyes that have witnessed the murders of at least five men that Will knows of, would-be informers, rivals, wrong-place-wrong-timers. Come on, motherfucker, he screams inside his head. Come on!

"What's that?" Ritter says after an eternity.

"Jacks. Princes. Second bananas. Third, really, after the queens. Knaves. You know what a knave is, Ritter?" Will tosses the cards back in front of him.

"Fuck you, Meyers."

"Yeah, when?" Will quickly waves him off. "Nah, screw it. We both know the answer's whenever McKenna tells you."

"Maybe that time's now." Ritter performs his own sleight of hand, a pearl-handled razor materializing from nowhere, the Sweeney Todd of D Street and Old Colony. Messy, Will thinks. And as slow as Ritter could manage it.

"I don't think so." Will forces his mouth to smile, his eyes to blot out the vision of the blade. "And if the time comes, I don't think you'll be the one doing it."

"That right?" Ritter tilts back in his chair, but the cover of his smoke has lifted.

"So like I was saying, jacks. The only royal with two one-eyed cards, and you're looking at them now. King has only one Cyclops; queens none at all, because the ladies, they see everything. And the kings, they're armed to the teeth, with the exception of the one-eyed diamond, but even he's got a blade within reach if he absolutely needs to get at it. But jacks got shit, hence the phrase. The diamond and the club look like a pair of bellhops at the Mirage. And the pair of one-eyed retards you're holding, well . . . Knave means fool, by the way; don't let anybody tell you the joker's the only fuckup in the deck. On top of that, it's got to be hard to sleep with one eye open all the time."

"You should know."

"Me? I sleep like a baby. Anyhow, I'm not saying jacks are a guaranteed loser; let's see." Will flops an ace and a pair of threes into the middle. Ritter shows not a glimmer of interest, but the razor's evaporated. "Do you believe in luck, Richie?"

"What? Who gives a fuck?"

"So only games of repetition and skill, then? Chess? Checkers?"

"No. No fucking games."

Will burns another card, turns over a nine of clubs. He hasn't even peeped his down cards because he's in the game now, whether he likes it or not, and anyhow, as any pro will tell you, the stakes get high enough, you play the man, not the cards. Only, Ritter's eyes tell Will nothing.

"When's he want me? Now?" Now would not be good. Will is not prepared for now.

"Tomorrow. I'll let you know where right before. Make sure you stick around so's I can reach you."

"Shit," Will says, arms open wide. "Where would I go?"

There it is.

Ritter's mouth twitches, Will hitting the nerve he'd been probing for: Ritter is out of the loop on the interstate cash drop locations, McKenna's moneyed exit route a one-lane highway. Which means McKenna's killing machine is as expendable as he is, a loose end when *the time comes to hit the road. It's not information that can help right at this moment, but Will stores it away for a later hand, turns over his two down cards to show pocket sevens and burns the last card under the deck.* "To the river we go. Luck be a—"

"And get yourself a sitter. The wife comes with." *Ritter grinds his smoldering cigarette into the felt, blows into his well, a cloud of ash exploding over the table and into Will's face.*

Will is still hacking as the door clicks shut, his hand hovering over the deck as if he could Uri Geller that last card by force of magnetism alone, by some special power that could change whatever it is into the only card in the deck that can bail him out of this shit. What are the odds? Actually, those numbers he can calculate in an instant, but why bother looking? The game is meaningless when played alone.

Will brushes at the misshapen ring of fire eating away at the table.

Think. No, don't think. Feel. Find the angle. McKenna has already leveraged Diane's identity, proven the length of his reach: Diane was untouched by the FBI even as her political contemporaries were swept up and jailed. Surrender was not an option when Diane was first pregnant, as she is again now.

Will flops the river card into the center of the burning hole; he hasn't wiped out the flames, only fanned them. The card is a king of hearts, naturally.

Yes, Will has the feel now. And what he now knows, he knows for sure: Lady Luck is a cunt. And the king of hearts, both eyes wide open, has a sword stuck through his fucking head.

FORTY-TWO

Lee punches the car's interior light so I can get a better look. One picture I'm already familiar with: Sullivan leaning into oblivion against the armored car. The other photos are new, except I'd already had a front-row seat for the slim black man with diamond studs in his ears laid out in the lane under a basketball hoop. The third body I don't recognize, but maybe that's because he's bent facedown into a plate of food, the back of his head a dark indented mess, a fine spray of blood reaching a hand-sized Jesus icon nailed halfway up the wall.

"Okay, I recognize the baller, on account of Wells dragging me to the scene, but before that I'd never seen him in my life. Same goes for that mess in the kitchen, and you know my Sullivan connect. What're you trying to tell me, Darryl killed these guys?"

"No," Lee says. "In fact, I know he *didn't* kill them. In no small measure because we have been following Darryl Jenkins and his subordinates for some time now."

"Come again?"

"Are you familiar with SIS, Zesty? It stands for special investigations section. Depending somewhat upon the city in which they serve, they are tasked with running long-term surveillance on criminals whom they suspect of committing or planning violent or serial crimes. Often they work with fugitive section detectives, whom I'm sure you are much more familiar with."

Fugitive section detectives specialize in tracking down and apprehending wanted felons considered armed and dangerous.

Like my mother. Except at this point, if she's still alive, she'd be considered armed and rusty.

"So you're telling me these guys saw Darryl's men grab me?"

"Off the record? That is correct."

"And they didn't do anything."

"It was not foreseen. But yes, we allowed it to play out. To intervene would have jeopardized an ongoing investigation. But we were close by, if that makes you feel any better." Something akin to amusement twinkles in Lee's eyes. "You are upset?"

"Whatever. Get on with it. No, wait. Has SIS been tailing me too?"

That actually causes Lee to laugh.

"Originally, that was the plan, only it proved to be a difficult task, much to the consternation of the SIS men, who pride themselves on covert ops, the art of the tail. I'm told you bike with no regard for the rules of traffic, which made tracking you problematic, even for SIS. Cars were of no use. Placing a bug on your bicycle wasn't deemed viable, and anyhow, you ride them as if they are disposable. Eventually, they put a man on a bicycle, only he was not quite as adept as you are on two wheels or as eager to take some of the risks you do," Lee continues. "You're not color-blind, are you?"

"No. Why do you ask?"

"Just wondering if you see red lights."

"I see them. I just forget what they mean."

"Perhaps if you had adhered to traffic rules, you wouldn't be in this situation to begin with."

"That's cold," I say.

"Yes, perhaps. These three men." Lee points at the photos on the seat. "Sullivan, the inside man, Derrick Coney on the basketball court, and Shaun Stavros were contracted to rob the armored truck by an individual who provided them with the weapons, the planning, and the change of vehicles after the robbery. As far as the bureau has been able to piece together with the invaluable aid of Detectives Brill and Wells, none of these men knew each other prior to the robbery, and if there was contact, it was most likely under aliases. Both Stavros and Coney had New York driver's licenses on their persons when they were killed, but under different names and Social Security numbers. Not the easiest thing to acquire these days, with all the computerization and paperwork required."

"They were criminal geniuses?" I say.

"Hardly. But they were organized and effective. Though not very loyal, as Sullivan discovered in the worst possible way."

"Less people, larger cut." Math was never my strong suit, but put anything into pizza or pie form, and I'm a genius. "Until there's only one left."

"So it appears. Sullivan was a Charlestown native, though the Town's not quite what it used to be. Coney was from Roxbury, and Stavros, East Boston. Arrests for assault, auto theft, witness intimidation. In and out of Walpole and MCI. Quite a diverse crew."

"Welcome to the new world order. You left out the part about the Asian FBI agent."

"Chinese. Yes. New world, only same as the old. Three men with no local gang affiliations and no ties to organized crime. Coney and Stavros with extensive records, but nothing in their makeup to suggest they were capable of taking down an armored car in broad daylight."

"But you know who hired them," I say, trying to draw Lee to a close, my arms numb from the shoulders down now, the smell of the patchouli mingling with my sweat and making me nauseous.

"Yes, I'm reasonably sure of who organized and recruited them."

"So case closed. Or almost, right?" A couple of arrests away,

Darryl sounding good as gone on money-laundering or corner-dope-slinging charges, a triple killer in SIS and FBI sights, Gus reduced to collateral damage, in over his head and paying for it with his life; Black Hole Vinyl destined to be a no-hit wonder unless Gus's posthumous album goes platinum. As for Britta Ingalls, if she has a brain inside that bleached blond head of hers, she'll cut her losses, ditch the traceable cash, and never be seen in this city again.

"No, not quite." Lee returns to frowning. "We still need to locate whoever hired these men and make an arrest, which has in the past proven quite difficult. See, that's where you come into play. I have one more photograph to show you."

Lee drops another picture on top of the three dead bodies, a card my father would have referred to as the turn or Fourth Street.

"Get fucking serious," I say, looking at the equivalent of a black king.

"So you know who Devlin McKenna is."

"Agent Lee, if you know anything about me, then you probably know I like to get stoned sometimes. Only that doesn't mean I live under a rock. Anybody who's grown up in Boston knows who Devlin McKenna is."

Even a decade after ducking an indictment that dismantled his crew, McKenna's name is still spoken in hushed tones, at least by the men in Zero's employ who've done time behind federal bars, close enough to rub tattooed elbows with those in McKenna's sphere. That McKenna avoided arrest on the indictment was not surprising in itself. His political connections ran deep, and he was a resourceful man who'd obviously planned an exit strategy. The more shocking revelations came later, when it was revealed that McKenna, in addition to his duties as crime boss, had also been a longtime FBI informant given an extraordinarily long leash by the bureau, which allowed him to wreak havoc and murder unabated and unpunished for decades while ratting out friends and enemies alike.

When McKenna's double life was exposed, his killing crew beat a path toward the prosecutor's office, Richie Ritter cutting the sweetest deal of all; leading investigators to cemented corpses under building foundations in Southie and bullet-ridden victims excavated from community gardens in the South End, the Big Dig shovels made their own unwitting contributions, turning over unmarked graves by the handful—the aftershocks of McKenna's disappearance reverberated through the New England FBI field offices all the way to Washington.

When McKenna's former handlers were sentenced to lengthy jail terms on corruption and murder charges, the Boston offices of the FBI were restocked with out-of-town agents, who had to navigate steep learning curves as they acclimated themselves to the local scenery. My father heard about it from the unaffiliated players having a hard time adjusting to the lockstep bureaucracy, the cold Midwestern faces and flattened accents of the new G-men working by the book.

My father suffered his first conviction on gambling charges in this transitional period, and though he still had enough political juice to keep him out of prison, his card games were sharply curtailed, his former network of bars and clubs no longer willing to risk his presence. This, in turn, meant admittance to his games became highly restricted, amounting to fewer fish for the sharks at the table and a tightening of the cash flow. Call it trickle-down crime fighting at its best.

"What do you want me to say, Agent Lee?" I use my leg to push the pictures aside. "You think Devlin McKenna's back in town?"

"I don't think. I *know* he is back."

"And what, he hired these three amateurs to take off an armored truck? You're out of your fucking mind."

"Why are you so certain he has not returned, Zesty?"

"Because it's a death sentence is why. He's got no friends here. Probably every hood from Charlestown to Southie wants to see his head on a pole on account of all the people he's fucked over, let alone collect whatever reward's still out there on him. Why risk it?"

"Why, money of course. Money in a city he knows like the back of his hand."

"*Knew,*" I clarify. "Like the back of his liver-spotted hand. Nothing's the same anymore. They don't keep you guys up to date once you graduate Quantico? Money? He's been on the run for, like, thirteen years; money hasn't been an issue yet."

"Money runs out." Lee collects the photos and slips them back into his jacket. "People get desperate and then they get sloppy. In fact, sometimes they just get sentimental. Are you a sentimental person, Zesty?"

"I can cry on command," I admit. "It's one of my many talents."

"That's not what I meant. I mean do you ruminate over things you have missed or paths you haven't chosen? Do you find yourself looking inward as the people around you change, wishing things could revert to the way they'd once been, the way you remember them? Are there things you long for the way I long to see Devlin McKenna face justice?"

"No. What is it you want from me, Agent Lee?"

"Insight," he says flatly.

"Into what? Into who, McKenna?"

"Not McKenna. McKenna I understand fully; he is just an animal bent on survival. And what better place to hunt than in the environment he once dominated so fiercely? Some things have changed, of course: Time marches on, the players are different, the neighborhoods, parts of them, unrecognizable. Even some of the streets are gone, I'm told. But the game is still much the same as it was when he left, and after all, he has done this sort of thing before. Do you see what I'm driving at, Zesty?"

"No."

"Then allow me to rephrase. Nineteen eighty-six. Allston. Bank of Boston. Any of this ringing a bell?"

"Fuck you, Lee."

Lee cuts the overhead light, hunches forward, the crime scene lighting washing his face in shadow, his features all but vanished, except for feverish eyes burning hot and bright, like a poker player on tilt, all his chips in the middle and relying—no, not relying, *believing,* with a near-religious fervor—in the power and mercy of the river card to bail him out.

"So again, Zesty, insight is what I seek."

"Wrong mountaintop," I say.

"No, I don't believe so." Lee draws a small notepad from his breast pocket, flips it open, and molests himself for something to write with. "So," he says, "when did you last hear from your mother?"

FORTY-THREE

Will knows there are two things you can't do at a poker game and expect to come out ahead: You can't sit at the table with a limited time-frame in mind—say, three, five hours, whatever—and expect the cards to fall into that little box you've drawn yourself. Time doesn't like to be dictated to, nor does it give a fuck about your schedule; the cards, even less so.

The second thing you can't do is come in with a hard plan, say, playing only tens or better, three to a flush, wired trips of anything, because the cards have to be massaged sometimes; they need the action or they're liable to go to sleep on you. Come in with a script carved in stone, you might as well cut your nerves at the roots because you'll have no feel for the game whatsoever, that moment requiring bold action lost in the rigidity of your losing formula.

Poker's a game where you have to be willing to lose often and be sanguine enough to learn from it, which is a hard thing to do while still licking bleeding wounds. At the same time, you also have to forget the bad beats, the unexpected setbacks; wipe the slate clean and free your mind, not just to calculate how many outs are left when the time comes to river a pull, but to feel the cards, absorb the game's flow.

Ritter calls with a location, and though Will long ago began to prepare for a moment like this, as of right now McKenna has him playing blind, groping for a hand that eludes him at every turn. What are his choices? None.

To the river he goes.

FORTY-FOUR

"This sucks," Brill says.

"It's the only place I could think of that's open and nearby." I keep busy rubbing cuff-indented wrists, the paraffin test I'd taken after my chat with Lee leaving my hands powder slick. We're sitting in a back booth at the Blue Diner, waiting too long for the moonfaced waitress to take our order. The joint's half empty. Or half full, depending how you look at it.

"The only other option was cold tea and dim sum in China-town, and I'm not really in the mood for Chinese after Agent

Lee. By the way, cold tea"—I make quotation marks with my fingers—"is really a euphemism for beer. Did you know that?"

Brill stares at me deadpan. "Like I said. This sucks."

"I like it." Wells settles in. "It's got a nice retro feel to it."

"It's bullshit," Brill says. "How's the coffee?"

"Poor. But the food's mediocre and overpriced. You know you can't smoke in here."

"Does it look lit to you?"

"It stinks like it's lit."

"Christ, Zesty, do you ever stop?" Wells says, perusing the menu.

"You should talk." Brill wrinkles his nose at me. "You ever hear of deodorant?"

"Stop what?" I sniff under my arms, smelling only patchouli.

"Antagonizing people. Cracking wise." Wells sets the menu aside. "Or do you have, like, some kind of punning Tourette's type thing going on?"

"What he's trying to say, Zesty, is stay away from open-mike nights."

"So now it's contagious?" Wells looks askance at his partner, not a lot of love in his eyes. As a matter of fact, I've yet to really see the detectives on the same page. Even in the hospital they were stepping on each other's lines, and here again, small digs are brewing with a side order of asides. Then again, maybe this is how they renew their daily courtship, a constant tuning up doubling as foreplay.

"Not very friendly." Wells examines the waitress retreating after taking our orders. With his cultivated rough looks and swag shoes, he's probably used to more positive attention.

"You know her, Zesty?" Brill grins around the unlit cigar. "The whole time she jotting our order, she shooting you the evil eye like you stole her tip money."

"I think we made out once at a Black Crowes concert?"

"Zesty do get around, that's for sure."

"Perk of the job."

"We'll make sure they splash that on your tombstone," Brill says. "That'll explain everything."

"Almost everything. How about you bring us up to speed on that private sit-down you had with Lee."

"What, the FBI doesn't keep you guys in the loop?"

"FBI?" Wells rears back in his seat. "What FBI? It's just Agent Lee out there on his lonesome if you hadn't noticed. Everybody else is BPD. What kind of foolishness did that man pump into your head?"

I tell the detectives about the photographs, leaving out the questions about my mother to gauge what they know. From what I've read in the crime novels my father lovingly dog-eared, the FBI and local police rarely work in harmonic concert, the FBI swooping down to take control of cases as they expand in breadth and importance, getting the lion's share of the credit when things work out, the locals looking like little more than cooperative younger siblings smart enough to step out of the way as the chiseljawed professionals do their jobs.

Only, Agent Wellington Lee neither has a chiseled jaw nor appears to be relegating Detectives Wells and Brill to the bench while he does all the glorified heavy lifting. In fact, all he seemed to be doing was stacking bodies and stepping aside to let Brill and Wells run their leads. So what's the beef? And what does Wells mean by Lee being out on his own?

"That's all?" Wells sniffs a gap in my retelling as my dormant head static returns, reminding me I still need to get a hold of Sam to hear what he's learned.

"Lee seems pretty confident this is all one story." I tilt forward, trying to see if the signal strength changes. "That kind of clearance should make you happy, no?"

"And your friend Gus Molten fits in where?"

"He didn't say. You got a theory?"

"You mean one that doesn't involve Lee's pipe dream of the big bad wolf Devlin McKenna returning to his old stomping grounds? Absolutely. Darryl Jenkins, our man in the streets, is feeling the pain of overextending himself and trying to clean up loose ends. The gang unit and vice guys are convinced Jenkins screwed the pooch and flooded the market, and now it's just in the process of correcting itself."

"The medical examiner give you a time estimate for when Gus was killed?"

Brill and Wells glance at each other a moment before Brill answers. "Little after one A.M., thereabouts. We can pinpoint it like that, not on account of the ME, but we might have caught a break with a witness, dishwasher in one of your cold tea joints, taking a standing nap in a doorway on his way through another eighteen-hour shift. Doesn't speak a word of English, so we're waiting on the translator to show at headquarters where they have him stashed. Guy's probably crapping his pants, thinking he just punched a one-way ticket back to Shanghai."

"Did he?"

"Not if he saw something and draws us a picture."

"Even if he does, it won't be of Jenkins."

"Maybe not in person, but he could've farmed it out."

"I don't think so. Darryl's circle is pretty tight, and we cut a deal that he'd give me twenty-four hours to try and find Gus. And anyhow, doesn't SIS have Darryl covered?"

"That what Lee told you?" Brill barks a laugh. "He's full of shit. DJ's our man with the plan, and when everything shakes out, you're gonna see your friend Gus falls out of the same tree. Darryl Jenkins's move to the big time is going to be a short one, mark my words."

"Did Agent Lee speak to him?"

"Who?"

"Your witness, the dishwasher."

"Why?"

"Lee's Chinese," I say.

Brill and Wells look at each other again, an unspoken conversation passing between their eyes. "Cocksucker!" they say in unison, Wells slipping out of the booth punching buttons on his cell phone, nearly knocking the waitress over as she brings our food.

Brill and I eat in silence, chewing on more than just our meal, until Wells returns to continue a wordless discourse with his partner, the food now just fuel for the fire, the refilling of the coffee cups gas on the flames. I wonder if they've even slept the last two days.

Apropos of nothing, Wells says, "We think Lee has some of it right, actually. Sullivan, Coney, and Stavros are connected, not the least because the slugs taken from Sullivan and Stavros are a match from the Python we lifted in Roxbury. Coney's a little harder to figure, on account his ticket got punched the way it did, but if you hadn't noticed, it's been like a shooting gallery in some of these neighborhoods lately."

"He means *black* neighborhoods, by the way," Brill says.

"Don't listen to him," Wells tells me. "Your man there lives in Newton."

"That's because this black man's *earned* it."

"Absolutely. So the way we see it, Coney's the shooter for both Sullivan and Stavros and then fate plays her hand and Coney gets it where he least expects it."

"You're telling me Stavros was killed *before* Coney?"

"No doubt about that. The man was not fresh when he was found. A neighbor called the super about the smell; super dialed 911."

"I'm still eating," I say.

"Shit tends to even out." Wells shrugs. "Coney was the

makeup, outdoors, night sky, fresh air. Hell, you were there. Coney must have been a piece of work, playing hoops with a Python jammed down his shorts. It's a miracle he didn't shoot off his own balls grabbing a rebound."

"No hustle," Brill concludes. "Boy probably all dribble, no shot."

"Yeah, you would know. Lot of run out in the burbs?"

"Hey." Brill drops his fork on his empty plate and points to his crotch. "Did I tell you I was shooting a home movie? It's called *Suckit,* and auditions start in five, four, three—"

I get up to leave, but Wells clamps down on my wrist.

"What did I tell you, Zesty? Ignore him. Or better yet, don't listen to the actual words, listen for the subtext."

"I think the subtext was suck it," I say.

"It's just how we communicate." Wells waves a white napkin toward his partner in mock surrender. "When we do the math, all of this is going to add up to Darryl Jenkins, whether you had a deal with him or not. We have money from Black Hole that matches the Fargo truck and Sullivan. We got some of that same money *and* the gun off of Coney that he used to kill Stavros. I have a gut hunch that you know something that ties Molten to all of this deeper than what we already know, but you're holding pat. So what's left, what'd I leave out?"

Brill points his cigar toward his partner. "Lee's McKenna conspiracy."

"Right. Question being, is Lee going to fuck us when we try to hang this on Jenkins, because if there's one thing we've learned around these parts, it's that where the FBI and Devlin McKenna are concerned, things get fucked in a hurry. Which is where we think you can help us out, Zesty."

"How's that?"

"For starters, you can tell us what turned you into a ghost when we took you out of the car back on LaGrange. Lee hang something over your head that we don't know about? Something federal-y?"

"No," I say. "He asked me when was the last time I heard from my mother."

"You serious?"

"Rarely, but there you have it."

Brill: "And your answer was?"

"Too long ago to remember." Wells and Brill both frown at that, the look painfully clear: Even homicide detectives have mothers.

"I used to get postcards, sometimes a phone call. It's been a while."

"That was it?" Wells begins obsessively scratching his two-day beard, maybe realizing the time has come for another trimming.

"That and what he said about McKenna."

"What, that McKenna organized these guys to hit the truck?"

"Pretty much."

"And you think?"

"Who cares what I think?"

"He's got a point there," Brill says.

"Nah, I kind of want to hear it. Something's not right about Lee pumping Zesty for intel. He's reaching, but he's a slim motherfucker, and we're this close to clearing four bodies with one arrest, and we need to make sure he doesn't screw it up."

"You think Lee's holding out on you?"

"On both ends."

"Who, me *and* you?"

"Not you." Wells shakes his head. "You're practically part of the team here, breaking into suspects' houses, turning over clues and shit."

"Emphasis on shit," Brill laments.

"But by both ends I mean *us*." Wells makes a large circling motion with his hand. "And by the other end, I mean Lee's field office at Center Plaza. Because if I know one thing and one thing only, it's that the Boston chapter of Fart Barf and Itch wants nothing more to do with Devlin McKenna if it can help itself, and if you throw your mother, the radical, dangerous, and once—if you don't mind my saying—quite beautiful Diane Meyers into the mix, it becomes a two-for-one shame-and-failure spectacular. Lee doesn't strike me as a dummy, but he could be a fool, because if he thinks he's on to Devlin McKenna back in Beantown, he's on his own with nothing more than a wing and a prayer. McKenna's been in the wind going on thirteen years. He's not just going to come waltzing back to town to fit himself for a pair of bracelets and a shank in the neck the second he sets foot in a cell. And as much public noise as the bureau makes about wanting to get ahold of him, what they'd prefer is his liver-spotted corpse stinking up a motel room somewhere far away, like Brazil. And—no offense, Zesty—the same goes for your mother if she's still out there. Nobody wants to rehash the eighties and nineties again, especially this town. What with the Big Dig almost finished, you got the new waterfronts, property values going through the roof, and most of your bodies dropping in places your average taxpayer will never see.

"So Agent Lee? Fuck him and his theories. He's out there on his own, so don't think for a second you're in the middle of some massive manhunt or bureau reversal all-hands-on-deck-type shit. Lee got a couple days' SIS support to work on DJ because we went out on a limb for him, because it's three, now four bodies, the Wells Fargo job, and money laundering through Black Hole. And the powers that be want this shit wrapped up quick before it cuts into the tourist and convention trade. Not for a fucking nanosecond is this about Devlin McKenna and Diane Meyers, no way, nohow. If Lee's going to reach for the brass ring, he's going it alone. A wing and a prayer, dude. A chicken wing and a fucking player."

Wells looks at me and then gathers Brill for a stare-down in my direction, their eyes glowing despite the weak coffee and lack of rest, the full force of their collective gaze working on me like Vulcan mind meld. If we were playing cards, I'd probably lay down a good hand and second-guess myself into next week.

"Chicken wing and a fucking player." Brill sits back chuckling, impressed by his partner's play on words, the love growing in his heart. He beams me his first real smile, the cigar tilting toward the ceiling as the waitress drops the check, barely concealing her middle finger extended toward me.

"You following me, Zesty?" Wells's eyes are electric coils. If he looks at Brill, his cigar might catch a flame. "Out on his motherfucking own." He nudges the check in my direction. "Now, pay the damn bill. You're right, this place does suck."

FORTY-FIVE

The outer walls of the machine shop are corrugated metal panels dripping green tears off copper screws. Will's heard whispers about this place, about men who've entered on their own two feet only to exit via the drain at the center of the sloped cement floor. Stairs lead to a cluttered back room. An array of firearms and explosives are laid out on top of wooden packing crates.

"Just Diane." McKenna, his back to a plate glass window overlooking the machine shop floor, barely acknowledges Will before Ritter muscles him down the stairs, past Leila Markovich and a man

sporting an outdated handlebar mustache. Will gets in his car, turns over the ignition.

"Hey, Meyers." Ritter puts a flame to one of his cigarettes, motions with his hand for Will to roll down the window. "That heads-up game last night?"

"What about it?"

"That last card. What was it?"

"You really want to know?"

Ritter eviscerates him with butcher's eyes, reduces Will's anatomy to a diagram with dotted cutting lines.

"I didn't look."

"Like hell you didn't." Ritter rasps a cold laugh through smoke. "You're a degenerate, Meyers. You couldn't stop yourself if your fucking hands were tied behind your back."

"It was my third seven," Will says, swallowing hard.

Ah, so that's what a catbird smile on Ritter's face looks like. Hopefully he'll never see it again.

"You're fucking pathetic, Meyers." Ritter's cigarette glows like a stick of lava between his long fingers. "What was it?"

"A king of hearts." Will gives Ritter the fullness of his black eyes.

"Get used to the feeling." Ritter flicks the cigarette off Will's forehead.

It's true. Will acknowledges he's lost this game and will lose again, but what Ritter has yet to learn is knowing you are going to lose provides a serenity that allows you to absorb that bad beat on the horizon, that flush on the river that paralyzes those trip-nines you had on the turn. There's freedom in loss, the empty well. And anyhow, Will's plan has always been liquid because nothing lasts forever.

When Diane returns home, she'll provide the details, though at this juncture they hardly matter. For one reason or another, McKenna is making his move right now and has them both drawing dead.

Which means the time has come to change the game.

FORTY-SIX

Back at the loft, nobody's home. Nicolette could be anywhere, and David's left a note saying he'll be at his girlfriend's until the power is restored. In general, roommate notes tend to be exercises in passive-aggressive communication; I've opened the refrigerator door to find death threats related to cheese consumption, peered into mirrors to read lipstick scrawls detailing the sanctity of personalized towels. What David means by "I won't be back until the electric is on" is really "don't make *me* pay this bill, because you won't be happy when you see me in the light."

There are candles throughout my room, and I light them. My bed's half stripped, my two Persian rugs bunched and shredded at the corners courtesy of the cat, who has the uncanny ability to find the most expensive item in a room and ruin it.

The candle glow is soothing, the lights flickering off the worn spines of the plays and novels plucked from my father's once vast collection: Steinbeck leaning heavily on Arthur Miller, leaning on Tim O'Brien; the crime and mystery writers he enjoyed— Chandler, Cruz, Parker, Block—lurking in dark corners with Carver and Burroughs teetering drunkenly over the edge, competing to see who can hang the farthest off the shelf without falling down and out. Books are heaped on the floor, piled in corners; take a ticket, maybe I'll read you next.

Actually, that's a lie. I'm not nearly the reader my father was. My sole motive for salvaging his collection is rooted in a desire to stay connected to him. See, my father didn't just read books, he folded pages he enjoyed, circled whole paragraphs in pen, wrote responses, comments, and questions in the margins as if the stories were ongoing conversations he was having with the writers, arguments with the characters. I read my father's books to talk to him still, to resurrect a voice that's mostly gone missing, to remind myself of the man who lived on the sharp edges of a city that changed the rules on the fly, playing the middle in a lifelong game where the margin for error was as thin as the blade of a razor.

How much has changed? My father grew up in the West End, a neighborhood razed and replaced by parking garages and sterile high-rises that taunt commuters with a sign outside the gates that reads IF YOU LIVED HERE, YOU'D BE HOME NOW and that Zero and I would occasionally vandalize in his honor with alterations such as IF YOU LIVED HERE, YOU'D HAVE NO SOUL NOW or IF YOU LIVED HERE, YOU'D BE SUCKING DICK NOW. Who remembers the West End anymore? For all I know, my father resides there again—the distant past is so much closer for him than the present, the neighborhood streets alive and calling to him, the echo of the dead still ringing in his ears.

Was my mother's voice calling out to him too? She certainly wasn't calling out to me. When was the last time I heard from my mother? That's a cruel question to ask someone whose family history you have stuffed deep on a hard drive in some bureaucratic office. I can smell her, though, her scent familiar to me still because my father kept articles of her clothes when I was younger, the alchemy of her skin and perfume—rosewater and something like chamomile—a forever scent in my memory.

The bottle from her perfume is on my father's dresser, empty now, and it was years before I realized that every so often he'd been spraying my pillow, his covert way of keeping her present for me and maybe for him as well, her scent lingering into my teens as if she was always nearby, watching over us all. If my father still retains that olfactory memory, would the scent spark something in him if he caught it nearby, would he recognize her in mist, invisible, alive?

What I'd told Wells and Brill about my conversation with Agent Wellington Lee was the truth, but it wasn't the complete conversation by far. Lee had an interesting story to tell me, most of which I already knew, but parts of which read like some Bizarro World parallel universe: Following the Harvard bombing, my mother fell off the FBI's radar as if she'd suddenly stepped into a black hole and vanished off the face of the planet. Until Bank of Boston.

Bank of Boston changed everything for my mother, because even as former activists surfaced to resume their lives, she stayed under the radar, maybe traveling across the country, precursor to those sporadic postcards I would later receive when I was a boy, stamped in different states and then, without fail, confiscated by the FBI, who were also listening in on the static-filled phone calls I would sometimes get from her up until my tenth birthday, every word bugged and recorded; my mother playing with the FBI's feverish desire to find a rhythm to her contacts, a deep code as she defied habit and predictability.

She would call on Christmas Eve, even though we are Jewish. Three days after New Year's. Twelve days after my sixth birthday. Nine in the morning. Eleven thirty at night. Happy Kwanzaa. Mommy loves you. Take care of your father. He needs you.

Agent Wellington Lee is a fresh face, but the FBI is no stranger to me. Their presence, ironically, is one of the few constants in my life, something I could depend on. In a way, the FBI made missing my mother easier to deal with—her powers to thwart such a vast and organized entity breathed life into my imagination, my ability to cope with a highly irregular upbringing.

By 1980 my mother was living full-time in Boston—a fact that must rub salt into the wounds of the local FBI who failed to apprehend her—which is a few years before Zero, abandoned and left to the streets, was rescued by my parents. My father's deep connections in city and state government facilitated his legal adoption, but the paperwork was a mere formality; fate had thrown them together, and my brother's loyalty to my father has always been unyielding.

Some of this history is what the FBI has pieced together from a variety of sources, Lee admitted; some by what my father had proffered in his yearly debriefings, the FBI a constant presence in his life as well. He met my mother at a bar named Jack's on Mass Ave., where he ran a weekly Thursday-night poker game and my mother waitressed. A year later, they were married and living in Joan Baez's former apartment on the corner of Bow and Arrow Streets in Cambridge.

My father either never knew of my mother's radical past—unlikely, considering the personal narrative Brill shared with me in his car—or he knew and never spoke of it with us. Zero and I opted not to press him for any information in any capacity, our adolescent fears being that he would interpret our curiosity as a rebuke of the sacrifices he'd made to raise us on his own. Everything makes sense. Nothing makes sense. When was the last time I heard from my mother? How about when was the last time I cleaned my room?

I start by marrying trash and bringing it to the kitchen barrel. I stretch fresh sheets on the bed and light a stick of pine incense off a melting candle. I carry stacks of my father's books and find places for them on the shelves, pausing once in a while to reflect on a lurid cover or obscure subject I'd never known my father took an interest in.

"More books," I say out loud as the cat saunters into the room, fresh off a twenty-hour nap. "Less cats. Whattaya think of them apples?"

Not much. But he does regard the room with a quizzical

look, trying to figure out how to take up three quarters of the blanket now that it's spread evenly over the futon. When he figures it out, I join him with an edition of *Hamlet* I pulled from under the novel *My Ántonia,* good company even for a Danish prince.

My father folded many of the play's pages, and there are notes written in the margins in his loopy script, but there's no message in his words, no discourse on betrayal or loyalty; they're just notes, an *aha!* here, a *not to be trusted* there. By the time I skip to the ghost of Hamlet's father crying out for revenge, the cat's gathered the lion's share of the blanket.

"Murder?" says Hamlet. *Wake up!* wrote my father.

The candles dwindle. The cat rolls over and sticks his nose between his paws. Ophelia drowns herself in the stream. *Cry me a river,* scribbled my father. The queen drinks poisoned wine. Laertes and Hamlet take turns cutting each other with poisoned swords. My father's parting words: *An empty stage.*

It strikes me how simple those words are, yet in the context of his torturously slow exit, the observation is prescient. Only the ghosts remain. Or maybe I'm giving him too much credit, bending his words to fit the mess I've written myself into.

In 2004, when the Red Sox won their first championship in nearly a century, someone printed up T-shirts that read *What would Johnny do?,* a playful note referencing Johnny Damon, the messianic-looking BoSox center fielder who bore a remarkable resemblance to Jesus Christ. This is the question I would ask my father if I knew he could truly hear my voice. What would you do, Pops, if the legendary Boston mobster Devlin McKenna was back in town, dropping bodies and desperate enough now to trust someone like Darryl Jenkins to wash his blood money, yet still vicious and calculating enough to chase it down like a terrier going after a cornered rat? I'm listening. What would you do?

Well, here's what *I* do. I blow out what's left of the flames, nudge the cat, reclaiming my turf, and look toward the night sky on the second of what feels like the longest two days of my life. Though it'll be light in a couple of hours, the moon is still hanging in the corner of my window, a few clouds transparent as gauze drifting past, as stars surrounded by stars flicker high up in the heavenly distance, like Wells and Brill and Lee, just doing their goddamn jobs.

FORTY-SEVEN

I dream of my father.

He is in his element, whole again, sitting in the dealer's slot of an oval poker table, green felt, black border, smoke. I sit directly across from him, men in dark suits filling the other seats, their faces hidden inside a darkness that envelops the table's outer ring. Equal piles of black, red, green, and blue chips sit on the table just inside the border, stacked neatly in front of each player. My chips are a mess; that's how I always play them.

Superstitious.

"Seven Stud." My father spins cards around the table, the corners sticking like ninja stars. Another round makes two down and then he dishes faceup. Seven players. My up card is a three of spades; lowest card showing is forced into the initial bet. I throw in two black chips. I have no idea what they're worth.

"In the blind," my father says, meaning I've yet to peek my down cards. He smiles at me, the long crooked scar under his lip glowing. The table calls. My father deals another round of up cards. I get a black king to go with my three. A spade.

"Schizoid," my father says to me, "but spading." He taps the felt in front of the player directly to his right, showing a pair of queens. "Ladies," he says.

Ladies bets a stack of greens. I look at my down cards for the first time. Four of spades. King of diamonds. I have the queens beat. I call. The whole table calls.

"Family pot." My father peels off another round of up cards. Queens gets the king I was looking for. Somebody pairs up tens. I get a seven of hearts.

"Tens are new," my father says. He smiles, his off-color front teeth showing. "Queens still high and betting."

"It's good to be the queen," I say. "She gets high *and* she gets to bet."

"Shush." My father's smile is gone. "Queens high." He taps the space in front of the queens with a king.

"Queens high," I say. "I know someone who went to Queens High. Didn't graduate, though. I heard he was the joker of the class."

My father stares at me. I mime locking it up, tossing the key. Queens bets five blacks. Everybody calls.

"Pot's right. Last up card."

I get a five of spades. I have four cards to a flush, a gut-shot pull of any six to get a straight; a pair of kings. Queens gets another up queen.

"Triple ladies," my father says. "Betting."

Triple Queens pushes his whole stack forward. The table folds out of turn, grunts, and curses, the darkness and smoke swallowing the men whole. Except for me. I look at my down cards again.

"What are you thinking?" my father says.

"Lotta outs," I say. One more card coming if I call. A spade of any kind would give me a flush, the six would bring a small straight like Waltzing Matilda, and another king would make it triple kings. Any pair to go with the queens, a king or another queen has me beat even if I river one of the cards I'm looking for.

Devlin McKenna hunches forward over his cards, staring at me under lids frozen at half-mast.

"What are you thinking?" There's no judgment in my father's voice, just asking. I stare into McKenna's dead eyes, see my reflection.

"Pot value?" I say, calculating the pile in the middle, the odds.

Devlin McKenna's fingers are bony claws. He bends the cards as he holds them. His pupils dilate into skulls.

"Zesty?" my father says.

"All in." I push my mess into the middle. McKenna leans back into darkness.

"Last one down," my father says.

FORTY-EIGHT

Britta slips into my dream on a wave of vanilla surf, navigating the obstacle course of my room as if she's been here before, can pierce the dark with her vampire eyes. I breathe her in before I sense her physical presence, before I hear her clothes falling off like the rustle of a breeze through dune weeds, before she slips through the darkness into my bed and I open my eyes to see the eclipse of the snub-nosed revolver in her hand, feel the warmth of her body molding to mine, her bare chest pressed tightly against my back. We lie that way in the dark, the gun held loosely over my shoulder, the warm metal brushing against my chest, until the rhythm of our breathing becomes one, her warmth flooding my wounds, my pain evaporating, the tug of the stitches melting into flesh.

I want to tell her that Gus has been murdered, that Darryl will kill her if he finds her, that their greed has set into motion events that have spiraled out of control, forced me to make promises I can't keep, write checks I can't cash.

"Britta—"

"Shhh. Not now." She slips the gun past my head under the pillow, runs her hand down my chest, flat-palming the ridges of my stomach.

"They're looking for you," I say.

"But not here."

"Darryl—"

"What part of *not now* don't you understand?" Her hand slides lower, finds me. "This part of you understands just fine. You always ready this quick, Zesty?"

"Fastest messenger in Boston," I remind her.

"I hope not."

I turn over and she straddles me, bends forward and plants her forehead squarely between my clavicles under my chin, her hair splayed over the top of her head, exposing the white nape of her neck. Her elbows dig into my chest. With one arm she reaches under herself, the back of her wrist brushing me as she shudders and starts grinding her hips, the flesh of her thighs clamped tight against mine.

"You sure you need me for this?" The top of her head forces my chin toward the ceiling. I try to crane free, pulling her hair back hard.

"I want to watch," I say in a voice that belongs to Kermit the Frog.

"Don't, you'll go blind. Hold my hips." With her free hand, she pries my fingers loose from her hair. "Tighter."

She slides her hands under my waist, digs her nails into my

lower spine, searching my eyes in the darkness, swaying in pred-
atory rotations as I hold her. Her lips glisten. If she touches me, I
swear this will be over in an instant.

"I've been a baaad girl, Zesty," she purrs, her nails sinking
deeper as she slides her tongue around my ear. "Can you handle
a bad girl, baby?"

"I committed three felonies yesterday." I arch my back trying
to avoid puncture wounds.

"Not bad enough," she says, suddenly driving all her weight
backward, pulling me off the sheets on top of her, her hair whipping past my face as a liquid heat envelops me. Too fast! Her
movements are way too fast, her hips arched too high, too tight,
and it's been way too long.

"Oh no, not yet!" she pleads, pulling me down to her breasts,
as if that'll help prolong things.

Distraction. I need distraction, bad thoughts: Desk job. Kha-
kis and polo shirts. Telemarketing. Retail sales. Not good enough:
Collin Sullivan, a bloodied Cyclops splattered across a Wells Fargo
truck. Derrick Coney bled out under a rusted hoop. Gus sprawled
out in his piss-stained foyer on a bed of broken glass. An intersection marked with my own blood.

Not good enough. What the hell is wrong with me? But it
doesn't matter; she's already in the throes, already moving beyond
me, her whole body slick with sweat.

Does Britta hear the same thing I do, the thundering between our chests completely off tempo? Or is it just me, my awareness sharpened by the smirk of the moon glowing in its predawn
brightness, spotlight on poor choices, unprotected sex with vam-
pires and the self-loathing that accompanies the unspoken admission that if given the chance I'd probably do it all over
again.

Britta produces cigarettes, flicks the trigger of the gun, igniting a blue lick of flame from the barrel, and lies across the foot of

my bed propped on her elbows. Beside her sits an open gym bag crammed with tightly bundled wads of cash, the cat curled against her narrow milky waist, the round slope of her rear mooning the moon. Her nakedness is without modesty, and I figure it can go either way, her exposed body the absence of anything to hide or the ultimate distraction, a full-body bluff.

Does she know Gus is dead? Would I have slept with her if I didn't? It's the worst type of question: one that can only be answered with lies you're willing to believe yourself, like holding great cards but ignoring that sick feeling you're heading toward a bad beat and Brokesville. Sometimes you just *know*.

"Ashtray?" I can only see her face in the momentary glow of the cigarette.

"I don't smoke," I say.

"You're angry?"

"I tend to get moody after I've been taken advantage of."

"I *forced* you?" Britta finds this possibility amusing.

"Angry at myself."

"Don't be. You're not nearly the fastest messenger in Boston."

"I wasn't talking about that. Whose idea was it, yours or Gus's?" I say.

"What part of it?" Her voice is raspy, tired, and I realize that I'm not going to be the one to tell her that Gus is gone, that I'm too selfish, too emotionally spent to comfort her if she truly cares. At the moment, my sperm count's probably hovering in the dozens.

"I don't know. You can start with the dealing, work your way up to the hard stuff."

Britta lights a fresh cigarette from the old one, two flares, like fiery eyes alighting her face, the vices she'd claimed to be kicking returning in spades.

"Gus was already dealing when we started dating. . . . Did I just say *dating*? That's so quaint. When we hooked up. Not a whole lot of courtship, but there you have it. He'd started with a few of his accounts, stockbroker types. I guess fleecing the market isn't enough of a high. I don't think your dispatcher knew."

"She didn't." Martha unwittingly running point, living within the same rules that govern her couriers—don't ask, don't tell.

"Gus was fed up with Black Hole." Britta hides behind the smoke and darkness. "Even though it was Ray who signed him to a record deal in the first place, which on the surface sounds great if you're trying to pick up girls at a bar, but whatever money Gus had coming was tied to the record release. And Ray kept pushing the date back."

"Why?"

"I don't know. They had a pretty stormy relationship, and after a while Ray used the recordings to bait him. And since Gus had the company account, he had to see him practically every day. Sometimes Ray just had Gus pick up shit to torment him, remind him that all he'd ever be without him was a messenger." Britta blows smoke in my direction. "No offense."

"Offense taken," I say.

"Yeah well, when Gus bankrolled some decent money with the coke, he got it into his head he could buy back Gizzard's master recording, offer Ray something above what the advance amounted to, and Ray could pocket the difference for basically doing nothing."

"You told Gus that Darryl Jenkins was boss?"

"Only after he got curious enough about the runs that he finally opened one of the packages."

"Gus told you he did that?"

"Not right away. But when he did, I told him he should talk to DJ, go over Ray's head about the record, but he was too intimidated. DJ always had these two scary guys with him, and he was legit street. He wasn't very approachable. And Gus also figured if

Darryl found out he was dealing coke to people he met through the Black Hole account, there'd be trouble."

"Because you knew Darryl was washing money?"

"I don't even know what that means."

"He was running drug money into the business."

"Or something. Why have Ray acting boss if everything's on the up-and-up, right? That's why Gus figured he could buy back the recording. DJ didn't have day-to-day dealings with the business; me and Darcy took care of things like that, contracts, concerts, advertising. If Gus could convince Ray to sell back the recordings, then anything above the advance money paid out for studio time and producer's fee was Ray's to keep, free and clear. And DJ didn't need to know anything about it."

"But Valentine refused," I figure out loud. "Why?"

"Because he was too scared of what would happen if Darryl found out."

And rightly so.

"How often did large amounts of money come in? Had to be a lot, considering the move to Newbury."

"It was pretty steady from all the club shows we've been promoting. And we reissued a couple of Lobster Rock compilations that started selling, so there was that. There was always a lot of money moving around from the ticket sales and merchandising. Gus had made multiple runs to Roxbury where you were heading before he . . ."

"Ran me over with your car?"

"That wasn't the plan. Not exactly. It's true Gus wanted the money he'd been delivering, but mostly he wanted to put Ray in a bind over the missing cash. He figured that if DJ was really the OG type he looked like, then he'd make Ray repay whatever was lost. Or else. Ray doesn't have that kind of money, so Gus figured he'd create a seller's market, force Ray to sell him back the master recordings."

"And if he refused, then you'd keep the money and what, take over for Ray when Darryl demoted him into an unmarked grave? That's pretty cold, Britta."

"Yeah? Well it's the music business, Zesty. If I was in charge, Gus would have gotten his record cut and promoted like it should've been." Britta drags, glows, fades to black.

"How'd that work out for you?"

"It didn't. But it's not too late. Gus and I'll split the money with you. There's almost a million dollars in that bag."

I try to read Britta's eyes through the smoke, see only my reflection in the glow of the cigarette. "No? I guess I'm not surprised. Gus said you were different. He admires you, Zesty. You ought to know that. He respects you because you're real, you know, *content*? He said you knew who you were and that you'd never change, no matter what. Didn't need to change. You get what I'm telling you?"

"I think so."

"He also said that you could get hit by a truck, brush yourself off, and walk away like nothing happened. That you've done it before, you were a pro. He freaked when you went down like you did and the money went everywhere."

But not enough to stop and check on me.

"How much money was in the safe when you gave me the fifty?"

"Everything that's in this bag."

"Why did you take it?"

"I don't know! I panicked after you got hit and expected the police to show up any minute."

If I survived the collision. Though she wasn't too panicked to call Martha and tell her I never showed to make the pickup.

"Did you know the money came from the Wells Fargo robbery?"

"I figured it out."

"How?"

"Like I said, money had been coming in steadily, but it started picking up last week like crazy." Darryl's money rolling in as the flood of drugs was converted to cash. "I knew something big had happened, and the armored car thing was all over the news."

"And you figured Darryl was good and fucked as soon as the police got involved, that there'd be nobody left to claim the money."

Britta's unaware that the money has more than one owner, that, if Agent Lee is to be believed, the whole thing has been orchestrated by Devlin McKenna, back in town after more than a decade on the run and, for reasons I can't even begin to fathom, crank-calling my senile father from the abyss.

So who killed Gus going after the million now sitting on my bed? Darryl? Otis? McKenna? They were all after it.

Britta's cigarette goes dark as she finds something to stub it out on, and I'm suddenly beyond tired, a delayed postcoital fog rolling heavily across my eyes, and though I can hear Britta saying my name, I let my lids close to black, not interested in any role she might have concocted for me to try to make things right. It's too late for that, as she'll find out soon enough. But not from me—not my girl, not my problem—too late and Nyquil blood running through my veins. Too little, too late, Dilaudid sleep. Morphine dreams. Never count your money when you're sitting at the table.

Story of my goddamned life.

FORTY-NINE

"There are five of us," Diane says, gently taking Will's hand from her belly. Already? She is preparing herself and Will is reminded: She's done this before. "There's a girl inside that's just come through their teller program. When the bank is at the peak of their holdings, she'll place a call. That man with the mustache you saw coming in, his name's Michael Drain. His girlfriend showed after you left. Then there's Leila and me."

"That's too many," Will says.

"By one at least. The girl on the inside's a given. Drain and his girlfriend can both handle guns, but so can Leila and I."

"Not you. McKenna wants you for explosives, Leila and Drain for the guns. The girlfriend will drive. What're the explosives for?"

"Diversion."

"Where?"

"Police station on Washington, across from St. Elizabeth's. There's construction on the front stairs at the main entrance."

"They're closed off completely?"

"Only on one side. It's all wrong."

Will understands she's talking about the danger posed to bystanders, innocents.

"How does Leila fit into this?"

"I don't know. We split ways after the Harvard thing—you know all about it. She wanted human targets, and I was done at that point. I thought she'd surface, cut a deal like everybody else. . . . McKenna must have something on her like me."

"It's a suicide run." Will sees it clearly now, open to the game.

"He's gathering expendables and taking a shot in the dark. Maybe with the exception of Drain, nobody's robbed a bank before. If you pull it off, he'll let Ritter loose on whoever makes it back with the money. If you fail, he washes his hands of it. That's why he wants to blast the police station, to make sure every cop in Boston shoots first and asks questions later. Cop killers don't make it back to the station house."

"But why? Why now?"

"I don't know. Maybe he's getting ready to run." Will's heard rumors before; there's always talk. And then somebody disappears, and it's not McKenna.

"We can run," Diane whispers, but her heart's not in it. McKenna's found her once, perhaps found Leila too in the same way. "So that's it, then? We do as he says and then he kills us, our baby? What about Zero and Zesty? That's it?" She allows the tears to flow freely now, not for herself, because in actuality, she has lived longer than she ever imagined she would, fuller, happier.

"No," Will whispers in her ear, taking her into his arms. "That's not it at all." The game will go on. Just not the way McKenna planned it. "I've made arrangements."

FIFTY

I wake to the sound of breaking glass, a rock skittering across the floor, Britta gone, the cat perched atop the money still at the foot of my bed. "Zesty!" From the littered field behind the loft. "Goddamn it, I know you're in there!"

I stick my head above the ledge and spy Tom Foley crabbing grass, hunting another missile. Tom runs Honeycomb Rehearsal on Harrison Avenue in one of the few buildings not owned by Spagnola. He rents relatively soundproofed rehearsal spaces by the month—think padded eggshell foam cubicles— and maintains a recording studio at the back of the building in case a band generates four minutes of alcohol- or drug-fueled inspiration and wants to burn a disc before the genius eludes them.

"What the fuck, Tom!" I pop up before he reloads. "I have a doorbell!"

"No you don't. Albert says he disconnected your buzzer from the battery. Said it was sending him weird signals. Hell of a doorman you got!"

"Put that fucking rock down! What do you want?"

"Does that guy Sid still work for your brother?"

"What?"

"Hulk Hogan. Does he—"

"What about him?"

"The fuckin' jamook's in my studio right now holding down guys from Cliff Note like hostages at the Munich Olympics. He already put a beating on Gary G, and now he's playing with my soundboard like he's Dr. Dre. He don't seem right. I don't know if he's always like this or he's on something or what."

"So?"

"So it's like the inside of a fucking bong down there, but as soon as the place airs out, which is like real soon 'cause I've been running the fans, I'm calling the cops."

"So call them," I say. "Or call Zero."

"You still got pavement stuck between your ears, Zesty?"

"Listen, Tom—"

"You gonna come help me out with this or what? The last time someone with a badge walked through the studio, I bought my lawyer an outdoor pool. And I can do without your brother pulling on my ear if Hogan gets busted, but I got expensive equipment in that studio, and I know he ain't paying for it if it gets broke."

"Broken," I correct him. "Broke is when you have no money."

"You should know."

"You going to pay for this window?" I say.

"Who're you kidding? I hear you're out of there end of the month."

"Where'd you hear that?"

"Word gets around. A little birdie told me Spagnola's already got Realtors walking through your loft, creaming their pants. You coming or not?"

There are two battered vans parked in front of the studio loading up for a road trip somewhere, the drummer getting the worst of it, the most moving pieces, set it up, break it down, watch as the singer or guitarist cherry-picks all the front-row girls.

It's a little past noon, and bands are already rehearsing, the hall leading to the rear studio vibrating with the collision of percussive beats. The door to the recording room's closed, and a kid with questionable piercings is leaning with his ear pressed to the wood, his eyes wide with either horror or delight.

"Oh shit, I think he just shot Dave's drums. You know this guy, Zesty?"

"Zesty knows everybody," Tom says. "He's like the mayor of Shitsville. You've got ten minutes, and honestly, I don't give a fuck if this place gets shut down. You hear those guys rehearsing?"

"Which guys?"

"My point exactly. Doesn't matter. A month of the same shit, and nobody's gotten a lick better. Who am I to step on another man's dream, but somebody needs to break a reality check over some people's heads before I lose my hearing."

Sid is at the soundboard, perched on a high swivel stool, playing with dials and switches, giving everything a whirl. I don't see a gun. The space is tight but lush, Persian carpets, filtered stand-up microphones, and Sid's captive audience looking aggrieved and distracted, too self-possessed even in their state of siege to give Sid their full attention. Only Gary G has any marks on him, a bloody nose and a bruise on the side of his cheek; the other guys just look disheveled, but then again, that's their look.

Sid flips a switch, says, "Take five, guys," and swivels to me. "Goddamn, Z, I've been looking all over for you."

"I'm just around the corner, Sid."

"Your buzzer's not working. You ever check in with your office? I left messages too."

"Let's get out of here, Sid."

"What's the rush? I was just getting started. You know these dorks?"

"Yeah. What's the problem?"

"You know Jhochelle's friend, Mo, works the stick at the Franklin? Well, a couple months back, she had her cousin staying with her for the weekend, brings the kid to this all-ages show at the Paradise? These idiots are on the bill, haven't even gone on yet; Mo's cousin goes missing. She's what, sixteen, lives way out in the boonies, you know, like where they burn their garbage instead of throwing it out. Half an hour, they don't see her. They gotta practically claw their way backstage to find her in some storeroom. This asshole, the one with blood coming out his nose, is feeding her wine coolers out the box, her shirt's over her head, and this punk's pants are unzipped. He's lucky security got there before Jhochelle got ahold of him. I'm just squaring things, making sure something like that don't happen again."

I have to smile, this coming from a guy who yesterday was advocating sex with dead women in bushes, one last twirl before eternal chastity.

"What about the other guys?" I say.

"They thought they were tough guys."

"You mean they aren't?"

"Where you been, Zesty? Really, I been to all your spots. Your name's poison in this town, by the way. What the fuck *you* been up to?"

"Walk with me, I'll tell you. How'd you end up here?"

"Took a detour when I spotted these chuckleheads."

"Time to let them go," I say.

"You asking or telling me?" Sid looks at me hard but can't keep a grin from taking shape beneath his blond Fu Manchu. "Shee-it, Zesty. Who's the tough guy now? Hell, they could've left anytime they wanted. I was just fucking around with the board. The door ain't locked. What am I, a zookeeper?"

When we get outside, the sun is beaming directly overhead, the glare off the sidewalk causing us to shade our eyes. "Man, look at this place. They can't build shit fast enough. What's with the bag?"

"Don't worry about it." I shift the money to my other shoulder.

"You own the building you live in, Zesty?"

"For Chrissakes, Sid, spit it out."

"It's your dad." Sid squints painfully into the sunlight. "He's gone missing."

FIFTY-ONE

Change the game.

It's hard for Will to veer from what he does best, but the cards he's holding can't get him out, no matter how well he plays them. See, the trick in this game is to get the mark to that warm fuzzy spot where, down to the marrow in his bones, he thinks he's got everything all figured out.

Three years Will waited before switching locations on the first bundle of McKenna's money, practicing what he preached, playing the long game. He had no doubt McKenna would check the early spots, double-verify the pictures and storage bills, the treasure maps and stash houses. He was too careful, too cunning not to, and Will knew he didn't even trust Ritter enough to let him in on the retirement drive. There might be prying eyes on McKenna, but if he didn't have the ability to go ghost once in a while, he would have been dead or in prison a long time ago.

So Will was forced to play it blind, odds or evens, heads or tails; it hardly mattered. Saint Paul. Oneonta. Glendale. Closer to home too. Orchard Beach. Montpelier. Why not? As far as Will is concerned, every dollar moved, hidden someplace else, is house money. Does Will believe in luck? No. What he believes is that McKenna will kill him and Diane whenever he decides the time has come. And in that he's right. The time has come.

Change the game again.

FIFTY-TWO

Alzheimer's is a losing disease, the car driving off to park itself on a different street, the keys turning to Mexican jumping beans, never where you left them last, your unlaced shoes a mystery to behold, like cracking Nazi code. The physical tells come next: hygiene, hair, the same clothes worn day after day. And then one morning a walk around the corner ends up as a picture on the back of a milk carton. *Have you seen this man?*

According to Sid, my father wandered off around the time Gus was killed on LaGrange, as sudden an ending to his life as my father's drawn-out decline, Gus's spirit—if you believe in such things—joining the walking ghost of my father beating bricks in pajama pants, a blue Gap sweatshirt and tennis sneakers with orthotics to ease his arch pain as his walk has turned into a flatfooted shuffle that quickly wears the bottom of his soles. If my father walked through a dirt field, you would swear they were laying train tracks behind him.

"You give all that to the Brookline police?"

"See, Zesty, here's the thing." Sid grimaces, tugs his walrus mustache with both hands. "My piece is missing."

"Your *piece*?"

"My gun," Sid explains.

"I know what a fucking piece is, Sid. What I wanna know is what you're doing at my dad's with a goddamn gun." I feel awkward talking to Sid like this, not the least because he could snap me like a twig, but also because he's my elder and someone I respect. Only nothing he's telling me is coming off right.

"Just following orders, Z."

Meaning Zero's. Why Zero thinks Sid needs a hammer while caring for my dad totally eludes me. My father lived his whole adult life working a very thin margin, but those days are behind him now, maybe even forgotten. Did he have enemies, people who held grudges? It's not unlikely; after all, somebody had to lose at my father's poker games.

"Jesus. This is like a shitty country song. My dad's crazy, and he's got a gun."

"And I don't gotta tell you, it ain't registered. Let's just hope he keeps it out of sight."

"Is it reliable, Sid? Loaded?" I don't know why I hadn't thought to ask that sooner. My own brain must be working at half speed, the first of its daily caffeine injections way past due.

"Course. What good's an empty gun?"

"Right."

"Hey, don't get all fuckin' pissy, Z. If you're asking me does it got, like, a hair trigger or anything, the answer's no. But it's a solid piece."

And my father knew where it was kept. Or did he just stumble across it?

"Did you notice anything out of the ordinary, Sid? Anything that might have caused him to do something different, out of his routine? Was he worked up over anything?"

"We was watching *Rounders* again, just like when you stopped by." Sid stops to think, makes a face like he's cracking a safe. "He got another crank call late, after I put the movie on. That same dead-air motherfucker I was telling you about, only this time he's yapping. Wants to speak to your dad. After I told him again how I was gonna fuck him up, I finally let him know your dad has Alzheimer's, but he didn't care, said your pops would remember him."

"You put him on?"

"I figured one time, so the prick would finally get he's wasting his breath. Only your pops just stood there listening and then we went back to watching the movie."

"And you got no idea who this guy is, Sid?"

"Not a fucking clue, Z. You ask me, maybe he's a little touched himself, got his own wires crossed."

"Why do you say that?"

"On account of I could hear the fucker, and all he kept saying was 'I want my fucking money. Bring me my fucking money.' Over and over. Fuckin' loon probably thinks he's calling his broker at Morgan Stanley."

"And my dad didn't say *anything*?"

"Well, nothin' that makes sense. Something about channel eleven."

"And . . . ?"

"The fuck hung up, and that was that. Only your dad kept saying it, channel eleven. So I change the channel to eleven." Sid laughs and pokes me lightly in the chest. "And your dad, he almost bites my head off. Fuckin' Matt Damon."

FIFTY-THREE

The men who have clocked long hours in my brother's employ, meaning those who've resisted their recidivist tendencies—the thrill of the caper, the call of the gun—walk as if they've taken a Cro-Magnon step backward on the evolutionary chart. There's a stoop to their shoulders as if they're bracing for a body shot to the kidneys, as if their spines have been compressed, not so much by the weight of the world as the weight of their collective hauling—narrow staircases, awkward life turns.

As Charlie pointed out, with the police it shows in the way they carry themselves, though I can read it just as clearly in their cynical eyes and downturned mouths. With the men and women who ride a desk and computer, log too many hours in hotel and airport lounges, it's their flattened rear ends and outsized bellies that tell their stories, limited range of motion, aching backs, carpal tunnel hands. My point being, you do something long enough, eventually the job becomes you; the body *is* the work.

For the man sitting in the client chair across from Jhochelle, it's the orator's posture and chalk-white mane, on its own looking capable of spinning a compelling argument to a skeptical jury. Plus, I've seen a handful of Andrew Tetter's press clippings over the years, so there's that.

"Where's Zero?" I ignore Leila Markovich's celebrity defense lawyer as he pulls himself to his feet with some difficulty.

Jhochelle blinks, taking in my new haircut, bending her words around me when she speaks. "Sydney, would you be so kind as to get us all some coffees?"

"*Sydney?*" I crane to look at Sid behind me grinning like a starstruck tourist. Jhochelle has that effect on men. Lithe and dangerous in camouflage pants and an army green T-shirt, she's olive skinned, of Yemenite descent; a pinup girl of the Mediterranean who can assemble an Uzi with her eyes closed. Who could want anything more from a girlfriend?

"Watch your mouth," Sid warns me with a raised finger.

"Zero's downtown," Jhochelle says, impatiently. "Zesty, this is—"

"Sid told me Zero was out looking for Dad."

"He is. Sydney, those coffees please?"

"Screw the coffees." I can't believe I just said that. "This is bullshit. Listen, counselor, leave a card. Now's not the time for whatever you're selling."

"You know who I am?" Andrew Tetter lets drop the hand I neglected to shake. For someone who must be on the far side of seventy, he's still a big man, his age showing mostly in his thin legs, which seem to cause him pain as he straightens them.

"Yeah. Give your press secretary a raise. What's Zero's plan? Where're the crews looking?"

"Sydney?" Jhochelle sighs heavily, and Sid grabs me hard by my shirt collar and wraps me in a cobra embrace, his tree-trunk arms making even Cedrick's outsized guns look like kindling.

"You'll have to forgive the kid, Mr. Tetter. I don't think he's had his bong hit this morning."

"Now is the time for listening, Zesty." Jhochelle fixes me with sniper eyes. "Which means with your mouth closed. Our guest can explain just about everything you need to know if, by some miracle, you manage to hold your tongue for a couple of minutes. Do you think you're capable of doing that, so we can discuss what needs to be done, or are you just content with making a scene?"

"I'll shut up," I say. "But I want Sid to hold me. He smells like Aqua Velva, and I like it."

Sid plants a rough kiss on my cheek and pushes me away.

"*Nu,* first order of business." Jhochelle rolls an empty seat beside her, motions for me to sit. "Your brother is downtown, as I've said, ostensibly to enlist other resources that might aid our search for your father."

"What's that supposed to mean, resources?"

"Just that. Figure the rest out yourself."

"A bunch of fucking crooks," I say.

"My, what an imagination you have. Mr. Tetter, would you be so kind as to update Zesty on what is occurring?"

"Certainly. First off, Zesty, you need to understand everybody in this room wants the same thing, to find your father before any harm comes to him. But his disappearance is far more complicated than you suspect."

"How?"

"You know your father is armed?"

"Yeah, armed and forgetful, great combo."

"How forgetful?"

"*What?*"

"Has he ever, to your knowledge, fired a gun before?"

"Jhochelle, counselor, what the fuck is this crap? Just get to the point so I can get out there and look for him."

"And where would you look for him?" Tetter abandons any effort to keep the frustration from his voice, probably unaccustomed to being interrupted by anything less than somebody in a dark robe banging a gavel. "Is there someplace specific you would go to find him? Someplace he's talked about returning to?"

"No."

"So listen, then. And answer the questions that are asked of you. Has your father ever used a gun before?"

"Not as far as I know. That a good thing or bad?"

"Hopefully we won't have to find out. Here's the short of it, Zesty, since you're in such a hurry: Your father is indeed missing, only I'm not so certain he's just wandering around aimlessly."

"Then you don't know shit, counselor." I spring to my feet. "And you're wasting our time. My dad's got Alzheimer's in the worst fucking way. He doesn't even know what *year* it is, let alone day. The world we live in, those streets out there, none of it's there for him anymore, you understand that? It doesn't exist. For Chrissake, he has conversations with people who've been dead for thirty years. He's lost."

"No, I don't think so." Andrew Tetter's deeply lined face is painted with a smile that's so kind, so understanding, all I want to do is rip into it with my fists.

"Your father may be out of time perhaps, but I'm not convinced he's entirely lost. And though I can't say for certain I know exactly where it is he's heading, I'm reasonably sure I know who he's looking for and what he expects to find."

"So that's a good thing," I say.

"No," Andrew Tetter says, shedding his lawyerly demeanor and shaking his head. "It's the worst fucking thing possible."

FIFTY-FOUR

These are the questions Will asks himself now: What is that weight in his pocket throwing his step off balance? When did he become invisible, people walking through him as if he didn't exist? Where is he? The psychedelic CITGO *sign, a triangular beacon, points him toward Commonwealth Avenue, helps him find his bearings toward the South End. Warren Avenue . . . Columbus Avenue . . .*

Home . . . Zero smiling at him beside the bed, Zesty still asleep.

"Why are you crying, Daddy?"

"Am I crying?"

"Are you scared?"

"Yes, I'm scared."

"Of what?"

"It doesn't matter, but it's okay to be scared. As long as you're ready for what's next, scared is good. Scared will keep you on your toes."

Devlin McKenna helps. He doesn't make it right, of course, but he makes it real when it dawns on him that Diane will not be acting in this snuff film he's directing. McKenna's rage helps, because it is Will's rage too that McKenna is channeling as he smashes Will's front teeth with a cut-off length of pipe, the pain only coming as the electric air rushes in to hit the exposed nerves dangling like loose wire from Will's gums. The blood helps too, because there has to be a price to pay for something that hurts so deep beneath the surface; something has to show, and when the pipe rips Will's jaw so wide he can actually feel his bottom teeth jutting through the hole, through the gushing red, he thinks to himself, Yes, this feels about right. This will serve as a reminder every time he looks in the mirror, every day his tongue finds this raised worm of flesh. This he will never forget. This scar will be his gift.

And the beauty of it all is on that very next October day, the pain helps him focus as he sits idling in front of Bank of Boston, the lipstick of a drunken clown smeared on his swollen face. Glance in the mirror: At least he shaved before the beating, but don't kid yourself; even without the bruises and swelling, Will does not make a pretty woman.

FIFTY-FIVE

"Perhaps the best way to start is by explaining Leila Markovich's parole to you." Andrew Tetter regains some flexibility in his legs moving about the office. Like me, he's more comfortable when he's on the go.

"I read the *Globe* article a couple days ago."

"Then you know her initial appeal was rejected, only to be reversed weeks later."

"Pissing off the governor."

"By all appearances. Which is the public face one would expect him to display considering the difficult position he finds himself in, eyeing a run for the senate next year. Only, it was the governor himself who ordered the board to grant Leila's early release. All the Sturm und Drang about a recission hearing was nothing but smoke to feed the media and sate the public outrage. There will be no hearing, mark my words. The board sits at the governor's pleasure; you think they'd actually buck him on such a high-profile prisoner, a former self-declared enemy of the state?"

"Why should I be interested in this?"

"Because it's more than local politics I'm explaining to you."

"Then I don't get it. What does Leila Markovich's parole have to do with my dad?"

"You've met Agent Lee of the FBI?"

"Yeah. So has Zero. But what he's dealing with has nothing to do with my father. It's a completely different mess."

"Or one that's spilled into the other. Agent Lee is not quite what he appears to be, and from what I can tell from my discussion with your brother, he has vastly misrepresented himself."

"He's not FBI?" My temples start to throb, either caffeine withdrawal or my internal DJ angling for a return to the airwaves.

"No, he's a legitimate FBI agent. But in many ways he is also a radical quite in the vein of other radicals Ms. Markovich has associated with and whom I have, in the past, represented. By which I mean that Lee, if you haven't deduced this on your own, is a fanatic of the most dangerous sort. Dangerous in part because he is resourceful, yes, but mostly because his obsession runs so deep it has obliterated every other aspect of his life, to the point where it has compromised his judgment."

"You sure we're talking about the same Lee? The guy I met looks like an accountant."

"Yes. On the surface, to look at him, Lee is all glide. He appears to function as a bureaucratic cog within his organization, but he burns with a fever that, at the very least, will cost him what remains of his career."

"Really? I know a couple of homicide cops who'd tell you his only problem is he's got a Devlin McKenna fixation."

"I would argue that 'fixation' understates Lee's pursuits. Though Leila would be the last to complain, seeing how he is solely responsible for the parole board's turnaround and her release."

"How?" Jhochelle pipes in from behind the desk, caressing a cigarette without lighting it. "How does an FBI agent who seems to be chasing the tail of a ghost influence the governor of Massachusetts to override his own appointed board and release a convicted murderer? I don't mean to echo Zesty's impatience counselor, but could you get to the fucking point already?"

"But I have, my dear. Agent Lee *is* the point. In his dogged pursuit of Devlin McKenna, it appears Lee has gotten ahold of sensitive documents belonging to the bureau. Documents that would prove damaging to the FBI and therefore the governor's national ambitions if made public."

"Gotten ahold being a euphemism for, what, stolen?"

"So it seems."

"And you know this because?"

"Lee contacted me prior to Leila's second hearing and informed me he was in possession of these documents. He told me what the outcome of Leila's second parole hearing would be if I called for one."

"So you did."

"Yes. And you know the result."

Jhochelle and I take a minute to connect the dots: Lee to Markovich to McKenna to my father out wandering the streets. All I come up with are more questions.

"Why would Lee steal something that belongs to his own organization, and then use it to free your client?"

"Former client," Tetter clarifies. "I no longer represent Ms. Markovich."

"Whatever. Why bust Markovich out of prison if his only goal's finding Devlin McKenna? What's in it for him? And why tell you about it?"

"My suspicion is that whatever Lee has unearthed in connection with Ms. Markovich's case and by extension, I suppose, your mother's poses a problem for the governor and the FBI, a problem to the degree that Leila's release was orchestrated as it was. I think Lee considered the deliverance of Leila's parole as a down payment on authenticity, a validation of his pursuits. He wanted to show me how powerful these documents were without actually showing them to me. Initially, I took Lee's ramblings to be those of a madman. But the board acted just as he said it would. Obviously, these documents, whatever they contain, are quite valuable to the FBI."

"Then why do you look like you just lost a case, counselor?"

"Because, to be perfectly honest, I'm not sure Leila's altogether sane after all she's been through and because I have the nagging suspicion Lee's set into motion forces that are spiraling out of his control, your father's wandering being an unfortunate offshoot of that."

"You think Ms. Markovich is dangerous?" Jhochelle finally tosses the cigarette aside.

"Yes. Certainly to herself. To others . . . ?"

"*What* others? Can you be more specific than that? And how does it tie Mr. Meyers to Devlin McKenna?"

"I'm not so sure it does. Zesty, when your father was running his poker games, was he ever compelled to pay tribute to McKenna or any other outfit operating at the time?"

"You mean protection money?"

"Yes. Was he extorted?"

"I'm just speculating here, but I know the DiMasis took a piece of everything back then. My dad's games moved around a lot but not really into townie neighborhoods like Southie or the North End, so I don't see why he'd pay McKenna a dime. Most of my dad's influence and protection came out of city hall, at least when Kevin White was mayor. Only they called it doing business in those days, not extortion."

"As they still do. I often heard in chambers that your father was a poker player to be admired."

"My dad was good at a lot of things," I say.

"My intention was not to insult. I ask about the prospect of tribute payments only because after the DiMasis' organization was dismantled, there was a power vacuum in the Boston underworld, which we all know was quickly filled by McKenna, whom we later learned was protected by the FBI. I'm just trying to establish a link between McKenna and your father, that perhaps he continued payments to McKenna in the DiMasis' absence."

"Like the transfer of a debt?" I give the prospect some thought but don't really see it.

"So Mr. Meyers paid or didn't pay McKenna to operate. Why does it matter?" Jhochelle gives us her back, staring out the window toward the lumberyard behind the warehouse.

"It probably doesn't. But it's long been Leila's contention that McKenna orchestrated Bank of Boston and the station house explosion that she and her cohorts committed, your mother included, of course. That would be a direct link. I looked into her claims years ago, even went so far as interviewing McKenna's former bodyguard Richard Ritter in prison, but I could find nothing that linked the robbery to McKenna."

"Ritter could have been lying," Jhochelle says.

"Absolutely. Ritter already had his federal deal. Any new revelations of crimes committed could be held against him."

"So he wasn't compelled to tell the truth," Jhochelle says, sharply. "There was nothing in it for him except more time behind bars."

"Unfortunately, that's correct."

"Where's Ritter now?"

"Part of his deal was admittance into the Federal Witness Protection Program upon his release. I assume he's still under their protection as of this moment. Where, I couldn't tell you."

Jhochelle swivels back to us. "So then what would Markovich

gain by tying the robbery to McKenna? Certainly not leniency from the court. What was her angle?"

"I wish I knew. Her surrender a few years after the robbery was out of what I took to be, at the time, a serious case of paranoia, an irrational fear of McKenna. So much so that I harbored reservations about even representing her. It was only when she was attacked in prison that first week that I reconsidered and thought there might be some merit to her assertions."

"Does Ms. Markovich have any inkling Agent Lee is behind her release?"

"If she does, the information didn't come from me. But if she knows even that much, I don't think she fully comprehends that Lee's orchestrated her release only to bait McKenna back to Boston, the cat following the rat following the mouse, as it were."

And with Leila Markovich meeting my dad at his house, throw in the paranoid leading the lost, the thin gauze of my mother's ghost hovering over everything but keeping her mouth sealed tight. Or not. Maybe my mother is talking to my father this very moment, her siren song leading him through Boston's crooked and ill-marked streets, her voice whispering sweet nothings as he shuffles toward his own personal abyss. Not happy thoughts, I know, but at this point I'm surprised the sky itself hasn't caved in.

"And of course there's also the matter of the money. As I'm sure you're aware, only a few thousand dollars from the nearly one-million-dollar haul from Bank of Boston were ever recovered. Ms. Markovich has always claimed she had no knowledge of where the bulk of the money ended up. Perhaps she was lying."

"Or maybe she thought Mr. Meyers had some knowledge of where the money would be," Jhochelle says. "Why else would she meet with him immediately upon her release? To rehash old times?"

"All she could've gotten from my dad *is* old times, Jo, you know that as well as anyone. So bear with me here, counselor, I want to make sure I have everything lined up. Special Agent Lee stole a file from the bureau and then used it to blackmail Governor Hibert into springing Leila Markovich from prison?"

"Precisely."

"Because he thought she'd be the perfect bait to bring Devlin McKenna back to Beantown? Is he fucking insane?"

"Even if he is, it makes his plan no less viable. Either it will work or it won't."

"Swell. And Leila, meanwhile, might be hunting for the money from BOB that might or might not still be around. And now my dad's wandering around packing heat because, what, she's infected him with her special brand of paranoia, his head now back in the Boston game, all of a sudden a player again?"

"Perhaps."

"Then that, counselor, in my neck of the woods is what we call a clusterfuck."

"Yes, that's an apt description, made no less so by what you've left out."

"Yeah, what's that?"

"Isn't it obvious?"

Maybe, but Jhochelle gets it past her lips before I do: "The FBI wants its file back."

"In the worst possible way, I imagine. And we need to see that file before they do, because they will most certainly destroy it if they get their hands on it."

"*We?*" I say, looking to Jhochelle. "What's with the *we* all of a sudden?"

"*We* have retained Mr. Tetter's legal services."

"For what? Is Zero in some kind of trouble?" Like maybe not coming clean about his connection to Sullivan, Darryl Jenkins, and the Wells Fargo takedown, or is it something totally different, like yesterday's ATM beat-down? Are Zero's fingers still in a lot of shady pies, despite his lukewarm denials to the contrary?

"It's not Zero we're concerned about," Jhochelle says. "It's you."

"Then you're wasting your money. I haven't done anything wro—" I stop short, recalling my last forty-eight hours of felonies, misdemeanors, and predictable moral failings.

"Perhaps you're not in any legal quandary yet," Tetter points out with the jovial spirit of a man who gets paid a retainer. "But Lee's contacted Zero again; he wants to hand the file over for safekeeping, as insurance, in case something happens to him. Namely, before his own organization can silence him. He has stressed that the file is of vital importance to your family."

"How?"

"Lee wouldn't specify. Only that whatever he has brings new light to Bank of Boston. I understand you are concerned about your father, but Jhochelle and your brother's men are on that right now. What we need for *you* to do is get that file from Agent Lee, Zesty. Before the bureau catches up to him and everything disappears."

"Why me?" I say, but it's a moronic question. I already know the answer before it leaves the lawyer's mouth.

"Who better?" A gleam in Tetter's eye coincides with a wide grin on his jury-swaying face. "You're a messenger by trade, and I'm told quite a fast one at that."

"*The* fastest," I say. Or at least the most reckless.

"Then I can only hope you manage to live up to that exalted reputation, because speed will be of the essence. But if you fail, rest assured, I'll visit you in prison as soon as I'm summoned. And I don't mean to tell you how to do your job, Zesty, but may I suggest wearing a helmet? It seems you've already taken your lumps, and something tells me this is going to be a very bumpy ride."

FIFTY-SIX

Will hears the low rumble of an explosion, followed by shots from inside the bank, soft, but he knows the sounds for what they are. It wasn't in the plan, but Michael Drain and Tara Agostini are both strung out, too long off the needle; McKenna made sure he'd know where Drain could be found scoring when this is over.

Rachel Evans is the first to exit, carrying a canvas bag, her steps small and hurried like a wind-up toy bird. Leila is behind her, pushing Rachel toward the car, her gun held loosely by her side close to her body. Tara Agostini follows, pulling the cap off her head and shaking out her black wig like she's the lead in a Breck commercial, looking every bit like Diane from a distance, except for her junkie-slim waist and the drug hunger in her eyes. Will hears two more pops, and Drain, like a black leprechaun who's just strangled a rainbow, actually jumps for joy as he exits the bank, both hands holding large canvas bags.

Focus. Rachel Evans is in the front seat beside him, but she is vacant, her spirit gone. Drain and Agostini, manic-panic, for now the adrenaline pumping through their veins enough to see them through their drug hunger; they imagine they're Bonnie and Clyde, but Will suspects they will not have such a cinematic exit from this world.

He drives Washington to Market, switches the cars as planned in the lot on Converse. There's no hurry; he hears sirens but knows they're converging toward the blasted station house less than a quarter mile from the bank.

Drain and Agostini stash their guns and coats in the trunk of the waiting Dodge Dart. Rachel Evans has to be moved from the

Impala like a statue, and as Will places her in the front seat of the lime green Volkswagen Bug, he actually thinks she might crumble to pieces, and he's never been any good at reassembling puzzles.

Will loads the money into the small trunk, rips off his dress and wig, and wipes off the makeup with the hem of the housedress before dousing them both in gasoline and setting them aflame.

Before Drain realizes what is happening, Will shoves a thick wad of bills into his chest and points a gun in his face. "You have two choices," he says. "Drive or die."

And Drain actually thinks about it, actually weighs his chances against Will's finger caressing the trigger. Drain lives for the blast, and the money will be plenty for that, only he wants more, always more. But when his eyes fall into the ink pools of Will's pitiless gaze, he folds as Will knew he would, and the Dart's tires kick gravel into Will's legs as Drain peels out.

Will turns to Leila Markovich, to the business end of a gun with a barrel as wide as the mouth of a cannon, and it's just about what he expected. Will feels the weight of his own gun held loosely at his side, but he doubts he could raise and fire it before Leila does, and anyhow, it was never his intention to abandon her to face McKenna alone and empty-handed. Will hopes she realizes this as he slowly turns away, reaching past a frozen Rachel Evans to retrieve one of the bags of money from the back of the Bug and tossing it gently toward her.

"Here's what it is." Will tries to find Leila's eyes, such pretty eyes, over the outsized barrel. Thick green stacks of banded cash have tumbled out of the bag and lie at her feet. "You can take your share of the money and go it alone, or you can come with us and I can deliver you someplace safe. But you need to decide now."

"Is that right?" Leila probes past the gun, looking as deeply into Will's black pools as he will allow her. "I do need to decide now. But those aren't my only choices, are they, William?"

"No," he concedes, looking toward the sounds of sirens, his eyes landing on a pair of fire-red cardinals watching from a high limb of the yard's only tree.

"It's not like there're any rules to play by, obviously. But you think you're the only one at the table who knows how to play a shitty hand?"

"What do you want, Leila? The rest of the money? Take it if you think you can go it alone, that Ritter and McKenna won't find you and stick you in a fucking hole. This isn't about the money."

"No, it's not," Leila agrees, cocking the gun and raising it so Will can no longer find her eyes, her finger twitching on the trigger. "It's not about the money at all. Where is Diane?" she says.

FIFTY-SEVEN

A half hour later, it's just me and Jhochelle in the office with four empty Dunkin' Donuts cups, Sid rejoining the hunt for my father—Zero's Zen Moving shuttered for the day—a colorful dragnet of tattooed thieves and hard cases fanning the city looking for a doddering old man packing heat.

On speakerphone with Zero, I relayed our meeting with Tetter and pretty much everything else that's happened the last couple of days. Zero listened in a stone silence that conveyed neither surprise nor worry, the workings of his mind like our father's, calculating players and pot value, looking for that moment of opportunity every game eventually presents itself with.

"That's all?"

"Everything I can think of. You think I should call Brill, let him know Dad's on the loose? He knew him back in the day; maybe he's got ideas."

"Are you a fucking retard, Zesty? Call nobody." I didn't need to see Zero to know he was crushing the bridge of his nose in irritation, a crimson tide rolling across his face. "Let everybody make their play with whatever they're holding. I'm cutting over to Charlestown right now. We'll find Dad. Your only job is to get that file from Lee so we can figure out what it means to us."

"You don't know?"

"I have my hunches. None of them good."

"Is it even remotely fucking possible Dad had something to do with McKenna?"

"Talk to Jhochelle," Zero said.

"What?"

"This is not something we're going to talk about over the phone." Zero's voice crackled from the speaker. "Jhochelle will tell you everything I know."

Jhochelle now takes a black phone and a hard pack of Marlboro cigarettes from the desk drawer, studies the box for longer than it takes to read the Surgeon General's warning, and lets fly toward the trash can, the pack exploding the remaining cigarettes to the floor.

"I assume you shoot a gun better than that," I say.

"Let us hope we don't have to find out. *Nu,* don't worry about your father. Zero will handle it, and you have other pressing matters to contend with. How adept are you with technology?"

"Technology? I ride a bicycle. Sometimes I even fix my own flats with goo and an air pump. Why?"

Jhochelle palms the phone and tosses it to me. When I touch the screen, it lights up greenish-blue.

"What's this?" The device is smaller than the stolen phone in my pack but with a sturdy rubber casing to absorb any drops.

"What you're holding is pretty much a standard cellular telephone, but it is disposable. Press that button there. What do you see on the screen?"

"Three phone numbers. One of them is Zero's cell."

"And the others belong to Special Agent Lee and Darryl Jenkins, respectively." Jhochelle leans back in her chair, studying my face. Or maybe she's just looking at my new lock-cutter haircut.

"You're shitting me."

"I am not."

"You know who Darryl Jenkins is?"

"Certainly."

I nod and look at the phone, welcoming the static building up behind my eyes, another song sifting through to my ears, Lee, DJ, and Zero all together now. Nothing will ever make sense again, so why not some Looney Tunes to go with the madness.

"There are only three people who have the number of that phone," Jhochelle begins to explain. "It can receive and send text messages, but we'll try and refrain from using it in that manner. The fewer records that exist, the better."

"That's it?" I say. "There's nothing else programmed, like *this message will self-destruct in twenty seconds* or *if you choose to accept this mission*—"

"This message will self-destruct in twenty seconds," Jhochelle says.

"Really?"

"No." Jhochelle inverts a sniper's smile, makes a gun with her thumb and index finger, and shoots me dead.

"So what am I supposed to do with this thing?"

"You're to wait until Agent Lee calls."

"Does it have any music programmed?" Not that I need it, Aimee Mann singing "Save Me" loud and clear now.

"Be thankful it does not. With my Israeli sense of humor, I would have downloaded endless Yanni or Cher for you. Lee will contact you when he feels it is safe to do so. Remember, besides Lee, only Zero and Jenkins have the number, so rest assured, if it rings, it is one of them and you must answer right away."

"What if I go to a movie? Can I put it on vibrate?"

Jhochelle stares at me. "Is it an inability or just the unwillingness to stop, Zesty?"

"You know, you're the second person in the last twenty-four hours to ask me that."

"So the answer is unwillingness. It's a shame vaudeville is dead. Do you have any questions beyond the technical?"

"Darryl Jenkins," I say.

"Yes, I was wondering when you'd get to that. I'm not at liberty to say at this point."

"Really? Is it an Israeli thing—loose lips sink camel ships? What the fuck do you mean, you can't say?"

"I understand your frustration, Zesty, truly I do, but you, *we,* are in uncharted territory right now. All your questions will be answered when the time is right."

"Does Zero have something to do with the Wells Fargo job? What is it you're not telling me?"

"Now is not that time. What I will tell you is that Darryl's and Zero's interests have intersected in the past, and now due to you, and *only* you, they've crossed once again. Zero is involved because *you*"—Jhochelle jabs an accusatory finger in my direction—"have entered into a bargain that is impossible for you to hold up on your end. You know of what I speak."

"You mean Zero's bailing me out."

"It wouldn't be the first time, no?"

Not by far. Nor would it be the first time Zero recognized an opportunity to profit from somebody else's plans gone awry. But at this point I must be an open book, because Jhochelle addresses the thoughts bouncing around my head before I put them into words.

"The only question you have to answer for yourself, Zesty"—she shakes her head disdainfully, her long raven hair dusting her shoulders—"is do you trust your brother? Do you think—" Jhochelle's voice cracks, and she breaks off to look longingly at the lone cigarette between her fingers before snapping it in two, the brown tobacco scattering between her feet. She takes a deep breath, looks down at the mess she's created, and when she looks up, there are twin tears streaming down her face. "You know I love your brother," she says, looking at me unembarrassed.

"I know."

"It makes no difference to you that he's adopted, does it?"

"No," I say. "He's just my brother."

She nods. "And it's the same for him. I should not have asked you whether you trusted Zero. It's an insult you don't deserve. You are unlike each other in so many ways, but in this you are the same, without doubt in each other. Loyal. People use that word loosely, but in your family, it defines you. More than you know."

"Zero's always been there when I've needed him," I say.

"And you for him, he tells me. Though he does not need you very often, does he?"

"He seems okay the way he is," I say.

"Hmm. *Beseder.* You know what that means, *beseder*?"

"It means okay?"

"Yes. He is okay. A hard man, your brother, hard in the way that the first years make you who you are, the way you have to be to survive when nobody is caring for you. But yes, okay. He is also going to be a father soon." Jhochelle smiles through clouded eyes.

"You're pregnant? Mazel tov. You're happy about this, right? Why are you crying?"

"Grandparents," she says.

"What about them?"

"You know my parents are dead, and yours . . . well, yours are more complicated." Fresh tears slide out of Jhochelle's eyes onto the floor between us. "Your father obviously did the best he could raising the two of you, considering the circumstances, his personal liabilities. But children need their mothers, especially boys. I've seen this with my brother, Shai. Boys shed their childhood skins and assume the form of adulthood, but they don't become men, most of them, fully or whole, and therefore don't know what to do with the women who come into their lives, don't know what space to clear for them. Am I striking a chord here, Zesty? Zero told me once that your father was raised mainly by *his* mother, which explains his many virtues, his perseverance, certainly his patience with you two maniacs." Jhochelle offers me a weak smile.

"I know Zero said to talk to me, but what he really meant was we need to talk about your father in a new way, now that matters have progressed to where they are. Do you think you can do that, Zesty?" Jhochelle reaches over, touches my cheek where Sid left his rough mark. "Are you ready to perhaps see your father in a different light, even as he steps back into the shadows of his former days?"

"Jhochelle," I say, gently taking her hand off my cheek, holding it lightly to my forehead as I close my eyes, "I don't know what the fuck you're talking about."

"Then I'm not making myself clear. What I'm asking is, are you ready to forgive your father, Zesty?"

"For what? What the hell's he done now?"

I open my eyes to look at Jhochelle, and for the first time, I notice she has eyes the exact same color as my father's, radiant in the way the pitchest of black glows from a dark star, impenetrable. Zero always told me Jhochelle cleaned up at the occasional poker games that would break out at the garage when the men were flush with cash. Now I see why.

"I don't understand what I'm supposed to do," I hear myself saying, my vision gone blurry. "I just don't get it." I make a mess clearing my eyes with my fingers.

"It's really very simple, Zesty." Jhochelle hands me a tissue across the desk, a hint of a smile breaking the drag of her lips, her eyes softening but still unreadable. "You just need to do what all good Jewish boys have been doing for centuries. You need to listen to the women in your family. And now, in lieu of a mother, that would be me, mother in waiting. So be a good soldier, and do as I tell you, and don't ask why, okay? And a little chicken soup couldn't hurt. Have you eaten anything at all today? My God, you're practically skin and bones."

FIFTY-EIGHT

Will navigates the Bug into Cambridge via Western Avenue, skirts the Charles, and satisfied he's cleansed himself of any possible tails, hits the Mass Ave. Bridge and turns right, crossing back toward Boston proper. Will's grandmother, on more than one occasion, told him of her presence on this very same bridge when the Great Houdini, draped in heavy chains and handcuffs, jumped the rail into the frigid water only to surface minutes later free of his bonds.

Of course everyone called it the Harvard Bridge in those days, its given name, and Will can't help but smile—though it pains him— at the symmetry of it all, because his escape from McKenna's grip will have to be every bit as calculated as Houdini's plunge going forward, the weight of his metaphysical chains just as likely to drag him to the bottom of a cold and airless grave as the heavy links and padlocks worn by the magician.

He's at the hundred-Smoot mark when the radio tuned to WBZ 1030 AM comes on with the story, and he reaches past a vacant Rachel Evans to turn it up.

This just in: We've received word of a bomb detonated in front of District Fourteen police headquarters in Allston, the blast coinciding with the armed robbery of the Allston branch Bank of Boston. Police and paramedics are at both scenes, and a police source confirms at least one death at the bank and one person in critical condition with gunshot wounds to the head. Names are being withheld pending notification of next of kin. The police station has sustained damage to the front stairs along with windows blown out on the Washington Street side. There are reports of casualties from flying glass and debris, with the wounded being rushed to St. Elizabeth's Hospital directly across from the station house. A spokesman for Bank of Boston could not yet confirm the sum stolen from the bank, but police are said to be on the lookout for four, possibly five individuals, at least three of them female, in a blue Chevy Impala witnesses reported seeing fleeing the scene. The suspects are to be considered armed and extremely dangerous. We'll have more on this story as it develops. This is Jorge Quiroga reporting from—

Will changes the radio frequency to FM, spins the dial to Charles Laquidara doing his Duane Ingalls Glasscock routine on The Big Mattress Show—*Will is possibly the only listener in Boston not doubled over laughing. At a red light, he ties a yellow ribbon in Rachel Evans's hair and grips her hard, turning her to face him; her eyes are as lifeless as marble. Will explains the ribbon has to stay in her hair, that he's made arrangements for her to be recognized by this ribbon.*

"Do you understand what I'm telling you?" He slaps Rachel across the cheek, and redness floods her face; she blinks like she's coming out of a deep trance. "Do you understand?"

"Yes." Rachel looks down at his fingers pressed into her arms. "You're hurting me."

He hangs a left onto Commonwealth, a right onto Arlington, passes the plate glass window of the Ritz-Carlton, the Commons on his left, the willows by the pond heavy from recent rains.

"When we get to the station on Franklin, you walk inside, head straight for the back where the buses board. There are seats arranged back-to-back with coin-operated televisions attached to them. Someone will meet you there, is already there wearing a yellow blouse. She'll be watching the television. There'll be a bag at her feet. It has money, a ticket for the Greyhound to New York City, a change of clothes, a wig, a small mirror, and a book. Sit next to her. When the time on her television runs out, if she thinks it's safe, she'll put another quarter in and start adjusting the dials. If she does this, pick up the bag, go out to the New York gate, and try to be one of the first ones on the bus. Do you understand everything I've told you?"

"Yes."

"Sit toward the back, off the window. Put the wig on—the seats are high, so you should be able to duck down and do it without being seen. The wig already has the same yellow ribbon tied into it. It'll take some time for the police to get a picture of you out, but they might have it by the time you hit New York. The wig will be enough for now. Someone will meet you at the station, recognize you by the ribbon. Go with this person."

"And then what?" Rachel Evans says, but Will doesn't answer her. "Then what?" She begins to shake, though no tears come to her eyes.

Then she will spend a few days in a borrowed East Village apartment while documents are prepared—a license, passport, a new Social Security card. She will have her hair dyed and cut and be given a tattoo, before being moved even deeper underground and into anonymity, until one morning she will wake to look in the mirror and won't even recognize her own face. If she's lucky.

But Will doesn't tell her that. That is for later. Rachel doesn't realize it yet—the shock has been too great, the unraveling of her life too swift—but Will has rescued her from the nightmare of Devlin

McKenna, spared her from the syncopation of the shovel digging her grave, from the defiling of her body before the bullet in the brain or the vise-tight grip of Rich Ritter's calloused hands around her throat. Yes, Will has saved Rachel Evans's life. Of this he is sure.

Perhaps, one day, she will even forgive him for it.

FIFTY-NINE

There're still no empty parking spaces in front of 38 Newbury, but that's on account of the two police cruisers, Wells's Audi, and a Boston Police van hogging up the metered curb. Either there's a knockout sale going on at Alan Bilzerian or Brill and Wells are moving in fast on Darryl's crumbling kingdom, putting an end to his nascent real estate dreams. There's a new doorman on duty, his hands jammed deep in his pockets like he's afraid to set them free for fear of what they might do on their own.

"Hey, how are ya? Where's Charlie?"

"Charlie quit." The doorman squints at me. "You Zesty?"

"Yep."

"Yeah, well, Charlie told the boss to shove the job up his ass. Whaddaya think about that?"

"Not very professional," I say.

"Professional what?" The doorman smiles. "He also said something about maybe riding a bike for work. Any money in it?"

"Barely. But the dry cleaning bills are tiny, and you have to beat the secretaries off with a stick."

"Sounds swell. You going up to Black Hole?"

"Yeah. You want me to sign in?"

"What's to sign? The cops are taking everything. That van there's already packed with boxes. Charlie told me he was bored shitless here, but I don't know what the hell he's talking about. Between the cops and all the tail on this street, this joint's a live wire. Here, let me get that for you. You know the floor, right?"

There's no music playing inside the Black Hole offices, no computers on the reception desk, nobody to greet me except for a female officer stacking boxes onto a hand truck just inside the glass doors.

"Place is closed," she informs me.

"I work here," I say.

"Dressed like that? Boy, did I pick the wrong job."

"But you look good in blue, Officer."

"Aren't you a honey. And a gentleman too." She wheels the hand truck past me as I hold the door.

"Well, look who it be," Brill says when he sees me coming. "Zesty, you know Darcy? She was just telling us she's your biggest fan."

"Only she uses curse words to express it," Wells says. "Explain that."

"Why should she be any different?" I say. "How are you, Darcy?"

"Unemployed, I think. Thanks to you." Darcy waves what might be a search warrant at my face.

"Aw, now that's a little harsh there, young lady. Zesty's just the messenger, remember? But he sure does pop up in the middle of a lot of shit. Why're you here, Zesty?"

"I saw your car out front."

"Darcy, would you excuse us a moment?"

"Gladly." Darcy heads back up front.

"You get inside Valentine's safe?" I say when she's out of sight.

"You mean Darryl Jenkins's safe? Sure. It was open when we got here. What, you expected we'd find Darryl's money?"

"I don't know, you're the detectives. I just make shit up as I go along."

"We've noticed that about you. Safe was empty, but really we just came for the paperwork and the computers, let the forensic eggheads figure it all out, run a line back to Jenkins, who's hit the mattresses, by the way."

"Ducking you?"

"Ducking somebody," Wells says.

"What's that supposed to mean?"

"We heard Jenkins has street-level issues to deal with. You wouldn't happen to know anything about that, would you?"

"I've been spending time with family," I say.

"Word has it maybe the street will take care of Darryl before we get a chance to."

"That how you'd prefer it?"

Brill looks at me and then to Wells with something close to malice in his eyes. The detectives are apparently back to cranky love between them.

"You're piping a little judgmental to my ears there, Zesty."

"I told you Darryl and I had a deal when Gus was killed. You're after the wrong guy."

"Nah, Darryl's our man, maybe not pulling the trigger, but pulling the strings. Seriously, though, all I want is to close this case and move on to a homicide a little less complicated than czarist Russia so I don't have to see your face every day. You are for real starting to wear on me, Zesty."

"And to think I was *this close* to getting deputized. You ever get a translator for that witness?"

"Eventually." Wells steps in, Brill wheeling on his heels but staying within earshot. "But first we took a run at him ourselves.

Guy doesn't speak a word of English, just keeps pointing at this poster we've got hanging in the squad room advertising Liberty Bonds. I figure he's making his case for the land of the free, give us your tired, your poor?"

"Where's Agent Lee when you need him?" I say.

"Shee-it. Lee already had a what, three-hour head start knowing what this wit knows. And don't make me say his name out loud, I'll get written up for racial insensitivity. Anyhow, the guy keeps pointing, and finally I give him paper and pencil, and it turns out he's a regular Chinese Norman Rockwell. And you know what he draws for me?"

"Not Darryl Jenkins," I say, looking over at Brill rolling his unlit cigar between his large hands.

"Right. It's a picture of some generic white guy deep in shadow, like one of those old-time noir movie posters. And his hand's on fire—Lady Liberty's torch. It was dark, and the guy was asleep standing up when he heard the pops. The translator came, but it was pretty much what the picture told us, a thousand words. As for Lee? We put in multiple calls downtown to the bureau but keep getting stonewalled. Nobody wants to talk to us. Now, why do you think that is?"

Poker face, I tell myself. "The usual reasons?"

"Maybe. But I'm not *sans* resources. I reach out to a supervisor who owes me a little something, and he practically chokes at the mention of Lee's name. Seems Agent Wellington Lee is persona non grata at the bureau right now. You remember about a year back, organized crime squad and joint task force hit this house in Mattapan looking for guns, narcotics, only they kick in Granny's door by mistake?"

I shrug a *maybe.*

"Bad enough, right? Only Granny's got a gun and knows how to use it. Anyhow, the whole thing's Lee's operation, and he screwed the pooch but *good*. Lee's partner takes one in the shoulder, one in the vest; Granny takes about twenty rounds, and that's all she wrote."

"Except you're leaving out the part where Granny's dirty." Brill feels compelled to speak, rounding back to us. "Running her own thing next door to the home invasion crew they were aiming for. Guess Social Security wasn't cutting it."

"True. But Lee's still holding the bag on the wrong intel, so it's on him. Following the usual hearings and a short suspension, Lee gets knocked down to, wait for it . . . Devlin McKenna sighting duty."

"That's a punishment?" I say.

"Are you kidding me? That's like no notice, be on the red-eye to Wichita—somebody just reported seeing McKenna buying a six-pack of Budweiser in a town with two streetlights and a seed store every fifteen miles. Then it's off to Cleveland for more of the same. That's no kind of life. Only here's the wrinkle. Lee put in for vacation a little more than two weeks ago, and here he is all tangled up in blue and way up our ass on this Wells Fargo thing. My guy actually asked me if *I* had a bead on him. They can't even keep track of their own agents?"

"Lee's chasing Devlin McKenna for a *vacation*?" I say.

"Different strokes," Brill puts in. "Fifty ways to fuck your lover."

"Been that kind of case," Wells says. "One sad song after another. Lee maybe the saddest—one mistake, and his career's circling the drain. And the impression I got, he was moving up the ladder when the chow-foon hit the fan."

"Can you imagine? Lee's out there seeing Devlin McKenna in everything, like it's all one big conspiracy. He probably figures the only way he's getting his career back on track is to nab Boston's number one bad guy and do it on his own, because the bureau sure as shit isn't in on it, and like I told you before, they'd prefer if McKenna stayed gone, a million miles away from Lee's redemption fantasy. So unless you got something new for us, this looks like sayonara, Zesty, we'll be in touch if we need you. Wish I could say it's been fun, but ever since I met you, my tan's faded and now I need new shoes. Any last words to remember you by?"

"Sorry I couldn't be any more help?" I say, keeping Lee's contact number and what I'm pretty sure is Darryl's hideaway address to myself.

Lee might be a loose cannon, but if so, he's a cannon with a radar attached to it. And as for Darryl, what can I say? He's a shady cat, no doubt, but I don't think he's killed anybody, and I like playing ball and smoking weed with him, and where I come from, that just about makes us friends.

And in this town, a man can use all the friends he can get.

SIXTY

The entrance to Chinatown is flanked by a pair of enormous foo li-ons guarding a pagoda gate that faces toward the Paifang and Beach Street, where Will finds a parking spot to shoehorn the Bug as a ma-roon Cadillac slides by, trailing exhaust and bad parking karma.

The money is noticeably lighter now that Leila has taken her cut, but she could have taken more. Under the cover of the blanket, he consolidates what remains into one duffel bag, lifts it out, and places it between his feet at the curb. From his pocket Will pulls a few coins, gripping them between the joints of his fingers before sliding them into the meter, though he knows he'll never drive this car again, the pile of tickets that will sprout on the windshield adding to the cliché of Boston décor. Diane has taught him well; he's careful enough not to leave any prints on the coins or the meter appendage, which he twists with his knuckles, the purchased time popping up behind the curved glass window and providing Will a moment of uncalled-for bemusement as it hits him that what he's doing, for Rachel Evans, for Diane, is exactly that: buying time as he calculates the next move.

Will picks up the bag and curses himself because while he'd been forced to factor Leila into the hand, he didn't have time to read her play, couldn't possibly know how tight a grip McKenna had on her. He'd assembled a puzzle of leveraged pieces, the whole only coming together on the outer edges, McKenna filling in the picture when the time was right for him, and Will realizes now that he had Leila all wrong, made her for a player content to come along for the ride, justify her inevitable losses with the caveat that, if nothing else, she'd played at the highest level, swum with the roughest of sharks.

Hell, he'd seen it before, the fish drawn to the current of the game, already inured to the fact that they're bound to lose, that perhaps the game itself is rigged against them. Lady Luck's orphaned children. After all, the entire ocean can't be stocked entirely with sharks. Diane had warned him that Leila was possibly unstable; she had wanted bodies at the Harvard bombing, a message in blood. Diane managed to rig a miracle, the bomb detonating prematurely before the students filed in, the charred remains of a century-old lectern the only fatality.

This was where they had parted ways, Sparhawk effectively disbanded even before the smoke had cleared over Harvard Yard; Leila evading the FBI dragnet for years, something not even Diane had managed; McKenna, up to this point, true to his word, running interference with the feds. Only now as Will navigates the winding Chinatown streets does he realize that Leila is improvising recklessly, the revolutionary's handbook replaced by something more selfish. So much for the commune, time to ditch those Che Guevara T-shirts.

So where does that leave him? Quite simply, playing catch-up in *a game he's always taken great pains to avoid, the wild card messing with the variables, creating a risk that leaves him now, like a rank amateur, praying on runner-runner.*

Leila's changed everything. Will's liar's eyes can't help him in a place where all is black, where every face has turned to stone. The time for calculating odds in this new game has passed. This is the hand he's been dealt. These are his cards. Now it's only a matter of deciding just how much he's willing to lose.

SIXTY-ONE

I stop at the front desk on the way out. Darcy has a box at her feet and paperwork the police either neglected or didn't want spread out in front of her. At the edge of the desk is the black-and-white sketch the dishwasher drew, a shadow-faced figure with sunken eyes and high forehead. Wells is right, the drawing's a work of art, the underlying message that it could be practically anybody, a composite blank caught in the strobe of a gunshot flash. I slide the copy into my pack without Darcy noticing. It's just the two of us now, the remaining staff out filing unemployment claims or chasing down job interviews.

"What are all these?" I say to her.

Darcy keeps her eyes on the paperwork, her tongue working her cheek, contemplating curses. I've heard stories about Darcy's tongue. Apparently she's one of those gifted women who can tie a double knot in the stem of a cherry.

"Band contracts mostly," she says finally. "Appearance obligations. I don't even know why I'm going through them. There's no company left, no deals. It's all worthless shit."

"Local bands?"

"Mostly." Darcy looks up from the paperwork, her face a little sad. "There're a few from New York, a couple from Europe. That one's Gizzard's contract. Talk about worthless. I'm gonna miss Gus." Darcy takes a deep breath, tears welling and blackening to ink drops as they pick up her mascara.

"You know a lot about the local music scene, Darcy?"

"What?" A black tear drops with a loud click onto the paper. Darcy smudges eyeliner with the back of her wrist.

"I mean you're always out going to shows, seeing new bands?"

"Yeah, so?"

"You know the business? Bookings, promotions, those sorts of things?"

"Hell, yeah." Darcy wipes the contract ink, the black streak on paper a mirror reflection of her skidmark eyeliner. "I've been doing this stuff since I was sixteen. It's all I ever really wanted to do. I can't sing, and I don't play an instrument. . . ." She trails off into a shrug.

"So?" I say.

"So what?"

"No more Black Hole, but there're all these bands with no label and no valid contracts."

"Yeah. And half of them I never would've signed in the first place."

"Exactly my point. You'd know, right? And here you are, vacant office, nice address."

"This street bites. I wouldn't put my office here if you paid me." Darcy smiles and looks at me with a fresh set of eyes. "You think I could do it, Zesty?"

"Who better?" I say.

"You really think Britta and Ray aren't coming back?"

"I'd bet my life on it." Britta cutting her losses, smart enough to step away from the million dollars in blood money, and Ray most likely putting some distance from Darryl and Black Hole. "And anyway, it doesn't seem like Ray knew what he was doing in the first place, does it?"

"I guess not. Listen, Zesty, I'm sorry I've been so mean to you. And thanks."

"For what?"

"Giving me a new perspective on this. I'm not sure I would've come to it on my own."

"I'm glad I could help. Usually I don't get that sort of insight without a bong hit or two."

"Yeah? We can do some of that." Darcy tilts her razored bangs toward the lounge. "I don't think the cops are coming back, and they didn't confiscate the couches. You gonna answer your phone?"

No, something inside my shorts says.

"I think I have to." I pull out the phone and look at the screen. Zero's number flashes.

Darcy smiles at me, licks her lips.

"I'm sorry, I have to jet. I'll call you soon, though, okay?" I bang through the glass doors, touching the screen as I go.

Zero says, "Tommy called in, thinks he spotted Dad in Chinatown near the Pagoda Gate. I'm on my way now."

"I'll meet you there."

"No. Wait on Lee's call. Where are you?"

"Back Bay. I can be there in, like, two minutes."

"What I fuckin' tell you? I'm on it. Jhochelle show you how to take pictures with that thing?"

"Yeah. What's that noise?" I hear a loud crunch of metal, a chorus of horns and car alarms.

"Oh shit, Jeremy just took off somebody's fender and—*watch out!*—almost killed one of your biking brethren."

"In one of *your* trucks?" With ZERO'S ZEN MOVING plastered all over it.

"Hell no, that's why I'm laughing. Jeremy boosted the Giants's box delivery bus outta their yard. There's gotta be, like, ten parked cars on Beacon Hill with purple paint scraped up their sides. That won't be good for business. Left here! Listen, whatever Lee gives us, use the phone to take pictures. Of everything. You got that?"

"Find Dad," I yell over the screech of brakes.

The phone goes black in my hand.

SIXTY-TWO

Will carries the money from Summer to Washington, Franklin to Arch, the morning rush hour congealed to a steady crawl, the sidewalks full of the daily paycheck grind. Would Will take this type of life now if given a choice?

What does it matter? His choices have brought him here to the expanse of the Summer Street Bridge and Fort Point Channel, the Boston Wharf sign shining in the cold, hard sunlight atop the rounded red brick curve of Melcher. He turns into the industrial canyon of the Leather District, Necco to Necco Place, skirting the bins beside the black box of the Channel, dead at this hour, cases of Bud and Miller empties stacked against the club's side wall.

This isn't the most private of places he's chosen, but the symbolism works for him, and besides, it's a place that's barely changed in a hundred years. It will do. At this point, it'll have to. Will's already missed the rendezvous in Everett; McKenna and Ritter are undoubtedly out looking for him. He tamps the soft ground, pushes aside the condoms and Twinkie wrappers as a song takes hold inside his head, prompting him, despite the pain in his mouth, to move his lips and sing along:

Love those dirty waters,
Oh Boston you're my home

No matter the Standells had been singing about the Charles River, an entirely different cesspool from this narrow industrial canal.

It's a bit of a ways, but Will can see clear across the channel to Dorchester Avenue, which means he can be seen too, but that's the risk he takes, coming here right under McKenna's nose, more of his damned symbolism, South Boston, firmly in McKenna's iron grip just a block down A Street. Still, the place is deserted; nobody wanders back here aside from the random drunk to piss in the polluted waters, Channel staff, groupies and bands to blow a joint or blow each other before or between sets. But it's always dark, and nobody pays attention to the scenery; they're more concerned with avoiding the long-tailed, red-eyed rats scurrying along the channel's murky edge.

Will finds the hole easily, counting each step as he makes his way to where he'd dug it late last night before getting his butchered stitches—not the easiest thing to do bleeding all over the place, half his front teeth missing. But there it is, one hundred and eleven steps from the back of the club, already lined with black plastic trash bags, covered with garbage, undisturbed. The hole's not too deep—it's not like he dug a grave or anything—just big enough to drop the bag in, fold over the black plastic, and cover with his hands and feet, followed by the trash.

At the water's edge, Will looks over the splintered piling lining the channel walls, holding back its poisoned muddy waters. They look like shit, but they've probably got another fifty years in them easy. What, somebody's going to build something around here? Stuff a giant cork in Boston Harbor and sift through this toxic sludge? Be a scary thing if they dredge these waters, turn over this land. Better get ready for the Year of the Rat if they do. This place is fucking crawling with them.

SIXTY-THREE

Junior White's has four customers as I wheel my bike through the door, two scruffy white guys in lightweight hoodies and headphones, an old man perusing the jazz section in a green jumpsuit with his name stitched over the front pocket, and a pretty college-age girl near the back door with a tiny backpack strung over her shoulders and a giant afro held high on her head with a bright orange headband.

Junior White does most of his business from what he refers to as Mount Never-Rest, an elevated platform where he can see the entire floor below him, his heavy-lidded stare more than enough to discourage any boosters from plying their trade in his store. Junior's longtime manager, Seldon, is manning the counter, separating records from a stack and dusting them off with a rag. Seldon's tall and wiry, and he's wearing a white dust mask and disposable latex gloves for the task.

"Anything good?" I say to him.

"Got a couple old Ella discs and Prince's first album that's pretty fine, probably worth the price of the bundle. See what else shortly, but it don't look promising." Seldon wipes his brow with the back of his wrist. "Really, I don't understand people. How can you have this here Chet Baker, then the rest of the shit's Jody Watley, Kansas?"

"Eclectic," I say, half saluting Junior at his perch.

"If you say so. You dropping something off?"

"I need to see Darryl," I say.

"Who?"

The back door where the girl's flipping albums is plastered with old Roxy showbills, a gray metal plate screwed in at the corners around the doorknob. It could be a storeroom, or it might lead to stairs, although there's no exit sign as would be required by law.

"It's a dust mask, Seldon, not earplugs."

Seldon looks at me for a long moment, flicks his eyes up behind him. "Talk to Junior," he says. "I don't really care for your tone, Zesty."

"Okay," I say, heading for the back door instead. "Excuse me." I edge past the girl and try the knob.

"Keisha!" Junior's voice rumbles from his perch, and when I turn my head, the girl's looking at me with hostile curiosity, her afro tilting to one side, a long-barreled silver revolver in her hand, which she presses deep into my cheek like she's trying to poke a hole through it.

"Keisha, no." Junior shakes his head, motions to the two guys in headphones. The old man in the jumpsuit looks over with raised eyebrows but decides it's none of his business and goes back to examining a Cannonball Adderley album.

"Girl," I mumble, half my face bent out of shape by the gun, "please tell me you did not have that thing hidden in your hair."

Junior reaches below his desk. The door clicks audibly, and Keisha opens it with the palm of her free hand, pushing me through with her foot into Cedrick's thick embrace.

"Ho, shit! Lookit what pussy dragged in. You know Zesty, Keisha?"

"How would I know this fool?" Keisha says.

"Zesty *every*where, girl. This muthafucka musta been cloned there so many of him. He a dangerous cat too. You done good."

"That mean I get to shoot him?"

"Hell no! Take a ticket and wait in line like everybody else.

And you best believe I got first dibs on that. Now, get your skinny ass back on the floor."

In no particular order, Keisha looks disappointed and offended but does as she's told.

"Nice to meet you," I call after her. "And no worries, your ass isn't all that skinny."

"Fuck you, Casper."

Cedrick laughs, pushes me against the wall and pats me down. "Keisha doesn't like white boys lookin' at her ass."

"Oh good," I say, turning around. "I thought it was just me. I'll come back when I'm tan. I'm usually super dark by July."

"Too bad you ain't gonna make it to July, then." Cedrick opens my bag, maintains a solid poker face looking at the money. "Get on up them stairs. End of the hall. Darryl waiting on you."

"You're not coming?"

"Second line of defense," Cedrick says by way of explanation, pointing my way up. "And, Z, I meant what I told Keisha. You one slinky muthafucka. That was some nasty shit you slipped me the other day, had me tripping my damn head off near half the night, then lights *out,* nigga. You cook that up yourself?"

"No."

"Yeah, well, whoever did be a damn genius. You get out this mess alive, you gonna hook a brotha up, right?"

Unreal.

The room where Darryl is waiting smells like a mixture of sweat, french fries, and machine oil from the arsenal spread out on a long table set up in front of Darryl's hard leather club chair. Darryl might have been waiting on me, but that doesn't mean he looks happy to see me. A half dozen sullen-faced teenagers take their cue from him, staring daggers from under the lids of their black "B" caps. Only Otis, greasing the chamber of a blue-gripped .38, looks content, but for all I know, he's just won the I Get to Shoot Zesty lottery.

Without a word, the teenagers scrape themselves off the walls and shuffle into the stairwell, the door swinging shut behind them.

"That's some army you got there," I say. "Some of them might even be shaving soon."

"How'd you know I'd be here?" Darryl's voice is hoarse like he's been doing a lot of yelling recently. There are half-moon eggplants under his eyes, and his normally pumped physique is wilting like a plant left too long in direct sunlight.

"It's hard to explain. But when I mentioned Junior's earlier, I read something, like a shift in energy." I shrug.

"Energy," Darryl says, eyes wide, looking toward Otis.

"Force field," Otis says, but he looks serious.

"Like a poker tell?" Darryl says.

"Pretty much. I just filed it away. Didn't know what it meant at the time but figured I'd just follow the music and see where it led me."

"Police follow you?"

"Not a chance."

"You mean you here all on your own, nobody knows where you're at?"

"Zero," I lie belatedly.

"Nuh-uh. You already played *that* card." Darryl picks a gun from the table and lazily points it in my direction.

"I thought you and him worked something out," I say.

"Yeah. Well, shit done changed. Why're you here? Most people like to commit suicide in private."

"Consider this a heads-up, D. Forget your corner troubles, I got it on good word homicide's aiming to pin four bodies on you."

"Bull*shit*."

"Gus and everybody connected to Wells Fargo: Sullivan, Coney, Stavros."

"*Who?*"

"Yeah, right, whatever. Here's hoping you got a good lawyer."

"Shit, Zesty, I got me a Jew on retainer."

"Those are the best kind," I say. "I keep mine in a desk drawer with my rolling papers."

Darryl turns to Otis, something like a dark light working in his eyes. Otis maybe shakes his head.

"Let's talk about Coney," I say. "Honestly, I don't figure you for anybody but him. The Rumsey courts are your turf now, right?"

Otis shakes his head visibly now, barely half a rotation but his eyes are focused elsewhere, maybe looking somewhere into the future, not happy with what he's seeing.

"That's how the money finds its way to you, right? Coney's the connect. He approaches you, says, what, he's got some massive score and word is you can clean it quick for a price? Put it through all those legit businesses you got going. How'm I doing?"

"Keep talkin'. I'll let you know."

"At first you've got to figure Coney's full of shit, no way this fool's going to bring you seven digits to launder. But he shows up, doesn't he?"

"Yes."

"Steps up."

"Yes."

"And he's not alone."

"No. He's got some cagey old white guy with him."

"And you don't know who it is?"

"Not right then. But I ain't without some due diligence. I have him followed a couple days, and we get what we need. Meaning we know he ain't police so . . ." Darryl lets his words hang.

"You know who he is now, though."

"Yes." Darryl bites down on something in his mouth, not enjoying the taste.

"But it's too late, you already took his money. Two million

dollars that you're going to rush-clean through Black Hole. Time is of the essence, the man's in a hurry? That's why your cut's so high at fifty percent. Except you get greedy, figure you knock off Coney, what's McKenna going to do? You knew where the money came from, didn't you?"

"I knew. I couldn't believe Coney took down an armored truck, but the man was good to his word."

"And then you took him out. Made it look gang related."

"No. I'll admit I thought about it, leave the old white dude out in the cold, but Coney's practically blood. We go way back; I couldn't do him like that. The streets took Coney, plain and simple. Young blood making a rep, and Coney always did have a mouth on him. But I shoulda known—the street giveth and the street taketh away. You got hit on delivery, my man on the wheels of steel, Valentine, getting sloppy at the office, not doing his job pushing the money through like he's supposed to; Gus and Britta play their own game trying to take me off for a chunk; the police all up in my legit businesses, and all the money coming off the corners gone. And now finally, Gus, maybe the only real talent I got, goes and gets himself killed."

"But not by you." I say this more as a question than a statement.

"You hear this cat, O? Like if I did Gus, I'd just come right out and say it. I know Cedrick searched you for a hammer downstairs 'cause he ain't gonna make that mistake twice, but he check you good enough for a wire?"

"He damn near molested me," I say. "And for your information, I'm your only alibi for Gus, but I need to know for myself—you order it done?"

Darryl and Otis just glare at me, neither one of them saying anything.

"So I'll chalk that up as a maybe."

"*Chalk* it any way you like, but *I* didn't kill no-*body,* you hear me? Why you think Otis here looks so damn disappointed?"

"So then what's with the mattress diving? The corners blowing up on you too now?"

"Looks like it. I lost two crew chiefs last twenty-four hours and then I pulled everybody in. Fuck hitting the mattresses, we sleeping on floors till this shit get sorted out."

"Where're the bodies?" I say.

"It make a difference?"

"I guess not."

"Nah, I know what you're thinking, Zesty. You think I don't care about my people, they're just replaceable slingers, chose the life, so fuck 'em, right?"

"That's how they do it on *The Wire*," I say.

"Yeah, well, there's limited choices out there, and the ones choose *my* way know the dangers of the business. But my boys weren't just killed, Zesty, they were cut up like you hear about in South of the Border shitholes—hands cut off, their eyes cut out, a message in every slice."

"You moved into Mexican cartel territory?"

"Maybe Colombian. Hard to tell."

"What the hell's wrong with you?"

"Fuzzy borders," Darryl says, palms up. "The crews strayed."

"You should've known better than to throw in with McKenna, kick-start this shit."

"Nigga was before my time. And I had to raise capital to clean Wells Fargo. The whole goddamn two million was hot off the presses. I'm talking numbered. I needed one million in clean, untraceable cash, and I needed it fast. I had a chunk of it from Black Hole, but I needed more quick."

"That's why you stepped up your street sales."

"Exactly. I wanted the man paid and out of my life, only because I don't believe for a second he ain't still wired into the feds. Nobody stays gone that long without help. Anyhow, like I said, shit done changed. Right now I got my people on ice, and when we're through this, when *I* got Devlin McKenna's dentures on my desk as a muthafucking paperweight, I'll give them a proper burial."

"But meanwhile you lose market share," I say, looking ahead, the blood tide that started with Wells Fargo picking up bodies along the way. "Your corners gonna be empty when you get back to them, or is this the start of some turf war too, your competition smelling blood in the water?"

"We'll see. Legend be McKenna like a ninja, here one minute, gone the next. Only he's wasting his time sticking around, seeing as I ain't got his money."

"Except you do," I say, overturning my bag on Darryl's desk, the bundled money tumbling over the array of guns.

"What'd I tell you? The kid specializes in long shots." Darryl addresses Otis, who somehow looks disappointed without changing his expression. "Only that don't look like a million dollars, Zesty."

"It's not," I say. "It's half."

"And the rest of it?"

"Comes after," I say.

"After what?"

"A favor," I say. "I need a favor."

"And what, pray muthafucking tell, would that be?"

"That burner you're holding will do."

"That's it?"

"No. I also need a shadow. Preferably one that can shoot and doesn't mind doing it."

Darryl looks again at Otis, who is smiling, finally, a shiny white crescent glowing in a midnight face, a flower blooming on the hard black lava of a dormant volcano.

"Now, I *know* I can help you with that."

SIXTY-FOUR

I answer Lee's call on the fourth ring.

"What took so long?" he says.

"Stuff and things. The more I'm nagged, the slower I work."

"You'll make somebody a great husband one day. Are you familiar with the bridge overlooking the swan boats in the Commons?"

"Quintessential Boston," I say. "We going for a ride?"

"In a manner of speaking, but not on the swan boats. How soon can you be there?"

"Five minutes."

"Really?"

"You've never heard the legend of Zesty Meyers?" I say, hanging up.

It's past rush hour, people taking the time to smell the tulips, happy hour running into overtime. Lee looks like he could use a few drinks. His suit's wrinkled, and he's lost the tie but gained a silver briefcase that ought to be handcuffed to his wrist.

"Pretty public place." I ride the pedals to a stop in front of him. Outdoors, in the fading evening light, Lee doesn't appear so one-dimensional anymore. "You're not worried about being seen?"

"Being seen?" Lee doesn't look at me as he speaks, his eyes scanning past my shoulders, tracking people and spots around the park. Stocky brunette pushing a running stroller. Man smoking a cigarette on the dock by the swan boats. A couple arguing in stage whispers. "Doing what?"

"You know, touristy things. Selling state secrets. Whatever it is I'm supposed to be doing with you."

"Zero did not tell you?"

"See, that's the thing. You, my brother, Leila Markovich, Devlin McKenna. None of this makes a whole lot of sense to me."

"Then stop thinking and just do what you're told," Lee says coldly.

"You're one to talk. I hear you're supposed to be on vacation. How's that working out for you?"

"Very relaxing."

"Sure. You look primed to party. You still in contact with Leila Markovich?"

"No." A look of confusion crosses Lee's face. "Why do you ask that?"

"Did you ever consider that maybe Ms. Markovich was in prison where she was supposed to be? That maybe she's a little off?"

"No, that never occurred to me. Nor do I care. Why do you?"

"Because my dad went missing after she visited him."

"Missing how?"

"He's got Alzheimer's. He's wandered off the reservation."

Lee squints in concentration, maybe trying to connect dots. "I didn't foresee that happening."

"How could you? Springing Markovich as bait for McKenna is what my dad would've called trying to river a pull. The odds don't favor you."

"Unlike many Chinese, I'm not a gambler," Lee says. "But I caught that card, didn't I?"

"Yeah, even the losers get lucky sometimes."

"I am sorry if I played a role in your father's wandering. It was not intended. Do you trust me, Zesty?"

"Trust you? Shit, Agent Lee," I say, "as far back as I can remember, I've been visited by the bureau and asked questions about my mother. Trust is out the window. At this point, I'm just following orders and trying to get back to the kind of work I understand."

"You've been given instructions?"

"You have something for me?"

From his briefcase Lee springs a faded green folder roughly the same size as the package I lost delivering for Black Hole.

I'm starting to put it in my pack when Lee says, "You're not going to look at it?"

"Actually, I was told to photograph it, but Courier Code," I say. "I just deliver shit."

"There is no bliss in ignorance, Zesty," Lee says curtly. "Open it. You will understand so much more if you do. Is that not the goal of all this for you—knowledge?"

"Sure, grasshopper," I say. "Wax on, wax off."

"Now you are being racist *and* disrespectful."

"Then I apologize for one, take your pick." And against my better judgment, I open the folder and see my mother's name handwritten on the front of the file next to four other names: Michael Drain. Rachel Evans. Tara Agostini. Leila Markovich. I look at Lee as I sift through the papers, the edges disintegrating, dry and brittle, the folder obviously stored for years.

"This is the FBI file on Bank of Boston," I say, my voice suddenly as dry as the papers.

"Yes."

"It looks like it's been sitting somewhere a long time," I say. "Untouched."

"So it seems."

"You had access to this file?"

"No. Until a few weeks ago, I did not know it even existed. When I spoke to Agent Grossman, he did not know of it either. Or at least that is what he informed me."

"That's his story, and he's sticking to it."

"Yes. And I have no reason to doubt him. The file was not easy to find. I'm surprised it even still exists. When most of the old files were digitized, they were disposed of safely. This, apparently, was not. I have also seen your father's file. It appears there are some documents overlapping between the two, but certain pieces are missing."

"And you got this where?"

Lee looks down at the swan boats, his face back to flat inscrutability.

"You stole it," I say. I can't help myself. I probably look like an idiot, but I have a giant grin on my face.

"I think your mother would have preferred the word 'liberated,'" Lee says.

I sit cross-legged, leaning my back against the rail, and shuffle through the stack on my lap. The sun's beginning to dip into the horizon, the light soft on the yellowed pages as I flip through them. There's plenty of federal busywork to pore through, witness statements, bank forms, supervisory summaries and stamps, the paperwork building as it climbed the bureaucratic ladder to its final resting place, heavy, as if they figured they could successfully try the case by file weight alone.

"What exactly am I looking for?" Even though it's probably not the case, I feel like I've been through half this stuff before, most of it already in the public domain.

"The bank photographs," Lee tells me. "From the surveillance cameras."

"I've seen them all before. They printed them in the papers. I can look at this shit online, for Chrissakes."

"No you can't. I know the quality of the photographs is poor, but that is the point. Look at them again. Closely. Particularly the photographs of your mother. Open your eyes, Zesty. What do you see?"

What do I see? I see grainy black-and-white video stills of

Leila Markovich, Michael Drain, and my mother entering the bank, an elevated shot; their long black coats flap as they step inside with their weapons. I see my mother's face turned to the side, her shoulder up, as if she knew she was being recorded and didn't want to give the camera a clear view. In another photo, I see Rachel Evans holding the bank guard's wrist as he reaches for his sidearm and the teller one window over, her hands shielding her face as if they could ward off bullets. I see my mother in the far corner of another frame as Michael Drain, his arm extended, aims his gun point-blank at the bank guard.

What do I see? I see dark sunglasses, long black hair under a black knit cap, black leather coat over a long slim body, black leather riding boots stopping just below the knee. I go through all the photographs that show my mother in full frame and squint at her face as if it's my eyes, not the photographs, that are blurry. I look up at Lee, who maybe thinks he looks like just another tourist but has a glow around him as if he's leaking nuclear waste.

"My mother was six months pregnant when they hit the bank." My hands are shaking, and I can't control them. I point at the clearest of the photographs. "The woman holding down the customers is thin, and her coat's open, and there's no bump. Nothing. That's not my mother," I say. "She never robbed the Bank of Boston."

"So it seems."

I look at Lee, who's still studying the park around us.

"She could have been the getaway driver." Why am I suddenly compelled to play devil's advocate? Trying to justify my mother's flight following the robbery, trying to process what Lee's handed me? What could have driven my mother to run if her one major crime—the Harvard bombing—was almost a decade old at that point?

"Yes, she could have been." Lee breaks away to look at me for a moment. "But she wasn't. The getaway driver was identified as an ugly blond. Harsh words for a witness statement, but that is a verbatim account. And that 'ugly blond' was seen smoking cigarettes, which your mother was never known to do and most likely did not do while six months pregnant. It is my belief that your mother did not rob the Allston branch of the Bank of Boston."

"And the rest of the bureau?"

"I think that file speaks for itself," Lee says. "The crime has never been attributed to anyone else. What's done is done. But you are missing a key component, and we are running out of time. They are coming for us."

"Who?" I say, looking around, but it's suddenly very clear who "they" are. The tourists and joggers are no longer passing through; the swan boats are empty but not stored properly, one of them drifting aimlessly at the opposite end of the pond, its bloodred benches devoid of passengers, the white swan at the head blocking my sight of where the person who pedals sits. There's nobody coming in or out of the gates within our view; the Boston Edison work crew that was digging a ditch parallel to Arlington Street has abandoned the equipment, long wooden planks still leaning over the top of the fence. I shove the folder into my pack and fling it around to the small of my back, the extra weight of Darryl's loaner gun noticeable but not quite reassuring. I mount the bike.

"What you did not have time to see in the file is this." Lee talks quickly, looking at the woman with the stroller, who hasn't tended to her child since I arrived. "A confidential informant led police to Michael Drain, who was scoring heroin in Revere just hours after the robbery. That informant's name has been redacted on more than one report in that file. That same informant identifies your mother as the lead planner for Bank of Boston and the

bombing of the police station. Do I have to tell you whose initials
have been redacted?"

"Only if it's someone besides Devlin McKenna," I say.

To my left I see a figure move off the path and disappear
somewhere under the bridge at the other end of Swan Lake. A
Latino man with lacquered black hair who'd been reading the paper drops it into the wastebasket and lazily reaches to scratch the
small of his back. His chest seems unusually boxy like an umpire
about to call balls and strikes behind the plate.

Lee's words start to run into one another. "Two days after
Drain's timely arrest, he was burned alive in his cell at the Charles
Street Jail by a trusty with kitchen access who'd fashioned a
crude but effective Molotov cocktail. Tara Agostini, Drain's girlfriend, was pushed in front of a train at Dover Station in the South
End. Tara Agostini looked a lot like your mother—had the same
build, same coloring—only her hair had been dyed blond for years.
Her killer was never found, but the description of the man who
pushed her matches Richard Ritter to a T."

"Okay," I say. "Everybody knows McKenna was a snitch and
the FBI protected him for just about anything he did, including
murder. Old news. Why steal this file and put yourself behind
bars or worse? What's in it for you?"

Lee looks momentarily stunned by the question, flicks his
eyes at me to answer. "Why, Devlin McKenna," he says. "Isn't that
obvious?"

"And *this* was the best way you could figure to flush him
out?"

"You have a better plan? No, I thought not. Understand this,
Zesty, your mother has not gone undetected for so long without
learning certain skills in order to survive, as has McKenna. It is
not inconceivable that their paths may have crossed in their jour-
neys. After all, there are a limited number of people who are capable of producing the documents and false papers they would

require to change identities and locales on a moment's notice, if necessary."

"If that's the case, then my mother's long dead, Agent Lee, like Rachel Evans, and Drain, and Agostini."

"Perhaps. But I think not."

"Why?"

"Because it wasn't purely guesswork on my part that McKenna was coming back to Boston."

"We already covered this. You baited him with Leila Markovich."

"I'm not being clear. Returning to Boston even *before* Ms. Markovich was freed. Even before I came to be in possession of your mother's heavily redacted file. I'd been contacted anonymously, sent time-stamped video of McKenna in what looked to be a storage unit that I was able to trace to Topeka, Kansas. I use the term *trace* loosely. The film cut to a town sign and then into the storage unit."

"You were being told where it came from."

"Yes. The film was not from the storage company's footage. It seems to have been set up surreptitiously by someone who had access to the unit, someone who didn't care if I found the hidden camera left behind. Any guesses who that might have been?"

"No," I say, meaning it. "You get papers on the unit?"

"You mean did I subpoena them?" Lee flashes me a crooked smile. "I didn't have to. A federal badge, no matter how tarnished, still goes a long way in some places."

"How long's the unit been rented?"

"Thirteen years. And from what I could see from the video and my visit, there seemed to be nothing stored but an empty box or two."

"Who rents an empty storage unit for thirteen years?"

"I was hoping perhaps you could answer that question."

"How were payments made? Not in person, I'm guessing."

"Yearly, forwarded from a post office box address in Somer-ville held by LP Enterprises. That name mean anything to you?"

"No. Did you get into the PO box?"

"The postal service is not as easily intimidated by a badge."

"And you didn't share any of this information with the bu-reau," I say, still trying to process what Lee's feeding me. "Didn't get official clearance to open the PO box."

"No."

"Because they'd either bury it as they had this file or pull you off the case. They don't want McKenna found. But you need him."

"Yes. To reclaim what I have lost. The bureau and, by asso-ciation, Governor Hibert cannot afford another black eye in con-nection with Devlin McKenna or your mother, for that matter, so he is my bargaining chip, whether they want him or not. McKenna is my all-in, as your father would say. I think it's time you took your leave, Zesty."

"One last question. Who do *you* think sent you the video of McKenna?"

"Must I really answer that for you, Zesty?" Lee's eyes burn into mine, but it's hard to trust someone blinking on full tilt.

"Nah, fuck that. Why would my mother deliver McKenna to you if she's gonna have this file to prove her innocence? And how would she even be able to track him in the first place? No. You know what, fuck it, and while you're at it, fuck McKenna too. Every mook from Southie to Charlestown wants to see him dead or disappeared. My mother's got nothing to gain by McKenna's capture."

"Yes she does. Don't you see, Zesty? That file isn't enough on its own. The bureau never intended for the Bank of Boston robbery to reach trial, preferring to let the public convict your mother and her misguided principles. Your mother, Zesty, was a revolutionary caution tale the supposedly new FBI could pull out and wave around, the aging radical, out of touch with the country's direction, certainly no longer a credible voice of any opposition. You see, Zesty, your mother needs Devlin McKenna too. Alive. Bank footage aside, they could still pin the station bombing on her—that was her specialty, after all. Aside from your father, who can no longer speak for himself, McKenna is the only other credible person alive who can exonerate her for the Allston robbery, especially if you're right about Leila Markovich's instability."

"So what?" I say. "I'm not here for her. I'm here for my father."

"Then perhaps I have done you a disservice. Unfortunately it is too late to change any of that now. I suggest you take your leave."

SIXTY-FIVE

The first shots come whipping out from under the willow trees to our right, flashes in the dusk, tulip beds exploding orange and purple. The Latino umpire hits the ground heavily, his gun skidding across the path and onto the edge of the grass. I look at Lee, who's as surprised as I am, his eyes wide as he ducks below one of the granite stanchions.

"Go!" He points toward Beacon Street as more bullets whang off the oxidized copper railing, a fragment exploding into the side of Lee's face, blood spilling out from just below his cheekbone. More shots come from a different direction, a machine gun *brrrpt brrrpt* spitting out of the mouth of the drifting swan at the far end of the pond. The chunky woman with the running stroller yells "FBI!", pulls her baby out of the carriage, unwraps her, and pumps a deafening round in our direction but under the bridge. The water near the spitfire swan erupts like charges were detonated beneath the surface, rocking the boat violently, nearly upending it. The globe lights above us rain pearly white glass over our heads.

Lee's on his elbows and belly, crabbing to get out of the crossfire, and I'm on my bike, hugging the frame, leaning into pole position, but not toward Beacon, where he'd directed me—there are men in Windbreakers crouching at the corners, boxing us in. My wheels rip into grass, dirt flying up behind me as I sprint toward the iron bars fronting Arlington; bumper-to-bumper traffic rubbernecking the shoot-out on the other side, a chorus of horns leaning heavily into their notes. Out of the corner of my eye, I see the drifting swan's head burning, the water around its fiberglass feathers rippling with small-arms fire. As the boat bumps onto the far shore, Otis disembarks gracefully and moves toward Charles Street, a zipper of pavement separating the Commons from the Public Garden.

I don't have that option. I opt for the fence, but maybe too late, the chunky blonde ditching her weapon and taking a short angle to cut me off. What I mistook earlier for pregnancy fat is obviously muscle, a former college sprinter blasting out of the block. She sees what I see and changes direction to meet me at the fence-leaning slats, but she's too long out of training; I've had too big a head start and hit the makeshift ramp hard, the wood springing up like a diving board, the kickback launching me airborne onto the front hood of a green Range Rover.

I don't hear any more shots as I drop to the street and start cutting in and out of lanes against traffic, trying to get a look at Lee through the heavy curtain of willows as Cedrick's black Pathfinder motors up the sidewalk collecting street signs like an

Alpine skier hitting poles, the hood inverting to a deeper V with every impact. Bullet holes pock the passenger-side doors. The back windshield's blown out, but the stereo bass is still pounding a wicked beat as it flies by, shaking the street.

Lee's nowhere to be seen, and I check behind me one last time to make sure the blonde stayed a one-heat track star, didn't add the pole vault to her résumé, leaving me on my own and, I realize, pretty much back where I started, the horn section in full swing, police strobes spinning blue ghouls into the dusk.

It's darker now, the mayor and maybe even Governor Hibert himself only an hour or two away from being trotted out in front of the park to preside over a news conference where, in no uncertain terms, they'll decry the violence, declare the city safe for one and all, and then prove the point by strolling through the park with their lovely wives. The FBI, for their part, will issue a terse statement and present someone respectable-looking to read it, and by the end, after declining further comment and ducking reporters' questions, the public will know even less than they did before.

But that's okay. The Sox are home from Seattle, and the Indians are in town. Aerosmith is playing three sold-out shows at TD Garden, and Legal Seafoods just received a fresh batch of monster crabs off the Bering Sea. Hell, there's probably someone out there right now sweeping the Freedom Trail, polishing Paul Revere's pewter mugs, dusting Red Auerbach's giant cigar in Faneuil Hall. The gears keep turning. Boston is a well-oiled machine. Always has been. Why should tonight be any different?

SIXTY-SIX

I already have the phone out when Zero calls. When I put it to my ear, I hear drums, whistles, the zip-screech of firecrackers.

"What the hell's going on over there?" Zero has to yell over the noise. "The police scanner's blowing up, shots fired, officers down. That you and Lee?"

"Pretty much."

"You have the file?"

"Right here."

"You take pictures like I told you?"

"Nope."

"Why *not*?"

"Old school," I say. "I pick shit up, I deliver it."

"You're a fucking bonehead."

"You find Dad?"

"No. There's some kind of parade going on in Chinatown—it's like dragon city, only you ask me, they all look like giant rats. If it was actually Pops Tommy spotted, he's gone now. Where are you?"

"Almost at Tetter's office."

"No! Break off. At this point you gotta figure the feds got him covered. Take the damn pictures like I told you and stash the file someplace safe."

"Then what?"

"I dunno. Lay low. Let's see what comes out of this mess."

"You ever hear of an outfit called LP Enterprises?" I say.

"What?" Zero says after a beat. "No."

"You have Sid with you?"

"Yeah."

"Put him on." I hear the phone changing hands, the hard scrape of Sid's unshaven face scratching plastic out of the receiver.

"Ya?"

"When you were watching *Rounders,*" I say. "That call my dad got."

"What about it?"

"When he hung up, what was it he said to you?"

"I dunno, something about changing the channel."

"To what?"

"Eleven?"

"What was on eleven?"

"Nothing. Like I said, he nearly bit my head off. . . . Hey, Zesty, you still there? Zes—"

SIXTY-SEVEN

Two hours. That's a lot of time to drink coffee, and I spend most of it fueling up at Peet's, refilling the same cup until my fingertips start tingling, a steady crackling of caffeine lightning sounding in my ears, tightening a band around my head. I've never heard of a coffee shop having to cut somebody off, but I'm coming close to being that guy. The scruffmeister behind the counter is eyeing me with a nervous crooked grin that makes me think he's looking for some way to eighty-six me from the establishment.

"Last one," I say disjointedly, extending my cup to him, my jaw floating on its hinges.

"You sure?"

I scratch distractedly below my ear, under my chin. I haven't shaved in a few days, and what's come in feels rough to my fingers.

"No worries." He refills my cup, and I start to walk away, but then turn back to him. "You know that today, as a nation, we drink way less coffee than we did in the nineteen-fifties *and* the coffee was stronger. This country was built on coffee after the Second World War, a cup or two after every meal, including dinner, and nobody griped or whined about whether they'd sleep with all the caffeine in them; they just did what they had to do. People wonder how so much got done in those days, why they worked so hard? They were fucking wired to the gills. Coffee, cigarettes, booze. They lived. It's called living."

"Okay," the barista says.

"Okay *what*?"

The kid takes a step back from the counter, tugs at his small hoop earring, and tries to find a place to rest his eyes so they're not looking directly at me. Something about the way I'm holding my bag makes him nervous.

It's dark outside, the moon blanked by thunderclouds, everybody taking their purchases on the run, trying to beat the rain spattering the sidewalk. I hear the low rumble of thunder, and trash starts to blow in the street against the smudged storefront window obscuring our view.

"I apologize. I should've been drinking tea. Let me just use the bathroom, and I'll get out of here."

It's my second trip to the back of the store and the second time I can't find a place to put the gun comfortably within reach. I drop it back into my bag next to the file and the phone. Lee hasn't called back. Zero keeps calling, but I don't answer. My father is somewhere out there getting pelted by the rain, pushed around by the wind.

There had been a small window of time after my father had

received his Parkinson's diagnosis when he was still able to walk on his own and his doctor recommended the purchase of a cane to help steady his already shaky gait. To our surprise, my dad heeded the doctor's advice and dutifully began carrying the cane Zero bought him, albeit upside down, the rubber tip held in his hand, the curved handle scraping the ground as he shuffled along. At first I thought he carried the stick in this fashion to subvert the implication of the cane—old age, infirmity, a doddering fool—but when I walked with him, I saw it served a more utilitarian role; he used it to slow his churning forward progress, hooking the handle around street signs at busy crossings, between the split tops of parking meters when the sidewalks were active with other pedestrians, the cane horizontal, his two-handed grip on the rubber end, by all appearances, the only thing preventing him from being pulled into the middle of the street, to the sky, as if gravity had lost its hold on him, threatening to lift him into oblivion.

The cruel irony of my father's unchecked momentum was not lost on me, nor I suspect on him either. He was aging rapidly, Parkinson's followed by Alzheimer's speeding forward as his mind retreated in reverse. My father hasn't been out on the street alone for a year. He didn't take his cane with him. What was it Jhochelle said about listening to the women in the family? I would if Jhochelle called, but it's my father's voice I hear in my head as I cross the Summer Street Bridge, the retelling of one of his thousand Boston nights—they were always nights, as if nothing noteworthy happened during daylight hours—this one, Zero's favorite, the night Boston burned.

In 1872 a fire broke out in the basement of a commercial warehouse on Summer Street, its flames launching glowing butterfly embers, which ignited the wooden French mansard rooftops of nearby buildings. Maybe the fire could have been contained to Summer Street, but the Boston of old had been built with no unifying plan, fireboxes were kept locked to prevent false alarms, and a horse flu epidemic had immobilized the Boston Fire Department's horses, meaning all the firefighting equipment had to be pulled on foot by volunteers. Combine all that with fire hydrant couplings that weren't standardized, steam engine pumps that couldn't draw enough water to reach the rooftops, and narrow streets packed with looters, and the result was a blaze that killed at least twenty people, consumed 776 buildings downtown, and could be seen lighting up the night sky by ships as far away as the coast of Maine.

It wasn't a total loss, though, as they used the rubble from the fire to fill in Atlantic Avenue, widen Congress Street, and shore up the walls of the Fort Point Channel, the 260-foot-wide strip of muddy and polluted water that separates downtown from South Boston. Why did my father repeatedly regale us with a story about this part of town? Aside from Zero's penchant for fire and destruction, it was probably also because Fort Point was home to the Channel, one of my father's favorite hangouts, an unruly, misshapen black rectangle perched on the banks of the muddy waters, which was torn down to accommodate the Big Dig, its footprint temporarily occupied by massive 120-foot booms that loomed over the city like mechanized carrion birds.

Now there's a slatted boardwalk running alongside the Fort Point Channel and the view of the downtown skyline is magnificent. But when I accompanied my father just after it was built, after the Parkinson's had morphed into early-onset Alzheimer's and it was suggested that Zero and I take him to familiar places, he became agitated and sweaty, his tongue darting between his teeth and lower gums, the scar beneath his lower lip protruding as his tongue pushed at the crosshatched lines of a talentless stitching job.

When I asked him what was wrong, he spat into the water but wouldn't speak, and I realized I'd made a mistake bringing him there—nothing was the same in my father's world anymore. The Boston of his youth had been demolished to make way for the iron behemoth of Interstate 93, and then the Boston of his adulthood reconfigured once more, rendering him a stranger in the city where he'd lived his entire life.

The rain's coming down in sideways panels as I roll across the bridge's black pavement, the stolen Trek painting a wet stripe up the middle of my bag and across my back. The Boston Wharf sign glows like a red beacon atop 263 Summer Street, its letters taking on the impression of movement as the rain sweeps across its front. In passing, I can see the boardwalk below, usually busy at this time of night but empty now except for an old man limping slowly with his cane, trying to get under the bridge and out of the downpour, and the dark figure of a woman leaning against the railing, seemingly oblivious to the rain soaking her short jacket, long limp hair covering her downturned face.

I can't tell if it's my heart thumping inside my chest or just the Doppler vibration of my wheels across the Harborwalk slats, but when I'm maybe twenty yards away, the woman turns to look at me, and I see a waxen face of crosshatched scars, which is to say, I see Leila Markovich as Sid described her to me. She opens her mouth when she sees me, but I don't hear her words until it is too late, see the plastic cuff hooked around her wrist attached to the railing, the old man losing his stiff-caned hobble as if touched by the dry lightning of an evangelical miracle, his cane slashing through the night rain across the back of my neck, an unnatural heaviness to the blow like the end's been weighted with metal ball bearings.

I think Leila Markovich yells, "You're not supposed to be here." But her words sound like a cartoon character talking underwater, her voice popping out of air bubbles breaking the surface. I'm on the boardwalk, my legs tangled in the bike, as the cane comes down again and a red mist explodes in my eye. I feel a pressure in my ears, followed by a small pop, and suddenly everything's hyperamplified, the heavy rain machine-gunning the boardwalk loud as golf balls peppering the hood of a car.

Devlin McKenna straddles me standing, thin silvery hair like matted foil crowning a face assembled from a toolbox: rusted screws for eyes, a crowbar mouth with nails for teeth. McKenna uses his cane to raise my chin, squints in the rain to bring me into focus, and rears back laughing, a look of sheer malevolent delight in his face. Blood and water drip off the cane onto my neck.

"Just as I've been cursing the fates," McKenna sneers, "they turn around and give me the proverbial son. Oh, I would have much preferred your bitch mother, but this will have to do. How does that song go, Leila? It was a lovely tune, something about a reunion."

"Fuck you, Devlin," Leila says from a crouch, her tethered hand extended above her head.

"You can't remember either? So we'll skip the reminiscences, then. Where's my money, son of a cunt?"

"Not here," I say, tasting familiar blood, a heavy gob dropping to the boardwalk over numb lips.

Devlin McKenna drives the butt of the cane into my front teeth; the back of my head bangs off the slick wood. I turn my head and spit sharp fragments onto the boardwalk.

"Now, isn't that a familiar look. Son, is your entire family made up of degenerate gamblers like your mush-brained daddy? I'm done playing games." McKenna presses something in the rounded handle of his cane, and a blade snicks out the end, its shiny point catching the red reflection of the Wharf sign high above his shoulder.

"Medicare covers *that*?" I say through the blood rushing inside my mouth. I turn my head away from the blade, but keep my eyes on it through the rain. I can feel the gun through my bag, wedged into my lower back. "Does your walker come with a machine gun?"

McKenna looks to the sky and drives the blade into my shoulder, a spastic fire erupting through me as I scream into darkness, blood flooding slick through my fingers clutching the hole as the blade exits.

"I'm sorry, boyo, did you say something? I promise you, I'll only ask this question one more time, and it just might be the last thing you ever hear if I don't like your answer. Where's my fucking money?"

"Darryl Jenkins," I groan.

"What? What the fuck did you just say?"

"Darryl. He has your money now."

"I'm not talking about *that* money, you fucking cocksucker. I want the money your parents have been stealing from me all these years." McKenna drives the blade into the boardwalk by my face and leans contemplatively on the cane end. "Oh, lordy." He turns to Leila. "Nobody told him?"

"He's not a part of this," Leila says. "Enough."

"No, I don't think so. Zesty, is it? Is that what Leila called you? Oh my, this will be hard to hear; I'm so glad I didn't kill you yet like I did Agent Chink Lee. Ah, yes, I see it now—you have your mother's eyes, you know that?"

"No."

"No, I suppose not. How could you, she's been gone so long. Life is cruel, and the truth only makes it that much crueler. Well, let me make this as painful as possible before you go, Zesty, seeing as you're the loyal son. Your parents are a couple of lying thieves, and your oatmeal-for-brains father robbed Bank of Boston for me twenty years ago and then stole my money whilst your mother robbed me blind one dollar at a time."

"You're a fucking liar." Dark shadows close in around my eyes. I start shivering, the raindrops slivers of sharp ice.

"Am I? Tell him, Leila, before I slit his throat and have him drinking channel water through his fucking neck. Tell him how his father looked driving a getaway car in drag, another family trait maybe, a little homo running through your genes, boy? Tell him!" he roars.

"It's true," Leila says, but there's a measure of triumph in her smile even with the blood streaked across her teeth. "But not in the way McKenna wants you to believe it. Your father drove, but only to take your mother's place. As for the extended larceny, well, there's more truth to that, I'm afraid. Your father was beholden to McKenna and hid his money as McKenna padded his eventual run."

"But why?" Half my body feels like it's packed in dry ice, but I manage to roll onto my side, the bag coming along.

"I had to trust somebody, boyo, didn't I? I knew I wouldn't be on top forever in this town full of rats and backstabbers. Even Richie gave me up, and once I was so sure he'd go down in a hail of bullets before betraying me."

"You should know about rats." I can feel the heft of the gun shift, no longer pressed against me.

"Yes, well, survival of the slickest. And you know what they say about keeping your enemies closer. What I should have done was kept a closer eye on your father. But your father was sly, or maybe just lucky. I have to give him credit for that. He was also playing the long game and figured right I didn't intend to let him or your mother live once I'd decided I had enough stashed away. As for torturing a confession out of him? My, but I would have enjoyed that, only it wasn't possible either."

"LP Enterprises," I rasp, my voice going.

"Ah, so we're wasting time. You know all this. What your father and I ended up with was what you might call a stalemate."

"It was better than that," I can hear Leila Markovich say from far away. "As long as your mother stayed safely out of McKenna's reach, your father would release one more location to him. You know what LP stands for? It was the designation given to long-playing records when they first came out. That's what your dad designed, the long play, the endless automatic payments to those storage units that housed McKenna's blood money. Also, your mother once told me that, knowing your dad, LP also probably stood for 'lucky pull,' something he hated to find himself relying on but at some point did. Finally, when it was McKenna's turn to run, your dad was, in effect, communicating with two of Boston's most wanted, and McKenna, too long the alpha dog, was now on your father's leash. You want to know how your father bluffed so well, Zesty, how he lied to everyone? He wrapped the lie in a little bit of truth is how. Bank of Boston was your father's lie, and it was also his payback for the exile McKenna forced on your mother. But McKenna kept tracking me. He found Rachel Evans, thought once that he'd found your mother in Los Angeles and killed an innocent girl."

Jane Orr, the alias my mother had once used.

"McKenna's evil, make no mistake about that, and we're sullied in association with him, but we were forced into Bank of Boston, and though I had access to McKenna's blood money and sometimes used it—"

"You stole from me, cunt."

"Yes." Leila smiles satisfaction. "It's a shame I could easily manage to live with."

"Dream on, bitch."

Leila shrugs noncommittally. "With your mother taking her cut, Devlin's money ran out early—he was never hoarding to share, remember—and so he returned to pursue me and the Bank of Boston cash when he saw the parole board was granting me an early release. By this time he must have realized I'd only taken a small cut of the BOB money when I ran to Diane for protection. Your mother had maintained her underground connections, while I tended to burn my bridges in the move-ment. I had nobody—"

"She helped you."

"Against her better judgment. She saw me through at the beginning—documents, let me in on some of McKenna's money."

"You fucking cunt. I'll be taking my time with you."

"The rest I can only guess, Zesty, but once your father's Alzheimer's worsened the communiqués to McKenna and your mother must have stopped. Lee lured McKenna back to Boston dangling me, figuring the same thing that McKenna did, that I had the rest of the Bank of Boston money stashed somewhere because that's what your father told him. But he got greedy again and sped up the timetable on something he'd concocted much like the BOB robbery, with throwaway players. Am I getting this part right?"

"The Wells Fargo truck," I barely manage to get out, the blood in my mouth tasting like a fistful of loose change.

"Your father would have referred to that play as a side pot," McKenna sneers. "A little something on the back burner while I was in town."

I moan, blinking water out of my eyes, having trouble just keeping them open. The bridge overhead is a black line over the channel, an occasional streak of light, followed by a hiss of wet tires crossing over the top. McKenna follows my gaze to the bridge.

"Don't believe in miracles, cuntboy. Like I said, your Chink's already leaking stomach bile into the channel and if the stick didn't do the job, he's bound to choke on one of Gillette's billion razor blades they dumped in there. Stop struggling with the cuff, Leila. You've never proven yourself to be one of those mother-bear types who'd chew off her arm to save her own cubs, let alone someone else's."

"Go to hell, McKenna."

"Only after you, darlin'. But let's complete this story first, no? Hey, stay awake, Zesty, I'm getting to the punch line."

I cough up blood.

"I can't tell you how disappointed I was, letting your parents get the edge on me and now letting that nigger Jenkins screw me, even after I gave him solid points on cleaning the cash. But what choice did I have? I'm not spending marked money and leaving a trail of bread crumbs for the FBI to peck at. They'd be happy if I never showed my face again, but they'd have no choice but to follow if things were that obvious. And I've some years left in me still. What a hassle this homecoming's been. Least I get to finish things here. Eeny, meeny, miney, moe." McKenna starts waving the gun between us. "Catch a—"

"I can get you your money."

"Tiger by the toe. If he hollers, let him go." The gun stops on Leila. "My, that would be an interesting turn of events. But I don't believe a word either of you say. So, where was I? Oh yes. . . . choose the very best one and you are—"

I'm already rolling over, trying to burrow my way between the boardwalk's slats, as Leila Markovich screams and McKenna swings the gun in my direction, firing two shots into my back, snapping my ribs with the force of a mule's kick. My breath's gone out of my body, the sound of Leila's scream stopped like someone's pulled my plug, and I can't hear her, can't hear the rain or feel its touch as it falls into my open eyes as McKenna rolls me over and says something, the gun pointing at my face.

What do people see when they die a violent death? Their lives flashing before their eyes? Loved ones who've already passed to the other side? Or does a final drop blur their vision, a mixed blessing of blood or tears thrown up to shield them from the horror of what's happening?

This is what I see as I die: Leila Markovich thrashing at the rail, blood covering her wrist as she fights to free herself from the cuff's restraints, her rain-soaked hair whipping around her head in a darkened halo. I see a lightning bolt rip the sky in two, black clouds roiling in their swirling fury, and I see the mirage of my father, a dripping shadow in darkness wearing pajama pants and unlaced tennis sneakers, welcoming me to the other side with arms extended, his shrunken frame illuminated like a strobe-lit angel first by the flash of the lightning and then once more by the bright fire leaping from his gun as he shoots Devlin McKenna again and again and again until the air above me settles into a mist of blood, the chamber of the gun clicking in silence, dry and empty until there's nothing, absolutely nothing, left.

EPILOGUE

I lost consciousness after seeing my father shoot Devlin McKenna, I'd lost too much blood and had gone into full-blown shock, but I've since learned that when the police arrived, followed quickly by the FBI, who tried and failed to wrangle control of the crime scene from Detectives Brill and Wells, Leila Markovich was gone, the plastic cuffs dangling off the rail, washed clean of her blood by the pouring rain.

Why had she run again? Perhaps to limit her prosecutable culpability to just the necessary tidbits implicating McKenna for Bank of Boston, or maybe to secure the file Lee had stolen from the bowels of the Boston field office, which ended up in Andrew Tetter's capable hands. Perhaps to dispose of the .38 Darryl had loaned me, which had been damaged when the bullets from McKenna's gun ricocheted off its barrel, drilled through my tin of weed and finally lodged into my lower back only millimeters from my spine.

I don't know if Leila tossed the gun into the Fort Point waters, but if she did, I'm pretty sure that's where it'll stay for another hundred years or until Boston's civic trust decides to build another superhighway to replace the eleven-thousand-foot, eleven-lane tunnel now running beneath the Fort Point Channel—at two billion dollars, the most expensive highway mile anywhere in the world.

Also, Leila being one of those stubborn yet practical-minded individuals, she probably wanted to surrender to the authorities with certain assurances already in place. And after she turned herself in, a year is what the court sentenced her to, and if I play my cards right, maybe I can get the same judge to take care of the thousand-dollar fine the Boston Licensing Board slapped me with for working under an expired courier permit.

As for Darryl Jenkins, he did indeed have a Jew on retainer, and a pretty good one at that. Darryl is doing some jailing on laundering and tax-related counts, but something tells me his re-introduction to the hood will be a relatively smooth one—it seems my buddy Sam Budoff's officially out of the hallucinogenic business, his secret formula sold to Cedric Overstreet, the new king of trip-hop, holding it down for his homey at MCI.

In a game of five-card poker, there are 2,598,960 possible combinations, the odds of making certain hands rising and falling depending on how many people are left in the game and what cards have already fallen. A player's chances of, say, pulling an inside straight on the last card dealt—in poker parlance, on the river—is somewhere between 10 and 11 percent. In other words, as strategy, it's an efficient way to go broke. Agent Lee, against all odds, was pulled out of the river with a winning hand. That is, still breathing. Not only did he survive the stab wound deep in his stomach, but all the diseases the channel waters could muster against him as well.

For a short time, Lee and I shared the same floor in Beth Israel's intensive care unit, and when we were downgraded and sent to our respective rooms, I would join him to watch the Sox snatch defeat from the jaws of victory, the bullpen imploding on the rare occasions they carried a lead into the ninth. Needless to say, Lee's room was cushier than mine, his nurses better-looking and friendlier, a fringe benefit of the FBI's insurance plan and Lee's newfound status as Boston's favorite son. Never mind that the bullets pulled from McKenna at autopsy were from a different-caliber gun than Lee's company-issued Glock 23, the only bullets that match Lee's gun being the ones extracted from my back, which I now keep rattling around in the punctured tin that used to hold my weed.

I can't say I'm surprised. The FBI will always have its secrets; that's the nature of the beast, and it hasn't changed. But for public consumption, Lee's a hero, and I was present when the director of the FBI, the mayor, and Governor Hibert bestowed upon him various accolades and a key to the city, the FBI director looking like he was sticking needles into his own eyes as he shook Lee's hand for the photographers. But much later, well after visiting hours were over, there were only four of us gathered in his room, Brill and Wells opting to stand as Lee and I reclined in our recovery, all ears and narcotics.

"Just to be clear, we're not here to play politics," Brill began, his trademark cigar stinking up Lee's room. He'd shaved recently, even suffered a haircut, but still exuded tired and grumpy. "Governor Hibert and the brass played the tune the way they wanted to hear it, but let's not bullshit each other, okay?"

"What he means is we're not here to fuck you." Wells looked every bit as sharp as the day I met him, his George Hamilton glow matched only by the gloss of his chocolate wingtips. "Mess with whatever arrangement's got you both keeping your mouths stitched about what really happened out there on the board-walk."

"I cut a deal in the high three digits." I turned lazily to Lee. "You?"

"Shut up, Zesty."

"That's what I figured."

"Damage control from the top was expected. And though you obviously got a wild streak in you, Lee, we figure you're most likely getting back up that career ladder, a company man through and through; just needed a little adjustment. But what got us thinking, what kept eating at us, knowing Zesty like we do now, is what could the bureau possibly have that could compel Zesty here to keep his big mouth shut, knowing what he does all the way back to 1986, especially considering Papa Meyers is beyond reach of the courts, on account of his Alzheimer's, and Mom's still in the wind. Ain't nothing to hold over Zesty at the federal level, seeing as they can't prosecute him over a file that doesn't exist, and all his, ah, poor choices more or less local chickenshit no DA in his right mind wants to touch."

Lee: "So you've concluded what?"

"Zesty's protecting someone," Brill said. "Ain't that right, Zesty?"

"Spell it out for me. They've been diluting the morphine drip daily, but it's not exactly Starbucks they're pumping through these tubes."

"LP Enterprises. It was pretty smart, your dad playing the game like he did, paying out the storage units, arranging for the coded ads in the *Times*—one more cash location released to McKenna as long as your mother was safe. But at some point, the sicker he got, he must have realized he couldn't keep doing it on his own, that he had to hand responsibility over to someone to protect your mom from McKenna, keep her out of his reach but still dipping into his money. Isn't that right, Zesty? It's got to hurt a little, maybe a lot I figure, your dad looking at Zero as the responsible son, still feeling the need to protect you from his past? But the thing is, the thing me and Wells admire about you, Zesty, is you got no bitterness in your heart, no jealousy whatsoever. You've been kept out of the loop for years, and just as it's about to close around Zero's neck, you cut a deal with the feds to protect him."

"He's my brother," I said. "What kind of deal?"

"Oh, I don't know. Something along the lines of your mouth closed about your mom's file, how McKenna was fished back to town by Lee, and who really put the bullets in him. And in exchange, Zero doesn't see bars, no aiding and abetting, no felony mail fraud and money laundering charges; that Wells Fargo cash is nowhere to be found, and Britta Ingalls is in the wind. Take your pick, there's probably more. Hell, Zesty, someone could even make the argument you coldheartedly chose Zero over your mother, considering she's off the hook for Bank of Boston. Not that the public knows anything about it or likely ever will."

"It wasn't a choice. I don't even know if my mother's alive."

"No, I guess you don't. Although Lee thinks she is. Unless he doesn't."

"I don't understand," said Lee.

"No reason you should," Wells said. "But really it's all about the video and what you did for Leila Markovich and why."

"Lee doesn't know who sent him the video," I said, and then I got it, their visit clear to me then. "But you do."

"That we do," Brill said. "And, Zesty—believe me when I say this—I'm sorry it wasn't your mother. True, your mom, if she's still out there, knew all those storage locations paid out by your dad through those LP Enterprises ads, knew where the money was and helped herself to plenty of it. Just not the money in the Kansas locker."

"You can't be sure of this," Lee said. "The storage facility has no video of its own, and nobody knew of the location except for her. She could still be alive."

"No, that's where you're wrong, and you know it. There was one other person who knew, had to have known. Maybe only this location, but one was enough. But we figure it just wasn't in your best interest at the time to go knocking around to find out for sure."

"Yes." Lee acknowledged the point. "I had my suspicions. But I couldn't be sure Zesty would aid me if he did not hold out hope that his mother might be actively involved. I'm not proud of that."

"I'm lost. If my mother didn't send Lee the video, who did?"

"That is a question you could ask your father, Zesty," Lee said. "If he truly lives in the past, perhaps he still remembers. If you recall, when McKenna fled the indictments, he left all his associates behind, including Ritter. While Ritter fared better than everyone else McKenna betrayed, his ten-year deal followed by admittance to witpro, he never forgave McKenna for abandoning him. Your father must have known Ritter on some level, and known McKenna was only securing money for his own solo run. . . ."

"Somehow," I said, "he got inside Ritter's head."

"That would be my conjecture."

"And I guess Zero knew where McKenna would pick up the next bundle of cash, so he got word to Ritter, led him to the locker."

"Yes. Hoping Ritter would either kill McKenna—though it would be difficult since he's watched closely—or do as he did, which was to rig the camera and send me the video to renew the dormant bureau hunt for him, at least unofficially."

"And, Zesty," Brill said, "like I told you before, I knew your father. But I also got some face time with Ritter back when I was a patrolman, and I'm not exaggerating when I tell you he was the coldest motherfucker I ever laid my eyes on. The fact that your daddy put a screw inside Ritter's head and twisted it all these years later is the damndest trick I've ever seen. Fuck poker." Brill points his cigar in my direction. "I wouldn't sit at the table with your daddy for a game of Go Fish. And by the way, in case you're wondering where the feds have had Ritter stashed these last few years? Just click your heels, Toto. Ritter was an army brat. He was born in Leavenworth. Who says you can't go home again?"

Well, Mario Spagnola for one, who made good on his threat and evicted my roommates and me from our Thayer Street loft. David and his girlfriend packed up and moved to San Francisco; Nicolette opted for Northampton, and I haven't had any contact with them since.

For now I'm subletting a one-bedroom apartment overlooking Union Square, but it's more of a glorified closet than a place to live, the rent is astronomical, the cat resents the low ceilings, and I'm beginning to realize that the South End of my youth is no longer there, that with all the money, all the new people moving in, I've become a stranger in my own neighborhood. To my surprise, I'm not bitter about it. I guess I'm learning to accept change, to embrace the uncertainty of the future; it keeps me moving, and movement for me is life.

Mercury Couriers is still in business, though my time on a bike has been limited since that three-day span in which I was run over, doored by my man Cedrick Overstreet, and stabbed and shot by Devlin McKenna. There's only so much abuse a body can take. I hired Charlie, the former doorman at 38 Newbury, and a couple more experienced couriers to fill in for me until I'm able to get back up to speed, and I've been helping Martha out in the office, though I doubt she'd characterize my presence in that fashion. I still have a soundtrack that plays in my head intermittently; the MRI Sam wanted me to undergo came up with some unusual electrical activity, but nothing definitive or worrisome unless the format changes and starts cranking out Rihanna or the Black Eyed Peas.

Speaking of music, Darcy's started her own little indie label, running it for now out of her North End apartment. We hang out from time to time, but I've yet to get another couch invitation. Our get-togethers all fall under the banner of the newly formed Celibate Slut Club, which I'm trying my hardest to quit. Don't believe the hype: Not all celebrity comes with groupies.

As for my dad, he's still sticking around, though where exactly he is on a day-to-day basis is anybody's guess, myself, Zero, Sid, and a couple other guys still providing him with the round-the-clock care he needs. It's not an easy job, caregiving, even just for a few hours at a time. The task is made more difficult by my father's continued decline, his inability to do some basic self-sustaining tasks, and the long bouts of silence where he seems to withdraw even farther inside himself, a look of fear and confusion playing on his scarred and weathered face. A face that mine now mirrors—a lightning-bolt scar under my lower lip, off-colored bonding on my shattered front teeth.

To be honest, it's downright heartbreaking, and I can't help but wonder whether he forever replays those steps he took on that sunny October day with the duffel bag crammed full of the stolen Bank of Boston cash and then retraced twenty years later to do what he probably wished he'd done in the first place: stick Devlin McKenna into the ground and let the rats chew through him as they eventually chewed through the cash itself, a million rabid nibbles shredding a worthless dream.

But I like to tell myself this isn't the case, that my father's recollections are happy ones, that his mind is busy reliving the short but joyous times with my mother, his loyal and resilient children, the ghosts of his family and friends, and poker games where all the cards fell just right, that confluence of luck and skill that sometimes takes you on a run that falls only a pixie dusting short of magic.

Zero claims I'm one lucky bastard, that he twice almost found and derailed my father before he reached the banks of the Fort Point Channel—there was that sighting of him in Chinatown and again at the corner of Arch and Summer Streets, but he disappeared in the downpour—and that maybe I should consider taking a run at the World Series of Poker in Vegas (Zero would front me the ten grand buy-in for a percentage, of course), that my very existence defies the odds, makes a mockery of Lady Luck who, for me, turned monogamous.

It's an unusually optimistic thought for Zero, and I'm inclined to roll with it. But reality doesn't play out like that too much around the octagonal green felt table we bought for our father and where we sit with him and a deck of cards as often as we can manage. Our father seems at peace at the poker table, more present, clicking the heavy clay chips between his fingers, shuffling the cards absently with his badly shaking hands, every so often spinning them expertly across the table to where we sit, spinning them through the smoke, through the years, an act as familiar to us as a bedtime kiss, a tug on our ear. Once in a while, out of the blue, out of his silence, he announces the hands before us in a voice much younger than his own.

"Seven Stud, gentlemen," he says, the brightest of lights shining in the darkest of eyes. "Poker. Get your lies ready. Not that they matter, the cards speak for themselves. Queen bets. Queen. Luck be a lady tonight."

ACKNOWLEDGMENTS

This book doesn't get written without the safety net of my family—my boundless gratitude for letting me do things the hard way.

To my mother, Devora Abramowitz, first reader and moral compass, and the entire Gleich clan of Brighton Third, not a conformist among them.

To the Doctor of Good Ideas and the funniest man I know, my father, Martin Abramowitz.

To Yosef and Susan, support and encouragement bordering on ludicrous.

To Blake Voss, dad #2, always ready and willing.

To Ralph Parks, who gave me my first inside look. To Lee Grove at UMass Boston, who woke me up. To Deborah Dapolito, my ticket to the South End and Thayer Street.

To Irene Wagner. To Pat and Pat Ansalone.

To the editors at St. Martin's Press: Jamie Levine, who

recognized the potential, and Will Anderson, who made me turn the screws.

To Meg Ruley and Rebecca Scherer, true believers and agents extraordinaire. To everyone at the Jane Rotrosen Agency even as the house was burning.

To the Monday night poker crew: Eddie Brill, J. R. Havlan, Hank Gallo, William Stephenson, Pat Dixon, Jon Keim, Joe Mulligan, Vic Henley, Bruce Smolanoff, Costaki Economopoulos, Louis C.K., Sarah Silverman, et al., no better place to hold a losing hand.